PRAISE FOR

TELL ME EVERYTHING

Named One of the Best Books of the Year
by Good Housekeeping

"A compulsive page-turner with shades of Donna Tartt's *The Secret History* peopled by a new generation."

—CATHERINE STEADMAN, *New York Times* bestselling author of *Something in the Water*

"Gripping . . . [Cambria] Brockman paints an unnerving portrait of the power people hold over one another—especially as they blur the line between protective and obsessive."

—*Time*

"Brockman's novel of secrets and murder at a New England college will undoubtedly remind readers of Donna Tartt's *The Secret History*. Dripping with drama and mystery, *Tell Me Everything* is a page-turner to the last."

—*Newsweek*

"The development of Malin as a narrator is truly inspired. . . . [She] draws riveting attention to humankind's vulnerability to evil. . . . A truly chilling thriller with a twist so quiet, you never hear it coming."

—*Kirkus Reviews* (starred review)

"Tension builds in a narrative that switches back and forth between Senior Day and freshman year, punctuated by flashbacks to events in Malin's childhood, and the tension is amplified by the focus on an insular group in an isolated setting. . . . Brockman's first novel will appeal to readers looking for another *Gone Girl*."

—*Booklist* (starred review)

BALLANTINE BOOKS
NEW YORK

TELL ME EVERYTHING

A NOVEL

CAMBRIA
BROCKMAN

2020 Ballantine Books Trade Paperback Edition

Copyright © 2019 by Cambria Brockman
Book club guide copyright © 2020 by Penguin Random House LLC

Published in the United States by Ballantine Books, an imprint of Random House, a division of Penguin Random House LLC, New York.

BALLANTINE and the HOUSE colophon are registered trademarks of Penguin Random House LLC.
RANDOM HOUSE BOOK CLUB and colophon are trademarks of Penguin Random House LLC.

Originally published in hardcover in the United States by Ballantine Books, an imprint of Random House, a division of Penguin Random House LLC, in 2019.

LIBRARY OF CONGRESS CATALOGING-IN-PUBLICATION DATA
Names: Brockman, Cambria, author.
Title: Tell me everything : a novel / Cambria Brockman.
Description: New York : Ballantine Books, [2019]
Identifiers: LCCN 2019003779 | ISBN 9781984817235 (paperback) |
ISBN 9781984817228 (ebook)
Subjects: | BISAC: FICTION / Coming of Age. | FICTION / Suspense. |
GSAFD: Suspense fiction.
Classification: LCC PS3602.R6267 T45 2019 | DDC 813/.6—dc23
LC record available at https://lccn.loc.gov/2019003779

International edition ISBN 978-1-9848-1993-2

Printed in the United States of America on acid-free paper

randomhousebooks.com
randomhousebookclub.com

987654321

Title-page and part-title-page images copyright © iStock.com/yenwen

Book design by Victoria Wong

For Lo

PART ONE

HAWTHORNE COLLEGE

Senior Day, January 29, 2011

This is the end of us.

The voice in the back of my mind.

Jump.

I suck in a shallow breath; my chest rises. The impending snow-storm gathers above us, the air cold on our bones. Below us, stagnant black water whispers our names, excited to seep into our pores. We pant, heavy and even, our hot breath billowing in tight clouds above our heads. Even if we want to run, we can't.

The chanting grows louder. The six of us grab at each other's hands, clumsy and drunk, and bring our half-naked bodies together in unison. Shoulder to shoulder. The white hairs on my arms stand on end, reaching for the clouds. Gemma and Khaled exhale, inhale—nervous, apprehensive.

Jump.

I close my eyes, feel Ruby's delicate fingers laced tightly with mine. Max, on my other side, squeezes my hand in reassurance.

John, tall and steady, begins to count down. Tricking us into thinking we aren't about to sacrifice ourselves to the frozen lake. His confidence solidifies our momentum, no turning back now.

"Four, three . . ."

I stay calm, and my father's voice rushes into my head. With my eyes closed, the noise from the outside world lessens, and I can see him leaning down to whisper in my ear. He is dropping me off at college, saying goodbye to his only child. He must leave her with some wisdom, must ensure the first steps she takes are the right ones. I see my mother, blurry, behind him. She stares longingly at the crowd of incoming freshmen, a sad line drawn on her lips. I know she will be focused on the boys in particular, the ones with freckles and sandy tufts of hair. She will want to see my brother's face in that crowd, and then she will look at me, and that sad line will slowly crack into a forced smile. My father leans closer, his hand gripping my arm. He has my attention. His hold is tight, but it doesn't bother me. He says one word, and then pulls back, reading my face. I know he is trying to see if he has made some sort of impression, so I nod. I follow his cue, an obedient child. As my parents walk to the parking lot and drive to the airport, as they arrive in the heat and humidity of my birthplace, and as they walk into their empty house, the word he whispered echoes in my thoughts. It binds my every move for the years to come, setting the rhythm to my beating pulse.

I feel a pull on my hand, and my eyes startle, open and wide.

"Two . . ."

Jump.

John's voice gets louder and more powerful. "One!" Our bodies lurch forward and upward.

For a brief second, we are suspended in the air, and I wish we could stay there. My friends shriek and recoil. I hear the exhilaration in their screams. They have waited their turn to jump for so long. After four years in the backwoods of Maine, we are finally here. This is what every freshman, sophomore, junior observes the seniors commit to, winter after winter.

Three years ago, we witnessed the Jump for the first time, huddled together in a tight group, passing around a flask filled with cheap vodka. It burned our throats, but we welcomed the warmth in our bellies. The Jump meant your time at Hawthorne College was coming to a close. Our picturesque liberal arts education was almost complete. The hole in the ice represented a rite of passage, the beginning of the end. It was impossible to explain to outsiders, to students from other colleges, to family members back home. It was ours, and we were possessive of its strange nature.

A thunder of cheers and claps envelops us. Our classmates are watching. I know they are observing our faces, reading the terror and joy that simultaneously merge with the ice-cold water. I am acutely aware that this tradition is supposed to be enjoyed, and I squeal as my naked heels plunge through the black hole.

The cold water rips daggers through my skin, and as I sink, my body is shocked into submission. I close my eyes in the murky water, voices drown out.

I sense thrashing as my friends kick to pull themselves out of the lake and back onto the ice, eager to warm themselves. The silence is inviting. Quiet, peaceful. This is where I belong.

I hear Ruby's voice calling my name. She sounds so far away. I see movement above me through the surface. Ruby's face pixelates in the watery blur. Her arms cling to her chest, thighs pressed tight, willing the warmth to stay contained.

"Malin," she calls, her voice out of tune and drawn out in the bubbles. I force my arms and legs to pump in unison, propelling myself upward. It is only when I crack the surface and gasp for air that my breath resumes. I swim to the rough edge and place one of my hands against the chiseled ice. It has been bitterly cold this winter, but almost no snow, not yet.

Ruby pulls me from the water, her chilled teeth rattling. Max is kneeling behind her, one hand steady on her back, the other reaching toward my slippery hand. He grabs it and pulls me up and over the jagged edge. I spot the others, John, Gemma, Khaled, slip-sliding toward the edge of the lake, grabbing for towels and hot chocolate.

The air is thick with alcohol and weed and the excitement of tradition. I hear laughter and the roar of cheering as we complete our jump. My blood works in overdrive to warm my body, my toenails a deep blue, braided hair frozen solid. I want my socks and boots, and I scan the shoreline for the clump of reeds where I left them with the rest of my clothes. Everyone talking and laughing through chattering teeth, purple lips. Ruby hugs me, and our goosebumps mesh together on our bare skin. I smile at her and the others as we retreat together, the hole in the ice behind us. Ruby tells me something, but her voice fades away as I wrap a towel around my body and lead us in the direction of the bonfire. I make sure to look like I am paying attention. I am too cold to talk, but I smile at her, as I always do.

There is something imminent surrounding us, and we have no idea it's there. Tomorrow morning, we will sit down for breakfast at the dining hall, as we always do, and realize one of us is gone.

Police will arrive on campus. Ambulance lights will flash across the snow-covered woods. We'll watch as a body is wheeled away on a stretcher, the police telling us to stay back.

They will ask us questions, run us through the night. Our memories will be fuzzy. We were drinking, out of our minds, typical college kids. They will look at us, figuring out whether they should believe us or not.

They will be right to question us.

We all have secrets about this day, and our group will be disbanded before graduation even begins. With a piece missing from our puzzle, we will fall apart.

Ruby talks about the cold, the Jump, the adrenaline, but all I hear is my father's whispered word, beating in my head.

Pretend.

CHAPTER ONE

Freshman Year

Those first weeks at Hawthorne appear in my mind as books might sit on a shelf, neat and ordered, separated by genre. I wonder if the others remember it as I do. Bits and pieces of memories, scattered moments, things we said, things we did. The reasons we became so close; it came down to those first few days, insecurities and nerves unifying us as one.

After my parents hauled my belongings into my bare room and escorted me to the dining hall, I was alone. I knew nobody, and I lived in a single in a dorm. It reminded me of the first day of kindergarten. My mother had dropped me off, her scent still lingering in the air after she left. She wore a perfume that defined parts of my childhood, every memory laced with that fragrance. I sat at one of the miniature communal tables, quiet and calm, while my peers panicked, cried and screamed, threw tantrums. College was similar, minus the show. Everyone older now, capable of hiding their fear—but the pits of their stomachs gnawed at them, and I saw the same panic in their eyes. They wondered if they would make friends, if they would find a place to belong for the next four years of life.

I looked up at the shiny new dining hall, construction having barely finished over the summer, its glass walls reflecting warm light in my eyes. Posters taped to the outside promoting campus clubs and athletic events. I thought about my parents, who would be crossing the Maine–New Hampshire border, driving the speed limit down Interstate 95 toward the airport in Boston. My mother was probably staring out the window as my father drove, watching the trees pass by, wondering when they would begin to turn.

I MET JOHN first, before anyone else came into my life at Hawthorne. Everyone pegged me as Ruby's best friend, her sidekick from day one. I didn't argue otherwise. Besides, people were drawn to Ruby, her bouncy ponytail of chestnut hair and enduring smile attracting the attention, not me. Everyone wanted to be close to that kind of perfection. People assumed she plucked me from the crowd of girls willing to be her friend when, in actuality, I chose her.

The dining hall was packed with new students, and a few jostled by as they made their way to empty seats. I stood still, eyeing my options. Students were introducing themselves, talking about their summers. I didn't have to choose a seat quite yet. The talk would start in ten minutes. I could grab a coffee from the cart outside. I turned on my heels and left, relieved for open space and fresh air.

"Iced coffee," I said to the barista behind the cart. She looked older, maybe this was her campus job. A junior perhaps. "Black, please."

"Same," said a voice from behind me. I glanced over my shoulder, looking up to see the face that belonged to the voice. It was rare for me to feel short.

Clear blue eyes stared down at me. He smiled, one of those half-smiles, charming and quirky, and had a handsome face, with thick blond hair sticking out from underneath his hat. I looked back at the barista, perhaps a little too fast. She stared at him, too, until he cleared his throat and she handed us both the coffees.

"It's on me," he said. Before I could protest, he had already handed over four dollars.

"Oh, um," I mumbled. "Thanks. That was really not necessary."

"No prob," he said. "Keep your friends close, enemies closer, right?"

I looked at him, confused. His mouth curved into a sly smile.

"The sticker," he said, pointing at something on my book bag. "Texans?" He pointed to his brimmed hat. "Giants guy."

I looked down at my bag. My dad had smacked the sticker on my bag after the Texans won two games in a row last winter. It was a big deal because they usually lost, by a lot. My dad was so excited, his face like a little kid's. I hadn't seen him like that since I was young, so I didn't take the sticker off, in fear of his face falling back into that grief.

"Right. Go Texans," I said. "I don't think we're much of a threat, though."

"Hey, you never know, with some good draft picks," he replied with a wink.

He spoke in that relaxed, teenage-guy kind of way. Dopey and sweet. I smiled a little, hoping to seem grateful and pleasant. But really, I was annoyed. I hated being indebted to people. Especially guys like this, who I knew would give me some pet name and high-five me whenever he saw me, or hold out his fist for a bump, leaving me guessing which one he would choose. I'd rather buy my own coffee.

He held the door to the dining hall open for me, and I slipped inside, eager to get away so we didn't have to talk.

"John," someone called from the path outside, and John the Giants fan released the door and let it close between us, already giving the other guy a loose handshake and slap on the back. They looked like athletes, the way their bodies moved with grace and precision, despite the slight air of nonchalance they both carried in their shoulders. Tan lines on their shins. Soccer, I guessed.

I got in line for my orientation packet and watched them through the glass. I wondered if they had just met, or if there was a preseason, or if they knew each other from home. It was curious watching people interact, watching them decide what to say, how to act. Their first impression the most important. I noted their body language, the attempts to look carefree. I tried to relax my shoulders, but they were stuck in permanent intensity.

John and I locked eyes, his mouth curling into that suggestive smile I would see a thousand times. He gave me a wink, and I turned fast, pretending not to see. I preferred to go unnoticed, but I had inherited my mother's porcelain fair skin and green eyes. My facial features were symmetrical and soft, and no matter how much I ate, my body remained thin. The Texan sun spun my hair gold, despite my urge to be plain and anonymous.

I turned my head away, but I could still feel his eyes on me, taking me in. His laughter rumbled as the glass doors opened and closed for other students.

There was a familiarity about him—in the way he smiled, how he wanted to do something nice for me, the coloring of his skin and hair. I swallowed and forced the memory to pass.

► ► ►

"THE FRIENDS YOU make this week will become friends you have for life."

I listened to the girl speaking in front of us, but my feet itched to move. I could never sit still long and was already dreading the rest of orientation. I didn't understand why we couldn't just read a manual for Hawthorne and be on our way. My appetite was eager for class, schedule, routine. I hoped they wouldn't make us do team bonding exercises.

The girl to my left picked at her cuticles. I watched her pull back the irritated skin on her thumb with her pointer finger. Pull, scratch, pick. She repeated this until the crusty pink flap dropped to the floor.

"Basically, don't get too shitfaced, okay, guys?" the girl in front of us said. "We like to call it *comfortably buzzed.*"

A few of my peers laughed. I wondered if the administration thought it would be more influential to have a senior talk to us about drugs and alcohol. It seemed to be working.

I shifted my gaze to the tops of the pine trees contrasting against the hazy summer sky, where I could make out the top of the chapel steeple, and the tippy tops of brick academic buildings. Edleton, Maine, was an idyllic location for a small liberal arts college, nestled between forests of maple, pine, and oak. When my father and I had visited my junior year in high school, the tour guide told us about the small mill town, how logging trucks dotted the roads and trundled the lumber to be processed into pulp, or wood pellets for heating. Sometimes floorboards. My father was more interested in the logging than Hawthorne and insisted we drive around town afterward, taking photos of all the timeworn brick mills and the dilapidated river watermill that once powered them.

During the tour, I had overheard another prospective student whispering about how the townies hated the privileged students. A student was stabbed a few years ago when a bar fight broke out at the local pub. They didn't get him to the hospital in time, and he bled out on the sidewalk.

Cuticle girl next nudged my arm, staring at a guy in front of us. I followed her gaze. The boy's hair was jet black, his arms flexed as he played a game of Tetris on his phone, his dark skin a welcome respite in the sea of white. He wore a hoodie and expensive dark jeans. His feet were planted solid on the ground, clean new high-tops meeting the cuffs of his jeans.

A whisper in my ear, "He's a prince."

I looked over at the girl, her face exploding with uncontained excitement. Her eyes brightened, mascara clumped on her eyelashes. I scanned the rest of her body out of the corner of my eye. Her features were dark, the opposite of mine. She had tan skin, like she was born with it, and dark eyes, dark hairs on her arms. I wondered if she was one of the international students, maybe from India or Sri Lanka. Her fingernails were painted with chipped blue nail polish, her black hair cut in silky layers around her face. What surprised me was the large size of her chest, which protruded from her small frame.

She leaned in closer to me. "I stalked him on the Facebook group. He's got like ten Lamborghinis. He's from the UAE. Dubai, or Abu Dhabi, or whatever . . . Abu Dhabi, I think. Yes. Because his dad is the finance minister there. I may have also been a bit of a creeper and stalked him on Google, don't judge," she whispered, her accent lilting. British.

I had never been impressed by wealth. I came from a comfortable household, where we never longed for anything, but never bought luxury items. I wanted money for myself one day, real money, but I never felt jealousy toward those who were born into it. There always seemed to be too many strings attached in those situations.

"We should be friends with him," she said, maniacal grin spreading across her face.

Her forwardness was surprising. She spoke as though we were friends—*we*, as in us. I didn't even know her name yet. The only thing we shared was where we sat, in a long row at one end of the dining hall. She let out a loud sigh and sank back into her chair, wrapping her flip-flops around the metal legs. I watched her pull something out of her bag, a stick of gum, and she handed it to me.

"What's your name, then?" she whispered.

"Malin," I said. "You?"

"Gemma." She smiled and squeezed my arm. "My roommate and I are having a party, you know, sort of a welcome do. It's tonight, you should come."

"Sure," I responded.

"So, are you from England?" I gave myself a mental pat on the back for continuing our small talk.

"My mum went here in the seventies. She's American, my dad is Pakistani. It's a whole *thing*. They're always competing to show me their own cultures. Anyways. They did agree that I should get a proper American education to help *round me out*, whatever that means. I think I'm pretty well-rounded already," she said, patting her soft belly and rolling her eyes. "But I don't really mind. You have cuter boys here. With much better dental hygiene."

She stopped, considering something. "Well, not that that matters for me."

Gemma pulled her vibrating phone out of her bag, spilling a pack of cigarettes onto the floor next to her flip-flops.

"That'll be the boyfriend now," she said, giving me a wink.

A few minutes later she texted me her number and just like that, we were friends.

► ► ►

THE PAPER PLATE dipped forward in my right hand, lobster juice dripping onto the manicured grass. I clutched the plastic fork and knife to my stomach. Someone jostled my shoulder, and the lobster lurched forward, its claws outstretched toward the sky. A silky haired girl yelped "Sorry!" as she moved past me, her voice cheerful, genuine. I watched her disappear into the line of students at the buffet, falling into the march for food and drink.

I stood at the shoreline of a sea of students sitting in small clusters, making introductions, forging friendships. In the distance, I spotted a shady patch of grass under a large tree. The ground would be cool beneath me, and there would be nobody asking me questions, trying to figure me out. But I recalled the deal I made with my father and forced myself to walk into the middle of the waves. I stared down at the lobster, dead eyes like black marbles.

As much as I believed college would be the same as high school, I was surprised at the lack of obvious cliques. There were no jocks, no sorority-type girls, no goths or nerds. At my feet, everyone wore flannel shirts and chinos. My mother had suggested I wear jeans and a plain T-shirt, and I noted her tendency to be right in these situations. The girls were decked out in casual apparel, their hair tied back in ponytails or braided over their shoulders. It was as if everyone had tried to look the same, consciously choosing a uniform, eager to fit in. I waded my way through the clones, a preppy-outdoorsy catalog, each group ripped from its pages and placed on the campus quad.

I reviewed my options. There didn't seem to be a place for me, and I received a couple pity smiles as I trudged forward, nobody willing to risk their spot in fear of losing it to me, or because of me. Our personalities were all tightly lidded, hoping they would find a match with whoever we glued ourselves to on the first day. I glanced back over at the tree. Maybe I could put this off a little longer. My father would never have to know.

"Heya!" a voice called out from behind me. I didn't think it was directed at me, so I kept moving.

"Hey! *Maaaay-linn*?" A British voice.

I looked over my shoulder—Gemma waved at me, patting the

ground beside her. I hesitated. This was it, if I sat down, this was where I would stay. I looked at the others with her—two boys and a girl. One of the boys had his back to me, but I recognized the broad shoulders and blond hair. The other girl was bright and shiny, thick hair looped into a bun on top of her head. Elegant, relaxed. Her eyes looked to me, where I was standing surveying their group, and she smiled, waving me over with Gemma.

"You looked so lost," Gemma said as I sat down cross-legged in between her and the other girl. I noticed a piece of corn stuck in her molars, the shiny yellow kernel bright against her teeth. I smiled at the others, who were all staring at me, intruder to their circle.

"This is Malin," Gemma said.

I turned, facing the blond guy, the one from earlier at the coffee cart. He gave me a knowing smile and reached out his hand immediately, taking mine in his, shaking it. A strong handshake.

"John," he said, and then nodded to the boy next to him. "My cousin Max."

"Hey," I replied, plastering a wide smile on my face.

Max and I made brief eye contact, but he remained quiet, his gaze distracted and somber. He was smaller than John, skinny and compact, dark hair parted neatly. He probably combed his hair after he showered. He was athletic, but not bulky and built like John. Even though we were sitting, I was taller than him, but I was taller than most people. The cousins both had those bright blue eyes, the only physical resemblance they shared. Gemma made a hand motion toward the other girl, who was still smiling at me.

"Fabulous new friend Malin, meet my equally fabulous room-mate, Ruby," Gemma said, smiling between the two of us. She enjoyed this, bringing us all together, as if we all needed to thank her for matchmaking.

Ruby's smile cracked into a wide grin, her teeth white and perfect, lips full. She looked so young, if I had seen her on the street I might have mistaken her for a high school student. In the back of my mind, I remembered we *were* in high school barely four months ago, on the verge of graduation, in the awkward and gradual shift between baby and adult.

"Hi," Ruby said, smiling wide, her brown eyes clear and unguarded.

I smiled in return, not sure how to respond to her joyous affect. Up close, freckles scattered like confetti across Ruby's nose and cheeks. Her face was proportional, a real-life manifestation of the golden ratio. Nature had made her perfect, each side of her face mirroring the other in prettiness.

"So you must be who Gemma sat next to at orientation?" Ruby asked. Her voice was softer than Gemma's. I was grateful she led the conversation so I didn't have to.

"Yeah, we stared at the prince for a while," I replied.

"Oh my God, *Gemma*." Ruby groaned, then leaned in toward me. "Did you tell her to leave him alone? I swear, she is such a little stalker."

"Shut up! I am not," Gemma rebutted. She pulled out her phone and started texting someone. Without looking up, she continued, "But hey, if we become friends with him, you'll be thanking me."

Ruby leaned in over Gemma's shoulder. "Who do you keep texting? Is that Liam? Let me see."

Gemma smiled, shielding her phone from Ruby's prying eyes. "Yes . . . He misses me. Poor guy."

"Who's Liam?" I asked.

"Her boyyyyyyfriend," Ruby responded.

Gemma smiled, putting her phone down beside her keycard chain. "I told him we should break up before I came here, but he insisted we give long distance a shot."

I thought fast for something to say. "So, you guys are having a party tonight?"

"Yeah," Ruby replied, forking some potato salad. "You should totally come. Hawthorne College, no parents, right?"

The motto *Hawthorne College, no parents* had graced the "about" on our class's Facebook page for several months over the summer. I imagined an overly excited student had thought it up as he raced to create the page upon receiving his welcome letter. The thought of a party made my head hurt, and I stared down at the lobster on my plate. I prodded it with my fork.

John's eyes were on me. "Never had lobster before?" he asked.

Everyone looked at me, awaiting my response.

"Um, no," I replied. "First-timer."

"It's delicious," Ruby said, dipping a piece of white meat in butter.

"Where're you from? Even the queen of England over here knew what she was doing," John asked, slight head tilt toward Gemma.

Gemma winced, as if being good at eating made her self-conscious. She sucked in her stomach and sat up a little straighter. Unfortunately, this only made her chest stick out more.

"Houston," I said. "My mom is allergic to shellfish so we didn't eat it."

"Ah," John said, scooting closer to me. He smelled like deodorant and soap. I looked behind him, at Max, who still hadn't spoken to me, although he watched us as he ate.

John reached down to the lobster on my plate, and I grimaced as the antennae wobbled in his hands.

"Start with the tail," he said, sliding the body into his hands with ease.

There was a sudden crack as he pulled the white meat out of the tail. He took the shell in his fist and smashed it down onto the plate, sending splashes of body fluids onto Ruby and Gemma. A fleck of watery substance splashed across my wrist. Gemma squealed in disgust and punched John's thick arm. He ignored her as he used his thumb to loosen the meat. Ruby was more reserved, quietly taking a napkin to wipe the fluid off her sneaker.

"Then the claws," he continued, digging with the silver pick into the curved pinchers.

He pulled metal crackers from his back pocket and squeezed the claw between them, sending more juice onto my already soaked plate. John looked up at me with a satisfied smile.

"Welcome to Maine," he said.

I looked at him and then the eyes of the lobster, which were now upside down and helpless in their black stare. I could tell John wanted me to thank him for his help, so I gave him a smile.

"Great, thanks," I said.

He pointed down at a green paste that had started to ooze from the body portion. "You can eat that part, too; it's a delicacy."

"Don't," Ruby said. "That's the—"

"Shit," Gemma said, interrupting. "Literal shit. He's fucking with you."

John settled back into his spot where the grass had begun to stand up again. He leaned back on his palms and grinned. "It's the best part. And it's not the shit. It's the liver."

"So gross," Gemma said, throwing a claw at his chest. It bounced off and fell to the ground where it landed beside John's salmon-tinted chinos. He flashed her a grin, and her cheeks flushed. It seemed inappropriate for someone with a boyfriend to be flirting with another guy, but what did I know about romantic relationships? I had never had one. Gemma pulled a cigarette out of her bag and lit it, not bothering to leave the group. The smoke unfurled into my nostrils, and I resisted the urge to cough. I hoped Ruby wasn't a smoker.

"How do you guys all know one another?" I asked, confused at their apparent closeness.

"Oh," Gemma said, eager to answer. "We literally just met. Like, today." She looked over at John. "Well, I guess he already knew Max, duh, because of the whole cousin thing, and Ruby was with them here for preseason. They all play soccer. And I'm Ruby's roommate. Sounds so complicated when I explain it."

"And we talked on Facebook this summer," Ruby pointed out.

"Right, totally. So, it's like we already knew each other," Gemma said, popping a piece of corn in her mouth.

I looked down at the lobster carcass, my hunger dissipating. The others started discussing their freshman-year seminars, their voices growing distant. I picked up a piece of cold rubbery meat and dipped it into the plastic cup of butter. I thought of all the other lobster remains around us, how only a few days ago they were happy at the bottom of the sea, unaware that their lives would come to an abrupt end on an elite collegiate lawn. And our lawn wasn't even the elitist of the elite. We were the mini-Ivy crew. The ones who didn't get into Princeton, or Harvard, or MIT—the Ivy League rejects. I wondered if Harvard's campus had better lobsters.

I watched Ruby press her knee against John's in the familiar way a girlfriend would do. It was intimate, a moment I had interrupted by witnessing. The others were laughing about something, but I tuned them out, watching John's eyes trace from Ruby's knee to me. I knew he was trying to figure me out, find a way to get me to like him. He was probably wondering why I wasn't fawning over him like the other two. I looked away before Ruby noticed our eye contact, hoping the gathering would come to an end sooner rather than later.

CHAPTER TWO

Senior Day

For everyone else in the senior class, today, Senior Day, is about tradition. It's a Saturday in the middle of winter, and Hawthorne feels sleepy and cozy in the morning. I still don't understand why it can't be in the spring, when it will be warm and we'll be done with finals. My guess is that whoever thought of Senior Day was bored in the middle of winter and wanted an excuse to drink and celebrate for a weekend.

By midday, we are lined up outside the dining hall, where we gather at the beginning of the house crawl, which will lead us to a few of the off-campus houses, each decorated with its own theme. The crawl will then end with a jump into the frozen lake. The other classes watch us, drinking hard alcohol out of plastic water bottles on the sidelines.

In the evening, we will attend Last Chance Dance in the old gym, called the Cage. The dance is seniors only, but usually a handful of lusty freshmen weasel their way in. This whole day, this tradition, is somehow sanctioned and even organized by the administration. It makes them look cool to prospective students, and they have to keep us entertained somehow, when we live out in the middle of nowhere.

I don't care about tradition. I care about what has been happening under the roof of the house I share with my five friends. Things have started to fall apart. We should be tighter than ever, no gaps in our ranks. Instead, we have revealed gaping holes. Things need to go back to how they were, when we were always together, and it was easy. We have been close for three years, I'm not about to let it all fall apart in the last few months. I need this group; I depend on them. And at this moment in time, all I care about is finding a solution to my problem.

Earlier this morning I sat on the floor and leaned against Ruby's bed as we got ready for Senior Day. Her room is to one far end of the house, sharing a thin wall with mine. Gemma's is at the other end, with a view of campus. Khaled, "the prince," as we used to refer to him, owns the house. Gemma is the one who got him to be a part of our friend group freshman year. She likes to think we live in the house because of her, and not so subtly reminds us of that fact.

Khaled lives in the biggest room downstairs, with John and Max in two smaller rooms on the opposite side of the kitchen. The guys rarely come upstairs, respecting our "girl space." Except for John. I've heard too much of him recently, his voice barely muffled by the wall. Everyone in our class always comments on how lucky we are—to have a house, a renovated house, to live in together. We call it the Palace. It's ours, and ours alone. Most students live in senior housing, which consists of small dorm rooms, or they rent outdated houses on the outskirts of campus. We're lucky, I'm aware of that, but I don't feel that way.

Gemma and Ruby both put more attention into their outfits this morning, which consisted of the tightest and most colorful spandex they could find. I had put on my running shorts and Hawthorne sweatshirt, already dreading the rush of cold against my bare legs.

I watched Gemma do her nails in a rush, leaving smudge marks around her raw, scrappy cuticles. Her hair was dyed blue, for "school spirit" she explained. Ruby and I didn't say anything, but we made eye contact, the same thought running through our minds: another cry for attention.

Ruby's final touch was Tutu, a mangy, black tutu that had been a part of our group since the freshman-year eighties dance. Ruby had plucked it out of a bin at Goodwill, and had since found a way to incorporate it into other Hawthorne traditions. I shuddered, thinking about the sweaty dance floors it had seen, and late-night trips to the

Grill. It had even been covered in Gemma's puke at one point. Tutu had followed Ruby from event to event through our time at Hawthorne, a totem representing her once playful nature.

If someone had looked at us through the frosty second-story window this morning, they would have thought how picturesque the three of us looked. The best of friends, getting ready for the pinnacle of our college career: Senior Day. And, in a few months, graduation. Excited to be one step closer to becoming adults. Focused on squeezing out the last drops of friendship, savoring every precious moment. They'd be jealous of us, of our youth and closeness, of it all. Jealous of our happiness.

Jealous of a lie.

▶ ▶ ▶

GEMMA STANDS ON the edge of the bonfire, a cigarette in one hand, hot chocolate in the other, talking with a few of her theater friends. She's wearing her baggy Hawthorne sweatpants and sagging Uggs, a towel wrapped tight around her torso. I look for Ruby, but she is off with John and others, in search of more hot chocolate to spike with whisky. This is my chance.

"Hey," I say, sliding next to her, the heat from the fire biting my nose and cheeks. Gemma looks over at me, gives a smile as she flicks the cigarette into the bonfire. She knows I hate smoking.

"Can I talk to you?" I ask, making sure to sound concerned, reeling her into something important, personal.

"Sure," she says, her voice casual, nonchalant.

"I've been meaning to mention this for a while . . ." I drag my words, try to shift my body into an insecure, worried posture—something she could relate to.

Gemma looks confused, black eyes narrowed. "Everything okay?"

"I guess." I pause for effect, kick a frozen chunk of dirt with my toe. "I'm worried about Ruby."

Gemma loves drama; she is a theater major, after all. A proponent of the dramatic, on and off the stage.

"She's been acting so weird," I start, choosing my words carefully. "I don't like to talk shit, but she's been kind of bitchy recently, you know what I mean?"

There is a glimmer of recognition in her eyes. I know she understands what I am talking about. Ruby snapped at her last week when we were driving to Butternut Mountain to go skiing. We ended up driving twenty minutes in the wrong direction when the GPS failed to find a signal. Gemma kept telling us we missed a turn, but Ruby refused to go back. I said nothing, fully aware Gemma was right. When the navigator started working again and commanded us to turn around, Gemma offered to help Ruby navigate. Ruby's voice went nasty and cold. *Jesus, I'm sorry. If you know it so well you can drive us home.* Except she didn't sound sorry. After that, we turned up the radio and eventually found our way to the mountain.

I focus on Gemma now, hoping I can needle the right spots.

"I have a feeling John is going to break up with her. She's just been so distant and flirty recently. With other guys. And he's noticing. I feel bad for him."

Gemma's eyes widen ever so slightly.

"Anyway," I say, "if they do break up, she's going to be miserable until graduation, and everyone in our group will take sides, and it will be so awkward. I mean the six of us, we live together. We're too close."

"Right, yeah," Gemma says. She looks down at her fingers and starts examining her bitten nails, towel wrapped tight in her fists.

The wind changes and ash swirls around us, whipping at our towels.

"I don't know," I continue. "I don't think he would ever cheat on her or anything, but if it was going to happen, it would probably be today. I mean, he can only take so much, you know? I can totally see him getting drunk and doing something stupid. What do you think? You and John are still tight, right? I was thinking maybe you could say something to him. Make sure he's okay, see if he needs someone to talk to. And I'll talk to Ruby about whatever is going on with her."

"Me?" Gemma says, her voice uneasy. But I can sense the excitement. It's there, beneath her concern for Ruby. "You think I'm the person to talk to him?"

"Yeah, I mean, he always says you're his best girl friend," I say. It's a small lie. "I thought that was obvious?"

Gemma's cheeks flush. The corners of her mouth twitch. She feels special. She is special, at least for this job. "Right," she says, "I'll talk to him. No prob, love. I'm on it."

The others come around the side of the bonfire, heading our way. I watch Ruby carefully. She does her best to look happy, but I know better. Tutu is limp in her hand, dripping lake water as she walks. She and Max are carrying steaming cups of hot chocolate while John and Khaled share a joint between them, keeping an eye out for faculty.

"Don't say anything," I whisper to Gemma.

She nods in reassurance. So serious and sincere, grateful I shared something with her. I know she is feeling closer to me than she ever has before. It's funny how Gemma has ended up being such an essential piece. After all these years when I never needed her for anything. She is always so willing to please, desperate to be wanted. And I know the truth about Liam, which is why I am certain she will do whatever it takes to get close to John. I know I should feel bad for her. And if things were different, I might. But I remember why I'm doing this, and the thought evaporates.

"Hey, guys," Khaled says, giving us his wide, ever-present smile. He holds up a blow-up doll, her face frozen in that perpetual surprised expression. "Denise did great."

"I think Denise needs a break," Gemma says. "You've ridden her pretty hard today."

They laugh together. We hosted a Halloween party at our house junior year, and someone left behind a blow-up doll. Nobody knew where it came from, and Khaled decided we needed to keep her. He named her Denise, and she spent her days propped up in the window of the living room, watching us come and go. Khaled's Facebook profile photo was him with his arm draped around Denise's plastic shoulders, both staring at the camera with that same dumbfounded look.

Gemma takes the joint from him, and they fall into conversation. She looks over at me, her eyes full of understanding, knowing she must keep this secret for me.

I feel John brush my arm, filling the gap in our circle. He looks down at me, and we make eye contact. We've been avoiding each other for weeks. He needs to act accordingly today, or my plan won't work.

My phone buzzes in my palm. I flip it over and stare at the screen. New message from H. I open the text.

We need to talk. Stop pretending you are okay. Let me help you.

I click the phone off and press it hard against my chest.

I had to lie to Gemma. The problem—that thick, heavy thing I am carrying around—is something much worse. It isn't a question of Ruby's social status or our future as a group. It is a far more serious problem, but you can't trust someone like Gemma with something like that.

CHAPTER THREE

Freshman Year

Humidity clung to my shirt as I made my way across campus. I preferred the cold, the bitter air a comforting relief. Texas was still hot this time of year, nothing like Maine. Maine. My new home. I wore black jeans and a silk top held up by thin, delicate straps. The jeans were snug tight, and my shoulder blades were exposed in the blue evening light.

Gemma and Ruby lived in one of the biggest dorms on campus. Ivy hugged the brick siding, and music played from flung-open windows. From the outside, the clashing songs competed for the most attention. It was jarring in a comfortable way. This was what college was really like, walking to a party on a weekday night, meeting up with friends. *Gemma, Ruby, John, Max.* I repeated their names, letting them roll over my tongue. I couldn't believe I had met them all so fast. I needed to be a good friend to them so they would keep me. I reminded myself to be fun, relaxed, to ask them about themselves, to be a good listener. To be *cool,* not lame, and to understand how each of them worked, so I could help them if they needed it. I put a mental tick in the box next to *friends*.

A group of boys sat on the front steps and side-eyed me as I passed them. Smoke wafted in the air above them, a skunky odor filling my nostrils and lungs. On the top step, I made eye contact with one of the boys. The prince. He gave me a wide grin and jumped up to open the door for me.

"Thanks," I said as I stepped inside the cool hallway.

The prince beamed. He was cute, his face soft, kind eyes. A people pleaser. Probably trying to make up for the fact that he was a *prince*. As I got closer I realized he reeked of cologne.

"You heading to Gemma's?" he asked, putting his foot in front of the door to stop it from closing.

Gemma must have found a way to meet him already; maybe she would get to ride in one of his Lamborghinis.

"I am," I replied.

We stood there, sizing each other up for a moment until one of the other boys reached up with a blunt pinched between his fingers. The prince looked down at the other boy, and then up at me again.

"Want some?" he asked, a mischievous look in his eyes, daring me to join them. I knew better than to be the only girl in a group of guys. I knew the stigma attached to *that kind* of girl, and it wasn't the look I was going for.

"No, thanks," I said.

"Suit yourself. See ya up there," the prince replied, and he hopped back down to the top of the stoop.

The door slammed shut behind me. I began to climb the tiled stairs, my steps echoing in the old building.

"Oh my God, hi!" Gemma squealed as I stood in the entrance to her room, her breath fruity and alcoholic. The liquid in her red Solo cup sloshed up and out of the rim, spilling onto the floor. She didn't seem to care.

The door was hitched open to the long hallway, the air hot and thick from sweat-stained clothes. Music was turned up so high I almost didn't hear Gemma's greeting. The bass of the song vibrated up through the floor and into my legs, loud enough to fill the entirety of the hall, which was packed full of new students. I had arrived late on purpose, eager to avoid the small talk before the party really got going. I was relieved most people were already wasted, one couple making out at the far end, his hand up her shirt.

I handed Gemma a six-pack of beer. "I come bearing gifts."

"Where did you get this?" she asked. "We had to pay a senior to buy us a fifth today. Absolutely absurd. I think his fee was more than the vodka."

"My dad, before he left," I said. When she looked surprised, I explained, "He'd rather I get it legally."

"How cool of him," Gemma said, pulling me through the tight crowd. "I'm getting a fake soon, hopefully. It's such bullshit—I am totally legal in London, but not here. *Land of the free* my ass," she shouted over her shoulder. When we reached the corner of the room, she took the beer and shoved it in a miniature refrigerator, its contents consisting of alcohol and energy drinks.

Gemma and Ruby's room was small, the only relief found in the high ceilings. Posters lined the walls, and unpacked boxes and suitcases were shoved next to the walls. Students sat on them, their skin touching, beer cans and cups of vodka and gin gripped in sweaty hands. We pushed our way to the far wall, where a large window boasted a vista of the quad. The old-fashioned streetlamps lit up the pathways, and students walked in groups up and down the cobblestones.

Ruby perched on the windowsill, laughing with John. His bright yellow head tilted down to hers, yin and yang, so close they could touch. He whispered something in her ear before leaving, easily the tallest person as he shifted between students, everyone looking up at him as he passed—the girls eager to be in the vicinity of his allure, the guys adjusting their postures.

I looked over at Gemma, whose smile had faded at the scene in the window.

"So that's John, right?" I said. "I'm still trying to get everyone straight."

Gemma nodded, glancing at me, as if remembering I was standing next to her.

"And his cousin is Max, the shorter, darker one. Super cute, but too short for me," she replied, her voice trailing off as she looked around the room and in the hallway. I wasn't sure if she was joking. She couldn't be more than five feet tall herself.

"Huh," she continued, "he's not here yet. It's weird, him and John don't seem that close, but Ruby says they're always together. John is like an excited golden retriever puppy, and Max is . . . well, that's exactly it. Nothing, absolutely nothing comes to mind. He's a bit of a bore, I suppose. I can't explain it. You'll see."

"I got that vibe at the lobster bake," I said, recalling how Max didn't even speak to us.

"Malin!" Ruby shouted, waving from across the room. As we approached, she eyed me up and down, giving me a hug. I was starting to realize hugs in college were a thing I would have to get used to.

"I love your outfit, so chic." Ruby touched the silk between her fingers, her voice kind. I was used to girls' backhanded compliments. My high school was full of them, everyone complimenting one another and then rolling eyes behind backs. But Ruby was different. She meant it.

She laughed after a second. "Sorry, is it weird that I'm touching you?"

I shook my head no, giving her a hesitant smile.

"I wish I could pull that off, maybe if I lost some weight," Gemma said, nervously laughing between words.

I couldn't bring myself to assuage Gemma's insecurities, and so I looked out the window. I hoped it looked as if I hadn't heard her remark, as if it had floated out the window and disappeared down the well-lit pathways.

Ruby broke the silence. "Oh, Gems, you're gorgeous, and you know it."

"Thanks, babe," Gemma said. She smiled and pulled at her shirt to reveal more cleavage.

Their repertoire was so familiar already, as if they had been friends for years. When my father handed me the rooming questionnaire at the start of the summer, I requested a single room, thinking I would get more studying done that way. I never imagined a friendship would come out of it, at least not like the one in front of me. The only thing I was sure of was that I did not want to be stuck with someone I didn't like. I felt so strongly about that, it outweighed the possibility of an instant acquaintance.

"So, how did you get from Texas to Maine?" Ruby asked me. She cracked open a beer with her pink fingernails and handed me the perspiring can.

I wasn't sure why Ruby wanted to talk to me. In high school, I got away with being a loner. I knew I was pretty enough, definitely smarter than everyone else, and even though the boys gave up trying to date me in the middle of sophomore year, I could have been in the popular crowd. But I didn't want to try. Forcing conversation was grueling, and I didn't have anything in common with the other students. I liked to be alone, reading. I knew it kept my parents awake at night. *She needs friends,* I imagined them whispering to each other in the dark. It had been so long since I talked with people my age, I assumed everyone would rather act like I didn't exist. But now, right in front of me, were two live girls, wanting to be my friends.

Before I could answer, Gemma interrupted, "Yeah, um, I don't even know that yet. You know, you look *so* New York. Like the black-and-white vibes, I love it, and your hair is so straight and blond, that platinum color I've always wanted. But Texas? You don't even have an accent, you don't even say *y'all*—can you say *y'all*?" Her accent was swift and songlike, I could barely keep up. She liked to be the center of attention, the leader of the pack.

I smiled. "I do love New York," I said, deciding on which question to answer first. Both sets of eyes took me in. "We used to visit New England a lot, when I was younger. My parents are originally from Massachusetts, so here I am . . . a little change of scenery. Hanging out with *y'all*."

They both laughed. I didn't mention the truth because there was no point. It wasn't something you explained over a beer after just meeting someone. I spent the next hour with the two of them. We talked about our majors—Ruby for art history and Gemma for theater. They asked if I had decided yet (I had)—English as pre-law. We discussed how we liked how cozy campus was in the fall, and then Ruby was asking if I'd like to go with them to an apple orchard this weekend. I sensed a slight hesitation from Gemma, but I ignored her tight little pout and said, "I'd love to."

Things got blurry when I finished a third beer. I remember considering Gemma and Ruby, asking myself if they would be good friends. I was surprised by how simple it was to get them to like me. I focused on being *normal* and nice. I could play nice all day. Complimenting them, laughing at the right moments, saying the right things. I didn't want to be too extreme in any direction, but not boring either, so I did my best to color in the lines.

Gemma was a little too much of something, her drama exhausting, but Ruby was perfect. She kept conversations going, interested in every detail you had to say. I liked her; she would do. I knew I would have to be more social, more outgoing, more like Ruby, if I wanted the friendship to last.

I wasn't the only one to notice her effervescence. Everyone loved her from the start. She glided around the room, welcoming and introducing herself to the new faces. She handed people drinks and made sure they were happy, the perfect hostess.

It was clear everyone else in the room wanted to be around Ruby, drawn to the fun and light that seeped out of her perfect skin. When the boys weren't throwing interested glances her way, the girls were sizing her up, determining whether it would be more of an advantage to be her friend or competitor. They all reached the same conclusion: friend was the smarter play.

LATER THAT NIGHT, Ruby and I huddled on an unpacked box, giggling over a plastic fifth of vodka. Our bottoms sank into the cardboard, and our shoulders tilted together as we leaned against the wall. I had never actually been drunk before, but I had a feeling this was it. Sweat laced our skin, and I yearned for the ever-present air-conditioning I was accustomed to back at home.

The room had emptied out somewhat; there were only a handful of students still standing. From the corner of my eye, I could see Gemma talking to some other girls, eyeing us every so often. She was pissed off. She had invited me to her party, and there I was, glued to her roommate all night. People were already referring to us as inseparable, asking if we knew each other from "before." That was how Ruby was in the beginning. An open book. Once you knew her, you *really* knew her. I didn't mind spending time with her, being her best friend.

"Hey," a voice said on my other side. I saw Ruby glance at me and smile.

"Hey," she said back, her voice sweeter than it was a second ago.

I turned to see John standing above us, a Ping-Pong ball in his hand.

"You two down?" he asked, holding out the ball.

"You're gonna lose," she replied, pulling me up with her as she stood.

We followed John into the hallway. Max was leaning against the wall holding a beer bottle, and the prince stood at the opposite end of a folding table. Two triangles of red Solo cups were on either end of the table, each cup filled halfway with beer. The floor was covered in a sticky substance, and the air smelled of yeast.

The prince leaned over the table toward me and Ruby. "I'm Khaled, by the way," he said, holding out his hand. "We kind of met earlier."

"Malin," I replied, shaking his hand in return. His hand was warm and slick with sweat.

"The prince?" Ruby asked, causing all of us to stare at Khaled, the alcohol masking any form of politeness we might once have had.

Ruby's cheeks turned pink. "Sorry, I didn't mean to call you out like that."

Khaled sighed. "Don't worry about it. My dad's the important one anyway."

Ruby gave him a grateful smile. "What brings you to Hawthorne?"

"Well," he tried to explain, "I want to be a surgeon. I'm in the pre-med program." He stopped, looking over at Max. "Like Max, over here. Anyway, my parents would rather I stay in Abu Dhabi and get a job in the government, but they said I could come here—to the States—Maine or Minnesota or Alaska. Only the coldest of states. Pretty sure they think I'm going to give up after a semester and return home, especially once it starts snowing. I'm a warm-weather man."

"That's so cool," Ruby said. "I've never even left the country. I hope you don't mind me asking, but you seem so . . ."

"Not like I'm from the Middle East?" Khaled asked.

"Yeah," Ruby said.

"I went to the American School in London for a while—for middle school. My dad was reassigned there for a few years. So I partially grew up there," he explained.

Ruby held up her cup, beer sloshing from side to side. "Well, here's to hoping you stay with us and don't have to return home anytime soon."

Khaled smiled and lifted his cup to hers. "Cheers."

John brushed by me and handed me the ball. "Ladies first," he said.

I looked down at the Ping-Pong ball, not quite sure what I was supposed to do with it. I looked to Ruby for help.

"It's beer pong," she whispered. I must have still looked confused, because she added under her breath, "Throw it in one of their cups, if you make it, they drink, and vice versa."

I was pretty good at throwing balls in cups. Within five minutes, Ruby and I were winning. John and Khaled had chugged about five cups each. They were burping profusely, their movements loose and sloppy. John kept running a wet hand through his hair, which now stood on end, blond tresses shooting in different directions.

"You guys are crushing us," Khaled said, shaking his head with a smile. He didn't seem to care that they were losing.

Khaled carried himself casually, tossing grins and fist-bumping those who passed by the table. His happiness was intoxicating. I wondered what his demons were, if he even had any. I was curious about people like that, who didn't have anything weighing them down.

Ruby and I looked at each other and smiled, relishing our victory, when I felt someone hug me from behind.

"There you are," a slurred voice. Gemma.

"Hey, girl," Ruby said to her. "Wanna play?"

"God no, I'm far too sloshed." Gemma nudged between us, wrapping her arms around our waists. John looked over at Max, who was watching us. He still hadn't spoken to us. His silence was intriguing and irritating at the same time. I couldn't tell if he was shy or if he thought he was too good for us. John and Max started commenting on something, football, I guessed. John made a vague insult about a player, and Max murmured in agreement, leaning against the wall.

"Anyone want to talk cricket? Any takers?" Khaled said.

"What are they talking about?" I asked Ruby. She started to arrange the Solo cups again, pouring an inch of beer into each of them.

"Football. The Giants are playing the 49ers tomorrow."

"Football fan?" John asked.

Khaled was up first, and he sank the ball into one of Ruby's cups.

"Pats till I die," Ruby replied, picking up the cup.

"Oh," John said, "I don't know if we can be friends anymore."

Ruby brought the beer to her lips, hiding a soft smile. "Let me guess. You're from the quaint suburbs of Connecticut, wearing J. Crew and Patagonia, and you're majoring in economics. Giants fan?"

John gave a crooked smile. "You forgot the house on the Vineyard."

Ruby threw the ball, sinking it into his cup. She put a hand on her hip. "Of course. And drink."

"Cricket? Anyone? I could talk stats all day," Khaled said.

"Ohh, cricket! My dad watches—" Gemma started before John interrupted, as if he hadn't even heard her. She looked away, forced to swallow her dejection.

"Dude, you're in America now, cut it out with the cricket talk," John said, tone light, poking fun.

Khaled shrugged. "Whatever, man. It's the best sport."

Gemma watched John and Ruby interacting, their loose banter back and forth. She seemed eager to add something about football, racking her brain for a comment to make. I hoped she wouldn't.

"So you must be a Brady fan?" John asked Ruby.

Gemma added, "Is he the hot one?" She could barely keep her eyes open.

"Yes. Even better in real life. And a really good person, too," Ruby said. "He came to Dartmouth last year to meet the football team. And guess who snuck in to shake his hand?"

Both John and Max looked at Ruby, impressed with the girl who could speak sports.

Football. I didn't get it. I kept smiling, though; it was important to look like I cared, at least a little. I took a long sip of the lukewarm beer, the alcohol making my throat tingle.

"He's a pitcher, right?" Gemma said, her head now resting against my right breast, her eyes fluttering open and shut. She was very drunk.

Ruby gave Gemma a quick "Quarterback."

She glanced down at Gemma and shot me a worried look, as if we should put her to bed. We half carried Gemma to her bed, her feet dragging behind her, and placed her on her side, "in case she pukes," Ruby said. She grabbed a trashcan and put it on the floor next to Gemma's head.

"So you went to Dartmouth before here?" I asked, confused about her earlier remark. Ruby pulled off Gemma's woven sandals, tossing them toward the closet.

"Oh, no," she said. "My dad works there. I grew up on campus."

I adjusted the pillow under Gemma's neck.

"What does he do?" I asked.

We had started talking in whispers, hoping Gemma would go to sleep, although I think she would have passed out in the middle of a circus. She started to snore as we collected empty beer cans off the floor and piled them in our arms.

Ruby's face tightened. I didn't want to make her uncomfortable, so I added, "I looked at Dartmouth. It's beautiful there. Our tour guide didn't wear shoes."

She relaxed a little, relieved. "Yeah," she said, "they're a bunch of hippies. Really smart hippies."

Ruby regained her composure, at ease again. I thought about my home, and how I too did not like to think about it. I understood that, so I didn't pry. I was already dreading school breaks, thinking of excuses to stay in Maine.

Ruby circled back to Gemma, her head cocked to the side.

"I guess roommates are kind of like family. You don't get to pick them, and they're always there," she said. "And you love them despite their flaws."

We were silent for a moment.

"Only child?" I asked.

She laughed. "How could you tell? My idealized view of siblings?"

I gave her a small smile.

"Do you have any brothers or sisters?" she asked.

"Yeah, kind of," I said. I hadn't been asked that question in so long. Everyone at home already knew what had happened, so there was no need to ask. It became an avoided subject, its contents too uncomfortable to discuss. "I had an older brother, but he died."

"Oh," Ruby said, placing a hand on my arm, her bright eyes wide and sincere, "I'm sorry."

"It's okay. It was a long time ago."

"Are you close with your parents?" she asked.

I considered my answer. "More my dad," I said.

"Not your mom?"

"Not really. She shut down after my brother died."

"That must have been hard," Ruby said, her voice quiet. "My mom left when I was a baby. My dad raised me."

I looked at her as she tucked in the sheets around Gemma's arms and legs, making sure she was warm. We stood together for a while, watching Gemma breathe in and out, and then we shut off the lights and closed the door behind us.

A WHILE LATER, time distorted as we drank more, I watched as Ruby and John walked toward the stairs at the end of the quiet hall, his hand pressed against the small of her back. They giggled, hushed, too far for me to hear what they were saying. John had asked if Ruby wanted to go for a walk with him. Her eyes lit up, and she agreed, letting her body fall in line next to his.

Khaled sidled up next to me, his cologne only a little less powerful than earlier in the evening. Now it was mixed with weed and alcohol.

He put a slack arm around my shoulders and stood next to me so that we were both looking down the hallway. Normally I would have cringed from his touch, but I knew he was harmless. Innocent. Naïve. I am usually right about people.

"Cute couple," he said. "You think they're gonna date for real, or just fuck?"

"Um," I said, not sure of how to answer. "I don't know."

Sex was something I was going to have to face at some point. I knew it was a topic in college, something that people did and discussed. I wasn't quite ready to join in, at least not yet. The hallway was empty, and I crossed my arms, feeling a chilly breeze brush my skin. Khaled sighed happily, enjoying our quiet moment.

"So," he said, turning toward me, "you wanna make out?"

I looked at him, his eyes red from smoking, his grin sloppy and playful. Breath hot, laced with gin. I held back a laugh. "I'll pass, thanks."

Khaled smiled. "Yeah, kinda assumed that's what you'd say. Worth a shot, though."

"Friends?" I asked him.

"Sure, sure," he replied. "Want me to walk you home so you're safe?"

I shook my head. I could protect myself. Khaled gave me a sloppy kiss on the cheek and sauntered off down the hall, letting out a loud belch as he began to descend the stairs.

I wondered where Ruby and John were going, what they were going to do. Would they date? Or *just fuck* as Khaled had put it. I thought about that look John gave me earlier in the day, that wink, those playful eyes. I saw my brother, a younger version of John, what he would have looked like if he had gotten the chance to grow up. And then I felt sick and ran to the bathroom, throwing up all the beer I had so eagerly drunk.

CHAPTER FOUR

TEXAS, 1993

In one of my first memories, I am four years old. Everything presents in black and white. We are on a lake, and I am bundled snug in a life jacket. The wind is warm and comforting. I raise my hand into the sky, let the air ribbon through my fingers.

We are in northern Texas, in a rented boat. My father is driving, standing behind the wheel, smiling as we gain speed. His hair tucked underneath his baseball hat. He looks so tall. Everyone does. I am tiny, a little bug in comparison to my parents and brother.

As we start to go faster and faster, my mother is laughing, holding me close to her chest. Her grip is tight and full of love. She adores me in this moment. I am between her legs, and we are both facing the wind. Bo is there, too, still a puppy. He's tucked between me and the side of the boat, his furry ears flapping back from his head. His tongue is out, sending drool onto my shirt. My brother is on the other side of us, clutching a metal handle. He is six, already a big kid.

Bump. Bump. Bump. We fly over another boat's wake and round the corner toward our vacation house. The wind is stronger here, and I feel like I can't get the air into my mouth to breathe. My father's hat flies off his head into the wind and shoots far behind us and lands in the water. He makes a funny face, and my mother is laughing again. I look at my brother. Levi. He is laughing, too.

Everyone is laughing, laughing, laughing. I laugh along too, because I want to be like them.

This is my only happy memory of us. It fades more and more every year. What was once color is now gray. A waning snapshot of how things could have been, before everything changed.

CHAPTER FIVE

Senior Day

Ruby, Gemma, and I are gathering the rest of our things by the edge of the lake, the smell of bonfire fresh in our hair, when we hear an odd, misplaced silence. It spreads from the hole in the ice up along the shore. The crowd of seniors is quiet, a hush blankets the frozen lake. We stop and turn around, searching for the source.

A voice breaks through the silence. Amanda.

There are four hundred students in our class, it's rare to find a face I haven't seen before, on the pathway to class, in the dining hall, or at parties. Amanda's skeletal arms are crossed over her chest, and she leans over the hole in the ice. She's wearing a sports bra and black spandex shorts, her red hair in a damp ponytail. The red and black is jarring against the gray winter landscape, and the hairs on my arms prick back up again.

Amanda's intensity is not unusual—her opinionated smack talk, mostly about other students, has echoed around campus for four years. Besides that, she is a loud human, and alcohol only serves to raise her volume. I almost turn around and dismiss the scene, but I notice the cadence in her voice—unsure at first, almost accusatory, then panicked. She shouts again, her body angled down over the frozen ledge, a name escaping her lips in gasps: *Becca*.

Everyone crowds around, tighter than normal, growing curiosity magnetizing their bodies in one unit. A banner waves above the hushed crowd. The bold white letters ripple across the royal blue fabric: *Senior Day 2011*. I wonder if this will be the year the administration takes away the Jump, the anxiety over drunk college students jumping in freezing cold water taking its toll. It's surprising they even sanction it in the first place. Drunk seniors jumping into a hole in the frozen lake doesn't scream *safety first*.

There is a slight wind on my arm as John runs past us and down the slope to the lake. He glides across the ice, his tall, solid figure taking charge. We watch him push through the crowd and jump. Ruby's hand is tight on my wrist, and we are motionless, waiting for a sign.

"What the hell?" Gemma says, breaking our trance.

Gemma stops herself before she asks the question we are all thinking. Nobody has ever died doing the Jump. It is supposed to be a happy event. A rite of passage for all Hawthorne seniors.

Seconds pass like hours. The water is still, save for a few waves lapping against the cut ice from John's jump. Gemma presses against me, alcohol keeping her warm. She is scared, maybe for Becca. Definitely for John. But she's not allowed to be, not when we are standing next to Ruby. I look over at Ruby. My best friend. A shell of what she used to be, weakening over the past year, her once spirited personality hollowed out and replaced with a deflated version of her former self. I watch her now, her expression severe.

I don't like it. I don't like the unease that overwhelms her. Her arms are slack, and I notice how skinny she has become. Jaw clenched, eyes wide. She is afraid. Afraid her boyfriend of four years is dead, stuck beneath the ice. I wonder what it is like to be that frightened, heart pounding, stomach constricting, palms sweating.

Only a few seconds have passed since John dove into the cold water. The worst part is the silence. All four hundred of us seniors, holding our breath, waiting. We wait for John and Becca to surface, to get up and shake their heads, and embrace us in their arms.

I think I'm the first one to spot it, because I take a sharp breath of anticipation. There is movement on the surface of the water, like something, or someone, is about to appear. Ruby releases her grip from my arm, leaving behind a white handprint on my purple skin.

Before I can speak, Ruby is already running down the slope to the hole in the ice. She pushes through the crowd, everyone parting for her, because they know who she is, they know why she is in a hurry. She is fast—her dark hair and porcelain skin a blur against the slippery translucent ice. Gemma and I follow, making our way through the tight group of students, everyone talking at once.

John Wright, our crowning hero.

He is Herculean emerging from the water, pulling Becca over to the side of the ice. She pales in comparison to his godliness. Her bird-like bones weak and brittle. She gasps for air, quick and succinct, as if she can't catch her breath, the wind knocked out of her. The temperature of the water is so cold it must have sent her tiny body into panic mode. Becca, the fragile little bunny who senses danger and holds still, unable to move. There is relief in her dark eyes.

Amanda slides along the side of the hole to where John is helping Becca out, and she gets down on her knees, leaning over the water. The grooves in the ice cut at Amanda's skin and beads of her blood soak into the slippery surface. I'm always surprised by her strength as a friend. She proves her devotion to her own, a mother hen charged with protective fury.

A few guys from the rowing team pull Becca from the water while John supports her from below. He latches one arm onto the ice, the other on Becca's back. He keeps her safe, talks to her, makes sure she is okay, his voice low and encouraging. Amanda grabs Becca and pulls her close, and then pushes her away again, searching Becca's face for something. She is asking her if she's okay. Becca sucks air into her lungs. She looks disoriented. Embarrassed.

Amanda wraps Becca in a towel and rubs her arms, attempting to keep her warm. The dean of students, probably the most relieved of us all, hurries over and puts a steady arm around Becca. The trio leaves for the health center, balancing on the ice until they reach the reedy shore.

Ruby leans down to John and puts a hand on his shoulder. His muscles tense, and he twists himself into a sitting position on the ice, cracking a smile up at Ruby.

John is already beloved by everyone, and now he is a hero. The crowd celebrates, some release awkward laughs, relieved it's nothing serious. John stands, puts an arm around Ruby and gives her a kiss on the head. Ruby hugs him sideways, her tepid smile barely noticeable. Everyone watches them, thinks how perfect they are together. I'm the only one who senses her hesitation.

I watch Becca fade into the distance, making her way toward the parking lot. Amanda walks next to her, their thin figures mirroring each other.

Khaled and Max appear next to me. Max is quiet, but Khaled cheers for John, like everyone else. Max lets his arms hang by his sides but his fists clench tight. I put a hand on his arm, the fabric of his shirt stiff from the cold, urging him to stay calm. This isn't the place for a confrontation, but I can sense Max is losing patience.

Gemma's towel is wrapped tight around her body, her breath quickening in a desperate fit. She is overwhelmed by adoration for John, her fierce infatuation merging with an eager appetite. She catches me watching her and averts her eyes, but I know what she did only a few hours earlier. I watched her at the swim team house, her face illuminated by strobe lights, splattered blue paint on her cheeks. That look in her eyes.

I know her secrets.

CHAPTER SIX

Freshman Year

My friendship with Ruby was solidified by the second week at Hawthorne. I probably had Amanda to thank. The situation was serendipitous, and I took advantage of it. Afterward, Ruby defined me as her *best friend*. She trusted me, relied on me.

I waited for Ruby at the entrance of the dining hall, listening to the beep of keycards as students filtered in to eat lunch. I leaned against the wall and opened my phone to check my email. I was annoyed she was late. I was always on time. Nothing new in my inbox besides an unread message from my dad. I took a breath and opened it.

Hi Malin,

I hope school is going well—your mom and I think of you every day and miss you at home. We went to Antonio's for dinner the other night and thought of you—I got the chicken parm, I'm sure you're not surprised. I'll keep this short since I'm sure you are very busy. I wanted to see how your classes are going, if you've joined any clubs. And of course, I'd love to hear about any new friends you've made. I also did some research into the health center at Hawthorne, and I think the counseling center could give you some helpful tips to manage any stress you may have . . . Don't forget to ask for help if you need it. It will get worse if you don't address it. I am also here for advice, don't forget that.

Love you,
Dad

I typed out a quick response.

Yes, I've made friends. Clubs are not for me. All is well. Love you.

I ignored the part about counseling. He was always such an advocate for getting outside help, but I could take care of myself.

▶ ▶ ▶

RUBY, JOHN, AND I wavered in front of the pizza bar in the dining hall, staring at the multitude of options.

"I'm going to gain, like, twenty pounds," Ruby said, sliding a piece of mushroom and sausage onto her plate. "But I mean, whatever, isn't that supposed to happen when you're a freshman?"

She worked out too much to gain weight. Her soccer practices were always two hours long, at least, and she started her days with a thirty-minute jog around campus. Sometimes I joined her, and we would run in silence, our sneakers hitting pavement the only sound in the early morning mist.

"I'm sick of pizza," John said.

He gave Ruby a flashy grin and disappeared into the depths of the salad bar. Hawthorne had one of the healthiest college cafeterias in the country—something they liked to remind us about. We were lucky to eat their wheat-crusted pizza, though its texture was cardboard and there wasn't enough sauce.

Ruby stood next to me while I selected pepperoni. We always did our round of the dining hall together—it had become our thing. Hunting and gathering. We had a system—pizza bar first, and if it looked boring, we would move on to the towers of cereal and peruse the hot bar last.

As I turned with my plate, a skinny wrist jutted out in front of me, curling around Ruby's arm.

"Ruby?"

The girl pinned us between her and the pizza bar. She had red hair, the color of a turned maple leaf. There were two girls standing behind her, holding yogurts, both with long dark hair. I studied their faces. Skinny, bony. Hungry. I noticed one of them glance down at our pizza and then up at our faces, judging.

The girl stared at Ruby, a confused look crossing her face.

"What are you doing here?" she asked.

"Amanda," Ruby replied, a tiny, almost unnoticeable quaver in her voice. "I had no idea you go here."

I scanned the faces of the other two girls. They looked bored and annoyed. Everyone at Hawthorne was so friendly; it was weird to interact with zombies like this.

"I got in early decision," Amanda said, smug. "I had no idea *you* were going here. Though I did hear they have a fantastic financial aid program. Your dad must be so proud."

"Yup. Soccer scholarship," Ruby said, her face flushing. She didn't mention that she also got in early decision. I wanted to say it for her, but I stayed quiet, unsure of the dynamic unfolding in front of me.

Amanda eyed Ruby's outfit, slowly scanning from top to bottom. "And you look so different. I almost didn't recognize you."

"Thanks," Ruby said. She shifted her hips, the pizza sliding across the plate.

I chased the glances between the two of them. Had Ruby not always been so put together? She looked flawless, her hair shiny and loose down her back, light makeup, and snug jeans.

"How *is* your dad?" Amanda asked, wide smile crossing her face. I did not trust that smile.

Ruby never talked about her home life. Her nostrils flared, only slightly, and blood rushed to her cheeks.

"He's fine," Ruby said, angry almost. She nodded toward me. "This is Malin."

Amanda looked me up and down. "Oh. Hi."

Her tone made me want to stuff a dirty sock in her mouth. Or a loaf of bread.

"I'm Amanda," she said to me, overpronouncing her name, and I forced a smile. I would spend the majority of my time at Hawthorne avoiding this girl, proving to Ruby that, as a best friend, I was also an ally. "And this is Becca and Abigail," she said, motioning to the two behind her.

Amanda hitched a hand on her hip and stared at Ruby, considering something. "Was that John Wright you were talking to?"

Ruby's eyes softened. "John? Yeah, why?"

"So you know him or something?" Amanda asked.

"We're friends." She glanced at me. "All of us."

"That's so funny you're already close like that," Amanda said, her hand choking the yogurt container. Her eyes bulged out of her head, a horse bucking back against the reins.

"You know, I hear he's kind of a man-whore," Amanda said, fake laughing, "but you probably know that already."

Ruby's eyes narrowed. "I hadn't noticed. We're gonna go eat. Good to see you," she said, overplaying the niceties.

Ruby pulled away from us and disappeared into the crowd. She was gone so fast I didn't have time to disentangle myself from the zombies.

"Um," I mumbled, "it was nice to meet you." I didn't want to talk to this girl any longer than I had to.

I began to follow Ruby, but Amanda grabbed my arm.

"You should be careful with that one," she said, looking me in the eye, making sure I heard her. I maneuvered my arm out of her grip.

The one named Becca gave a weak smile, as if she felt bad, like she was regretting getting stuck in this clique. She was the smallest of the three; I could almost see her veins through her thin skin. She cradled the yogurt in two hands, and I wondered if she would finish it. The three of them stared at me, waiting for a response.

Amanda's eyes glared, ready to dissect Ruby, tear her to pieces right in front of me, urging me to be on her side. I knew this about girls. I knew how they fed on the weakness of others, how they broke each other down and talked shit behind closed doors. They wanted me to feast with them. But I wasn't like other girls.

"WHAT WAS THAT?" I asked when Ruby and I were both seated at a table. John still wasn't back from getting food.

"Oh, Amanda?" Ruby said, her voice quiet. "God. She hates me. We're from the same town, but she always went to private school so we only really interacted at summer camp one time." Ruby let out a loud sigh and pushed the tray of food away.

"Were you guys friends or something?"

Ruby was quiet, deciding whether to tell me something or not. *Tell me,* I wanted to say. *You can trust me.*

"Kind of. It's a long story."

I wasn't going to get it out of her. If I pushed her too hard, I'd push her away completely.

Ruby looked at me, trying to figure out if I was buying her story. "She just hates me. I'm not sure why."

This was my chance to prove I was best-friend material. "You know she's jealous of you, right?"

I knew this was a classic crutch that girls told one another to make them feel better. But in this scenario, it could be true. It was obvious Amanda had a crush on John.

I continued, "Amanda likes John, and she is jealous because John likes you. She's threatened by you."

Ruby's eyes shone. She liked what I had said. "I don't know. She's rich, smart, and pretty. Why would she be threatened by me?"

I answered, "Because everyone likes you; everyone wants to be your friend. And it's only the third week of school. Did you see anyone trying to be her friend? No. I mean, besides those zombie girls."

Ruby laughed a little. "Can we keep calling them that?"

"It's mean girls being mean, which is weird, because we are in college, so who cares? We're too old for that shit. You can't let it bring you down or you're letting them win." I remembered watching her with John, and added, "And I think John likes you."

Ruby smiled a little at the mention of John. "I feel badly. Now we're the ones talking shit. It doesn't make us any better than her."

"Whatever," I said, and then remembering a poster I saw in the admissions office, *"Everyone is fighting their own battle,"* I quoted. "There. We can let her off the hook a little."

"Except her only battle is being a total bitch," she said.

I laughed. "Feel better?"

"Yeah." She grinned at me. I considered asking about her father but decided against it. I didn't want to push her away, not when I had her this close.

Ruby's gaze shifted to my hands. I was wondering when that would happen, when she would notice the scars. I caught her eye.

"What happened?" she asked.

I looked down at my palms, crisscrossed with smooth lines. "Fell through a glass coffee table when I was little."

It was a necessary lie. I looked down at my hands. Remembered the police officers staring at me, their sympathetic glances.

We were quiet for a while, chewing on the pizza while the dining hall buzzed around us.

"Don't tell anyone," Ruby said. "About John. That I like him. More than a friend."

"I won't," I said. "I can keep a secret." That was true.

"Do you think he's a man-whore? Like Amanda said?" she asked me.

"I think a lot of girls have a crush on him," I said, "and he's nice, so he flirts back. It doesn't mean anything."

Ruby sighed, chewing slowly. "We've never even made out or anything. Maybe he's not into me."

"No." I was firm, deciding she needed a confidence boost. "He likes you. Be patient."

She was quiet for a moment. "You're always so sure of everything," she said, squeezing my hand across the table. "I'm so glad I met you."

"Me, too," I replied, wishing she hadn't touched me. I ignored the instant recoil I felt. "And seriously, if you need me to punch someone in the face, let me know."

Ruby laughed. It filled our space of the dining hall with warmth and joy. Her rosy cheeks crinkled her eyes, and the sound she made jolted my memory. It was a sound I hadn't heard in so long, and I realized who Ruby reminded me of—my mother.

CHAPTER SEVEN

TEXAS, 1995

I was six years old when I discovered that Levi was a problem. My parents had always paid close attention to him, but I thought it was because he was older, he was the boy. The first child, the golden child.

My parents looked tired on this particular day. My mother's once thick blond hair was pulled back in a messy ponytail. My father had new lines across his face. They talked in hushed voices in the living room. My mother told me to go play, but I didn't want to play so I sat on the floor in my room reading a book.

Levi had locked himself in his room. I pressed my ear against the wall we shared and heard nothing. Bo licked my toes, and I giggled.

"Shhh," I said to him, "we have to be quiet."

Bo wagged his tail and pressed his wet nose against my chest. I dug my tiny fingernails into the blue carpet as Bo pushed against me and tried to lick my ears. Bo always made everything better.

I heard my parents' voices, flat and low, but I heard them nonetheless.

My father's voice first, pleading, desperate. I didn't like hearing him like that, he was supposed to be strong. "Celia, he tried to hurt her. You saw what happened."

"He didn't mean to; he's a kid." My mother sounded weak, broken. "That's what siblings do, they roughhouse."

Bo's licks drowned out their voices.

We were supposed to celebrate Levi's eighth birthday the next day. A donkey piñata sat in the corner of my room, stuffed behind a rocking chair. My mother and I had gone shopping together earlier in the day. *We'll hide the party supplies in your room, baby girl, and then it will be a surprise!* Unopened boxes of wrapped presents were stacked against the wall.

I wanted to tell my parents that Levi didn't hurt me; I felt fine. I wasn't even mad at him. I didn't *feel* hurt; I didn't feel *anything*. I wasn't afraid.

I wanted everything to go back to normal. I wanted my father to finish mowing the lawn, and my mother to curl up in her chair with a book and watch us play.

I couldn't stop thinking about the look in my father's eyes. After he pulled me from the pool and held me too tight in his arms, he looked at me like I was something scary. I didn't like it. After I could breathe normally again, and the coughing stopped, I told him I was okay. *Daddy, did you see how long I held my breath?*

He had ignored my words, staring at Levi, who was still treading water in the pool. They stayed like that until my mother came running out with the telephone in her hand. She was so white, and her hands were shaking, tears streaking her cheeks.

She's okay, my father had said. He was calm as he spoke, but something seemed wrong. I looked between him and my mother. I didn't know why they were acting so funny.

That was before we went to our rooms.

I laid my head down on the carpet, which smelled of cleaning products. Bo snuggled into the crook of my lap so we were nose to nose, and I kneaded my fingers into his fur, smelling his warm, comfortable smell. I held him tight until we fell asleep, our breath synced together, even and light.

▶ ▶ ▶

LEVI AND I hunched over the naked baby bird, the sun warming our golden heads. I looked up, spotting the birds' nest, a woven bowl of twigs and leaves. The mama bird was nowhere to be seen, probably finding food for her babies. I wondered if the mama would be sad when she realized one of her babies was missing from the nest.

We were on the outer edge of the backyard, under the strong branches that held our treehouse. Spring had come early to Texas, and with it came baby birds that fell from trees and littered the streets and sidewalks. After a few days, the birds would disappear, their fragile bodies seemingly disappearing overnight. I wondered who picked them up, where they went. I asked my dad, and he told me they flew off to bird heaven, but I knew that was a lie. There was no such thing as heaven. I guessed they were eaten by coyotes or our neighbor's cat, who I often spotted with limp mice hanging from its mouth.

"Up there," I said. Levi followed my gaze. He picked up a pointy stick and poked the fledgling. The bird flopped for a second and then stopped, its chest fluttering up down up down.

"Is it dead?" I asked.

Levi poked harder, almost tearing through the fragile pink skin.

"Stop," I said, pulling back his hand. "Mommy's a doctor. Maybe she can fix it."

Levi knocked my hand away and continued with his prodding. "No, stupid, animals go to the vet."

"Oh, yeah. Well, we should take it to the vet."

Levi pushed the pointed end of the stick into the softest part of the baby bird. The bird's chest stopped moving.

"Levi, stop," I said.

"It's fine. Go away," Levi said.

I sighed and stood up, brushing the dirt off my knees. I placed my hands on the straps of my overalls so they hung in place. Bo ran up to me and licked my fingertips, panting in the heat.

I remembered our mother had given me a medical kit for my birthday. Maybe there was something in there that could help the baby bird.

"I'm going to get help," I said.

Levi ignored me. I left him and walked toward the house, the air-conditioning cool against my skin as I made my way to my bedroom and back out into the warm backyard.

I stepped through the grass, red medical kit in hand, Bo at my feet.

I stopped when I saw Levi pick up the bird. He held the bird in his hand, delicately at first, examining it. I thought maybe he was going to kiss it, that's how close it was to his face.

But then he squeezed hard, his fist clenched in a knot, and I felt an invisible hand choke my neck and suck the air out of my lungs. Levi stood, his eyes wide. He looked relieved, almost. Like a weight had been lifted off his shoulders. My mind flashed to what had happened in the pool, his fingers twisted in my hair. The sound of the lawn mower muffled underwater. I didn't struggle. He was supposed to love me, protect me. I thought it had been a game. When he had finally let go, my body climbed to the surface, and I gasped for air, chlorine burning my eyes. That was when my father reached in and pulled me out of the pool.

Levi and I stared at each other, but didn't speak. He tossed the bird in the grass and stomped past me, nearly stepping on Bo as he disappeared into the house.

I didn't look for the bird. I didn't want to see its pink, mangled body. I stood still for a few minutes and experienced something similar to mourning, not for the bird, but for the person I thought my brother was. That feeling was quickly replaced by something else. My skin prickled in the heat. Now that I knew Levi wanted to, *could,* hurt me, I knew I needed to find a way to survive.

CHAPTER EIGHT

Senior Day

After the chaos of Becca's near-drowning settles and our stomachs are full of cookies and hot cider, we gather next to the bonfire on the side of the lake. A few stragglers are still lining up to jump, their faces jittery and apprehensive. I take a breath, inhaling the scent of smoky campfire. I picture my family roasting marshmallows, Levi with melted chocolate around his mouth. I want to open my eyes and start from the beginning, but when I open them, I am standing with Khaled, Gemma, and John. They are laughing about something, so I smile, pretend to engage. But my mind is with my family, back when I was naïve, when I didn't know any better. I was too young to cherish those times, to know that they could end.

"You guys ready for a shower?" Khaled asks the three of us.

"Hell yeah," Gemma says, "I'm freezing."

Showering together is the next step in the day of tradition. Not fully naked, but in your underwear. Everyone seems excited about this, so I act like I am, too. The voice in my head tells me to follow the crowd, *pretend pretend pretend*. John argues that Parker, a quiet dorm, will be less crowded.

When we are halfway up the steep side of the hill, panting, I turn around.

"Wait, where are Ruby and Max?" I ask, looking over at Khaled, realizing I haven't seen them in a while. Denise is trailing behind Khaled, her plastic skin scraping against the ground.

Khaled and I turn around and survey the hill. Small groups of our classmates are scattering in all directions, anxious for hot showers. From our vantage point, we can see half of our small campus. Despite the bare winter, it's still beautiful and quaint with the brick buildings and wide pathways, the slope of the land rolling and calm. A part of me wants to bury myself in a book at the library, ditch the rest of Senior Day.

Khaled nudges me. "Over there," he mutters, so only I can hear.

I see what he sees. Ruby and Max, alone together on the edge of the waning bonfire, in what appears to be the throes of an argument. I look back over at John and Gemma, who are giggling together, try-ing not to slip in a steep patch of mud. Gemma hangs off John's arm, asking him what it feels like to be a hero. I need to stay on course.

"Let's keep moving," I say, "I'm sure they'll find us."

Gemma and John don't acknowledge my comment, and they con-tinue to saunter up the hill in drunken delusion. They are too wasted to notice anything.

Khaled catches my eye, and I shake my head for him to be quiet. He says nothing, flannel shirt slung over his shoulder, the booze keep-ing him warm.

I know he'll keep it to himself, at least for now.

► ► ►

WHEN WE ARE inside the dorm, I veer off to the women's restroom as everyone else heads toward the men's.

The bathroom smells fiercely of urine. College kids are disgusting pigs. There is a roll of unused toilet paper strewn across the floor, winding underneath stalls. Part of the roll is wet and torn, and I step over it as I make my way to the cleanest stall (always the first, no-body ever chooses the first).

I sit down on the toilet and pee, resting my chin in the palm of my hand. Cloudy light filters through the window. Day drinking is de-pressing, the sunlight underscoring our inappropriate behavior and making everything seem dirty and cheap.

When you go to school in Edleton, Maine, you get creative.

Edleton—one of the most beautiful towns in America, and also the most boring if you are a rowdy twenty-year-old college student. Decades ago, the men of Hawthorne College (strictly men-only until 1964) decided to do something about the lack of bars and restaurants, and so they came up with the house crawl, to start Senior Day with a bang. Once a year, five off-campus houses would serve as those sought-after watering holes. The seniors living there would pick a theme and dress up the house. It could be the Playboy Mansion, or a speakeasy, or you could even bus in some strippers from Portland and transform your sitting room into a club, whatever you wanted. On top of that, they decided to make it a competition. Everyone had to sprint from house to house, stopping only to socialize and chug some alcohol. Whoever ended up in the hole in the frozen lake first won. Not that there was a trophy or anything. It was about pride, and getting drunk.

It was so tiring.

I flush the toilet and turn on the faucet to wash my hands. I spot myself in the mirror, red cheeks and frozen white blond hair, dripping icicles onto the floor. While Gemma and Ruby tried to look pretty today (easy for Ruby, she always looked immaculate), I look like I always do—no makeup and natural straight hair. I don't like to dress up.

My mother's voice in my head: *Are you dating anyone, sweetie?*

I could tell the truth, that yes, I am dating someone, kind of. Was it dating? What were we doing? We didn't want to make it public, at least not until graduation, which was only a few more months away.

I clamp down on my teeth, my high cheekbones hardening. I step away from the mirror, choosing to wave my hands dry instead of using the sopping wet towel behind the trashcan.

I think about what happened earlier with Gemma, at one of the house-crawl stops. The dark living room was packed with seniors. Sheets of plastic covered the walls and furniture. Through the glare of the strobe lights, everything tinted blue, Hawthorne's color. The swim team had protected all their belongings in plastic sheets, and then filled water balloons with blue paint. Students were hurling them across the room, at each other and at the walls. I watched as Khaled ripped open a balloon above Ruby's head. She shrieked and recoiled, paint seeping into Tutu's tulle layers. Another flash of the old Ruby. I miss her. Not in a longing, emotional way, but in the way that you want a broken appliance to start working again. Max, hesitant, handed her a balloon, and she threw it against Khaled's chest where it burst open on his shirt, blue paint spilling on the floor.

Max and Ruby. I hadn't seen them like that since junior year. They were getting along, happy. Somehow the merriment of Senior Day caused them to forget whatever it was that was going on between them.

I searched for Gemma in the crowd, scanning for the blue hair. My eyes bounced over the faces of my classmates. I recognized everyone, though most of them were still strangers, even after all these years together.

And then I found John and Gemma, in a dark corner, behind an open door, cocooned in privacy. I assumed they would be flirting, like they always did when they drank too much. At least they knew to hide. They didn't see me, but I saw them. The strobe pulsed with the thundering beat from the music. I scanned back to Ruby. She was distracted. Her focus was on Max, the blue paint. The two of them kept catching each other's eyes, not bothering to suppress their grins. Their matching dark hair was streaked with blue paint, and then drenched when Khaled popped a balloon above them like mistletoe.

Gemma pressed her lower half up against John. She leaned backward, grabbing a balloon from a basket in the windowsill. Her pelvis was pressed hard against his. John pulled back, but he was drunk. His movements playful and clumsy. He didn't even look for Ruby. He probably didn't even think what he was doing was wrong, flirting with one of his girlfriend's best friends.

Gemma smiled up at him, giving him her sex eyes that she used to practice in the mirror freshman year. We'd laugh at her, never realizing she was actually serious. She squeezed the balloon in her hand and the paint spilled on her chest, her V-neck stretched down to expose the crest of her breasts.

Gemma took a small step toward him. She stood on her tiptoes and traced a blue finger from his nose to his lips, laughing.

John looked down at her, eyelids fluttering, nostrils flaring. I had seen that look before.

I looked back at Ruby. She was too distracted. Why wasn't she watching him? I thought about going over to her and warning her, but knew better. All I had to do was wait.

Now, IN THE dank dormitory bathroom, I hear Gemma's shrieking laugh from down the hall. My plan has been set in motion. It's up to her to follow through and put it into action.

CHAPTER NINE

Freshman Year

Professor Clarke stood at the front of the room during our third week of class. He was tall, in charge, confident, an athletic fifty-year-old who looked forty, and stood next to someone I didn't recognize. A guy, maybe a few years older than us. He was shorter than Professor Clarke, stocky and thick.

My phone vibrated against my foot. I looked around the classroom. Nobody noticed.

"This is Hale," Professor Clarke began. "He'll be your TA for the semester. He just started the graduate program here and attended Hawthorne as an undergrad."

Professor Clarke gave Hale a fatherly pat on the back. Hale stepped forward, giving us a wide smile.

"Hey, guys," he said, sounding more like our peer than teaching assistant.

He must have been early to mid-twenties, but he dressed like he was still in college, his shirt tucked in messy around his waist, Birkenstocks on his feet. Hawthorne had a distinguished English department that offered a very selective graduate program. Only fifty students were admitted per year. Hale must have been one of them. He didn't look organized enough to teach a class.

My phone vibrated again. I looked at it, annoyed, and leaned down to pull it into my lap.

It was from Ruby. We have another Gemma problem.

I glanced up. Professor Clarke had left the classroom, and Hale was unpacking his book bag, asking us if we had enjoyed the reading assignment. He couldn't see me. I sat in back, closest to the door.

"After the poem you read last week, I was thinking today we could continue with something a little lighter. Not that Russian poetry is ever light," Hale said.

I looked around. There were a few murmurs of appreciation.

I tapped out a response to Ruby: What now?

My phone vibrated. I switched the setting to silent mode.

Ruby: She keeps talking about how cute that guy Grant is, the guy in your dorm. What am I supposed to say? He is the worst. And she has a boyfriend!! I feel like she should at least break up with him before cheating on him!

Ruby was right about Grant. He lived a few doors down from me. Whenever I passed him in the hallway after his showers (which were rare, our hall monitor had to remind him to clean himself), he would give me a wink and ask *what's up?* I heard a rumor that he sometimes bathed himself with hand wipes.

I replied: She won't cheat. She's obsessed with Liam. And Grant's already hooking up with Becca anyway.

Ruby: Do you really think that will stop her?

Ruby had a point. Even though Gemma was dating Liam, she flirted with every guy in our class. I wondered how long her relationship would last.

Today was Thursday, which meant as soon as class was over we would take John's car to the Walmart a couple towns over. Khaled had a fake ID made for him before he even arrived on American soil and always made sure we were stocked for parties. Nobody partied more than Khaled, but he was somehow already the most promising freshman in the pre-med program. Max didn't seem to mind the competition, and the two of them would egg each other on with tests and labs. Khaled always said, *Work hard, play hard.*

My phone lit up. Ruby again: Whatever, I'll just keep reminding her about her BOYFRIEND.

"Malin." Hale's voice echoed in my direction.

I looked around, confused at how he knew my name already.

Hale smiled at me, and then the rest of the classroom, "Oh, yeah, I know all your names. I studied the student facebook, and I've already read all your papers from last week. Creepy, I know."

There were a few laughs.

"Malin?" Hale looked right at me.

"Yeah, sorry," I mumbled, shoving the phone in the bottom of my bag.

"You know the phone rules," Hale said, standing from his lean against the desk.

The other students looked at me, their eyes wide with relief it wasn't them who had been caught. Everyone texted during class. It was our job to cover for one another, but sitting in the back corner made that difficult. Hale picked a hardcover book out of his bag and placed it in front of me. I stared down at the book, the sepia-toned painting of a young man gazing off in the distance.

"Pick something," he said. He smelled like woodsmoke and Old Spice deodorant.

The room was silent as I fingered through a few pages, running my eyes down the list of poem titles. When I found the one I wanted, I pushed back from my desk and walked to the front of the room.

I cleared my throat and began, *"What's friendship? The hangover's faction, / The gratis talk of outrage."* I glanced up at Hale. His arms were folded over his chest as he leaned against the back wall, his expression encouraging. *"Exchange by vanity, inaction, / Or bitter shame of patronage."*

I finished reading and snapped the book shut in my hands. Outside the window, I watched a few crunchy leaves fall from a fire-red tree. The scent of cider and cinnamon lingered in the air, and each day grew colder with the promise of winter. Everything was better when it was cold. Hot coffee, a long run, a warm shower.

"A shorter one, but a great choice," Hale said, breaking through my thoughts. "A convenient topic for us to discuss in a first-year seminar."

He slipped through the desks at a relaxed clip, his Birkenstocks shuffling, wooden floorboards creaking under his weight.

"You can have a seat," he said to me as he passed by, his eyes meeting mine.

When he reached the front of the room, he wrote, "FRIENDSHIP," ALEKSANDR PUSHKIN on the whiteboard in bold, neat letters.

"Who wants to take a stab at this one?" Hale asked the class.

"Shannon," Hale said, calling on the girl holding up her hand, eager and desperate, "go ahead."

Shannon was always the first one to raise her hand. I was glad she liked to talk so I didn't have to.

"I think he's trying to say that friendship is superficial." Shannon paused. "He seems negative about it, too."

"Why superficial?" Hale asked.

"Well . . ." Shannon paused again, looking down to her right. She always did this when she was thinking out loud. "He is questioning the *idea* of friendship in the beginning of the poem. He's equated it with a hangover, which is like the bad leftover of an awesome night out."

There were a few laughs, and Hale continued, "Anything else?"

"Um, yeah, he is arguing friendship is not as great as it seems. Like after raging and having a good time, all you're left with is a headache. It seemed like you were having a great time because you were drinking, but really, the alcohol was deceiving your perception of reality. A friend can seem great at the time, but then, they're not as great the next day?"

Shannon looked confused as she sat back in her chair.

"You think Pushkin is arguing friendship is like a hangover; okay, I see what you're saying, but what about the rest of the poem? Do you think he is giving up on the idea of friendship altogether? Is there any point in having friends?"

Hale scanned the room, looking for one of us to answer him.

Someone in the front spoke up, "It's such a pessimistic view. He seems frustrated."

Another voice, one that I recognized, "Yeah, it's like he thinks friendship is fake and pointless."

Amanda. She must have transferred into the class right before the add/drop deadline. We made eye contact but she didn't acknowledge my presence.

"That would make things depressing, don't you think?" asked Hale.

Amanda smirked, pleased with herself for making a significant comment.

A few laughs and the room fell silent again. Hale looked at me and paused, our eyes locking. I felt a spit of adrenaline spike my blood. I gritted my teeth, staring back at him, willing him to break eye contact first.

"Malin," he said, smiling at me, encouraging. "What do you think? You're the one who chose the poem. Let's hear your thoughts."

My thoughts were that I didn't like speaking in class.

After a long moment, all eyes lingering on me, I began, "He's arguing most friendships are superficial. But, he believes real friendship exists in rare circumstances. And it's the kind where you stick it out through the hard parts and deal with people's baggage. And if you find that person, you should be loyal to them, and they will be loyal in return. That is what real friendship is."

Shannon snapped up from her seat, her palm slamming hard on her desk.

"Right," she said, as if something clicked in her brain. "A true friend will be there for you in the worst of times, and that's how you know they're real. And all the others—like, the people on the edge of your life—they don't matter in the end."

Hale nodded in agreement, thrilled we had gotten so far in our analysis.

"Keep that idea in mind as you navigate life here at Hawthorne. A true friend is a gift. Hopefully you know it when you see it."

I thought of Ruby and how she had started calling me her *best friend*. Nobody had ever called me that before.

I glanced at my watch. I hated staying in class past the allotted time. A few students started shuffling papers and closing laptops when out of the corner of my eye I saw a hand shoot up. It was Edison. It was always Edison. He had an exhausting habit of asking a broad question right before class was over, causing us to sit, anxiety-ridden, for five minutes after class, sometimes ten. I fought the urge to walk over to him and shove his hand back down. I hated when things ran late. I liked sticking to a schedule, a definitive beginning and end.

"Edison?" Hale asked.

There was a collective sigh from the class as everyone, all girls, shot Edison an infuriated glance. I watched something, amusement maybe, pass across Hale's face.

"So," Edison started, "is this a common theme in Russian poetry? Are there other poets who discuss friendship, and if so, doesn't it sort of go against the traditional antiquated motifs of Russian poetry?"

When class was actually over, a full ten minutes later, we were divided into groups of three and told to meet over the weekend to answer discussion questions. I dreaded group work.

Hale called out the study groups, Malin, Shannon, Amanda. *Amanda.* Ugh. I had avoided her so well until now. We let Shannon chatter away about meeting in the library on the couches, and I agreed, impatient to leave the classroom.

I packed my bag, stuffing my books and laptop into the tight space. I felt someone standing in front of me, and I looked up to see Hale. Up close, I noticed his soft facial features, the slight bulkiness of his body. Not fat, but sturdy. He was average height, his hair thick with waves, parted off-center. He wore a green plaid shirt, the cuffs rolled up carelessly around his forearms.

"What are you thinking of majoring in?" he asked me. Smiling. Did he ever not smile?

I didn't respond right away, and I took my time zipping up my bag. The quieter I was, the more uncomfortable it made people, which led to me being left alone.

"English," I replied, "for pre-law."

"You want to be a lawyer?"

"Yup." My voice came out confident, maybe a little annoyed.

He raised his eyebrows. In the fight between liberal thinkers and greedy corporate America, I was choosing the latter. I didn't want to give him a chance to save my soul and sway me in the other direction. I looked out into the hallway, signaling that I had to go.

"Well," Hale sighed. I avoided eye contact, making sure to focus on my bag. "I read your first essay on Tolstoy. It was really, really good. And great job today. Have you read Pushkin before?"

I shook my head no.

"Wow. You really nailed that analysis."

"Thanks," I said, shifting in place, looking toward the door. I could tell he wanted to talk more, but I had places to be, like meeting my friends to procure illegal alcohol.

"I gotta go," I added.

"All right," he said, "get outta here. Go enjoy the afternoon."

I finally looked at him, letting our eyes lock. Up close, I realized his eyes were a deep, pure blue, steeped in empathy I didn't want or need.

I left Hale standing in the classroom. He was watching me leave, trying to figure me out, probably wondering if I was a bitch or just shy. That's what people usually thought, at least that's how it was in high school. But there was nothing to see, really. I wouldn't give him anything else, and his curiosity would disappear. He'd soon learn that and forget about me, which was what I preferred. I liked living in the shadows, away from the compliments of teachers and professors. The limelight was not a place I wanted to be.

As I pushed open the double doors into the brisk fall air, I pulled my phone out of my bag. Five new texts. I always knew when Ruby was texting me because my phone would vibrate five times in a row, quick and succinct reminders of her presence.

Ruby: You know it's a bad sign when you put your jeans on and they don't fit. No more food. No more beer. Hard alcohol only, and no mixers. That fucking pizza bar.

Ruby: Literal rolls, everywhere.

Then, after a ten-minute gap:

Ruby: OMG. M!!!!!!?

Ruby: Why are you not responding???

Ruby: I HAVE TO TELL YOU SOMETHING, TEXT ME BACK!

► ► ►

JOHN HAD ASKED Ruby out. On a date. A real date, and not a walk back at the end of the night, at a restaurant in Portland. And this was a big deal at Hawthorne. Usually students hooked up on the weekends and did, or didn't, decide to be exclusive. The date meant they were a couple. The first to proclaim such a title in our class.

Ruby and I peeled off from the guys upon entering Walmart, making our way to the endless aisle of instant food.

"I think we're gonna go to the Thai place," Ruby said, pulling a box of ramen off the shelf. "I've been craving drunken noodles. And it's the best restaurant in Portland right now."

I took the container of ramen from her and added it to the pile already in my arms. I had started noticing Ruby's shallow tendencies toward money. John's money, specifically. The way he would talk about his house on the Vineyard, and how her face would light up even though she had never been there before. Or how she would check the labels of his clothes, as if approving of the designer, relieved to find out how wealthy he actually was.

"Does this mean he's your boyfriend now?" I asked.

Ruby continued down the aisle, scanning the shelves, smiling to herself. "I guess so."

"Are you sure you're cool with that? Being locked down so early?"

Ruby laughed. "Yes, M. That's what dating is. There's no one else I want to be hooking up with. And I definitely don't want to see him with anyone else. So, yeah, I am definitely cool with it."

I had watched John and Ruby closely over the weeks. The way they gravitated toward each other. Magnets. I didn't know what that feeling was like. I had never experienced it. I watched carefully, the excitement they felt toward each other, the way they held hands, gentle and protective. I wondered if I would ever have that.

"So are you in love?" I asked.

Ruby looked at me, curious. I knew I should stop asking questions, but I didn't get why she would want to be someone's girlfriend, especially so early in the semester.

"Maybe," she said. "What's with all the questions?"

"Oh," I replied, "nothing. I want you to be happy."

"Well," she said, sounding a little defensive, "I am."

"Great," I said. "That's all that matters."

I watched her get farther away, pulling a few boxes of microwave macaroni into her chest. They seemed like a good couple. They already had inside jokes and were plenty affectionate. John was nice to me, too. Whenever he got Ruby a drink at a party, he always asked me what I wanted, as well. I was somehow included in their relationship, an add-on to Ruby. But I couldn't shake the weird feeling I had about him. I knew it had to do with Levi and that I should just ignore it. John wasn't Levi.

"Oh my God, M," Ruby squealed from the end of the aisle, holding up a colorful box in her hand. "Gushers! My childhood in a box."

WE WAITED FOR the guys in the parking lot. It was better if we split up while Khaled bought the alcohol with his fake. Ruby and I perched on the back bumper of John's car, a BMW that once belonged to his mother. Both John and Max drove their parents' old cars, luxury vehicles with out-of-date interiors.

I pieced together that John's mother and Max's were sisters. It seemed like John's father was no longer around, and I assumed he had passed away, leaving the family with a lot of money. More money than Max's family. John never talked about his father, and I wasn't about to press him for details.

Unlike the rest of us, Max appeared homesick at times. He was constantly texting with his parents and younger sister. Smiling at the texts and then his face resigned afterward, thoughts elsewhere. Maybe wishing he was with them, and not us. Something I didn't understand. Maybe my family could have been that way, if Levi had been different.

Ruby's phone buzzed.

"It's Gemma," Ruby mumbled, pulling her phone out. "Checking in."

Gemma hated being left out, but her theater class was putting on a production this weekend and she was buried in rehearsals. She complained about being left out, and Ruby worked overtime to make her feel a part of the group. She tapped out a response, the wind picking up, cold air brushing through my sweater.

We were silent. We were at the point in our friendship where silence wasn't uncomfortable or awkward, and it had become peaceful almost, the rhythm of our interactions natural and comfortable.

Ruby shivered and rubbed her arms to generate warmth. "Hey," she said, remembering something, "did you know that Max has anxiety?"

"What do you mean? Like about something specific?" I asked.

Ruby and I often discussed the others in our moments of privacy. We dissected everyone's personality, making sense of who did what and why. Khaled hated being alone. He always had to be with one of us, if not all of us. When Max and John had soccer practice, Khaled would text Ruby, Gemma, or me to find out where we were. Even if we were going to an a cappella concert, a typically female-oriented endeavor, Khaled was by our side. When he studied in the library, he sat in the busiest section, craving the constant flow of human interaction. It was like he was afraid of being alone, or the silence that came with it. I didn't understand it—I liked solitude, it gave me clarity and a chance to recharge.

"You know how we have that class together? The biology one?" Ruby asked, rolling her sweatshirt over her hands and balling the ends into a tight plug. She crossed her arms over her chest.

It was funny to think of Ruby, the art history major, in a biology class. That was Hawthorne, the liberal arts education. We were all required to take a variety of classes.

Ruby continued, "We were in the lab super late the other night, and just ended up chatting about, well, everything. And I was telling him how I get so nervous before soccer games, like everyone watching me and stuff, and he said he gets the same way. Except he gets panic attacks. Said he's gotten them since he was in middle school."

"Does he know why?" I asked. Max was quiet, but I never got the antsy vibe from him. I thought he didn't like us. Then again, we hadn't spoken much. Never one-on-one.

"I didn't want to pry," she said. "But it seems like something happened, or changed, when he was a kid, because he said it was like a switch was flipped. One day he was fine, happy, and the next, he wasn't."

I knew about flipped switches. Despite the cold air, I felt the humidity of home hot against my throat.

"That sucks," I said.

"Yeah, it seems awful," she said. "You remember when we were at that party a few weeks ago, the boys' soccer team one?"

I remembered. A few of them had hit on me, unsuccessfully. I couldn't take them seriously, not when they were sloppy and drunk, their eyes going off in different directions when they tried to talk to me. Sweaty and wet with spilled beer, smelling like body odor.

"Yeah," I said.

"You know how Max just sort of, like, disappeared?" she asked. I remembered that, too. When we all went to leave, we couldn't find him. John shrugged, suggesting Max had gone home, *He's probably bored, only boring people get bored, right, Malin?* He nudged me in the arm, like we were good friends.

Ruby continued, "Well, I guess he did leave early. Because he felt like he couldn't breathe. And his hands went numb. So, he went *jogging*. Until two A.M."

I had never experienced anxiety or panic attacks. My father once told me my mother developed anxiety after the accident, but I didn't understand what it meant. She was distracted all the time, but other than that, she didn't act upset or anything. She eventually went to therapy. I remember the term *PTSD* thrown around in whispers, behind closed doors.

I tried to recall that night. The six of us had been together until around eleven. It was so crowded we never made it past the entryway of the house. The memory was fuzzy; all the parties had blended into one long string of binge drinking. An image of Max leaving flashed in my mind. He never looked comfortable at parties, as if he was counting down the minutes until he could leave. But that night he had been glued to Ruby's side, and he actually seemed happy. They kept laughing about something. Probably Gemma, who was wasted, per usual.

But Ruby was right; I did remember him leaving without saying anything. And there was something else. John had said something to him, too quiet for me, or anyone else, to hear. After that, I have no recollection of Max at the party.

"Do you think he gets therapy for it? The anxiety?" I asked.

She shook her head. "No, no, definitely not." She sniffed, all of us getting over the same cold. "And he asked me not to tell anyone."

Her voice inflected at the end, as if it was a question.

"Got it," I said. I understood. I could keep secrets.

The boys hurried out of the building, mischievous grins and heavy bags in their hands.

"Success?" Ruby asked as they got closer.

"Oh yeah," Khaled replied, placing a few bags into the trunk, glass bottles clattering.

"Holy shit. Did you guys see this car?" John asked, putting down his bags of beer, peering into a faded green sedan parked next to us. The bumper was hanging off the corner, and the sides of the car were covered in dents.

We all crowded around John, and I realized what he was talking about. It was filled with fast food containers, plastic bags, mostly trash. There was a water bottle in the console filled with cigarette butts. You couldn't see the seats—the driver's side was covered in paper, what must have been old food wrappers.

"What an animal," John said, backing away and opening the trunk of the BMW.

"Who lets it get this bad?" Khaled asked. He looked horrified. I'm not sure he grew up witnessing this kind of poverty, if any at all.

Ruby, Max, and I circled the car.

"Oh, no," Ruby said to us. I followed her gaze, to the car seat in the back. "So sad. Can you imagine what home must be like, if this is the car?"

"People make their choices, Rubes," John said, closing the trunk and heading to the driver's side of the BMW.

Under his breath, Max whispered softly so only we could hear, "Good thing you made the right choice being born into money."

Ruby and I looked at him, and he caught our glances, his expression embarrassed almost. Ruby cleared her throat. I knew she hated awkward moments, felt like she had to fill the gaps of silence. I heard footsteps behind us and found a man staring at us.

"Can I help you?" he asked.

He was in his mid-thirties, long greasy hair held up in a ponytail. He looked so worn, and I looked down at the bag of ramen in his hands—the same flavor Ruby had picked out. In his other hand was a stack of lottery tickets.

We all stared at him, trying to think of what to say, but John ignored him, climbing into the car. I heard him say to Khaled, "Oh good, townie trash paying the poor tax."

I glanced at the lottery ticket and the man's expression, unchanged. I was relieved he hadn't heard John. I didn't hear Khaled respond, and I wondered how he was dealing with the comment. I imagined he was going through some sort of internal dilemma about placating John but not wanting to be an asshole.

"Oh," Ruby startled. "Sorry, we'll get out of your way." I knew she was trying to imply that we hadn't been staring at his car, and that we were only trying to get into ours. But it was obvious what we had been doing. Max held the door open for her as she climbed into the back seat, and I hopped in on the other side.

The man watched us, walking slowly, hesitantly, to his car door. The BMW started up with a loud rev from the engine. Before we pulled away, John let out a laugh. "Shit, someone take that dog to a groomer."

I whipped my head around, knowing the window was open. I had hoped the man didn't hear John, but by the look on his face as we drove away, there was no way he had missed it. None of us laughed at John's "joke." If Gemma had been there, she probably would have. Ruby avoided eye contact with me and stared out the window until we got back to campus. Her mind was racing, with what I wasn't sure.

▶ ▶ ▶

IT WAS DARK by the time we got to campus and walked back from the freshman parking lot. It had never been an issue before, us bringing in beer and various hard liquors.

Campus security stopped us a few feet away from the entrance to the dorm. The chatter we had carried back from John's car came to an abrupt end as we peered out into the darkness.

"Hey! You kids!" the officer called out in the dusk.

We didn't even see him coming. There was no warning—no blue-and-white flash of his vehicle, or wavering cough to announce his presence. I tightened my grip on the two bags in my hands. One held a six-pack of beer, the other held two handles of gin. I maneuvered the hard alcohol behind my thigh, hoping it was somewhat out of sight. The officer made his way toward us, heavy boots shuffling on the asphalt path.

"Shit," Khaled said under his breath.

Both John and Max stopped walking, and looked at each other. I knew they were worried about getting a strike; they would be benched for the rest of the season. So would Ruby. I noticed Max took a step in front of her, as if to shield her from the officer.

We stiffened in unison as the security officer approached.

"You freshmen?" he asked us, hands on his thick hips, a fold of skin muffin-topping over his tight uniform.

"Yes, sir," John responded. Our unofficial spokesman.

The officer cleared his throat and grunted a little. I could make out his nightstick in the dark, not that he would ever use it, or have a reason to. He pointed to the plastic bag.

"Open it up," he said to John, his Maine accent thick and heavy.

John gave his warmest smile, chock full of charm, keeping the bag shut. Beer was legal on campus. He had a twelve-pack. Even if the officer found out, we wouldn't get in trouble. Ruby, Max, and I were the only ones with hard alcohol.

"Just some beer. Want one?" he said, his charm melting into the chilly evening air.

"Funny guy, huh?" the officer asked. He puffed out his chest, validating his importance as campus security.

As he rummaged through the bag, John shot Max another warning glance. The officer handed back the bag, grunting in approval. He eyed Ruby behind Max.

"Miss," he said, beckoning her over, and she walked forward, her eyes confident and alert.

John watched Ruby, his eyes tight with skepticism. I knew what he was thinking. Ruby was incapable of lying; we all knew it. She was too nice.

"Sorry if we are doing anything wrong," she said, her voice graceful with respect. "My dad was in town and offered us a ride to the store. We didn't mean to cause any trouble."

At the mention of her dad the officer narrowed his eyes, as if parental supervision trumped his position and he knew it. Ruby's power play worked, somehow, and he grunted again, this time the inflection nonchalant and accepting. Her sweet, syrupy words and wide eyes had worked their naïve, girlish magic. The officer gave her a slight smile and stood a little straighter.

"Don't do anything stupid," he said, still focusing on Ruby. "Administration is on our ass about strikes this semester."

"You got it," she said. "Thanks for letting us know. We really appreciate it."

The officer gave a final grunt of satisfaction and sauntered off, his bulky body disappearing down the dark path.

When he was out of earshot, we could finally breathe again, and laughed with relief as we started toward the dorm.

"That's my girl," John said, leaning over to land a kiss on Ruby's cheek.

She beamed. She didn't know he had doubted her for that small second, didn't see the critical look he gave her as she had stepped up to the officer.

Her bravery surprised me. Confronting authority like that, and lying so boldly, it wasn't the Ruby I knew. I watched how happy she was to have gotten us out of trouble and surmised the fearlessness was to impress John. I felt like I was seeing her without her clothes on and hung back, unable to stomach her apparent willingness to please.

Ruby flung open the door and started up the stairs, with Khaled right behind her. I paused to adjust the alcohol in my arms, and I think John thought I was far enough away, because I saw him turn to Max so they were face-to-face, a hand on Max's shoulder.

"Good job staying off your moral high horse, thought you were gonna fuck that up for sure."

I didn't look to see Max's reaction. I stalled on the bottom of the steps, adjusting the heavy bags, to make it seem like I hadn't heard anything. Out of the corner of my eye, I could sense Max looking at me, wondering if I heard.

"Can you hold the door?" I called, adding to the pretense, still not looking up.

John had already started heading inside, taking the steps two at a time.

"Sure," Max said, his voice quiet.

We walked up the stairs together, mirroring each other's silence. I wondered why he hadn't stood up for himself. Maybe it was a cousin thing, a part of their relationship I didn't understand.

I blamed John's remark on the scare, the fear of getting caught and the nerves firing in his synapses. People were weird; they said strange things when they were scared. Maybe he was in a bad mood that day. Maybe he got a bad grade on a test and was taking it out on the people around him. I convinced myself it was a one-time thing. I didn't need to get involved. My job was to be easygoing, relaxed Malin. *Be chill,* Khaled would have said. Get good grades. Have friends. Be a normal college student. I wasn't going to go down the other road.

▶ ▶ ▶

I CUT ACROSS the quad the next morning, setting a trail of footsteps in the dewy grass. Shannon wanted to meet before the weekend to avoid thinking on a hangover. Amanda and I had begrudgingly agreed. Anyway, it was a good plan to avoid Ruby finding out that I was spending time with someone who hated her.

My head rang from the night before. We had played quarters late into the night, laughing about our security guard encounter, relieved we'd avoided getting into trouble. Even Max cracked a smile toward the end, when Ruby teased him for looking like a deer in headlights. Gemma had been a little put out, jealous she hadn't been the one to save the day, putting her theater major to good use. She tried to hide her eyes darting between Ruby and John, but I noticed. Ruby spent the rest of the night linked around John's arm, fetching him beers until we went to sleep.

I rounded the corner for the library path and heard my name called from a distance. I spotted Max, who was waving from under a tree, the leaves flaring yellow and orange. As I got closer I saw a text-book balanced on his lap, thermos of steaming coffee in his mittened hand.

"What are you doing?" I asked, my teeth chattering. "It's freezing."

"I run hot," he said. "And it's quiet out here."

I looked around the empty quad, completely devoid of students this early before class. Max continued, "I'm studying. Want to join?"

"Um, no, I have a group thing," I said.

It was the first time we had been alone together, and I didn't know what to say to him. I looked over my shoulder at the library.

"You can go," he said, teasing a grin. "We don't have to do small talk."

I adjusted my bag on my shoulder. "Very funny."

I spotted a camera peeking out of his bag. "Taking photos of something?"

Max looked down. "Um, yeah. For the art elective."

"Anything interesting?"

Max took a sip of his coffee, considering whether he wanted to tell me or not. "The retirement home."

"Like the building, or . . . ?"

He laughed. "The people inside the building. I do portraits. And some landscapes. My professor seems to like the landscapes better, though, so I guess I'll stick to that."

"So you take photos of the people there?"

"Yeah, it started because they needed a volunteer to take photos for the bulletin board. Sort of a who's who of who lives there."

"That's cool," I said.

"Yeah. It's really sad, to see them all living there. The housing isn't that great. Did you know that the United States treats the elderly pretty terribly in comparison to other countries?"

I did not know that. "No," I said.

"It's pretty depressing. Sorry. Debbie downer, I know."

"No, it's nice. That you care. I bet they love you."

He shrugged. "I dunno. I think they just like talking to someone different."

I didn't know what else to say. Responding to people was so taxing. And then the bells began to ring. "I gotta go," I said, hitching my bag up higher on my shoulder.

"Enjoy that group work," he called out as I got back to the path, his voice playful, teasing.

I looked back at him, his slight frame bulky with the puffy jacket, head made smaller by the wool hat. I recalled my conversation with Ruby and wondered if he felt anxious right now. He looked the most relaxed I'd ever seen him.

There was something endearing about him, sitting there alone. It was familiar, reading in the silence. A part of me wanted to go back and sit with Max, but I trudged on to the library.

. . .

I PUSHED THROUGH the library doors, the metal scratching against the tile floor. The library loomed out of place on campus, the early nineties architecture clashing with the brick schoolhouses and stone walls. The foyer opened into a large common area lined with computers and desks. I spotted Shannon in the far corner by a window, curled up on one of the couches. Amanda sat next to her, her legs tucked underneath her body, fixing her hair into an oversized bun on top of her head.

"Hey," I said as I approached. I let my bag fall to the ground and slumped on the couch next to Shannon.

"Good morning, Malin," Shannon sang out, bright and cheery. I hated when people were too loud in the morning.

"Cute sweater," Amanda said with a smirk. My sweater was old, gray, boring, like the library.

"Thanks," I replied. "Should we—"

Amanda interrupted me with a flat palm in front of my face. "Before we start," she began, dragging out her words with suspense, "I heard the craziest thing about our TA last night."

"What?" Shannon asked.

"You know how he's dating that other grad student? The one who always wears prairie skirts, kinda hippie-ish?"

"Yeah?" Shannon replied.

I knew what she was talking about. I had seen Hale with a girl in the dining hall last night, his hand parting from hers as they made their way to the hot bar.

"Apparently," Amanda said, "she got caught fooling around with a professor."

"Seriously?" Shannon asked.

This was why I hated study groups. The inefficiency was frustrating and tiresome.

Amanda continued, "She was caught with one of the English professors."

She delivered the end of the sentence in a rush, as if her body could no longer tolerate keeping it inside.

"That is so bad," Shannon said. "Like so, so bad."

"I know. I was finishing up some work in the Greenhouse last night, and I heard some of the other professors talking about it. And"—she paused for maximum effect and lowered her voice to a whisper—"the professor is married."

The Greenhouse was one of the newest academic buildings, funded by rich old alums. Centered on an open floor plan of couches and fireplaces, it provided a comfortable respite from the library. It was common for professors and students to sit in the same space, supposedly facilitating an open atmosphere to discuss academia.

"Oh," Shannon said, her eyes wide, "poor Hale."

"I know, right? Who would cheat on that? I mean, he's obviously nerdy, but he's cute. Too nice for me, though. So . . . wholesome. I'm sure that gets boring to date."

"So, you're into dumb jerks?" Shannon asked, teasing.

Amanda rolled her eyes. "Shut up, you know what I mean."

"Is she getting kicked out?" I asked, trying to sound interested.

"Oh, I don't know. Who cares. It's such a scandal. Besides, I don't think you get kicked out for something like that. I feel like the graduate program is different than undergrad. If anything, the professor might get fired. People can fuck whoever they want, I mean, as long as it's consensual, obviously," Amanda said.

I leaned my forehead into the palm of my hand. We were all quiet for a moment.

"You know," Amanda said, staring at me, "Hale seems to like you, Malin."

I didn't respond.

Amanda persisted. "What did he say to you, anyway? After class?"

She was jealous that he hadn't approached her. I'd rather he had. Better for me if he paid attention to other students. Then I could go unnoticed.

"He wanted to talk about my major," I said.

"Well," Amanda scoffed. "You can tell he's impressed by you, or whatever. He probably likes the weird quiet types."

I ignored the blatant insult against my character, though she wasn't wrong in her assessment.

Amanda continued, "And now that he's single . . ." She raised her eyebrow at me, the insinuation clear.

Shannon's eyes widened. "But he's our TA."

"Like that fucking matters. *Clearly,*" Amanda said, still waiting for my response. "Besides, he just graduated last year. It's not like there is some awkward age difference."

"It's still five years," Shannon protested. She looked at me, gauging my interest, both of them wanting me to indulge in the fantasy.

I let the moment roll into an uncomfortable territory, and let it sit there, irritated and raw.

Amanda perked up, like she had thought of something more interesting. "Or do you have your heart set on John Wright, like everyone else in our class?"

"You know he's dating Ruby, right?" I asked, pulling my books out of my bag, stacking them on the table. I opened my laptop and the screen brightened in the early morning light.

Amanda rolled her eyes. "She doesn't deserve him."

Like before, in the dining hall, I could tell she wanted me to ask more. But I didn't. It was satisfying, bothering her that I didn't care, and made me feel closer to Ruby. Shannon looked back and forth between the two of us, a cat chasing light.

"So," I said, after I was pleased with how awkward I had made the moment. "Shall we?" I picked up the book, waiting for them to follow my lead, but they both looked at me like I was insane.

I sighed. Group work, the worst.

CHAPTER TEN

Senior Day

I am a fraud, a fake. If people knew my secrets, they wouldn't want to be friends with me.

For starters, I hate getting drunk. Wasted, hammered, shit-faced, tanked. I fake it, and I'm pretty good at it. Being sober during college would mean I'd have no friends. Zero. Everyone would think I was a freak. At Hawthorne, going to parties and drinking is all we do on the weekends. Even the quiet dorm kids get bombed once in a while. And when they do, it's entertaining to watch them lose control.

Losing control. That's the part I can't tolerate. Once that burn of alcohol settles in my throat, I try to fight the release of inhibition. I can even sense my body slowing down, relaxing. Random thoughts and comments fly out of my mouth, loose cannons of personal information. There are too many things, haunting and heavy memories. Things I need to keep inside.

During the winter of freshman year, I nearly told Ruby everything. We spent hours playing cards during a snowstorm. Around three A.M., Ruby asked me about my family.

The room spun, and I laid on my back on Ruby's bed. The others were watching a Disney movie on the other side of the room, John rolling another joint while Gemma and Khaled hyena-laughed at the screen. Max watched Ruby and me out of the corner of his eye. He had been cradling the same beer between his knees for hours, and he kept yawning, but he always stayed up until Ruby called it a night.

My body was limp, exhausted. My carefully constructed walls were down. So down that they had ceased to exist altogether. I was sassy, all my prejudgments about our classmates were flowing freely from my lips. Ruby was giggling next to me, egging me on, and my abs hurt from laughing so hard.

Tell me about your family, Ruby said. And I almost did. Thankfully I puked instead.

Five minutes later we were in the bathroom, and Ruby was holding my hair back while she stroked my back.

"It's okay," she said, her voice soothing, "You'll feel better soon."

I vomited into the toilet. The way she held me, I thought of my mother, when she would tie my hair into a ponytail when I was sick, *It's okay, baby girl, let it out.*

After that, I bought a flask. I still have it. Silver and sturdy, like a bullet. I blamed my refusal for sharing it with others on a fear of germs. Max understood. His anxiety came with a phobia of disease. I had my own flask at parties, and it wasn't to be shared. I announced I'd developed a gluten allergy so I had to stay away from beer, too, which meant I had to sneak pizza out of the dining hall and inhale it in the privacy of my room. Khaled teased me about the flask, but by the time sophomore year rolled around, people knew it was my thing, and it made me cooler, somehow.

These are the things I think about as I walk back to the house after the showers. Khaled and I walk fast down Campus Ave, our skin braced against the winter air. His legs tan and streaked with dark hair, mine stark white. Towels wrapped around our shoulders, damp clothes in our hands, forever stained a deep shade of royal blue from the swim team house.

We left Gemma and John in the freshman dorm bathroom. Khaled didn't seem to think it was a big deal that we were leaving them alone together, but I knew better. I hesitated in the doorway, watching as Gemma stripped down to her bra and underwear and hopped in the steaming shower with John. She almost slipped, but he caught her by the arm and yelled out to me, *Don't worry, M, I'll take good care of her*. Their laughter followed Khaled and me down the hall and out into the cold.

A group of classmates squeal from across the street, and we watch as our fellow seniors make their way inside a dorm. Only one more event, Last Chance Dance. Senior Day is halfway done.

We round a corner, and the Palace comes into view. Behind it, the sun lights up the dusky sky in orangey pink hues, a break in the clouds before the storm sets in hard. We pick up our pace, eager to be back inside the warmth of the house. I clutch my flask close to my chest, the cold metal pressing tight against the rough towel. Off in the distance, the snow clouds make their way across the rolling hills of Maine. The chill comes for us, the temperature cutting through our skin. This winter has been depressingly dull and ugly, and I am happily prepared for the sweeping white blanket of snow. I heard it was going to be a big one—three feet, at least. The kind of storm that can shut down a town of our size.

I know that Khaled wants to talk about Ruby and Max, and their argument, but I don't want him to bring it up. I don't want him to become a part of it. The situation is already too messy.

Khaled likes to know everything about everyone. It's a thrill for him, to talk to people, and talk about them. I think he also craves helping people, which is probably why he wants to be a surgeon. I know he would do anything for us, which is why he can't know about any of this.

It's odd, thinking about Khaled in the context of friendship. Even though we've been living together for years, we've never fully connected. We are roommates, but that's it. I was focused on Ruby, and John, so I didn't have much time for anyone else. Everyone thinks our group is so tight, the best of friends. Nobody doubts my part in that. Probably because I'm good at keeping up appearances.

"Dude, do you think Max and Ruby are okay?" Khaled says, his words cutting through the silence.

I hate when he calls me that. *Dude.* I notice he is carrying Denise by the space in her genital area.

"Can you not hold her like that?"

"Like what?"

"By her hole."

Khaled laughs and tucks Denise up and under his armpit.

"Okay, but seriously. What's going on?"

I knew he wouldn't be able to stay quiet. His thirst for knowledge and desire to help seep out of his pores. Sometimes I wish he would act rich and spoiled, like he is supposed to be.

"I'm sure it's nothing," I reply.

"What do you think they were talking about?"

"I don't know," I say. "They were drunk." *Leave it be.*

"It was intense. Ruby looked pissed." Khaled looks over at me, hoping I'll divulge something. "Never seen her like that before."

I don't respond. This always bothers Khaled. He requires validation and response, his brain unable to compute getting ignored.

"Whatever," he says, annoyed with me.

"You know how Max gets when he's emotional," I say, hoping it's enough for now.

"He's going to fucking crack one day," Khaled replies. "He needs professional help."

His voice is low and serious. His accent always adds a certain weight to his words.

"Remember that time freshman year? When we were at the hospital? And he freaked out at me about Shannon? I thought he was going to hit me. And he wasn't even involved. It had nothing to do with him."

"That was out of character. By the time we get to Last Chance, everything will be totally fine," I say.

Khaled doesn't say anything, but he gives me a skeptical look. We both know I am lying.

I need to change the subject. "Let's talk about something else," I say.

He is surprised. I don't usually indulge in conversation with him. "Like what?"

"Like . . . do you have any problems these days?"

I was starting to feel like everyone's shrink, but it was the easiest way to distract people.

Khaled looks at me, smiling. "Taking interest in someone other than Ruby?"

I shoot him a look. "She's my best friend."

"Fair enough," he says. "Ummmmm. Problems for me?"

"Yeah," I say. I am already counting down the moments until we will be back in the house so we can go our separate ways.

"Well," he says. His voice solemn. I look over at him, his eyes focused on the sidewalk. This is intriguing. I have never heard this tone from Khaled before.

"Okay," he says. "Don't think I'm crazy. Because I'm not crazy."

"Sure," I say. "Don't worry. What is it?"

"I know it's going to sound like I am a spoiled brat. I mean, let's be honest, I am spoiled. So let's get that disclaimer out of the way."

I roll my eyes. "Yes, okay, disclaimer heard."

"So my problem is that I have no problem. Look, like I said, it sounds crazy. But I love my life. I love my family. I love you guys. I love school. And I love partying. I am very happy."

"You're gonna have to explain this one a little more," I say.

"Okay, so I'm constantly worried that something is going to happen. Something bad. Like the other shoe is going to drop at any moment, and everything will go to shit."

Interesting.

"So recently, like ever since senior year started, I lie awake at night and can't sleep because I'm afraid my parents will die. Or my little sister. She's so innocent, you know? And then sometimes I worry we're all going to get some crazy plague or someone will nuke us."

I am silent. These are all things out of his control. I understand worrying about the things out of your control.

"Anyways," he continues, "I feel it looming over me. The feeling that something bad will happen."

"I get it," I say. I know this is the part of our conversation where

I need to offer advice. "But maybe you should enjoy your life while it's good. Because you're right, something bad will happen. That's how life works."

"Wow. Thanks, Malin. That helps so much," he says, joking.

"That's not what I meant. I think that you should try to focus on all these good things you have. Enjoy it. There is nothing wrong with that. And when something bad happens, *then* you can lie awake at night and stress out. But don't waste your life worrying about things you can't control. What's the point?"

As soon as I say the words, I know I should take my own advice. But I won't. I'm not made that way.

"Okay, yeah. You're right."

We get to the Palace and take quick steps up the porch stairs to the front door. I love this house. It is old and smells like childhood vacations at my grandmother's house.

Khaled pulls off his shoes in the entryway and heads toward his room. "See ya later, doom and gloom."

I look over at him, pausing as I use my foot to pull off my sneaker, bracing one arm against the wood-paneled wall.

"Just kidding," he says, tossing Denise onto the couch. "We all need you. We are all self-absorbed assholes, except you. Sometimes I think you're the only one who listens."

He gives me a smile and then disappears into his room, shutting the door behind him.

I do listen. I listen to everyone, and now I know things I wish I didn't.

I think about Ruby and Max, relieved Khaled seems to have forgotten them for now. The image of them arguing after the Jump replays in my mind. Max grabbing Ruby's wrist, pulling her to him, that fraught look on his face. And Ruby recoiling. The way she shook off his hand, it was almost violent the way she moved, so swift and afraid. What was she so scared of?

Everything is falling apart. I need to move faster.

I use my foot to kick open the door to my room and drop the wet clothes into the laundry basket. It's convenient we all have singles, where we can escape with our secrets and shake them off behind closed doors.

I open my flask and take a sip of water before tossing it onto the neatly made bed.

CHAPTER ELEVEN

Freshman Year

Parents weekend.

The entire campus erupted in blue banners and Hawthorne paraphernalia. We all dressed a little nicer, shoved the vodka bottles to the back of our closets, hid the bongs under beds, straightened our rooms. I didn't have to worry about mine—there was nothing to hide.

My parents were attending a seminar in the biology department; my mother knew one of the professors, and she wanted to catch up with him since they had been friends in college. My mother would have to explain why she didn't practice anymore, why she had given up on her career. She would probably lie, explain with a smile that she wanted to focus on raising me instead of spending time at work. I wondered if it was strange for her daughter to follow in her husband's footsteps and not her own.

A few weeks had passed since the rumors about Hale's girlfriend and the professor spread through the English department, flu-like and disruptive. Shannon and I had been some of the first students to find out, but thanks to Amanda, everyone knew by the end of the day.

My meeting with Hale was scheduled for three P.M., but I was early. Everyone in our seminar had to schedule a time to check in with him, a continuing part of the orientation that never seemed to end. The administration wanted to make sure we were set in Hawthorne's ways, that we were established, happy, any potential problems acutely averted. Parents were welcomed, but I didn't want them there. I wasn't ready for the worlds to collide quite yet. I preferred separation; everything in its own neat box.

I sat on the bench outside the TA room, staring at the bulletin board across the hall. There was a flyer for Ruby's soccer game pinned up, even a photo of her, front and center. She had developed into a mascot of sorts, the prized possession of the women's varsity soccer team. Their shiny new toy who led them from years of loss into victory. Kickoff was in little over an hour. I told my parents I'd meet them there, so we could watch the game together.

The door opened, and my head snapped up.

"Malin," Hale said, surprised to see me. "You're early."

I stood, smoothing out my shirt over my jeans. He didn't smile, but he opened the door a crack for me, retreating back inside.

Hale sat down at the large circular table in the middle of the room. He seemed distracted. I listened to the door click closed and wished I had left.

"So," he said. "How's it going?"

"Fine," I replied. I could be spending my time doing more useful things, instead of meeting here, to talk about my feelings, or whatever the purpose of this meeting was.

"Getting enough sleep?" he asked.

"Yup." I didn't sleep much, maybe four hours a night; it was all I needed. The rest of the time, when campus was quiet, I studied and wrote my papers. I needed to be at the top of my class, there was no time for sleep.

"Good, good," he said, distracted. He shuffled through some papers on the table and pulled mine to the top of the stack.

"Should I come back another time?" I asked.

"No." He cleared his throat. "Your papers have been great."

He flipped through my essays. A's on all of them.

"Let's talk about your goals," he said. "You still want to be a lawyer?"

I knew where he was going with this, and I didn't want him to. It was a waste of time.

He continued, "You sure I can't convince you to focus solely on English instead of pre-law?"

"I want to be a lawyer," I replied.

Hale leaned his head against a fist, his head tilted at an angle. "Why?"

"Well, I work hard and I can handle high intensity. And I like to be challenged."

"You sound like me," he said.

"And I want to make money," I added.

"Ouch," he said, deadpan. The corner of his mouth twitched. Almost a smile.

He continued, "I'm only saying this because you are very talented. You would probably be ushered into the grad program here."

"My father's a lawyer," I said. "It's what I know. I will be good at it."

"That is very . . . safe. A safe decision. Do what you know, I get it," he replied.

I was becoming irritated with him. He didn't know me.

"Keep your options open is all I'm suggesting," he said. "You don't have to take my advice. I'm here to encourage you to explore. It's that liberal arts spirit, I just can't shake it."

I hated the way he thought he was right in trying to convince me to choose a different path, that encouraging look on his face annoying. I didn't ask for his advice, and I didn't need it. I wanted to change the subject.

"Sorry about your girlfriend," I said. His eyes met mine. I almost felt bad, using his personal life for my own benefit.

"I assume everyone knows?" he asked.

"Yeah."

He sat hunched, staring at the table. He was so malleable. Breakups happened for a reason. Shouldn't people be relieved to be rid of someone who wasn't right for them?

"At least you know now," I said, trying to sound positive. "I mean, what if you got married, had kids, and *then* she cheated."

He looked at me, puzzled, like most people used to do in high school when I was blunt and honest.

"Well, that's true, I guess," he said, sitting up a little straighter. Had nobody said that to him yet? People were usually too sympathetic about these things.

"Also, nice try," he continued, "avoiding the subject. I see what you did there. Let's get back to you."

"I'm still going to law school."

"Okay, okay," he said, laughing. "Tell me about what you'd like to see more of in class, less of, that sort of thing."

We talked for a few more minutes, his good-humored attitude back in place. The good guy, the normal guy, happy-go-lucky. The opposite of me.

I felt giddy almost, being able to change him like that. He had responded positively to my candor. It was as if someone was seeing a glimpse into who I really was, and it wasn't a bad thing, he wasn't angry or disgusted. He was content.

I felt relaxed, at ease. My shoulders slumped as I sank farther into my seat. I watched myself let my guard down and didn't fight it.

▶ ▶ ▶

ON MY WAY out of the building, I ran into Shannon coming out of a classroom. She stumbled for a second and made a stern, scolding face at her shoes. She always looked like she was going to fall apart—bag, clothes, hair.

"Hey!" she said, sliding next to me, textbooks clutched to her chest. Her copper hair was pulled back in a messy bun. She glanced back at the door to the TA's office slowly closing behind me.

"How was your check-in?" she asked.

"Fine, I guess," I replied, then remembered to be polite. "Yours?"

"Good," she said, and we started walking side by side down the hall. "He's so nice."

We continued walking.

"Hey, so," Shannon said, dropping her voice an octave, as people did before they were about to say something secretive. "Your friend Khaled."

"Yeah?" I asked.

"Does he have a girlfriend or anything?" Her cheeks flushed a deep red, lighting her freckles on fire.

"Not that I know of," I replied. I considered telling her that Khaled would probably make out with anyone, but decided that might not paint him in the best light.

"Oh, cool. We're in the same chem lab; he's so nice. He's the only one that talks to me; you know, I just get kind of shy in group settings. And lab is all about group work. But yeah, he's chill."

I noticed how nervous she was. I wanted to tell her that she didn't have to act cool, or use the word *chill* when she had clearly never said it in her life. I wasn't going to judge her. I wondered if it was because I had a group of friends and she didn't. She was always with her roommate, another quiet girl. That was how I must have been perceived in high school. The quiet girl.

"I'll put in a good word for you," I said, filling the silence.

"You're the best, thanks." Shannon grinned and said her goodbye as we reached the crosswalk, her bun slowly falling out of its hair tie.

I checked the time, adjusting my bag on my shoulder, and headed to the soccer fields.

► ► ►

"HI, SWEETIE," MY mother said as she pulled me in for a hug, her bones edging into my clothes and skin.

She had been running again, not eating enough.

My father cleared his throat. "Your good friend is playing today?" he asked. "Ruby?"

"Number five," I said, pointing to the field.

The players were lining up in their positions, readying for the start. My father focused on the field, hands clasped in front of him. He was thinner, too, somehow. Maybe my leaving for Hawthorne had more of an effect on them than I previously thought.

"How have you been feeling?" he asked. I knew what he really wanted to ask, and this was his way of getting at it.

"Good," I said. "No complaints."

My brusque answer was rude, but he had already made his point before I left for college. I wanted to be left alone, to fend for myself. I wanted him to stop caring so much.

He cleared his throat. "We're going to go visit your grandmother in Deerfield tomorrow. Would you like to join?"

My mother tensed at the mention of Deerfield. She hated going there. She blamed my father's side of the family for Levi's death. I don't know why my grandmother still lived there, with everything that happened. I guess it was years ago, but still, our name was ruined in that town.

"Dad, that drive would be like five hours for me, there and back."

"Okay, just checking," my father said, disappointed.

"We're so glad you've made such wonderful friends," my mother said, her voice so quiet, almost a whisper.

I wanted to tell her to talk louder; I wanted her to be confident, and fun, and loud again. I wanted to breathe courage into her. But she hadn't been like that in years, and it was my fault, so I kept my mouth shut. I let her hold my hand, her skin paper thin.

I scanned the crowd in the bleachers. I spotted John, sticking out above everyone else. Khaled and Gemma sat in the middle of John and Max. My mother followed my stare.

"Is that them?" she asked. "Point them out to me."

"The shorter one with the dark hair, that's Max," I said, and then pointed to Khaled, "and Khaled's next to him."

"The prince?" she asked.

"Yes, the prince."

Now he was Khaled, the *prince* part having been dropped a while ago. We all wanted to meet his parents, but they were too busy to make the trip.

"Next to him is Gemma," I said.

"She's cute, like a stout little pony," my mother said.

"Maybe don't tell her that," I replied. My mother made a face, a glimmer of her humor shining through for a small moment.

I continued, "Okay, and then on the end, that's John."

I watched my mother trace John's face, making the small comparisons in her head.

"Ruby's boyfriend?" she asked.

"Yup."

"John," she said slowly, as if she was trying out the name for comfort.

I hoped she wouldn't make the connection, but her synapses were already firing. She was sizing up his thick yellow hair, tan skin. His charming smile. I felt my teeth clench together, my cheeks hardening.

"He's cute, looks nice," she said, looking away, but I knew what she was really thinking.

She glanced at me, as if I was interrupting her private thoughts. A hint of regret, anger, and then the look disappeared, replaced with her natural softness. She looked back at the soccer game, but her eyes were vacant, her mind elsewhere. She watched the players pass the ball back and forth, swallowing carefully, pretending to care about what was going on on the field, and the moment evaporated into the cool afternoon air.

A REFEREE BLEW a sharp whistle, and the crowd hushed with anticipation. I was squished between Max and Khaled, with Gemma and John on Khaled's far end. I left my parents on the sidelines. They were excited I wanted to watch the end of the game with my friends, their eager glances at each other irritating.

It was Hawthorne's throw-in. The game was tied with a minute left to play. Ruby jogged to the side of the field and scooped up the ball.

"She seems like someone else when she's playing," Max said. He sat up on the bleachers and leaned forward, elbows on his knees.

"Yes, so serious," Khaled said, joking, and making a frown face. "Is she gonna do that flip thing? Hope she doesn't break her neck."

"Can you not joke about that?" Gemma said, smacking his arm. She took a swig of gin and returned the flask to its hiding place in the crook of her arm.

Ruby needed to throw the ball down the field if Hawthorne wanted to get a final goal. She locked eyes with her teammate Bri. Ruby did a coordinated skip backward, away from the white line on the soccer field, holding the ball high above her head.

"You got this, babe," John shouted.

He clapped his hands together, thundering above my head. Ruby was focused. A warrior on the field. Tied up in a ponytail, her thick chestnut hair moved in sync with her body. Every sharp pass or fake out was marked by the hair whipping behind her. I looked up and down the sidelines, scanning the faces for recognition. Her father was supposed to be visiting today, and I was curious to meet the man who had raised her.

"Oh, shit," Khaled said. He covered his face with his hands. "I can't watch."

Gemma eyed him. "Seriously, stop."

Ruby brought the ball back an inch and picked up her right foot, bending it in preparation to run.

"Nope," Gemma said, her voice wobbly. "It's like watching a car crash. Can't."

She hid behind Khaled's shoulder.

"What happened to being supportive?" Khaled asked.

"Fuck off," Gemma hissed.

I squinted my eyes, reading Ruby's face. Max was right. She *was* different. Confident, fierce. She was always trying to please everyone, but now, I could see there was fight in her. I wondered why she tempered it off the field.

Ruby wound her body into a tight missile and launched herself forward. She sprinted toward the white line. We all caught our breath.

"Oh God, oh God, oh God," Gemma said softly, peeking out to watch the flip.

Ruby dove into the ground, holding the soccer ball tight in her hands. Her body braced for impact. She flipped over the ball and hurled herself upright, causing the ball to soar up and out of her hands.

We all cheered, clapping as Bri nestled the ball softly between her chest and her thighs, turning it delicately in the direction of the goal. Ruby flew back onto the field, sprinting toward the open net. Her blue-and-white uniform blurred as she dodged around the other players.

Bri came face-to-face with a player from the other team who looked mountainous in comparison. Bri secured the ball behind her, and Ruby shouted from the other side of the field. There was a small gap in front of Ruby and the goal. Bri smashed her foot into the ball, sending it toward Ruby, who caught it with the inside of her foot and tapped it into the loose net.

The blue-and-white crowd erupted into happy chaos. A whistle screeched through the fall air. Ruby's teammates rushed over and bulldozed her into a group hug. Hawthorne had won.

"Good play," Max said, his voice soft. "I wouldn't be surprised if she's captain next year."

Gemma and Khaled joined together in a quasi-hug-jump, the relief on their faces palpable. John made his way to the sideline, edging his toes against the chalk barrier. He began cheering Ruby's name over and over again. He looked so proud, so glad that Ruby was his.

AFTER THE GAME, we waited for Ruby by the sidelines. Gemma practically knocked her over as she ran to us across the field.

"That was fantastic, love!" Gemma said, after she had made a show of squeezing Ruby.

"Yeah, very entertaining, you know, for a girls' sport," Khaled said. Before the three of us could smack him, he added a quick, "Just kidding, guys. I mean, girls. You'd crush me out there, let's be honest."

"I would," Ruby replied.

John wrapped an arm around Ruby and pulled her to him. "I told you you could do the flip. But next time, watch your right foot when you come back down, it was looking a little loose. Gotta tighten that up. You'll get there."

Ruby gave him a sideways smile and wriggled out of his grasp, making it look like she was trying to get her water bottle out. But I knew he had bothered her with his critique.

John, Khaled, and Gemma started walking toward the road, heading to the Outing Club's barbecue.

When they were out of earshot, Max said, "You played really well. You're the best on the team."

She looked up at him, closing the top to her water bottle.

"Thanks," she said, giving him a smile.

"Want me to carry any of those?" he asked, looking at her gym bags, filled with her shin guards and tape. I knew she had already stuffed her sweaty clothes into a laundry bag, embarrassed we would ever think her anything but perfect.

"I'm good; let's go eat," she said, and the three of us walked to catch up with the others.

By the time we reached the main part of campus, my stomach began to rumble at the promise of a burger and hot dog. Maybe two hot dogs. It had gotten colder, and the breeze picked up. I flipped my hood over my head, protecting myself from the chill. The wind rustled the autumn foliage, and the leaves fell around us like snow. There was a cocktail hour for the freshman parents; they'd meet us afterward at the Outing Club, my father particularly interested in the vast collection of canoes and kayaks.

John put an arm around Ruby's shoulders and kissed the top of her head. She looked up at him, dripping in adoration, her hand swinging next to her hip, scuffed soccer cleats tied together by their shoelaces.

Next to me, Max grew quiet, the version from the soccer game buried somewhere inside him. I watched him sneak glances at Ruby when he wasn't staring at the ground in front of us, his shoulders slack, deflated.

"So," I said, "are you excited to see your family?"

Max's trance was broken, and he gave a small smile. "Yeah, my sister's here, too. I haven't seen her since she went to summer camp."

"That's great," I replied, leading toward my actual question. "It must be nice being here with John, though, since he's your family too and all."

His smile melted, and he chewed his lip. "For sure," he replied.

That was when I realized he liked Ruby as more than a friend. He wanted to be the one with his arm around her shoulders, the one kissing her congratulations. This was going to be a big problem.

► ► ►

THE LAWN OUTSIDE the Outing Club was thick with parents and students. I stood in a semicircle with Khaled, Ruby, and Gemma.

"It's probably for the best my parents couldn't make it. I don't think they could handle me drunk," Khaled said, patting his stomach and holding up his fourth beer. He let out a loud belch. "Not that they haven't seen it before."

"I can't believe mine didn't come," Gemma mumbled. "The flight isn't even that bad."

"They're not coming?" Ruby asked.

Gemma rolled her eyes. "My mum is terrified of flying." She held up her phone, tilting it back and forth next to her face. "But she's been texting me all day, says she is here in spirit. She's asking where we are so she can have a visual."

"Hey, where's your dad?" I asked Ruby. "I didn't even get to meet him."

Ruby fiddled with the top of the water bottle in her hand. "He couldn't come. Something came up last minute."

"That's too bad," I said.

She was lying. She did this thing when she lied, it was a tone, a slightly higher octave in her voice.

"At least he *tried*," Gemma replied, sarcastic, texting a response to her mother. The phone wobbled in her hands, threatening to fly out of her grip at any moment. Gemma vibrated with energy, causing her body to jerk in odd motions. "My mum *went* here for fuck's sake. She's the reason I am here. She could at least get on a plane and come visit me."

Ruby's father was still a mystery, my only clue to his existence the fact that he lived in Hanover. Her mother left them when Ruby was a toddler. It didn't seem to bother her. It was just a part of her, like the slight bump on the slope of her nose.

"Well, whatever, we can all hang out together and not have to worry about our parents judging our rooms and drinking habits," Ruby said with a forced smile.

"Totally," I said. I didn't want to push her.

In the uncomfortable silence, Khaled straightened up a little, puffing out his chest. He cleared his throat, like he wanted our attention.

"What?" Gemma asked him, eyes narrowed, skeptical. "Why do you look so weird?"

"I have an announcement," he said. He took a swig of his beer.

He was dragging this out, enjoying the suspense he had created.

"Well, stop acting like such a wanker and tell us what it is," Gemma demanded.

"I thought this would be a good opportunity to tell you, since it's *parents* weekend and all that—"

"Oh my God, Khaled. Tell us," said Ruby.

"Fine," he said, looking put out. "I already told the guys"—he nodded over to John and Max—"and they're in. So you three are the final hammer in the coffin, or is it nail in the coffin?"

Khaled always tried to include American phrases in his speech, but he often messed them up.

"What is it?" Gemma nearly shouted at him, catching the attention of nearby parents and students.

"Okay, okay," he said. "My parents bought a house."

"What?" said Gemma, her accent particularly more pronounced than usual.

"A house?" asked Ruby.

Buying a house was a big deal. Did Khaled really have that much money? My parents would definitely not buy me a house, especially one that could potentially be trashed by college students. I reminded myself Khaled was a prince. I kept forgetting that.

"You know that old purple one on Campus Ave?" he asked. "And you know how it's currently being renovated?"

We walked by the house every day. It was nestled between two corners of our campus, a beautiful Victorian on a hill. I had always admired it, wondering why it sat empty. I assumed it was the price tag.

"My parents bought it. For me. And my new friends," Khaled said, implying the last sentence, looking at us, raising his eyebrows.

"No," Gemma said slowly. "Really?" she said, her voice suddenly very squeaky. Khaled held back a smile.

"Us?" I asked.

"Yes, you three. And the guys."

"That's fucking insane," Gemma said, giddy at the idea.

"What's the rent?" Ruby asked.

"No rent," Khaled answered. "Well, we will split utilities, but that's it."

"Well shit," Gemma said. "Yes, a thousand times *yes,* I want to live in your fancy-ass house."

Gemma jumped onto Khaled, causing him to stumble backward. He was laughing, so was Ruby. How lucky we were, we all thought. A house. To ourselves. A house to live in with our best friends.

"When do we get to move in? And why? That is so generous of your parents," Ruby said. I was curious, too, why his parents would buy a house in Edleton, Maine.

I also realized this meant Ruby would be living with her boyfriend. I wasn't sure if that was weird or not, but nobody said anything about it.

"Next fall. I figured we'd do girls upstairs, boys downstairs. Everyone gets their own room. Of course, I imagine there will be some intermingling," Khaled said, winking at Ruby. "And I think my parents like knowing that I'm living in a nice place. They may not approve of me being here, but I'm still the favorite son, which gets you a lot of pull where I'm from."

"Aren't you the *only* son?" Gemma asked.

Khaled smirked.

"Well, that is really nice of them. And I am so in," Ruby replied. She didn't seem to care about the John part.

"Hey, so," I said, looking at Khaled, "how do you feel about that girl Shannon? I think she's in your chem lab."

"Shannon? She's a cool girl."

Gemma looked from me to Khaled. "Does someone have a crush on Khaled?"

Khaled shrugged. "Who doesn't?"

"Oh my God, you are so full of yourself," Gemma said, rolling her eyes.

"She's really nice," I said. "If you're into her . . . maybe hang out with her outside of lab."

Khaled took a swig of his beer. He didn't look excited, but I knew he would do me the favor. "Sure, yeah. Why not?"

"Oh, shit," Ruby whispered, shoving the water bottle into my hand. "God, I wish I had showered, how do I look?" She licked her palm and smoothed down her flyaway hairs.

We stood in a tight group, following Ruby's gaze to a tall older woman. She was presumably a mom, who looked like she had once been a model. Her hair silver-blond, body lean, defined muscles in her arms. One of those uber-rich moms who worked out all the time and always ate organic salads.

I scanned Ruby up and down. "I mean, honestly? You look like you just played a soccer game, why?"

"That's John's mom," she said quietly, adjusting her hair and uniform.

John's mom made her way over to the entrance of the building where John stood with a group of guys from his team. She reached Max first and pulled him in for a hug. Her nephew, of course. Another woman appeared behind her, shorter, but with matching blond hair and clear blue eyes. Next to her was a man who looked exactly like Max, and a teenage girl, presumably his sister. Max hugged the three of them, looking relieved to have them there.

"Cute," Gemma said. "Family reunion."

"I always forget they're cousins," Khaled said. "Weird. You guys think that's weird?"

We didn't answer him, continuing to watch the interactions. Yes, it was weird, I thought. Max and John were not close, but they were around each other all the time. Max always grew distant around John. I watched Ruby smile at both cousins. Max's half-cracked smile, hesitation holding him back.

Ruby took a deep breath and made her way toward John and his mom, her face plastered with that sweet outgoing smile.

► ► ►

As the afternoon settled into dusk, I hugged my parents goodbye and told them the best route to the highway. My mom hesitated before getting in the car, asking me one more time if she could meet Ruby. I wasn't ready for that; I probably never would be. I needed my two worlds to remain separate. I couldn't let Ruby get too close to my past. I looked at my father, and he understood. *Let's go, Celia, leave her be,* he said to her, tapping the hood of the rental car before they got in and drove away.

Our group was headed to a soccer team party that night. There was a guy who was going to be there, a sophomore, Charlie. Ruby thought we would get along, maybe hook up, she said, her excitement palpable. She wanted me to have a boyfriend so that we could go on double dates. I knew she felt bad when she would hang out with John and I'd go back to my single. She didn't know how much I needed the time alone. I needed that more than I needed a boyfriend.

Charlie was good-looking enough, cute and tall with curly black hair. And one time—*one time*—I mentioned to Ruby that I thought he was hot, only to keep her off my back about boys. Now she wouldn't let go of the idea of us—Charlie and me—as if we would meet and be hooking up within seconds.

"Sorry for the mess," Ruby said as I sat down on Gemma's bed. I looked around. Her side of the room was clean, it was Gemma who had shoes and clothes scattered across the floor. There was a definitive line between Gemma's side and Ruby's. Gemma had photos of her family and friends taped to the wall, but Ruby's side was sparse. Not even a photo of her dad. A few thumbtacked posters lined Ruby's wall, mostly architectural imagery and one photo that looked like southeast Asia. Her closet door was shut neatly, and I knew the clothes were hung and folded inside. Gemma's door couldn't have shut even if she tried, weeks of laundry unfurling from an even larger mountain inside.

"Where's Gemma?" I asked, sitting on Ruby's bed.

"With her theater friends. They're making Jell-O shots, I think." She paused. "I guess next year we will be making shots in *our* kitchen."

She was right. The six of us would be living together. It felt like we were pretending to be grown-ups, living in a sitcom of twenty-somethings trying to make it in the big city. Except we were eighteen-year-old students living in a mill town in Maine.

"Speaking of Gemma," I said, "has she calmed down with boys?"

Ruby looked at me out of the corner of her eye, pausing her hand in midair as she brushed her long hair. "Oh, sort of. I wonder when we will meet Liam."

"Do you think he'll come for a visit?"

"I don't know! I want to meet him. I tried to talk to him when she was on the phone with him the other day, but Gems got all pissy and went into the hallway."

"What does he look like?" I asked. "Have you seen a photo of him?"

Ruby nodded her head. "Yeah, she showed me one of them from this summer. He looked nice . . ."

"But?"

"I dunno. I don't want to be mean."

"Tell me," I said.

"Okay, but don't tell her."

"Obviously."

"There's just something about him. I can't put my finger on it."

"Hmmm, weird." I made a mental note to stalk Gemma and Liam on Facebook later.

"By the way, good job today, you shining star," I said, poking fun at her newfound glory.

Ruby braided her hair on top of her head, tapping her foot in time with the music playing from her laptop.

"Thanks," she said, blushing. Ruby made an excited motion and pulled her desk drawer open. "Want to see what John gave me?"

She pulled out a rectangular box and handed it to me. I held the soft velvet and opened the gold clasp. A delicate bracelet reflected silver in the fluorescent lighting.

"Are those diamonds?" I asked.

"Yes. He's crazy. I can't actually wear that. What if I lost it?" Ruby was trying to downplay it, but there was a feverish glow in her cheeks.

I fingered the row of sparkles and snapped the box shut. John was much wealthier than I'd previously imagined. So was Max. Their mothers came from old money and, apparently, new money, as well. It seemed those two went hand in hand at Hawthorne. The children of the wealthy. Academics amongst the rich. My parents were financially comfortable, but it wasn't from decades of steel or paper. My mother was a pediatrician, before she quit, and my father a corporate lawyer. They had done well for themselves, but the satiated wealth of the New Englanders I went to school with was new to me.

I assumed Ruby was the least wealthy of all of us, but I wasn't quite sure how financially secure her father was. There was something going on there, but it wasn't exactly socially acceptable to ask about. *Hey, how much money does YOUR family have?*

"How was meeting his mom?" I asked.

Ruby hesitated for a moment. "It was good, I think. She was really nice. I don't know; I can't really read her that well. I'm not sure if she's the kind of mother who wants her son with someone of the same social standing, or whatnot. Which is kind of . . . insulting. But whatever. She's not a witch or anything. John said I did a good job meeting her, so that's a relief."

I pictured John patting her on the back. *Good job, kiddo, meeting my mom, you nailed it.* It was weird. Like she had to appease him and his family.

"Where was his dad?" I asked.

"Oh, he's not around anymore. John doesn't like to talk about it," Ruby replied. She was quiet. "And he asked me to keep it to myself, so . . ."

"No worries," I said, noticing a definite rift between us. I spoke casually, like it was no big deal. "Well, I'm sure she loved you."

Ruby blushed, grinning, and excused herself to the bathroom. She needed the bright light to put on her makeup. When the door shut behind her, I got up from the bed and put my hands against the back of her chair. Her desk was a mess of printed articles on Italian Renaissance art and energy bar wrappers. I fought the urge to tidy her papers. She'd know someone had been there. I listened in the hallway. Silence. There was time. I opened the drawer closest to the floor and pulled out a small, black notebook.

I didn't plan to read Ruby's diary. But once I started I couldn't stop. I had seen her writing in it a few days ago, stuffing it into the drawer when I arrived at her door. It was the most convenient insight into her life. I knew all her secrets without having to ask her about them. I knew how to handle her, how to keep her happy.

How to be her best friend.

October 14

I love it here so much. I don't ever want to go home. It's nice to have real friends, people I can trust, and people who like me. I already feel like the friends I have here are way better than the ones in high school. I never really had time for friends back at home anyway, especially with working so hard to get the soccer scholarship. But here, I get to see them all the time. It's awesome.

Well. I wish Amanda wasn't here. I feel like she is always on the verge of telling Malin something about what happened. I know they're both English majors so they spend time together. I don't know *why* Amanda would say anything; what happened between us doesn't exactly paint her in the best light, either. Honestly, I think she just likes torturing me, watching me squirm. Thank God I never see her.

Last night John and I made out for forever. I haven't told him I'm a virgin. I should have had sex in high school and gotten it over with. John really wanted to last night. He was being so sweet, I felt badly. I think he is getting impatient, which I totally understand. I mean, I have to do it eventually. I want to do it. I do. But every time I think about sex . . . well. You know. He did say we could wait until whenever I was ready. But still.

In other news, I got an A on my antiquities paper. I applied to that internship at the Museum of Fine Arts Boston this summer. If I get it, housing will be covered, which is a huge relief. And John will be on the Vineyard, so I could visit him on the weekends. Fingers crossed.

Okay, also, I'm stressing out about Dad coming to visit. I think I might call him and tell him not to come. Since I got to Hawthorne, I haven't thought about all that stuff in forever, and I like it that way. I don't think some distance from him is such a bad thing. I'm just embracing my independence. I'm sure he'll understand. I still love him. Whatever.

I heard the bathroom door open and shut. Ruby's footsteps back down the hall. I closed the diary and placed it back in its drawer. I flopped back on her bed, fiddling with my phone, as if I had been there the whole time.

CHAPTER TWELVE

TEXAS, 1997

When I was eight years old, I kept to myself at school. At recess, I read in the corner of the playground. I knew that it classified me as a loner, and probably a loser, but I didn't care. My classmates were nice enough, but I didn't want to play. I didn't understand the concept of make-believe and tag and hide-and-seek. I liked playing sports and swimming in the pool, but I liked reading the most, so that's what I did.

A few of the girls in my class were playing ring around the rosy. We seemed too old for it, but then again, people my age always surprised me. I didn't understand them. I watched carefully as the girls laughed, held hands, singing, *we all fall down*, collapsing onto the hot tarmac. More laughs. Didn't they know that song was about a plague?

Whenever I was invited to birthday parties, my parents made me attend. I wanted to make them happy, so I put on a nice smile and handed over the pretty gift, and when nobody was paying attention, I snuck into the bathroom and snooped around medicine cabinets. I knew all the medical conditions of my peers' parents, and a few siblings.

I liked to be alone, watching from afar. I didn't tell anyone that, because they would look at me like I was a freak. Like I was broken.

Even my teacher, Ms. Little, stopped caring about getting me involved. She stopped coming over and asking if I wanted to join the

others, and I was happy to be ignored. Besides, school was almost out
for summer.

I balanced the book on top of my folded knees. *Walk Two Moons*
by Sharon Creech. She was my favorite author. This was my fifth time
reading the familiar pages. The edges of the paper were worn and
wrinkled in spots from reading by the pool. There was something
about the main character, Sal, that comforted me—the way she
searched for her mother, even though she was dead. Sometimes it felt
like I was searching for my mother, too, even when she was right in
front of me, fixated on Levi and all his problems.

In the shade, the breeze was a relief from the humidity. On the
hard-top playground, the air above the black asphalt waved like
bacon in cooked heat. It was so warm I could almost smell the asphalt. I looked over the top of my book and watched my peers. It was
like television, except the characters were real. I saw a figure discon-
nect from the crowd. Levi. Our grades, third and fifth, respectively,
shared recess. He was supposed to be playing soccer, but I noticed his
slight frame dart away from the game and toward the sidelines. In the
corner of the playground, he hunched over where the wooden fences
came together. No one else was watching him.

The girls jumped up, grasping at one another's hands, beginning
the song again. *Ring around the rosy.*

Levi was a star student and popular. To the naked eye, we were
complete opposites. I was the weird, quiet sister, and Levi was outgoing and friendly. All the other students loved him, his happiness infec-
tious. He knew how to compliment everyone, how to get girls to
blush and boys to want to be his friend. I had watched him for so
long. I was used to his game. He was a different person at home. He
was able to trick my parents, but he wasn't fooling me anymore. I
knew he was rotten, and I had given up hope on him "returning to
normal" a long time ago. My parents, on the other hand, still thought
it was a "phase" he would grow out of eventually. They hated any
slight overreaction. So we all pretended everything with Levi was
normal.

A pocket full of posies.

I strained my eyes to see what he was doing. There was a bag, a purse. Ms. Little's bag. She must have placed it there when she arrived—late—that day, meeting us and the substitute teacher on the playground. From a distance, her purse was bulky, and Levi rooted through it, looking for something. This piqued my interest. Levi, the perfect student, was *stealing.* Finally. This was the Levi I knew.

Whatever he was doing, he wasn't doing it fast enough, and I watched as Ms. Little surveyed the playground, eyeing Levi within seconds. Her stride was wide and fast. She always seemed like a giant in my eyes. So tall and strong. I knew she was twenty-seven, because she told us on the first day of school. Still young, but so old in my child eyes.

Ashes, ashes.

"Levi," she called as she neared him. He stood up and held something behind his back. Her wallet.

"Levi," she said again. When she reached him she grabbed his arm. Her grip was light, and she looked confused. All the teachers loved Levi. "What are you doing?"

Levi was quiet. Ms. Little gently twisted his body to the side to see what he was holding.

"Levi," she said again, this time sterner.

They stared at each other for a moment, Levi sizing her up, a meal he was about to devour. He looked excited, eager almost. He got this way at home sometimes. Last night our mother asked what we wanted for dinner. Levi requested shrimp. My mother had looked at my father pointedly. As if to say, *he didn't mean it,* but he definitely did. He knew she was allergic to shellfish. I didn't understand why he got so much enjoyment out of watching her squirm.

I watched Levi toss the wallet back into her bag. Ms. Little gave him an odd look, putting a hand on his shoulder, as if she was trying to figure out what was going on. And then Levi slapped himself, hard. The welt rose quick, crimson watercolor spreading across his cheek. He started to scream.

The other teachers on duty ran over; he had the attention of the whole playground now.

The teachers, and a few interested students, formed a U-shape around Levi and Ms. Little.

Ms. Little dropped her hand from his shoulder like it was fire. She began to open her mouth to speak, but nothing came out, her expression shocked and confused. Her eyebrows seemed to rise off her face completely, her mouth in a tight little O.

Levi ran over to another teacher, Mrs. Day, and pressed his face into her stomach, sobbing.

"What's going on?" Mrs. Day asked, her voice sweet and concerned. "Is everything okay?"

"She slapped me!" Levi screamed, tears already splashing his cheeks, his voice knotted in anxiety. "It really hurts," he cried.

"I didn't," Ms. Little said, trying to stay calm. The other teachers looked from her to Levi, and back again, the red welt blaring on Levi's face.

I think Ms. Little was too shocked to say anything else. The other teachers looked at each other, not sure of what to do.

Of course they didn't think he had slapped himself. He was *such a great kid. How unlike Levi,* they would have said to themselves, behind closed doors, meetings with the principal. I am sure my parents were no help, my mother probably demanded Ms. Little be fired.

I knew better.

We all fall down.

THE NEXT DAY, Ms. Little didn't show up. The same substitute took her place, as if she never existed, and we never saw Ms. Little again.

CHAPTER THIRTEEN

Senior Day

When I get to that point between consciousness and dreaming, I hear screams. Familiar screams. They are loud and distant at the same time. Screaming right into my ears, illuminating my brain cells. My memory racks with violent sobs. I fall asleep to the screams, and when I wake, they are gone.

My body jolts, eyes open. I look around the dusky room, and our house is still. I look at my phone. I've been asleep for forty-five minutes. I can't believe I slept. I'm glad I did; there is a long night ahead of us.

Everyone should be back by now. Last Chance Dance is starting in a few hours. Gemma and Ruby will be primping themselves, the scent of burning hair lingering in the air. I sniff. Nothing.

The house is quiet. Sometimes I wonder if the walls have gotten tired of soaking up our secrets, and one day it will collapse into the earth, taking us with it. I get up and wander into the hall. The doors to Ruby's and Gemma's rooms are open, devoid of their presence. I hear the front door open downstairs. Someone is back, and they are alone, the sound of salt and sand grating against hardwood floors. I peer down the staircase. A slender frame fills the doorway, one hand bracing on the wall as he kicks off his winter boots. Max.

"Hey," I say, my throat hoarse from sleep.

He looks up at me, expression grim. We communicate without talking. Something is wrong.

CHAPTER FOURTEEN

Freshman Year

"Hey, Malin, wait up!"

Khaled's voice rang across the quad as he and John started cutting over the grass. Their shoes left dewy footprints, and I gripped my thermos closer, stealing the heat into my hand.

"Fuck, it's early," John said as they approached, his voice groggy.

"I really don't mind the eight A.M.'s," Khaled replied. "Gets class out of the way for the day."

The three of us shared a microeconomics class. It did nothing for my major, but I figured it would be helpful to learn about for my post-college life, and math was easy. Professor Roy was in his thirties, one of the visiting professors. He was pretty boring, and very awkward, but I liked the readings he assigned. He was a tough grader, which most of my classmates hated. It didn't bother me since I did the work and got A's. Most of my classmates didn't seem to realize that if you actually studied and read, you could get good grades.

I usually enjoyed my walk to class alone, the silence invigorating. John and Khaled were up early, maybe they hadn't snoozed their alarms five times. They were rarely on time for this class, but somehow they always made it to the gym at seven A.M. on the days they had afternoon class. They liked to stroll into the dining hall for breakfast afterward, showing off their swollen muscles.

Students slowly made their way out of dorms, crossing the pathways to the academic buildings. Campus was silent, save for the birds calling above our heads, who probably woke up hours earlier with the sun.

"Did you finish reading the chapter?" Khaled asked me.

"Yeah," I said. "You?"

"Almost done. I, uh, got distracted last night," he replied, winking.

John laughed through a yawn. "You mean your dick got distracted. By Kelly Lee."

I looked away, ignoring the image of Khaled's penis.

"And what were *you* doing—no, sorry, *who* were you doing?" Khaled argued back.

"I was with Rubes," John replied, trying to keep his voice innocent.

"Mmmmhmm. Studying, I'm sure," Khaled said.

John punched Khaled lightly in the shoulder. They bantered back and forth for a while, until we reached the economics department. It was one of the oldest academic buildings on campus, brick faced and three stories tall.

"Okay, Malin, girl, so you gotta tell us what the reading was about," Khaled said, panting, as we made our way up the stairs.

I refrained from telling them I had finished the whole book, and it was actually good. I knew they would see me as a loser so I kept it to myself.

"Just don't act like idiots, and he won't make you talk," I said. "And read it later."

Khaled sighed, leaning on the railing. "Little Miss Perfect, never giving away her secrets."

"Did you really think she would tell us?" John asked, dragging his boots, laces casually undone.

I knew I had to recover somehow, to stay in their good graces.

"Oh my God, fine," I said. "If he makes you talk, just say something about cause and effect and social issues and how it does stuff to the economy. Like how after 9/11, people started stealing less because they were feeling more patriotic and empathetic. And then give your own example, like . . . if there was video footage of a homeless man getting beat up, there would probably be an uptick to shelter donations the next day. Or something like that."

"I love you, thank you," Khaled said.

"M, pulling through for her best buds," John said, with a sigh of relief. I hated when he called me "M," like Ruby did.

The classroom was empty. Professor Roy's laptop was open on the front desk, his bag laid haphazardly on the floor.

"First ones here, props to us," Khaled said, settling into one of the single-arm chair desks. The metal creaked beneath his weight.

I chose a seat closest to the door; I liked being able to leave class first, escaping the chatter of after-class discussions. The seat was cold through my jeans, and I took a drink of black coffee, still hot inside the thermos.

John placed his bag on the desk next to Khaled and circled around the room, ending in front of Professor Roy's laptop.

"Dude, what are you doing?" Khaled asked.

"Just seeing if there's anything interesting on here," John replied, placing a finger to the touchpad. "Answers to midterms, ya never know."

I looked at the door, and John glanced up, tracing my eyes.

"Malin can keep watch, right, M?" John said, more of a statement than a question.

I wanted to tell him to fuck off, no, I was not acting as a lookout, but I smiled back.

"Sure," I said, trying to sound nonchalant. He gave me a slick grin, and returned his gaze to the glaring screen.

John clicked a few times, his finger barely touching the touchpad. Khaled let out a long belch and looked at me, sheepish. His burp echoed around the classroom.

"Oh, shit," John said, his face cracking into a grin. "You guys, look at this."

Khaled jumped up and joined John at the front of the classroom.

"M, you gotta see this," John said.

"I'm on guard, remember?"

They ignored me, laughing at whatever was on the screen.

I watched the two of them. John hovered closely over the screen, while Khaled remained behind him, over his shoulder. Khaled kept glancing at the door, faking his interest in the laptop. Making fun of people was not his jam, but he felt awkward not appeasing John either, so he joined in with the commentary.

"So lame," John said. "M, he's looking at his Rate My Professors page, and he's only got one review. Two stars. *Avoid this class at all costs. If you do end up in it, sit in the back corner and take a nap. He won't even notice. The two stars are for the readings, it's the only mildly interesting part of his class.*"

"Damn," Khaled said, his voice always upbeat and positive. "I mean, they're not wrong. But still. Kind of feel bad for him!"

"Feel bad? No, man. It's true. The guy grades tough, and his class is boring as shit . . . What else do we have on here? Should we set him up on a dating site? Maybe that would help him loosen up. If he got laid."

"Guys," I said, "stop going through his things."

John ignored me. Khaled and I made eye contact, but he said nothing.

"He's got a Match.com profile. No new messages. I wonder how many times a day he refreshes this page," John said.

"Maybe we should give him a four-star review, you know, on the professor page, to up his average," Khaled said, trying to join in with the laughing, but failing.

I tried again. "Seriously. John. Stop."

I heard footsteps in the hallway. A part of me hoped it was Professor Roy, but the steps were slow, shuffling, like a tired student.

John sighed and clicked out of the page. "Fine, fine, relax. His fault, for leaving his laptop open like that."

Khaled didn't say anything. He looked at me, but I ignored him and opened my notebook. A student wandered into the class, and Khaled jumped away from the computer. John stayed calm, giving the student a relaxed head nod, the kind only bros do, and then retreated to his desk. He gave me a wink as he slinked by.

When the class was filled with students, everyone quiet, a few people taking long sips out of their coffee mugs, Professor Roy entered the room. John looked at Khaled and raised his eyebrows, and I could tell he wanted him to laugh, but Khaled pretended he was busy flipping through *Freakonomics*.

I sat up straighter, feeling myself on edge, the defensive walls growing taller. Professor Roy adjusted his laptop and a few books stacked on his desk and cleared his throat. He paused, if only for a small second, to look at the screen of his laptop. I wondered if John had remembered to leave it as he found it. I looked over at him, but he didn't seem worried, and he caught my glance, giving me a smug, satisfied smile.

I ABSENTMINDEDLY SCROLLED my Facebook, looking at a photo Ruby tagged me in from the weekend. The photo was dark, the flash illuminating only our faces, sweaty from the band that was playing in the old gym. I continued down the feed, Gemma's name flashing, tagged in a post from Liam on her wall. Miss you, babe, can't wait to be with you every day this summer. #firstdrinksonme. I clicked on Liam Weld, but his page was set to private, friends only. His profile photo was of him and Gemma, on a stage somewhere, probably from high school, or a summer program at a theater. I wondered if that was how they met, through acting. I should've asked her more about him, but I forgot. It didn't seem important at the time.

I watched Ruby and Max hurry in the entrance to the Greenhouse, their faces flush with cold, jackets dusted with snow. They were smiling at each other, talking about something, their heights matching in stride, her slender frame matching his slight athletic build.

I turned my gaze toward the windows facing the lake. A trio of cross-country skiers made their way across the frozen lake, their poles moving in sync.

The three of us were studying in the Greenhouse, the golden lamps lighting our study session before finals. The short days and cold temperatures kept us stuck inside, our brains fried with memorized notes and theories on this or that. One more day of exams and papers and we'd be home for winter break. I was dreading it already. Ruby and Max were returning from getting hot chocolate at the Brew, their cheeks pink from the outside. When they got closer to the couches where I was sitting, I turned my headphones to mute. I didn't acknowledge their presence and pretended to keep reading.

"Favorite color?" Ruby asked.

Max paused. "Blue," he said. He thought for a moment. "Favorite TV show?"

Ruby creased her eyebrows, considering her answer. She looked sheepish before she answered, *"Keeping Up with the Kardashians."*

"Yeah," Max said, "we can't be friends anymore."

Ruby laughed as she pulled out a textbook from her backpack. *The History of Tattooing.* I noticed the cover was a photo of a man's chest covered in black ink. I glanced down at the book in my lap, *Introduction to Criminal Law.*

They sat next to each other on the couch, Ruby cross-legged, back straight. Her pink pom-pom hat framed her heart-shaped face, dark hair spilling out from under it. Max was looking at her a little longer these days.

John didn't need to study. He had a photographic memory. Or so he claimed. He and Khaled were probably playing videogames in the dorm. Gemma would be studying beside them, claiming she couldn't focus in the Greenhouse, subconsciously attempting to flirt with John. I wondered how Liam would feel seeing her like that. I thought about Ruby, but she didn't seem to care that Gemma flirted with John. I don't think she even saw Gemma as a threat.

"Next question?" asked Max.

Ruby settled deep into the couch, the cushions cocooning around her frame.

"What are you most grateful for?" she asked.

"These questions are getting heavy," Max replied.

Ruby smiled. "That's when they start to get good."

Max cradled the hot chocolate in his hands. "My parents."

Ruby's face crumpled for a moment, but she composed herself before Max could notice.

"Aw," Ruby said, her voice teasing, "sweet."

"You asked the question."

"Your turn," Ruby said.

I flipped through the pages of *Criminal Law*, underlining things like *mens rea* and *retribution*.

"Where do you want to live after college?" Max asked. Their wild energy was slipping into something more intimate. I pretended to be deep in my book.

Ruby chewed on her lip. She did this when she was focusing. It would be pink and irritated later, scabbed over.

"Any big city, really. Maybe Boston or New York, or L.A." She glanced out the window. "I don't know how I ended up in the sticks for four more years."

"I'm glad you came here," Max said.

They looked at each other until Ruby's cheeks turned a deep red, at which point she stared at her textbook, flipping through photos of tribal art and modern-day tattoos. If she sped through the pages any faster, she would get a paper cut.

Ruby cleared her throat.

"If you weren't majoring in pre-med, what would you major in?" she asked.

"Photography," Max said without skipping a beat.

"What? I've never even seen you with a camera. Do you have any photos with you?"

Ruby leaned forward a little, interested, her flush evaporated. This was her area of expertise, looking at art. All art looked fine to me, but that was as far as it went for my appreciation. I folded over a corner of the page on trial procedures.

"They're all back at the studio."

"I want to see," Ruby protested.

"No, you don't. I'm not that good," he said.

I felt Ruby look over at me, making sure I wasn't paying attention to them. As if she wanted to keep this part of their relationship a secret. It was too late for that.

"What kind of stuff do you photograph?" she asked.

"Landscapes and people, the boring stuff."

Ruby laughed. "Stop with the self-deprecating act. I can't believe I didn't know this about you!"

Max brought a hand up to the back of his neck and shifted in his seat. "Yeah, I don't really advertise it. It's just a thing I like to do."

"How are you feeling, by the way?" Ruby asked, her voice lowered.

Max swallowed. "With the anxiety stuff?"

"Yeah."

Max was quiet for a moment. "I don't know. When I think it's getting better, an attack comes out of nowhere. My mom thinks I should be on medication, but I don't want to."

"Why not?"

"Because. It's admitting it's a thing. And I'd rather ignore it."

Ruby looked thoughtful, concerned.

"Do you know why you get anxious? I mean, is there something that makes it happen? One of my friends in high school used to get panic attacks around flu season because she was a hypochondriac."

Max's disposition changed when Ruby said this, a look in his eyes like he was doing something wrong. He stared at his laptop, considering something, and then finally responded, "No, it's who I am. How I'm wired."

"I really can't wait to see your work," she said, changing the subject back to his photography. "I'm going to hunt it down; you can't stop me."

"Don't get mad when you're disappointed," he said, trying to joke, lighten the mood. He was one of those people who didn't like uncomfortable situations. But something had happened, and he closed his laptop and grabbed his bag.

"I should go," he said.

Ruby placed her fingertips close to his, so close they were about to touch. Max's eyes lingered on her hand, and I thought he might place his on top of hers, but he didn't. Instead, he pulled away and zipped up his backpack. I focused on my book, but I could sense Ruby staring at me.

"Malin?" she asked me.

I pretended not to hear.

"Malin," she said, nudging me with her toe.

"Yeah?" I asked, pulling the headphones off my ears.

"Can you hear us?" she asked.

I looked up at them expectantly, as if I had been in deep concentration and they had interrupted me. "What?"

► ► ►

ON OUR WAY back to Ruby's dorm, we passed by the arts building. There was a light on inside, catching Ruby's attention.

"Let's go in," Ruby said, pausing in front of the door. "Maybe we can see some of Max's work."

"What do you mean?" I asked, playing dumb. Of course, I already knew this about Max, from our encounter on the quad earlier in the fall. But I had never told Ruby about that, and I didn't want her thinking I had been listening earlier.

"He's a photographer, apparently."

Ruby pulled open the door and we walked inside the foyer, a door to the right labeled STUDIO. There were photographs hung up in the long, open hall, and we slowly made our way through.

"Nope." Ruby sighed. She moved to the next photo. "Nope. Let me know when you find him."

I glanced at each photograph. There was one of a lake. It was dull, monotonous. Nothing spectacular about it, not sunrise, or sunset, and the line of the lake wasn't even straight against the horizon. It bothered me, and I moved forward.

The next photograph was of the boys' lacrosse team. This one was more interesting than the last; it was clearly taken during a storm, so the tones were dark and moody. I recognized a few of the blurry players as faces we saw at the usual parties we attended.

Ruby made an excited sound at the opposite end of the hall.

When I got closer, Ruby was bouncing on her toes, and she pulled me close.

"Look," she whispered.

The photograph had been taken on top of a mountain, the trees at peak foliage, orangey-red and yellow. The sky was hazy pastel blue, and the scene seemed to stretch for miles in the distance. There was a small outcropping of rocks in the lower right, which happened to be the most magnificent part of the photo. There was a tiny black figure on top of the rocks, a person looking out at the view. I could almost feel the wind on my face. Below the photo was a white label with Max's name written on it.

She moved toward the next photo in his series. It was another landscape, this time a lighthouse and an ocean, with a tiny person, the contrast between land and human subtle and monumental at the same time.

The last photo of Max's was displayed in the center of the gallery wall. Unlike the landscapes, this one was a face. Deep lines marked the woman's skin, her lips stretched thin, silver hair pulled back into a bun. One of his subjects from the retirement home.

"Beautiful," Ruby murmured.

It was beautiful. I couldn't stop staring at the woman's eyes, shy, nervous, but her expression on the verge of a laugh.

"He's good," Ruby whispered. "His are the best here, by far."

I watched her face soften, her eyes lighting up in that way they often did. By the time senior year rolled around, the spark would be gone. This version of Ruby would be a thing of the past.

As we walked out of the building she turned to me, her face suddenly drawn. "Let's not tell him we saw his work, sound good?"

"Sure," I said.

"I don't want . . . to give him the wrong idea, you know? We are just friends," she continued, reading my thoughts.

"No worries, our secret," I said.

Ruby was quiet for the rest of our walk, lost in her thoughts.

CHAPTER FIFTEEN

Senior Day

I take a step down toward Max, the wood floor creaking beneath my weight. He is anxious—his movements heavy, face pallid, expression distracted, like he's not fully there.

"I'm making hot chocolate. You want some?" I ask.

I descend the stairs quickly and glide into the kitchen. My slippers smack against the sticky tiles. Beer. I gave up on mopping the floor during our sophomore year. Filthy, gross, careless boys. A clean kitchen never stayed clean long, not at the Palace. I can't wait to graduate and live on my own. Max follows me into the kitchen.

I stick the kettle under the faucet, letting the sound of running water fill the room. The sink is filled with empty Solo cups, the stench of stale beer in my nose. I hold my breath as I wash two coffee-stained mugs.

Max settles on a stool at the island, staring at the marble countertops. We are the only students on campus to live in such luxury, thanks to Khaled. I am grateful for his mother's taste. She renovated the old house into a sleek and modern family home. Our family home. I wonder who will live in it once we are gone.

I think about what Khaled and I saw. How Max and Ruby were arguing, and the way he held on to her wrist as she backed away from him.

"Did you and Ruby end up going to Parker? To shower?" I ask.

I flip the burner switch on, and the flame explodes, flaring beneath the kettle.

"Not really," Max says. His voice low. He rubs his eyebrows. He does this when he is tired. "I still need to shower."

I notice his damp clothes from the Jump and wonder how he isn't shivering.

"Where's Ruby?" I ask, expecting her to enter the house at any moment.

Max doesn't look up, his brain consumed with restless energy. I open one of the cabinets and root around in the back, searching for the little box I keep hidden behind the mismatched plates. Nobody ever bothers to use them, in fear of having to actually wash them afterward. Even if someone did find the crushed pills, I would have no issue saying it was for my anxiety. A simple lie.

"We got in a fight, I guess. Or a heated discussion. Whatever you want to call it," he says. He is much less handsome when he's exhausted, his face pale, dark circles under his eyes. "But that's not the worst part."

"A fight?" I ask. "You guys never fight."

Max straightens his back. He always does this before he is about to confess to something shameful. As if it would compensate for his internal weakness, the imbalance in his brain.

"I told her I love her," he says. "It was stupid. Things seemed back to normal. I thought it was the right time. It wasn't."

I knew this would happen one day; I didn't know when. They were so entwined with each other, but never touching. It was an unspoken thing between all of us.

"What did she say?" I ask.

He looks up at me but doesn't answer. His silence speaks for him.

The tea kettle begins to whistle, and I flip off the burner. I dry the two mugs and place them by the sink, my back facing Max. A red ceramic one, and a larger blue one. I slip white powder into the red mug, without Max noticing.

I hand him the red mug, and he lets out a frustrated sigh as he takes a sip from it.

"Pretty sure she hates me now," he says, staring at the counter.

"Before, she was annoyed by me. But the look she gave me today, it was bad. Like I was a stranger."

I thought about how Max used to make Ruby laugh, relax, and be her true self. Like he is the weight she needs on her pendulum of stability.

"I don't think she hates you. She's confused," I say, although I have no idea what Ruby is thinking. I still don't know what happened to them last spring, what caused their drift.

I watch Max take another sip from his mug, his expression suddenly more serious, more focused. But he will relax soon, his shoulders will drop and his expression will settle, his pulse returning to its normal rhythm.

"I haven't told you the worst part," Max says, and he finally looks up at me.

"What?" I ask. *Did it happen?*

Max continues, "Well, I told her she deserved better than John. And then she ran off. I wasn't done talking with her. We knew you guys were going to shower, so she sprinted up the hill toward Parker. She said she needed to find John. I followed; I wanted her to understand what I was trying to say, or you know, why I said what I said."

He stares down at the mug, again avoiding eye contact. He does this when he's anxious.

"When I got to Parker, I opened the door—you know, the one that leads to the basement bathroom," Max says.

I know which one. It's where we left John and Gemma, who were throwing water at each other in the tight quarters of the dirty freshman bathroom. They were drunk, out of control.

Max clears his throat. "Ruby was standing outside the bathroom, in the hall. She was standing right outside the doorway. She didn't even look at me. When I looked inside the bathroom, John and Gemma were . . . together."

"Together how?" I asked.

"Well, they were naked in the shower, and I couldn't tell what . . . or if, you know."

I interrupt him. "Did Ruby see?"

If she saw John and Gemma together, she would have to break up with him. There was no other option.

"Yeah."

We are quiet. Max finishes his hot chocolate. He looks up at me, as if I will fix everything. He wants to be unburdened.

"And then what?" I ask.

"She ran off. I went to look for her. Unsuccessfully, obviously."

Max shoves the empty mug across the counter. As if it's filled with the disgusting image of John and Gemma, and he can't stand to be around it any longer.

"You don't seem surprised," he says.

I'm not. But I can't tell him why. "No, I'm surprised," I say, lying. "I'm in shock, that's all."

If Ruby saw John and Gemma, where was she now? Was she breaking up with John? Where was Gemma?

"He's such a dick," Max says, his expression serious and drawn. "He treats her like shit. Usually it's me he takes his crap out on. And I can handle it, I've handled it for years. But he can't do this to her and think that it's okay."

"What do you mean, 'Usually it's me'?" I ask.

I know what he is referring to. The condescending attitude, the bullying. I want to hear what Max thinks.

"Don't play dumb, Malin." He looks up at me, eyes sharp. "You hear what he says to me. He's hated me since we were kids."

I don't say anything.

"I've talked about it with my parents," he continues. "It's not like I'm oblivious. We think he's jealous of our family because of everything that happened with his dad, and he takes it out on me. I never thought it would spread to other people, like Ruby. It makes me sick. I should have stood up to him a long time ago. I actually felt bad for him. So I did nothing."

"You're upset," I say. "It's understandable."

"I remember this one time, at a soccer party freshman year. I was with Ruby the whole night. We were just having fun. John got pissed.

He told me if I didn't stop talking to her he would tell her I was obsessed with her, like a stalker, or some shit like that. I don't think she would have believed him, but I got the message. Probably another reason why she hates me, because sometimes I just straight up ignore her."

I glance outside at the gray clouds building in the sky.

"Why don't you take a nap before Last Chance?" I suggest. "It's going to be a long night. I'll find Ruby. Don't worry. Everything will be fine."

I need Max to take a break. He is getting worked up, and I'm unsure of what he is actually capable of. I consider what Khaled said, about what happened freshman year at the hospital. How upset Max got, emotional. I need him to calm down. I can't have him interfering with my plan.

"Yeah, okay." Max gets up, as if he has decided something here in the kitchen. At least the anxiety is gone. I hate seeing him like that, his body tensing with every pulse of adrenaline.

"I'll be in my room," he says. "Let me know when she's back, so I know she's all right."

I lean against the counter as he leaves the room. I hear his door open and shut, and the creak of his bed as he collapses.

I think about what Max told me during finals our freshman year. How had I forgotten? I had been distracted by exams, exhausted. Sick of everyone. Eager to be alone. I should've listened. Maybe we could have solved our problem a long time ago. Maybe John could have gotten help, or one of us could have told him to stop being a bully. In the dull light of the kitchen, I realize what I've been missing about Max. For so long, I thought it was just anxiety. A diagnosis I had heard from Ruby. Something he was born with, something that wasn't his fault. It still wasn't his fault. But there was someone to blame. A specific someone. John.

My phone lights up on the counter.

H: checking in. still worried. text me.

I think for a moment, then write back: all good. getting ready for last chance. see you later tonight?

My phone buzzes back immediately.

H: sounds good. and we'll talk. okay?

I don't respond. As I wash the mugs in the kitchen sink, I hear the front door open. Someone stumbles over the pile of shoes in the entryway and sniffles, hoping to avoid being detected. I can tell it's a girl, and by the way the shoes clunk awkwardly against the wall, I know it's Gemma. She is clumsy, whereas Ruby is delicate, athletic, quiet.

I glance at the clock on the oven. It's five thirty P.M. Three hours until Last Chance Dance.

CHAPTER SIXTEEN

Freshman Year

The dining hall pulsed with the stress and anxiety of finals week. The six of us sat together at the table we always chose—right in the middle of the hall, where we could see everything. On Sunday mornings, we watched all the walk of shames filter through the breakfast bar. We were in the eye of the storm, a view of Hawthorne's social stratosphere from all angles.

I read over my notes for my criminal law final. Gemma sat across the table, her eyes closed, visualizing a monologue for her theater class. Her lips moved silently, for once devoid of any sound. Ruby's face concentrated on her laptop screen; images of oil paintings flashed by. They all looked the same to me, but she could recite when and where they were produced, and by which artist. Khaled leaned over his anatomy textbook, chin in his palm.

John scrolled through emails on his phone, his face taut. He reached for his water glass and let out an aggravated sigh. "When do you think they're going to get some bigger cups around here? A man needs more water than this."

He held up the plastic cup between his thumb and pointer finger. It was comically small.

Ruby jumped up and grabbed the glass. "I'll get some, babe."

She squeezed his shoulder and disappeared into the cafeteria. Gemma looked at me, rolling her eyes. In the past few weeks, Ruby had increased her doting. She indulged John's every need. I knew it annoyed Gemma, the idea of catering to your boyfriend like that, but

I also knew that if Gemma was the one dating him, she'd do the same thing.

We fixated on exam material, quiet, but the rest of the hall filled with stressed chatter. Students sprinted in and out, grabbing mugs of coffee and handfuls of cereal. There was no time to eat this week, and I made a mental note to grab a few bananas on the way out.

John slammed a fist on the table and broke our unified focus.

"Fuck," he said so loudly a couple students surrounding us looked over, their eyes wide and bloodshot. They stared for a moment and then went back to their textbooks and laptops, unfazed by the disturbance.

We all looked up at him, and he lowered his voice. "I'm screwed."

"What's up?" Khaled asked.

Ruby returned and handed John the water. She looked at all of us looking at John, and she put a hand on his shoulder.

"What's going on?" she asked.

John looked at Khaled, ignoring Ruby, not thanking her for the water.

"Professor Roy. He's failing me."

Khaled and I looked at each other. If karma existed, this was it.

"He's warning me about receiving my final grade . . . saying that I got a C– on the final," John said, gritting his jaw so that his muscles clenched tight beneath his skin. "He probably hates that I have connections in finance and he never actually made it. He's stuck in this tiny-ass town in Maine teaching us what he could never do. Fuck. It's going to bring down my entire GPA. What if I get put on academic probation? What if I can't play next year?"

"You'll be fine," Ruby said, her voice calm, mothering. "Just make sure you get really good grades next semester." She sat back down next to him, sliding the chair even closer to him.

"Wait, why does this guy suck so much?" Gemma asked.

John sat back in his chair. "Because he wants to be us. And he can't get chicks."

"Okay," Gemma continued, rolling her eyes. "For real, though."

Khaled spoke. "He grades tough, on a curve. Nobody in the class has above a B. It brings all of us down. I think Malin has the highest grade right now—right, Malin?"

I chewed slowly, flitting my eyes between Khaled and John, not sure how to answer, not wanting John to spiral.

"I think so, maybe," I replied.

Ruby perked up, rubbing John's back. "Why don't you go talk to him? That always helps. A face-to-face. Then he can't fail you. If you are nice to him, he will feel bad and at least give you a C."

"Babe. I can't. I'm not getting on my knees," John said, flinching her off his back. "I'm fine. It's fine."

I wished they would stop calling each other *babe*.

Ruby looked away and went back to studying the notes on her laptop. If she was bothered she didn't show it. Max didn't say anything. He focused on his notes, as if he wasn't listening.

"So," Khaled started, "what are you gonna do?"

John stared intensely at the sandwich scraps left on his plate. "I have an idea"—he looked over at Ruby—"and it doesn't involve sucking his dick."

Gemma made a face. "Crude much?"

"Why did you get a C–?" I asked, and everyone else glanced in my direction, questioning me. "What? You must have gotten that grade for a reason. Professors don't just hate students and give them bad grades."

I already knew that John had blown off studying to go to a soccer team party the night before.

He smirked at me. "Unlike you, I have more than two friends and a social life."

I didn't flinch. Blood pulsed fast in my veins, excited by the challenge. Charming, friendly, sweet John. Nobody was that perfect. He loved to be loved, pretending to be the nice guy, but I knew there was something else in there. He was finally coming to the surface. Everyone else would see it, too.

Ruby and Gemma looked over at me, their gazes sharp and intent, waiting to see what I would do, how I would react. John's comment teeter-tottered on the edge of a cliff. I imagined Ruby panicking, not knowing how to respond, in the choice between me and John. Who would she choose? I wasn't sure of the answer.

I took a quick, conciliatory breath, knowing I needed things to get back to normal. For the sake of the group, I shouldn't have challenged him, shouldn't have started this.

Pretend.

"Not all of us have time to be socialites," I replied, teasing.

John's cheeks tugged on his mouth, and he gave a caged smile. The intensity subsided as quickly as it had emerged.

"If he's giving me a shit grade, I'm gonna mess with him," he said, a twinkle in his eye.

"Don't do anything stupid," Ruby said, exhaling slowly. "I would prefer you didn't get kicked out of school."

"Don't worry, babe," John said, sliding an arm around her shoulders, giving her a kiss on the cheek. Even though she pulled away from him, wiping off the spit, she smiled.

I looked over at Max, whose head was still bent toward the notes. He hadn't even glanced up at the friend comment. It was as if he lived in his own world, and we didn't matter.

▶ ▶ ▶

THE NEXT DAY, I left the library and sprinted through the freezing rain to the English department. Sharp flakes of glassy ice scratched my face and lit up my coat and boots. I took the stairs two at a time, heading for the TA's room.

I knocked twice on the door.

"Yup," Hale called out, and I entered.

"Hey," I said. "Just dropping off the final now."

"Handing it in early, nice," he said.

"Yeah, I'm leaving early, so." I riffled through my bag filled with notes and books, *found it.* I pulled out the essay, smoothing the edges. "Here." Hale took the exam from my hands, our fingertips touching for a slight moment. "Thanks," he said, grinning. "Good job this semester."

I smiled, adjusting the winter hat on my head. Yes, I had done a good job. I started to head toward the door when he stopped me.

"Malin," he called out, "um, can I ask you something?"

"Of course," I said, trying to sound relaxed. I placed a hand on the doorframe and turned back toward him. I didn't have time for this. I knew it wasn't a question about my academics. I got an A on the last paper, and the paper before that. And a 100 percent on the midterm quiz.

"Do you know anything about the thing that was written about Professor Roy?"

Shit.

"Um, no, what was it?"

"He's your econ professor, right?"

"Yeah, why?"

"I'm sure you've heard of Rate My Professors?"

What the fuck, John.

"Yes."

"Someone wrote something about him. It's not good. I just want to make sure you haven't experienced anything like that with him. You know, inappropriate."

I stepped back into the room and kept my reaction calm, collected.

"What do you mean?" I asked. "I haven't seen anything, sorry; I'm not sure I understand what you're saying."

Hale sighed.

"So someone, a student, a girl, wrote that he hit on her and insinuated that if she . . . traded a sexual activity, he would raise her grade."

I didn't know what to say. I knew it wasn't true. I thought back to John's outburst the day before. *I have a plan.* The grin that had spread across his face.

Hale continued, filling in the silence, "I don't think the administration has seen it yet. Sometimes things like this happen, it's a *he said, she said* situation and there's not much they can do, but it's still very awkward. Adam, Professor Roy, is a friend of mine. I don't think he would do that, but you never know, I guess." He paused, then looked back at me. "I just want to make sure he hasn't offered anything like that to you."

I shook my head, swallowing. "No, never. He's a good professor."

"Okay. Well, you can always talk to me, if there's ever anything . . . And if you hear anything . . . you know, students talk. If you know it's not true, please tell me, or someone. At this point, I'm not sure he will even come back next semester."

"I'll let you know," I said.

I didn't linger and headed out of the building as soon as I knew the conversation was over. I didn't think Hale suspected I knew anything, but I was annoyed he even had to ask me in the first place. I didn't want to lie to him.

Stupid, dumb fucking John. I stomped down the icy stairs outside and headed toward the dining hall.

► ► ►

I MARCHED UP to our table in a fury, my bag thumping against my hip, wet boots squeaking against the floor. Everyone was laughing about something, except Max, who had his face stuck in a textbook.

"John," I said, my voice stern. They all looked at me.

"Relax. It's all good," he said, smiling at the others. Ruby faked a smile, hiding her disappointment. She wasn't going to be on my side. I was going to be alone in this. Even Khaled looked weak, smiling under a lowered gaze.

I leaned in so the other tables couldn't hear and whispered, "My TA asked me about Professor Roy."

"Ohhh, Professor Royyyy," Gemma said, feigning a swoon. "Everyone's talking about him. What a creep."

Khaled let out a small laugh; he always laughed for Gemma.

"He's not a creep," I said.

Gemma winked. "We know that, but nobody else does."

I looked around the dining hall, everyone bent over their phones. I was sure the news had already spread.

"You can't do this shit; you could ruin his career," I argued.

"Relax," John replied, "it's harmless. Just a bit of gossip. He deserved it."

"He didn't do anything wrong. *You did*."

John put a hand on his chest, so proud, so obliviously vindictive. "Calm down; they will never know it was me."

"I don't want to get in trouble because of you," I said, anger lacing my words.

John looked up at me through the crinkled eyes, wide smile. He could tell I was angry. I wasn't even trying to hide it. His face fell, ever so slightly.

"Look, M, I'm sorry," John said, his voice now matching my tone, the others quietly staring at us. "I didn't mean for you to get in trouble or anything; it's just a stupid prank. It's not like I killed anyone."

I knew I should play along. Find it funny. But I didn't. I wanted to tell John what I really thought. I wanted to tell him he was cruel and immature. But I knew the others would see it as me being serious, boring, straightedge. Nobody wanted drama. Nobody wanted to deal with a fissure in the circle. I couldn't risk losing them, so I tried to relax, to bring slack back into muscles that were wound so tight.

I looked at Ruby. She couldn't approve. She couldn't possibly find this admirable.

She finally spoke when she caught me looking at her. "It's okay, M. Seriously, you won't get in trouble," she said, her eyes pleading with me to let it go.

She was on John's side, and for a brief moment, I wanted to shake her out of it. She was always going to defend John, never questioning him. Just like my mother with Levi. Loyal and weak.

► ► ►

AFTER LUNCH, WHILE the others bundled up in their coats and scarves, and headed off to their last exams of the semester, Max and I were alone at the table.

"Max," I said. He looked up at me, and I eyed the seat John had been in.

He followed my glance. "Not my business," he replied.

"He makes it our business. We are guilty by association," I said, surprised by his nonchalance. Besides having a group of friends, my grades were the single most important thing in my life at Hawthorne. I knew Max felt the same way.

Max turned his head toward the large windows facing the quad and flicked his eyes over the students hurrying down the pathways. He wasn't worth the effort. He clearly didn't care about me, and I certainly wasn't going to spend my time arguing about John's bad decisions. I started to pack up my things. I knew the Greenhouse would be crowded, but at least I could escape from John, and everyone else. I shoved my notes in my bag. Max looked over at me.

"He did that to me once," he said.

"Did what?" I asked. My patience balancing a very fine line.

"Well, it was a little different. When we were in middle school at a sleepover camp for soccer. For the last week of it, we had a tournament. Only one camper could be captain. John wanted it, like, *really* wanted it. I didn't care. I didn't want it, but there was a vote and I won."

I couldn't picture him in a leadership role. Not the quiet, reserved version of him I knew.

He continued, "I went back to my cabin that night and found that someone had shit in my bed. It was under the sheets, everywhere. The next day someone called me Captain Shitter. The name stuck for the rest of the summer."

Gross. Boys were disgusting. I didn't know what to say. I waited for him to say more.

Max looked back at the students rushing by outside, their arms folded over their chests, braced against the chill. "I didn't know who did it at the time. I didn't think he was so . . . spiteful. I guess I'm not surprised."

I sat back down, remembering something.

"What happened to John's dad?" I asked.

"I don't know all the details," Max said. "Things were bad in our family for a while because of him. He got caught for insider trading and went to prison. Then he got divorced from my aunt. It was a whole thing. I think he lives in Boston now. New wife, new kids. We never see him."

"So you think that makes it okay for John to do what he did?"

"No, it's not okay. But he doesn't even speak to his dad anymore. That would fuck someone up, don't you think?"

I didn't answer.

Max gripped his pen, his jaw setting into a firm, hard line. "I've learned to let him do his thing. Don't get in his way. I'm serious."

I ignored Max, spotting Ruby in the foyer to the dining hall. If I left now I could still catch her on her way to the Greenhouse.

"Fine, whatever," I said, slinging my bag over my shoulder and leaving Max alone at the table.

► ► ►

"RUBY," I CALLED, leaving the dining hall in a bubble of warmth.

She kept walking, and I thought I even saw her pick up her pace.

"*Ruby*," I said again, louder, running to catch up with her. I pulled her arm so that she was facing me.

She stopped on the sidewalk. Snowflakes melted into her pink hat. She didn't say anything, looking at me with defensive eyes.

"What?" she asked, annoyed.

"Ruby. What is going on? Aren't you mad at him?"

Ruby sighed, adjusting her tote higher up on her shoulder. She crossed her arms and looked out over the quad.

"Yes, I'm mad."

"Well, why don't you say something to him? He'll probably listen to you. You're his girlfriend. What if Professor Roy gets fired?"

"What John does is up to John. He is his own person."

"Seriously?"

"What?"

"That is such bullshit."

"What do you want me to say? I'm not his mother. Am I angry? Yes, of course I'm angry. But it's not for what you think. There are things you don't know about me. There are things you don't know about John. You think you know everything, but you don't. Just let it go. Okay?"

I had never heard her talk like this before. This was not the sweet, fun Ruby I knew. There was something else in there, another girl, buried somewhere inside. An angry girl, with something to hide.

"All right," I said, trying to relax, realizing she was becoming angry with me, too. I knew I couldn't lose her as a friend. She was my only strong connection to the group. I needed her. I needed to fix this. "I'm here. If you want to talk."

Ruby laid a hand on my arm, her eyes more sympathetic now.

"Thanks, M, but I'm just not ready to talk about it. I love you for understanding."

I hated her for saying that, but I smiled and linked arms with her as we headed toward the Greenhouse. I changed the subject, to how ridiculous Gemma looked in her moon boots. I needed to lighten the air.

I hated how Ruby kept things from me, how she alluded to things and then pulled back, as if she was teasing me, casting a line and then taunting me with her truths. Pulling me close and then keeping me at a distance. Her own special method of control.

CHAPTER SEVENTEEN

TEXAS, 1997

Summer hadn't even officially started but Texas was already hot and soupy. As Levi and I ate waffles one morning, we listened to the newscaster warn parents about hot cars and the danger of leaving their unattended children inside. My mother muttered something under her breath, something about the heat, how overwhelmingly early it was this year.

Levi and I spent our mornings at an accelerated learning program and our afternoons at swim team practice. My parents kept asking me if I had made friends with any of the other kids on my team. I lied and said I had. Twice a week Levi went to visit a doctor, at least that was what my mother told me. He always came back in a bad mood.

During that time, in the hours I spent alone with our babysitter, Lane, Bo and I went for adventures in our backyard. He was small enough that I could hitch him on my hip, up into our treehouse where we sat for hours. I wasn't allowed to bring Bo up with me, but if I didn't, he whined at the bottom of the tree. Lane didn't know this rule, or maybe she had forgotten it, so I got away with it. She was sixteen, but she seemed like she was thirty-five. So old, so mature. She let us do what we wanted, and I liked her for that. Occasionally she would yell our names, and we had to yell back to let her know we were alive.

Up in the treehouse, I read stories or watched the neighbors as Bo sat next to me, panting in the heat. When I could no longer stand the humidity, we jumped in the pool, cooling off together in the tepid water. Bo liked to lap back and forth, his dark hair fanning in the water. When he was tired, he clung to me, panting, paws digging into my shoulders. I liked holding him, making him feel safe, protected.

Bo and I were in the treehouse one afternoon when Levi ran into the backyard, screaming and kicking at the grass. I thought he had left for his visit ten minutes ago. They would be late if they didn't leave soon.

He was so loud, screaming as if someone was hitting him. He was in one of his bad moods. He yelled a lot. I never did; I was the behaved one. My mother followed him, pleading with him to calm down. She was still in her work outfit since she came home early to take Levi to the doctor herself. I thought they looked like pajamas, the matching blue top and bottom. I went to the edge of the treehouse, where there was a small gap for the ladder. It always worried my mother that there wasn't a gate, or some sort of barrier, but my father taught us to be safe. Besides, both Levi and I were athletic and coordinated. I crawled to the gap and looked down at the two of them.

I heard Levi yell words at my mother. I was pretty sure they were all swear words, which we were not allowed to use. The way he said the words made them sound bad.

My mother was begging him to come back to her. She kept saying it over and over again. *Come back to me, baby.*

Our mother was always so nice, to everyone. At parties, people always ended up around her, laughing at her stories. She was also very pretty. I wished I could be more like her. Sometimes I practiced smiling like her in the mirror, but it never felt right. Instead, I was like my father, who always stood to the side, avoiding people. I didn't think he knew I noticed, but I did. He also liked to walk around and offer people drinks so he didn't have to talk to anyone for too long. But he was always nice about it. He smiled a lot, too.

I don't know why Levi never seemed to like our mother. He played tricks on her and acted upset even when he wasn't. And then, every time my mother tried to love him more, he would get angry at her. He was lucky. She never tried to love me more.

My mother inched closer to Levi, but he backed away. They were now directly under me. I wanted to call out, but I didn't want to get in trouble for having Bo with me. His eyelids fluttered with sleep, but his warm eyes were trained on me, as they always were.

I didn't feel afraid, but I clutched Bo under my arm and he licked my face. His tiny paws were on the edge of the overhang, and I held him tight so he didn't accidentally wriggle off.

Levi, sweetie, I love you, please calm down.

"I'm not going," he hissed.

He screamed again. My mother lurched forward and tried to grab on to him, to bring him to her. I knew she wanted to hold him. She always did when we were upset. It was weird Levi never acted like this around our father. I didn't think our father would allow the behavior, and Levi knew it. Our father couldn't be messed with, not like our mother. She was too nice.

"I'll tell the doctor you're a bad mom," he said and then screamed again, as if to attract the neighbors' attention.

I cocked my head to the side. Our mother was *not* a bad mother. Would they take us away from her? I'd watched that happen in an episode of *Law & Order*. The mother was called "unfit," and they separated her from her kids.

And then Levi did something I'd seen him do before.

He started crying, like he did at the playground. He whimpered about how our mother hated him, *you hate me, you hate me, you hate me, don't make me go,* he said over and over again. My mother's face crumpled, and she pulled him into her arms. She dropped to the ground and cradled him for a long time. She was crying, too. *I'm sorry, it's okay, I'm sorry, we don't have to go,* she said as her body swayed back and forth.

Something inside me cracked open. I barely noticed it at first. The feeling was unfamiliar and strange. I wanted to tell my mother he was tricking her, that she didn't need to feel badly, it wasn't her fault. I wanted to hug her and tell her not to worry, but instead I stayed still and buried my face into Bo's fur, trying to drown out their voices, hoping she wouldn't notice us.

CHAPTER EIGHTEEN

Senior Day

People tell me things. I learned that useful lesson freshman year. I guess I am trustworthy, not caring about gossip or rumors; I don't feel the urge to tell secrets to get attention. Maybe I am so good at masking my judgments and opinions that they feel comfortable spewing their innermost thoughts. I never tell them what I actually think. They probably wouldn't like it. I used to find it annoying, everyone's opinions and feelings, a burden I didn't want to carry. Now it comes in handy. I am the secret-keeper of our little group.

I tiptoe from the kitchen into the doorway and peer into the hallway. Gemma is in the entryway, her chubby face red from outside. Her hair tied back into a blue knot at the base of her skull. I watch her proceed carefully, or as carefully as her alcoholic stupor will allow. She stumbles on a pair of shoes and creeps around the corner to make sure Khaled's door is closed. She doesn't want to be seen, not like this.

"Gems?" I say, stepping into the light. I need to know what happened. I try to sound concerned.

She snaps her head up. Caught.

Gemma and John. Max's words knock around my head, bouncing off my skull like bowling balls.

This isn't the first time I've caught Gemma like this. She doesn't remember. But I do.

CHAPTER NINETEEN

Freshman Year

"Okay, pick a hand," Ruby said, straightening in her chair and putting both fists in front of me.

We sat in the dining hall, our empty breakfast dishes still in front of us. It was a Tuesday, neither of us had class in the morning. The glare from the winter sun flashed through the glass windows. The twenty-degree day had us cozied up inside. Since the incident with John during finals, the prank he pulled, things were quiet. That's what happens during the winter in Maine. *Nothing.*

After my last exam, I had flown home to Texas. It was the start of my quiet winter. Our mid-century modern home lay flat and dull against the waning humidity. I had only been away for four months, but my parents already seemed older. After what happened with Levi, they aged prematurely, the joy sucked out of them as if by a black hole. That had been years ago, but it still wore on them. They both woke at dawn, their eyes shallow and tired. Every morning I set my alarm to drink coffee with my father before he went to work. He asked questions about Hawthorne, about my friends, my classes. This always ended with him recalling his days from college. Every story a reminder of what my mother once was—tenacious, joyful, witty.

I leaned back in my chair and rolled my eyes. Ruby looked so excited, holding both her hands out in front of me.

"This is not how people make decisions," I said.

"It's how I make decisions," she argued. "This is how I decided to apply early to Hawthorne, didn't I ever tell you that? I couldn't decide between University of Vermont, Boston College, or Hawthorne, so I drew out of a hat. Decision made."

"That is ridiculous."

"Whatever. Pick a freaking hand already. One hand is we go to Portland; the other is we go to boring class. I've picked which is which. So now you decide."

"Okay, the right one," I conceded.

Ruby flipped her hand over and opened her palm. "Ha! I win. Portland it is. Let's go."

"But I have class at one. I can't. Seriously," I responded.

I never skipped class, but Ruby was in one of those moods where she needed to *do* something. There was an exhibition at a gallery in Portland. Some photographer that she loved.

"Come on. Be *fun,* M."

I clenched my jaw. *Pretend. Pretend. Pretend.* Maybe if I said it a few more times to myself, I would change my mind about Portland. So far it wasn't working.

She continued, "We can get lattes and pop in a few galleries. Well, maybe skinny lattes. I feel so fat right now."

I didn't tell her she *wasn't fat,* even though she really wasn't. I was tired of saying it. I had secretly started tallying how many times she and Gemma made the *I'm fat* declaration since second semester had started. Gemma was in the lead by four.

"How do I know you weren't going to say Portland whichever hand I chose?" I asked.

"You don't," she said, standing up with her tray and a wink.

WE WERE IN Portland by noon. We caught a bus from Edleton and hopped off on Commercial Street, where we ran to the nearest coffee shop. It was one of those days where your snot froze in your nose if you didn't get inside fast enough. Even the usual chorus of squawking seagulls was subdued, every creature avoiding the bitter cold.

I liked spending time alone with Ruby. Without John or Gemma,

I had her to myself. I knew it was selfish, but she seemed more re-laxed with me, like she could say and do whatever she wanted. John wasn't there to distract her, and Gemma wasn't around to demand all her attention. With nobody to impress or please, she could breathe easy. In the back of my mind, I knew she was only so adamant about hanging out with me because John had mandatory attendance at a talk for his econ major. I was probably the second choice. I tried not to think about it.

"Okay," she said, taking a sip of her latte. "Let's go in Stafford's first and then Brooke Water, 'k?"

"Sounds good, whatever you want," I said.

"Thanks, M," she said, linking my arm as we walked the cobble-stones. "John never goes to galleries with me. You're the best."

I hated that I was missing a lecture, but I chalked it up as a "friend day." One point to the social category of my life. I was doing my job, being a good friend. It was almost as time consuming as schoolwork. My father would be proud. And I knew how happy it made Ruby, to get lost in paintings or photographs. Sometimes I felt like she needed it to escape. From what, I wasn't sure.

We walked up the granite steps leading into Stafford's, the gallery greeting us with giant glass doors. I saw our reflection, matching in our knit hats, Ruby's petite figure next to my taller one. The inside of the building was warm and clean. There were two people chatting in a corner, but their voices weren't above a whisper. One thing I ap-preciated about galleries was how minimal and quiet they were. I hated mess. And noise.

"Ruby?" a voice called out from the other side of the room. "Malin?"

We both turned to find Max, a Polaroid camera dangling from his neck, standing in front of one of the larger photographs.

"What are you guys doing here?" he asked. He hesitated for a moment, looking behind us, at the door. "Is John with you?"

"Are you serious? He wouldn't be caught dead in a gallery," Ruby said, unzipping her parka. "We're here for the Atwood exhibit. What are *you* doing here?"

"Oh, well, same," he said, letting out a smile.

Ruby looked intrigued and then delighted. She hopped over to him and clutched his arm. "Have you seen *Three by Sea* yet?"

They talked excitedly about this Atwood guy, the famous photographer, and his photo of three llamas in a desert (*three llamas in a desert?* I didn't get it. I made a mental note to do some research on appreciating art when I returned to campus), and made their way toward the back of the gallery. They were content, standing in front of the llamas. I heard Max laugh at something Ruby said. They looked so at ease together, I didn't want to disturb them. They reminded me of my parents, from some of my earliest memories, when I would watch them together in the kitchen, cooking dinner and sharing a beer or glass of wine.

After a few minutes of glancing at the photographs, I found a couch toward the far wall of the gallery, pulled a book out of my bag, and settled into the soft leather. Max and Ruby stood together, circling the room. When she moved, he moved, and when she spoke, he looked at her as if she was the best thing he'd ever seen. I was certain nobody had ever looked at me that way.

There was an invisible string between the two of them. They couldn't see it yet, but I could. It grew stronger the more they were together, winding tighter every day.

▶ ▶ ▶

MAX OFFERED TO take us back to campus in his car so we didn't have to catch the bus, and we happily agreed. The three of us wandered Portland for a few hours, Ruby and Max leading the way from gallery to gallery. I was relieved Max was there, to do most of the talking. And he seemed to bring out a happier side of Ruby.

Max and I were in the front of the car, semi-listening to NPR, the voices a sweet lullaby to our conversational silence. Ruby had fallen asleep in the back of the car, her mouth agape.

Max glanced in the rearview mirror. "You should try and throw something in there," he said.

"She'd die if she knew she was sleeping like that," I replied.

"Don't worry. It'll be our secret."

I was surprised by how comfortable he seemed. Max was so charming when he was with us, but quiet and awkward around the group. The others were too unpredictable, their emotions up and down, energy uncontrolled and wild. The uncertainty of their moods was stressful. But with the three of us, everything was so normal. I almost felt like I could tell him things, though I never would.

"So," he said, drawing out the o. "How are you feeling about skipping class?"

I smiled. "I hate it. I'll feel better when I watch the lecture online."

"That's why you're at the top of our class," Max said.

"I guess," I replied. "But it's fine. She was so excited about that Atwood guy, I couldn't say no."

"She's pretty good at getting her way, huh?"

I couldn't tell if he was joking.

"It's not a bad thing," he continued, reading the look on my face. "I wish I was like that."

"You don't think you're good at getting what you want?" I asked.

Since the accident, I made sure to work hard to get what I wanted. Of course, I failed when I didn't get into Yale, or Princeton, or Harvard. That's why I had to do better at Hawthorne. Everything was leading to getting into a good law school.

Max was quiet, his eyes flickering back to Ruby. "Not everything. But that's life, I guess."

My mind raced to find a question to ask him. People loved to answer questions about themselves. It was a quick way to get the focus off me, or other things I didn't want to discuss.

"When did you start taking photos?" I asked.

"Oh, um," Max started, "my mom bought me a camera when I was ten. I think she thought I could use a creative outlet. Something other than sports."

"Why something other than sports?"

Max cleared his throat.

"Because I was starting to get a little antsy, I guess. I started to dread going to school, and other random things. My mom has pretty bad anxiety and was always worried I would get it, too. Anyway . . . she's a photographer, a hobby thing, but it helps her calm down."

I thought of my own mother. Her anxiety. The way she would clam up at the mention of my brother, or the time we went to the hospital because she thought she was having a heart attack. She wasn't. It was all in her mind.

"And you like it? Taking photos?" I asked.

"Yeah, love it. Whenever I'm in the darkroom or editing, it relaxes me. I forget about everything else going on and zone out for hours. And you know, the actual photo-taking part, I like that, too. It's one thing I am completely in control of."

"I get it," I say. "That's why I like running."

"My mom would be so proud hearing me talk like this," he joked.

"What's with the old camera?" I asked, picking up the bulky Polaroid from the center console.

"It's sweet, isn't it? I found it at Goodwill and thought it would be fun."

"Well, your photos are really good," I said.

"You've seen them?" he asked.

Oops. "Um, yes." I glanced in the back seat to make sure Ruby wasn't awake. "We stopped by the art building a while back."

"Ruby's seen them, too?"

"Yeah, but I mean we walked by real quick," I lied.

"Oh," he said. I didn't want to disappoint him, but I also didn't want to tell him how impressed Ruby had been. I'd made a promise not to say anything.

When we got back to campus, Max parked the car outside Ruby's dorm.

"Hey," he whispered, turning toward me with a grin and holding up the Polaroid, "get in the back with her and I'll take a pic."

"You're a bad friend," I said.

"Do it!"

"Fine, fine," I whispered back.

I inched in next to her, so close that I could hear her faint snore. I wasn't sure what I should do; I hated having my photo taken. Posing always felt so forced. I remembered a photo from one of my parents' oldest albums—my mom and dad in college, her leaning in to give him an air-kiss. I shifted myself to do the same to Ruby, pausing a few inches away from her cheek.

Max pressed a button, and the photo started printing immediately. The click was loud and mechanical, causing Ruby to stir.

"It's a keeper," Max whispered, handing me the Polaroid. I watched the colors swirl to the surface, our faces slowly coming into view. I looked down at the photo. A funny moment between best friends. But that wasn't me, of course. That was who I was pretending to be.

"Ew," Ruby said, her voice sleepy, wiping drool from her face. "Was I drooling? Did you guys let me drool back here?"

We laughed.

"Don't worry; it was cute," Max said.

I watched as they made eye contact, Ruby blushing. I was an outsider to whatever they shared during those glances.

Ruby straightened her back and looked away as if the moment never happened.

"Ugh," she said, adjusting her hat, "I had a stress dream that I forgot to turn in my paper. Does anyone know the date?"

I looked at the date on my phone.

"January 29," I replied.

"Whew," she sighed, her voice still groggy. "Still have a week."

January 29. It was a meaningless date at this point in time, but it wouldn't be in three years. It was the death date. The anniversary before the anniversary.

I STILL HADN'T hooked up with anyone at Hawthorne. Technically, I was groped on a dance floor, and a guy from my ethics class tried to stick his tongue down my throat at a party. But I had not partaken in any mutual affection. People were starting to notice, cautiously eyeing me like a circus freak show. I knew they were wondering what was wrong with me, why I didn't want to be a part of it all. I was too attractive to not want sex. How could a face and body like mine go to waste? I knew that's what they were all thinking.

Ruby, Max, and I spent the majority of our time in the Greenhouse. An entire side of the building was made of glass, an atrium that stretched three stories up, allowing us to daydream out the window, watching the ice freeze up over the lake. It snowed five feet after the holidays, and our legs planked into the snow as we traipsed out to the shore of the lake to watch the Jump.

One day that will be us, Ruby had said, a look of wonder on her face. I knew she wanted me to be excited, too, so I had let her squeeze my hand and gave her a smile.

Our quiet and studious weeks were bookmarked by weekends filled with drinking and staying up late. I found myself caring less and less if I even attended the parties. I preferred the confinement of my room. I wasn't used to winter, the darkness of it, and it gave me a happy excuse to retreat to my cave often and without questions from the others. Somehow, it had even made my friends like me more. They begged me to hang out with them, to play beer pong into the early hours of the mornings, chugging beers and taking shots. I declined more often than not, realizing it made me more desirable. Somehow, I had become cooler by making rare appearances in their nightlife.

One evening in February, I was finishing up a paper in my bed when Ruby came barging in, letting the door slam behind her. She sat down next to me, one leg up on the bed while she stretched the other.

It was *Saturday,* she said in a firm, determined voice.

"Come on, don't make me go alone," Ruby said, pulling on my wrist. "You're more fun than everyone else; it's always boring without you. And you laugh at all my stupid commentary."

I was lying on my bed with my laptop open on my stomach. It was snowing (again), and the last thing I wanted was to get out of my cocoon and get dressed. And then go outside, into the freezing cold, and then go to a party.

"This one will be fun, I swear," Ruby said. "Gemma's already there. So is Max."

The last party I went to with Ruby was decidedly not fun. The six of us left early and headed to the Grill for mozzarella sticks and fries. On the way there, Khaled kept pushing Ruby and me into the high snowbanks flanking the sidewalk. We would scream in glee as he knocked us off our feet, sending us sideways into the powdery pillows of snow. I had to admit I had fun that night, but it wasn't because of the party. I did not like parties. Luckily, my *I'm from Texas and it's too cold outside* routine worked pretty well on my group of friends.

I heard John and Khaled giggling in the hallway. They were probably drunk already.

"Okay, you're clearly not going alone; you don't need me," I said, rolling my eyes toward the boyish squawks.

Ruby grinned. "Actually, I have to tell you something." She let go of my wrist and inched toward me, as close as possible to my face. I didn't like close-talkers, but it was a drunken habit of Ruby's that I had come to accept.

"John and I had sex last night," she said, whispering the words into my ear. She pulled back, her eyes wide and excited. I knew she wanted me to be as excited as she was, so I sat up and put on my biggest smile, pulling her into a hug.

I wondered what boys did in this situation. Maybe a high five? Or fist bump? Or a thump on the back? The whole process seemed so awkward.

"How was it?" I asked.

"The most perfect thing ever."

Ruby was still pretending she enjoyed sex. She told stories as if she knew about it, and everyone believed her. And why shouldn't they? She looked like the kind of girl who could know about sex if she wanted to. I was the only one who knew the truth, but not because she'd told me.

"I'm happy for you," I said. "I guess I could come out tonight. If you really want me to."

This led to a series of squeals as she dove into my closet, haphazardly digging through my neat collection of clothes. She held up a loose button-up flannel shirt, inspecting it, holding it over her thin frame.

"Can I borrow this?" she asked, casual.

"Um. Sure. It's not really going-out material."

"That's fine," she said. I raised an eyebrow at her. "John doesn't like this one."

I looked at her shirt, at the low cut, the way the fabric hugged her curves, the cleavage. She brought a hand to her chest, scratching her nails against her exposed skin.

"You know how protective he is," she said, avoiding eye contact. Defensive. "I love this shirt, though. Oh well."

I didn't say anything as she wriggled out of it and pulled the flannel shirt over her shoulders, taking care to button it up.

"I'll wash it, promise."

"It's fine," I said. "It's all yours." The shirt was tainted now. I didn't want it back. I swallowed the bitter taste in my mouth.

"Here," she said, smiling, "you wear mine. It will look *so* good on you."

I held the shirt in my hands, fingering the lace detail.

"Pajamas off, jeans on," she demanded. "I think Charlie's gonna be there," she added, looking at me out of the corner of her eye, cautiously testing the waters.

Charlie. She had been trying to get me to hook up with him for months. The last time she tried to get us to hook up, I had successfully avoided him all night by leaving the room every time he came in. I could play that game for hours.

"We could go on double dates," Ruby said, adjusting her hair in the mirror, flipping it over to one side of her face, fanning it out with her fingers.

I grimaced. "Oh yes, because the dating scene at Hawthorne is so hot right now. The dead of winter. Sign me up."

"Stop being so depressing."

When I was ready to go, she looked me up and down.

"You are *so* pretty. Even when you don't try. It's impossibly unfair," she said.

I sighed, choosing not to say anything. She threw the door open and pulled me into the fluorescent light of the hallway, where John and Khaled were sitting against the wall, their eyes slit into bloodshot beads.

"There she is," John said, his voice slow and drawn. He gave me that sneaky smile, and scanned his eyes up and down my body. His eyes lingered on the shirt. I zipped my jacket up to my neck, hiding from his stare. Ruby didn't notice.

"My queens," Khaled said, jumping to his feet. "Your carriage awaits."

THERE WAS NO carriage.

Instead, there was a twenty-minute walk to the opposite side of campus. We stuck close to the snowbanks. Cars drove by us slowly, the road slick and wet with snow. Ruby was loose, holding her arms out, hips swaying, palms up to the snowflakes. When a logging truck rumbled by us, the clanging of metal against metal and the shifting of tree trunks loud in my ears, I had to pull her back by the hood of her jacket so she wouldn't get hit. She squealed in drunken delight as chunks of snow hit us in the shins.

"You saved me," she said, grinning over her shoulder at me.

I didn't tell her she could have just died. The driver wouldn't have even noticed if he hit her, the truck was so loud and out of control. Each shift and jolt of a tree trunk could be a body under the wheel. I was annoyed at her for being so stupid.

Khaled offered Ruby a swig from the forty he was carrying with him. Ruby started to chug, and John pulled it from her lips.

"That's enough, babe, don't you think?" he asked. She swayed on the sidewalk, wrapping her body around him, bringing her lips to his, her fingers unzipping his jacket and finding their way inside his warmth.

He hated when she drank too much. She got flirty when she was loose and sloppy. He liked her all to himself.

"Ew, gross, guys," Khaled said, continuing to saunter along the sidewalk.

John looked at me through their kiss, his eyes glistening in the cold night air.

As we got closer to the senior house, I could almost see the clapboard siding vibrating to loud techno music.

"This looks promising," Khaled said as we took the steps two at a time. I followed the others, still considering a last-ditch effort to make a run for it. A few students were smoking on the porch. They ignored us. I recognized them as older, probably juniors or seniors.

"How did you hear about this?" I asked Ruby.

She was putting on lip gloss and puckered her lips before stuffing the shiny tube in her back pocket. She yanked open the door, and the music got louder.

"One of the girls on my team. It's a lacrosse party—I think," she said.

Ruby was always getting invited to upperclassmen parties. She was friends with everyone. I didn't know how she kept up with it all—their names, their stories, their problems. She was so popular that it was exhausting to watch. I knew she liked me the best though, because she told me often, usually after a heavy night of drinking. *You're my favorite, M, because you're the realest—not like fake girls—you're the most genuine, most realest friend, ever. You don't put up with bullshit. I love that about you.*

As soon as we entered the house, I wanted to leave. I looked from John to Khaled to Ruby, and they all had the same expression on their faces. Desperate to be a part of something. Someone squeezed me from behind.

"You caaaaame," a voice sang, and I knew who it belonged to. Gemma might have loved me more than Ruby did. She was drawn to the unavailable.

"Hi, love," I said, twisting around to hug her, even though we had seen each other hours ago at dinner. But this was drunk Gemma, and she needed the validation and attention that sober Gemma would never admit to craving.

I was slowly warming up to Gemma. Whereas I had taken to

Ruby immediately, Gemma was more of a slow burn. There was something about her, amidst the insecurity, that was charming and real. I had watched her over the past months, seeing glimpses of the real Gemma from time to time. She loved to act out scenes and sing, and be loud and annoying in a way that had become somewhat endearing. One day we were the only two to show up at lunch, everyone else busy with meetings and class. She told me about her strict private school in London, and the itchy uniforms she had to wear, and how she would walk home along Abbey Road, past the "Beatles wall" that everyone signed. She explained how it would get painted over every couple of months, erasing all the messages from fans in one fell swoop. It became her mission to be the first person to write on the clean slate, every time. She talked about riding the double-decker buses down Oxford Street at Christmas, and going out to pubs with her high school friends. I had learned more about Gemma in an hour than ever before. She never talked about her home life, as if she thought it would bore us. I wished she would try less to be someone she wasn't.

I spotted Max across the room, grinning with a girl from my philosophy class. Her hair was dark and long, similar to Ruby's actually, and her lips formed the perfect pout. She looked like a Disney princess, illuminated by all the other regular humans around her. Max leaned in toward her, their heads tilted together at an intimate angle.

"Who is that?" Ruby asked me, her grip tight on my arm. A little too tight.

"Greta," I said, looking over at Ruby. "She's from our philosophy class. Older. Sophomore, I think."

A disappointed look crossed Ruby's face. She was used to getting all the attention from Max.

"They've been together all night," Gemma said, throwing back a shot of some mystery liquid from a small cup that looked like it was from a dentist's office. "She's hot, right?"

At the mention of the word *hot,* John's head swiveled toward Max and Greta.

"Oh yeah, get some," Khaled said, pounding his fist into his palm. Both he and John snickered like schoolchildren.

"You are both idiots," Gemma said, and she grabbed my hand and pulled me into the suffocating crowd.

Ruby had her hand on my shoulder, and we followed Gemma, navigating our way through the herd. I smelled sweat and body odor, and a loose fart someone must have drunkenly let escape. I gagged and pressed forward.

I looked back and saw Ruby glancing over her shoulder toward Max and Greta, his lips close to hers, bent toward the dark wisps of Greta's hair. His hand was on her back. Greta *should* date him. And then maybe he would stop pining after Ruby. Maybe he could be happy.

A booming voice sounded from behind me. "Malin Ahlberg!"

Gemma, Ruby, and I turned around. Hale was standing with a group of seniors around a flip cup table. He stepped out and greeted us, hands on his hips, baseball cap perched atop his mess of curls.

"You and your friends want to join us?" he asked.

Gemma and Ruby looked at me; I knew they wanted me to introduce them. They were excited to have been invited to play. A grad student with a group of seniors, wanting to hang out with *us* put me in a good position on the social ladder.

"Sure," I said.

Hale pulled me in next to him, putting a hand on my shoulder. I expected to feel that wall go up, the one that always swept over me when someone touched me. But it didn't.

"You guys know what to do?" he asked us.

"Duh," Gemma said, a hand already on her cup. Ruby stood on her other side, all three of us in a row.

We all brought our cups up to the line of juniors on the other side of the table.

"Down, up, down, up, drink!" everyone shouted in sync.

I watched as the two dueling lines chugged their beers, one at a time, like the wave at a baseball game. After Hale swallowed his beer in one gulp, I brought the cup up to my lips, and the warm liquid slid down my throat. I made a mental note to rehydrate immediately after the game.

"Atta girl!" Hale yelled in my ear, clapping as I brought the cup upside down to the table and flipped it upright on the first try.

Gemma was already chugging when I looked over at her. She wiped the side of her mouth with the back of her hand after the game moved on to Ruby.

I kept a slight eye on Hale to my right, noticing his movements, listening to him interacting with the others. He was the team captain, leading us to beer-chugging victory. He knew everyone's name, even called a few of them by nicknames. Girls came up to Hale, flipping their hair and tossing their wittiest lines at him. He responded to every single one of them, made eye contact, made them feel special. But was respectful at the same time, somehow. He made it known he wasn't interested in them.

I wondered if his very public breakup made him more attractive to the junior and senior girls, or if it was that annoying positive energy that buzzed around him, following him like a cloud.

AFTER A FEW rounds of flip cup, the three of us found ourselves having to pee so we crowded into one of the tight bathrooms. Hale thanked us for joining them and making their team better.

"He's very jolly," Gemma said, panting from pushing us through the crowd.

Ruby laughed. "He is *so* awesome."

I rolled my eyes. "Nobody is that nice. It's weird. And why is he hanging out with undergrads?"

"Awww, my grumpy old man," Ruby said, squeezing her arms around my torso, my arms pinned to my side. "And probably because Edleton is boring as fuck and he wants to have fun?"

I shrugged, fiddling with my flask and rehydrating. I was a little dizzy from the beer, and I tried to focus on my reflection in the mirror. I was relieved nobody had questioned my "gluten allergy" when I chugged the beer with everyone else. They were probably too drunk to notice.

"Hey, so how's Liam?" Ruby asked. She sat on the toilet, always delicate, back straight. I looked away, focusing on myself in the mirror and smoothing out my hair.

Gemma didn't answer for a moment, her face drawn, as if the mention of Liam had ruined her good time. She leaned against the bathroom door, ignoring the banging from other girls outside, yelling at us to *hurry the fuck up, freshmen.* "He's great," Gemma said. "Misses me, as always. He wants to come visit."

"Really? Let's text him now!" Ruby said, overly excited. She stood up and flushed, her pee clear. Alcohol could fool you that way. Hydrating until suddenly it's not.

"No, he's definitely asleep," Gemma replied, firm.

"Oh, come on, who cares, I'm sure he'd love to be woken up by you," Ruby protested. She grabbed Gemma's phone out of her hands.

"I said *no,*" Gemma said, securing the phone and stuffing it into her back pocket.

"You're no fun," Ruby said.

I wanted to ask Gemma *why* we couldn't call him, besides the sleeping thing, but Gemma changed the subject so fast I didn't get a chance. I knew that tactic well.

"Hey, so," Gemma started, sitting herself down on the toilet, pee streaming like a pressure hose. "Serious question."

I could tell by the way she was talking that she had already drunk too much. And that she was about to ask us something inappropriate and personal.

"Yeah?" Ruby asked. She was adjusting her high ponytail next to me in the mirror.

"Not for you, Mrs. Wright," Gemma responded, using John's last name. She looked at me. "It's for Malin."

"Fire away," I said.

"Well, are you ever going to hook up with anyone?"

Ruby laughed. "Oh my God, Gemma. Rude much?"

Gemma smiled, flushing the toilet and giving me a wink. "I'm serious, love. You are gorgeous. Why don't you flaunt that bod?"

Before I could answer, Ruby interrupted, "I'm setting her up with Charlie so don't even think of interfering."

"Oh, Charlie, huh? He's a cutie," Gemma said.

They both stared at me expectantly. This was where I was supposed to do that thing. That thing where I confess that I have a huge crush on someone.

"Um, yeah, he is. We'll see," I said with a forced smile. I undid my jeans and hovered above the toilet. There was no way I was going to touch that seat. My quads burned.

"It would be so freaking cute if you guys dated. Your kids would be beautiful," Ruby said, a dreamy look in her eyes.

I ignored her, standing up and hitting the flusher with my boot.

"Ow, ow," Gemma hollered, opening up the door back out into the party, "Malin's on the prowl, ladies and gentlemen!"

Nobody acknowledged her. The party was far too crowded to hear anything. Gemma laughed and squeezed my hip.

"Maybe tonight's the night," I added, hoping the implication of sex would get them off my back.

"Oh, wow," Ruby said, surprised. "My Malin is all grown up."

I sensed a slight hesitation in her voice. She tried to cover it up but I saw right through her. There was something she was worried about, making her excitement feel forced and fake.

"Well, that's a relief," Gemma said. "I was worried you were like, you know, asexual."

"I'm not," I replied, trying to get my voice loud enough for them to hear.

Shit. I needed to hook up with someone, soon. I didn't want everyone thinking the same thing as Gemma. I had to act interested, at least a little bit, or everyone would think I was a weird anti-sex freak.

AN HOUR LATER, I began my routine. I would say I had to find someone, usually Max or Khaled was my fallback, and then I would leave. Nobody would notice, at least not at first, and by the time they did notice my absence, they'd be too drunk to care. It worked every time.

I didn't have to say goodbye to anyone and deal with the whines about my leaving.

"Going to find Khaled," I yelled to Ruby and Gemma, who had begun to sway their hips and swing their heads back and forth with the music.

Ruby jolted, grabbing at my arm. "Oh, no, you aren't," she said. "No bailing tonight, no way."

Gemma laughed, her head lolling from side to side with the music. "No way," she echoed in a drunken trance.

I smiled, tried to act clueless. "I'm not leaving," I said.

"I know you, Malin," Ruby said, her eyes suddenly serious. "Don't even try. You're staying. It's time you had some fun."

She grinned at someone behind me.

I looked over my shoulder. Charlie.

That was the thing with Hawthorne. Everyone believed you needed to hook up with someone to have fun. I hesitated. This could be my chance to show everyone I was normal. I wanted them off my back, so I turned around.

Pretend.

I gritted my teeth and showed off my wide Texan-girl smile.

TWENTY MINUTES LATER I was grinding against Charlie on the makeshift dance floor in the basement. We were so close to the rickety staircase that my shoulder kept brushing up against a maze of spiderwebs, probably decades old. With every motion, either from Charlie's thigh or my waist, I focused on spending enough time to prove my normalcy. Then I could leave.

Through the techno lights I spotted Max and Greta in the corner, making out against the crumbling brick wall. I watched their hands interlocking, him take a gentle step toward her, pressing her farther into the wall. I wondered if they knew about the spiders. I didn't like seeing him like that, and I looked away before anyone noticed me watching them.

I looked to the other side of the room, where I spotted Amanda dancing with Becca and Abigail. I liked that it was the three of them, no guys rubbing their crotches against them. They were laughing, delirious, their skinny bodies dancing in time with the music.

Charlie was good. A little bland, but he meant well. If I had to do this with anyone, I could deal with it being him. We had flirted for a little bit, making small talk. *The weather. Majors, minors. Dorms, houses.* I made sure to pull my hair out of its ponytail and laugh in all the right places. After I could no longer stand talking to him, I suggested we dance, and so we did.

He shouted something in my ear.

"What?" I yelled.

"Having fun?" he repeated, louder this time.

Instead of responding, I pulled him closer, so that the space between our bodies became smaller. I ran my hand under his shirt and up his tight back muscles. His sweat lathered my palms, and I felt him shudder beneath me. The closer we got, the slower his movements became. I leaned back and looked up into his face. His lids were heavy, and he drew his eyes from mine to my lips. This was easier than I thought it would be.

I knew what to do; I wasn't an idiot. He tasted like beer, and it wasn't terrible like I thought it would be. A guy should taste like beer. Hard liquor was aggressive and cheap.

Charlie tugged at my lip with his teeth, gentle and sweet. He stopped moving and put his hands to my face, so that he was cupping my cheeks in his large palms. We stood there, kissing, until the song changed and we kept dancing. He was a good kisser. Not that I had anything to compare it to. I opened my eyes to see Ruby pressed against John, so entangled I couldn't make out where her body stopped and his began. I looked past her shoulders and hair, into the space where John's face would be.

I held my breath for a moment, as John's eyes met mine. Charlie started moving again with the beat to the song. I kept waiting for John to look away, but he stared right back. Before he finally looked away, he took a moment to survey my body, his eyes thirsty. Even though I was soaked in sweat, I could feel the hair on my arms stand on end.

I pulled back from Charlie. "I have to go," I mouthed.

I pushed toward the base of the staircase, needing to get out. I felt his hand brush against my wrist, but he was too nice to pull me back. He'd let me go; he was respectful. I climbed the stairs and glanced back at Charlie. He shrugged his shoulders as if to ask what he had done wrong. I shoved my way out of the basement and into the kitchen and then out the back door, the frigid air a welcome relief against my hot skin. The sweat under my clothes froze, shocked by the change in temperature. I left my jacket in the house, but I didn't care. I started to jog and then picked up speed. The noise from the house vanished as I sprinted back toward campus, the snow crunching beneath my boots.

► ► ►

I NEEDED FOOD. The beer had made me weak, and I was craving carbs and cheese. I knew the Grill would still be open so I ran up to the doors, sighing as I came into contact with the dim lights.

I bought three slices of greasy pepperoni and spotted a deserted table in the far corner. There were a few students hanging out, laughing from their drunkenness, dissecting their nights. The Grill was a popular spot late night, but it would be another hour or two until everyone poured in before it closed at one A.M. John and Khaled always snuck bags of chips and candy bars in their pockets, attempting to steal as much as they could without getting noticed. This was always my cue to turn in for the night.

I must have zoned out while I ate, because a voice interrupted my thoughts.

"This seat taken?"

I looked up to find Hale grinning at me, a tray of cereal bowls and cups of milk in his hands.

"Um, no," I said, mouth full of pizza, and unable to think of an excuse. "It's all yours."

He sat across from me and began to pour one of the glasses of milk into a bowl of Froot Loops.

"So," he said, "have fun tonight? You're good at flipping cups."

I shrugged, remembering I needed to be nice, friendly. "Yeah, it was super fun."

He looked up at me, a funny look in his eye. "Super fun, huh?"

He finished his first bowl of cereal, burping, and started in on the second. I didn't say anything, picking at the pizza crust.

"How do you like class?" he asked. "Am I doing okay?"

Hale was leading another one of my English seminars, this time on Shakespeare. I thought about how messy he appeared in class, standing in front of us, lecturing with his shirt untucked, hair unkempt. He made up for it with challenging readings and by making interesting points, things I wouldn't have thought of if he hadn't mentioned them. It was the only reason he could get away with his appearance.

"Um," I said, his vulnerability catching me off guard. "Yeah, you're doing a good job."

"There has to be something I can improve upon. I feel like you have some good advice up your sleeve."

I hesitated. I wasn't sure if it was appropriate for me to actually critique him.

"Come on," he said, his spoon of Cheerios halfway to his mouth. He took the bite and looked at me, expectant and attentive.

"Well," I started. I looked out the window. I pictured Edison's eager, annoying face, his hand lifting as if on cue, two minutes before class ended. Unfortunately, he was an English major, too, which meant I would have to endure his routine until graduation. I sighed.

Hale laughed, reading my mind. "It's the kid in the front row, right? Edison. That guy has some serious timing."

I felt myself smiling. "You indulge him, every single time."

Hale pushed the two empty cereal bowls to the far edge of his tray.

"What am I supposed to do? The kid likes to learn. I'm supposed to facilitate his learning."

"I think he does it on purpose," I said, picking a pepperoni off the pizza and popping it in my mouth.

"Okay, besides dear Edison, what else?" He looked so eager.

"I think you're good," I replied. "Everyone pays attention to you."

"I guess. At least no one sleeps. That's my main goal. Keep you guys awake."

"I'm awake," I replied.

"That you are. Smartest in the class, too. I probably shouldn't tell you that . . ." He paused, chewing on his cereal, staring at me. "You're one of those people, aren't you?"

"What do you mean?"

"You're good at things. Everything, I assume."

I didn't say anything. Nobody had ever assessed me like that before.

Hale grinned, wide and mischievous, forgetting about his previous comment. "Want to see something cool?" he asked.

I hesitated. He wasn't giving me that look so many of the other guys at Hawthorne did. The drunk one, with bloodshot eyes and a lusty expression. But still. I didn't like being alone with guys.

"I should go home," I replied. I needed to make one more stop before I went back to my room.

"It'll take ten minutes, tops," he said. "I promise you won't be disappointed."

I considered his offer as he began to empty the bowl of dry Frosted Flakes into his coat pocket. Somebody putting cereal in their pocket was not a threat.

"Okay," I said. "But only ten minutes, and then I have to go."

I followed him to the tray return, where we placed our dishes on the conveyor belt and watched them disappear into the hidden depths of the kitchen. We walked outside, our breath unfolding into the cold air.

"Want my jacket?" Hale asked. I forgot I had left mine at the party.

"Oh, no, I'm fine," I replied, sucking the clear air into my lungs.

I followed Hale to the English department, a building I was already familiar with. He walked at a fast clip, looking over at me with a sheepish grin.

"What?" I asked.

"I like that I get to be the first person to show you this."

I followed him up the stairs, and he slid his keycard across the access point. The light went green, and we stepped inside the dark corridor.

"This way," Hale said, entering a side door. It was a door I passed every day and had never thought twice about.

We climbed up four flights of stairs, where Hale pulled a string from the ceiling revealing a ladder to a tight space in the attic. I looked at him, skeptical.

"Are you going to murder me?" I asked.

He laughed. "Yup, I'm gonna leave you in the attic and stink up the whole building."

When I didn't say anything, he smiled. "Go on."

I knew he wasn't going to hurt me. He was innocent. I placed my hands against the rough wood and ascended the ladder.

Except the attic wasn't an attic. It was a bell tower. The top of the old schoolhouse, I realized. Windows stood in as walls on all four sides. I brought my arms around my chest to stay warm, the space lit up by the full moon.

In the center of the small room was the rusted metal bell. Hale appeared next to me, grinning.

"You can see everything on campus from here," he said.

I stepped beside him and in the dark, I could make out the dining hall, the quad, and the street that led to Khaled's house—my future house. The line of brick freshman dorms dotted along the road. The night sky was a deep blue, the stars lighting up even the darkest fragments. I spotted a few students, toy soldiers from up here, walking across the quad, in a hurry to get out of the cold. I liked being up high, being able to watch everything, everyone, from a safe distance.

I pictured the treehouse in Texas, the dangerous fall that threatened us every afternoon.

"It's beautiful," I breathed.

"Worth the detour?" Hale asked, still looking out at campus.

"Yes," I replied. "Thank you."

Hale was still, taking in the view. I traced his face, the open book, now appearing calm and subdued. I wanted to know more about him, wanted to keep him talking. It was a craving that had to be satisfied.

"Why did you move to Maine?" I asked.

"Fresh air," he replied. "I'm from Boston. There never seemed to be enough of it there."

We were quiet for a moment, and then he asked, "Why did you choose Hawthorne?"

"I like how cold it is," I responded.

And the other reason. But I wasn't planning on telling anyone about it.

Hale looked over at me and smiled. "You're a curious one, Ahlberg."

I liked the way he said my last name like that.

"So, you don't like drinking, do you?" he asked.

"Sure, I do."

"No, you don't. I saw you chugging that water after flip cup. And you're steady as a rock right now."

"Fine," I say. "I kind of hate it. Yeah, it's super lame if I don't drink, I'm aware."

I was waiting for him to give me that look, that look that says, *oh, you're weird*. Well, at least he would realize who I am and leave me be. He could stop trying so hard to be my friend, or whatever it was he was doing.

Instead, he smiled at me. "Hey, you gotta do you."

There was something in his glance that was new, like he was noticing something on my face. It only lasted a few seconds, but I saw it. I was suddenly acutely aware that we were alone in the tower. I remembered that he was a TA, and I was his student, and it was time for me to leave.

"I need to go," I said.

"Of course, sure. Be careful on the stairs," he said, turning toward the hole in the floor. He held out his hand for me to climb down the stairs, but I ignored him. I was glad he didn't fight it.

We climbed back down the narrow stairs, and Hale held the door open for me back into the cool night.

"Well," he said, shoving his hands into his pockets. He looked like a little kid for a second, innocent and naïve. *Leave me alone,* I wanted to warn him. *You don't want to know me.*

"Thanks for the detour," I said, giving him a smile, hoping he would leave.

"No prob. See ya later, Malin," he said, taking off into the night. I watched him walk away, pulling out a handful of Frosted Flakes and leaning his head back to toss them into his mouth. I waited until the darkness swallowed him and then remembered what I still had to do. My night wasn't over yet.

► ► ►

I RAN THROUGH campus toward Ruby and Gemma's room. I hated walking. Running was so much more efficient.

Every student had access to all buildings until two A.M. I pressed my keycard against the plastic scanner, and the heavy door clicked open. A wall of heat enveloped me as I climbed the stairs to the second floor.

I knew their room would be open. Gemma had a habit of losing her key, and after they owed fees for her irresponsibility, they decided to forgo the keys and leave the room open. Everyone else did the same. Nobody was going to rob a college dorm in Edleton, Maine. The town was too sleepy for thieves. I wondered about this often, how easily our expensive electronics and clothes could go missing one night, but by the next day it would all be replaced by concerned parents.

Once I was inside, I evened out my breath and stood in front of Ruby's desk. I pulled open the drawer and tugged at the diary, stuffed in the back behind her textbooks.

February 28

Dad called today. I wish he wouldn't.

Things with John are . . . fine. That is the worst way to describe a relationship, isn't it?

Fine.

It sounds so . . . blah. Like there's a problem, but nobody wants to admit it, so you just say "fine."

John and I kind of had sex. The first time he was inside me for about ten seconds before I pushed him away. It hurt . . . I feel bad. We've been dating for six months. I wish I could just DO IT, and be good at it. I am so frustrated with myself. I am the best soccer player at Hawthorne, and I can't even have good sex? I am fun. I am normal. So what the hell is wrong with me? I can't be the last virgin on campus. I just can't.

Sometimes I feel like I'm just going to vomit on him because my stomach is tensed up in knots. I think if I get drunk enough, it can happen. I need to make it happen. This is ridiculous. I am ridiculous. I'm going to tell M we did it and it was great. Then at least maybe I'll be more motivated to actually do it. Or else I'm a liar.

I'm pretty sure I know what the issue is. But I can't even go there. I'm going to ignore it, and maybe it will go away, and everything will be fine (there's that word again, ha haaa . . . ugh).

On a different note. John has been acting weird. One second he is super nice and his normal self, and the next he's cold and distant. Like a completely different person. I think maybe he is overwhelmed by school (his grades aren't so great, but it's because he doesn't apply himself, I know it) and preseason started so I think the pressure of it all is making him—

A noise. I snapped the diary shut. Something was dragging against the hallway outside their room. I stayed calm, hoping it was a drunk couple, oblivious to everything else around them. They would pass and fall into a room down the hall. I went back to Ruby's diary.

But the noise was right up against the door, and someone fumbled with the handle.

Shit.

I darted inside Gemma's closet as the door swung open, the metal handle crashing against the wall. I held my breath and pressed into the back of the closet, making sure to avoid any clanging hangers. I ran my hand up against the wall, looking for something to brace myself with. Two bodies fell inside the room, breathless and desperate. I held the diary to my chest, looking around for a place to hide it in case I needed to.

I knew who it was in a matter of a few, quick moans. The door closed again, and it was just the three of us. Through the slanted cracks of the closet I could see the two of them, clumsy and groping.

"You're so hot," he said, which only caused her to release a gasp of delighted pleasure. His voice was husky, thick.

I surveyed my closet-prison. There was no way out, no way I could escape without them seeing me. If I stepped outside, we'd all be stuck, staring at each other. The awkwardness of the situation would ruin everything I had worked so hard for over the past few months. I stood so still I began to feel faint; I reminded myself to breathe.

They continued to suck at each other's faces, saliva slopping around their mouths. The rush of hands over clothing and skin.

"I need this," he said. "You have no idea." His voice was muffled, probably because he was sucking on one of her body parts, I couldn't tell which one, and I didn't want to know.

I tried to think of other things. I imagined I was in class, and we were analyzing a passage by Austen, or the Brontë sisters, or—*no.* I couldn't focus between the slaps of naked skin on the other side of the door.

"Oh my God," she whispered in a rush, only loud enough that I could still hear her, "John."

This was turning into a really bad porno. I was stuck in actual hell. I made a mental note to never go out, *never,* ever again.

I heard a sharp smack and then overwhelming silence. It was so quiet I could hear static buzzing in my ears, probably left over from the party's deafening music.

"Did you like that?" John asked, slow, succinct. He didn't sound like himself. This was different. Dark, almost. I would've missed it if not for the heavy silence.

No response. I pressed my nose against the slats, my eyes crossing as I tried to look into the room. *Did* she like it?

She finally spoke, and I could see her arm move toward him, as if she was grabbing at his chest. "Again," her voice demanded, playful, ignoring his change in demeanor. "Please."

Another slap, this time followed by a painful gulp from her throat, a gutted whimper. A wounded animal at the mercy of its killer. She laughed, trying to cover the pain.

"Again," she said, trying to sound sexy, purring her voice like a kitten.

John was quiet. He stepped away from her and stood in the middle of the room, panting. He made a grunt of regret. Her desperation must be turning him off. She was too eager to please him. He wanted to have to fight for it.

"What am I even doing here?" he asked under his breath.

"What is that supposed to mean?" she asked, wounded, taken aback, yanked out from her happy delusion of reality. She sat up. I saw her start to pull her sweater back on, her breasts still on display.

"Nothing," he said, stumbling toward the door. I pinched my eyes shut as his shadow passed the closet. He was so close I could smell the deodorant billowing off his body with the sweat and booze.

"John?" she whimpered. "What are you doing? I thought you wanted this?"

The doors shook. He was pacing, deciding where to run. "Shit. Shut up already. Nothing. This was *nothing*," he said.

Silence.

"Don't fuck up and tell Ruby. You'll ruin everything if you do," he threatened.

He was quiet for a moment, listening to the hallway, and then he pulled open the door and left. I heard his footsteps retreating down the hall, quick and succinct. He was running.

The room was silent, save for the rapid intake of breath coming from the other side of the room. I heard her rummage around under her bed and pull out something heavy. The sound of a bottle unscrewing, and then three long gulps. More silence. And then the sound of clenching and a short, guttural cry. She jumped up from the bed and ran into the hallway, where I heard her empty her stomach onto the linoleum floor.

Gemma.

I quickly made my exit from the closet and surveyed the room, the comforter a mess, clothes askew. I knew I had only a few minutes. *Where is it?*

I picked up Gemma's jeans and felt something heavy in the pocket. *Bingo.*

She had left her phone unattended. It was *her* room, after all. But anyone could wander in here. Clearly. As a friend, I wanted to tell her to be more careful, but as someone trying to find out the truth, I was relieved.

I scanned her recent texts and calls. Everything appeared normal, what I would expect for a long-distance relationship. A lot of *miss you babe*s and updates on school, friends, life. Then I found Gemma's laptop under her pillow, entered the name "Liam" into Facebook. This time I got onto his page right away, thanks to Gemma's automatic login. My suspicions were confirmed within three minutes. Liam was not Gemma's boyfriend. Yes, they had plenty of photos together. And if you didn't look close, you could definitely envision they were dating. Kisses on each other's cheek, hugs in front of various pubs. But if you looked closer, you saw the truth. Liam was certainly in a relationship, but it wasn't with Gemma. It was with Henry Miller. Liam was gay.

Gemma's *boyfriend* was a lie.

► ► ►

GEMMA SWAYED OVER a sink in the bathroom, the bottle of gin at her feet. She was in her underwear and a T-shirt she must have grabbed to cover her naked chest.

"What are you doing here?" she asked in a meek voice.

"I lost you at the party; I was trying to find you guys," I said, watching her breathe in and out, attempting to regain some sense of stability.

"Drank too much," she said. "So dizzy."

Parts of her words were cut off, falling into the sink in chunks. The gin racing through her brain, muddling her speech. I noticed the smudged makeup on her face. She caught my stare in the reflection of the mirror.

"I'm fine," she said. Her voice was wet with saliva, and her words were slurring together. "Rejected. Again."

I played dumb. "By who?"

"You can't tell anyone," Gemma said. She stumbled over to me and slumped against the wall of the bathroom and slid to the floor. I winced, thinking of all the germs, but I slid with her and made sure she didn't hurt herself.

"Okay, hang on," I said, steadying her next to me.

Gemma bowed her head toward the ground, her legs splayed out in front of her.

"I would've done anything for him, literally *anything*," Gemma whispered. "I can't help it. I don't want to feel things for him. But I do. I even let him hit me. I'm not even really into that stuff. I'm probably pretty boring in bed. Does that surprise you? I'm very vanilla. But I let him hit me. Is that fucked up? Because it sounds fucked up when I say it out loud."

I expected her to cry, but she didn't. Instead, she stared straight ahead.

"Who hit you, Gemma?" I asked. I needed her to make her confession.

She winced. "It wasn't *really* a hit. I mean, it hurt. Does that mean it's a *hit*?"

"Gemma," I said again, more stern.

"Fine, *fine*. It was John. *John*. I know, I know. I'm a terrible person."

I didn't react. There was no point in pretending anything, she probably wouldn't even remember this in the morning.

"Why would you do this?" I asked. "What about Ruby?"

I needed her to explain it to me. It was reckless, stupid. And it was Ruby she was hurting, not some random person.

Gemma mostly ignored me and continued to rant in her slurred speech. "I did what he *wanted*, and he still didn't even want me back. Well, he did, for like, a second."

She looked over at me, her eyes bloodshot and glassy.

"Poor, pathetic Gemma," she started. "I know that's what you're thinking. That's what you are always thinking. You and Ruby, taking pity on poor, pathetic Gemma."

"No, Gems," I said, not knowing what to say. I never knew she was aware of anything that passed between Ruby and me.

Gemma turned away and tried to focus on the tile floor.

"Gemma," I said slowly. "What about Liam? Will he be upset?"

Gemma was quiet, more tears welling in her eyes.

"You can tell me the truth," I said. Gemma sniffed, wiping snot from her nose.

"I made him up," she said. "I mean not really. He does exist. He kept texting me when we moved in, and Ruby saw, and just assumed he was my boyfriend. He's one of my best friends from home. But he's dating someone else. It's absurd, I know. But I wanted to look wanted, when we first started. I wanted to look normal. You won't judge me, will you?"

"No, no. It's fine. I understand. But why would you do that? I'm single. Nearly everyone is single. It's not a bad thing," I said.

"But you're so pretty. I'm average, at best. And I've never had a boyfriend," she said, her voice a whisper. "I've hooked up with plenty of guys, sure, but none of them wanted me like that. And when I said I had a boyfriend, I started to like the lie. It made me feel wanted. I thought that maybe if others saw me like that, someone would want me in real life, too. And what is that saying? Fake it till you make it? Yeah. Well. That's the story of me and Liam."

I leaned my head against the bathroom wall. "So John? Do you like him as more than a friend?"

At the mention of John, Gemma's face transformed.

"God, he's such a fucking asshole," she said angrily. "He always gets what he wants and doesn't fucking care what happens because he's Prince fucking Charming."

"Then why do you even like him?" I asked.

It made no sense to me. I couldn't sort through her emotions and place them in a box. She was all over the place. I wanted to cut into her brain and figure out what was going on, fix the wires and sew her back up again.

"Because he pays attention. He looks at me. Nobody else does that. I feel like—" but she stopped short.

"Like what?" I asked. I didn't mention that he looks that way at *everyone*.

Gemma stared at the sticky floor, her brain searching for the right words.

"I feel like he can't get away with this. He messed with me. Ruined my night. I want to punish him. I want him to feel embarrassed. You can't do that to someone and get away with it, but . . ."

"But?" I asked.

Gemma sighed. "Ruby."

She looked over at me then, her eyes unable to focus.

"But it would hurt Ruby. I mean, I already did hurt Ruby. She doesn't even know. He was all over me. He said I was beautiful. I know he has feelings for me, I can tell."

I knew he didn't, but I couldn't tell her that. She was already fragile enough. She glanced over at me, and a sense of guilt flickered in her eyes.

"I deserve to be punished, too. He and I—we're bad people, like really *awful*. She can't ever know, Malin, promise me."

She was rambling, sick, drunk. But she was aware—she knew she was desperate, and yet she didn't do anything about it. I didn't get how she could do that to herself, be willing to take part in it all. Gemma closed her eyes and took a sharp breath.

"Do you want to throw up again?" I asked, bracing to pull her up.

I held her hair back over the toilet, trying not to imagine all the bare asses that had sat on that seat since the last time it had been cleaned, all the shit clinging beneath the rim.

When Gemma's body stilled, I guided her back to her room. We stepped over her vomit from earlier, and she groaned in disgust.

"Sorry," she whimpered. "Thank you, I mean it, you're being so nice, you're never this nice to me. It's okay, I know you like Ruby more. You're such a loyal friend to her. I know you never talk shit about her, and you would never hook up with John, or even flirt with him. I wish you were like that to me, too. But I get it. You can only have one best friend."

"That's not true, Gems," I said softly, gently. I wanted her to relax and go to sleep.

"I keep trying, you know? I am trying to get you to be like that with me, like you'd do anything for me, like how you are with Ruby."

I didn't say anything. Gemma fell onto her bed, and I guided her under the sheets and helped position her head on a pink pillow. She grunted what sounded like a thank-you and then relaxed, limbs askew.

"Will you stay?" she asked. I glanced over at Ruby's bed, still empty.

"You know how I like my own room," I said. "And besides, Ruby will be back soon."

At the mention of Ruby's name, Gemma's face stiffened in fear. She looked up at me, desperate.

"Okay, I'll stay," I said. "I can sleep on the floor."

"No. Will you spoon me?" she whispered, patting the space behind her with heavy-handed thuds.

"Um," I said, trying to think of an excuse. I had never shared a bed with anyone, ever.

"You've no choice," Gemma said with a smile. "As the complete and utter failure of the night, I demand your full attention."

She pointed to the ceiling with a swaying finger and then dropped it back on top of her pillow.

In a softer voice she added, "Besides, if Ruby—if she finds out, I can't be alone. You need to be here so she doesn't kill me."

She looked so broken. She was right. I didn't know what Ruby would do if she found out, but I didn't trust Gemma to handle herself in an appropriate manner.

"Fine," I said, "but don't touch me or roll around too much."

"Yeah, yeah," Gemma said as I climbed in behind her.

She was asleep within minutes. I listened to her breath even out. I could hear students outside, coming back from parties, shouting into the winter night. I imagined their alcoholic breath sweeping into the sky in hot, puffy clouds, white mist gleaming in the rural darkness.

I had never felt obligated to Gemma. Not before tonight. I wished I could make better decisions for her, taking the pressure of perfection off her hands.

I fell asleep to images of Charlie and me on the dance floor, and that cutting stare from John, and the sound of his hand hitting Gemma's bare skin. I couldn't shake his gaze, and his crystal eyes followed me to sleep, where I fell into a fit of dreams, chasing after Bo, but never able to catch up to him. Eventually, my mind traced its way to a classroom. Hale lecturing. I couldn't hear what he was saying, but I watched him pace back and forth, his face animated and energized. Normal. A genuine happiness I hadn't encountered before. I was lulled into a sleep, trying to touch his happiness, to steal some of it, but I never got it in my grasp.

▶ ▶ ▶

I WOKE TO Gemma sitting above me, her eyes wide awake despite the sleep-encrusted lashes.

"What are you doing here?" she asked.

She was delighted, bouncing like an eager puppy, the room bright with winter sun reflecting off fresh snow.

"You asked me to stay after what happened," I said, turning over to face the wall.

My body felt stiff and tired, relieved to shift to a different position. I glanced over my shoulder to where Ruby should have been, but her bed was empty.

Gemma noticed where I was looking.

"Probs at John's," she said. "What do you mean, 'after what happened'? Shit. I must've really drank a ton, the last thing I remember is dancing in that god-awful basement."

I gazed at Gemma; my eyes narrowed. She looked back with earnest confusion. I thought of everything she'd said the night before, all the pain she had suffered through.

"Nothing happened," I said. "You got sick, and I brought you here. You made me sleep with you."

Gemma laughed. "You must've *loved* that."

She got up from the bed and padded over to her pile of clothes, pulling her phone out of the jeans pocket. She placed it on her dresser, the screen lighting up as soon as it started charging. I shifted again in the bed, stretching my arms and shoulders, considering my next move. Did she really not remember? Or was she pretending? She must have blacked out. Everyone always talked about blacking out, but I didn't know it could wipe out an entire hour.

We heard fast steps sprinting down the hallway, and Ruby flew into the room, a flurry of brown hair and jackets. She threw mine at me, not even questioning why I was there.

"You left this at the party," she said, her voice light, normal.

Everything was too normal. My hands were ice.

"Did you guys see someone puked right outside our door? Fucking animal," Ruby said, starting to change.

"That's disgusting," Gemma replied, as she snapped on a bra and pulled a sweater over her head.

I pulled the jacket onto my lap. "Where were you last night?"

"At John's," Ruby said with a soft smile.

I glanced over at Gemma out of the corner of my eye. She was at ease, her memory of last night erased. The alcohol must have worked its magic, the incident wiped from her mind. I held my gaze, trying to figure out what she was thinking.

"What?" Gemma asked me when she noticed my stare. "Do I have something on my face?"

"No, sorry, zoning out," I replied. I looked at the phone on the dresser. "I think I saw your phone light up. Maybe it's Liam?"

Gemma didn't even pause before she responded. "Oh, probably. He always checks on me in the morning. It's so sweet."

At the same time, Ruby whipped around toward me and gasped, "Oh my God, I almost forgot! M, you little minx. Making out on the dance floor, never thought I'd see the day."

Right. Charlie. I almost forgot about that. At least I could check one item off my list.

CHAPTER TWENTY

Senior Day

Gemma and I face off in the entryway. I try to look casual, but she's known me for too long. I don't want Ruby to see her if she comes home, so I suggest we go upstairs.

Gemma follows me up, her feet plodding as if they are filled with sand. She is crying so hard, harder than I ever knew possible. I wish she had a mute button. I fight the urge to tell her to stop. What could she be upset about? She got what she wanted, didn't she? I thought this was what she wanted.

When Gemma collapses on her bed, I shut the door and sit on the edge of her desk. Her walls are covered in vintage posters of theater productions; there is a photo of her family by my hand, her parents hugging her at what looks like the Globe Theatre in London. My legs perch on her duvet, and I lean forward, cupping my chin in my hands. I realize how tired I am. So tired of all of it.

Gemma starts rambling before I get the chance to say anything.

"I know you know. Somehow. I don't know how you know, but I know you do. I'm sorry. Okay. I'm fucking sorry. I'm weak, pathetic, stupid. I know, I know, I know," Gemma says, her voice filled with a mix of insecurity and strength. It's an odd combination.

I learned a lot from my mother's therapist in Texas, when my parents made me go to a family session. I knew how to lead the conversation, to never give direct advice, to lead the patient to an answer they deem suitable. To sound kind, caring. To never show your own weaknesses.

"Tell me everything," I say.

She leans forward and hides her face in her hands. She is really milking her theater major for all it's worth.

Gemma looks up at me. "John and I, I mean we—I feel so dirty, but he took advantage of me. I think I'm mostly angry," she says, biting her lip. "Betrayed."

I remember freshman year. I remember what Gemma does not. She was blackout drunk, her retches echoing in the dirty bathroom. How easily we repeat the same mistakes.

"I've always thought we had something," she continues. "He always gives me that look, you know? Like I'm important to him. After you guys left the showers, I knew we had to talk. Like about what you mentioned at the bonfire."

Our conversation at the bonfire. About Ruby and John. And how Ruby has been acting so weird since senior year started, cold and spacey. Moody. How Gemma was supposed to convince John to stay with her. For the good of the group.

I nod. She continues.

"So we talked, but he wouldn't listen."

I blink back skepticism. There is no way Gemma brought that up. I saw them with my own eyes, throwing water at each other with their bare hands, laughing and falling against the tile walls of the bathroom. She is covering her tracks.

"He said he was glad we were friends, glad that I was so trustworthy," she says.

I wonder if he was talking about how trustworthy she was the first time. Since she blacked out, there was nothing for her to tell Ruby, no reason to betray John.

She continues, "And then he started kissing me. I know, it sounds bad. But in the moment, it felt so right."

I wince a little inside.

"And," Gemma argues, "you said yourself that Ruby wasn't that into him anymore."

Not what I said, but I am not surprised Gemma interpreted it that way.

"Anyways, he kept telling me he wanted me."

I clench my jaw, the embarrassment for Gemma screeching in my ears.

"And then, well, I couldn't get Ruby out of my mind. I felt terrible. So I told him to stop."

Her eyes well up again. This is the second time I've ever seen her cry. The first time was when we were freshmen, in that sterile hospital room, before we left for summer break. Her tears gather, shiny and contained.

"I really asked him to stop, I promise," she says. I believe her. I know that side of him, too. "I said that I wanted to wait until he and Ruby were broken up. It's only right."

She sounds so matter-of-fact. She actually believes John has feelings for her.

"That's big of you," I say, although the words are hard to get out.

"Right?" she says, her eyes wide. "Anyways, then he said he wasn't going to break up with her. He said that we were just playing around. He said I wasn't serious."

I'm not sure what else to tell her. I don't feel bad for her. She made a bad decision, twice. I wasn't really sure if she would, but she's so predictable. A small part of me is disappointed in her.

Gemma buries her head in her hands. My back is aching so I straighten it and sit up, stretching my arms out and upward. I crank my neck back and forth, forcing the blood to flow.

"I'm so mad," Gemma says. "I can't believe he would do this to me."

I can.

"I know," I say.

"I just want to get shitfaced and forget this ever happened," she says.

That's what you did the last time.

She gets up and walks over to the opposite side of the room, pulling a handle of gin out of her closet.

"Maybe you should wait," I say, "until Last Chance."

"Yeah, maybe," she says, taking a swig anyway.

"Question for you," I say.

"Yeah?" Gemma asks. She looks at me with her bloodshot eyes.

"Did Ruby see you?"

"Oh." She pauses. "God. I hope not. I really hope not. Do you think she could've?"

I am glad she has no idea about this part. One less thing I have to deal with.

"No," I answer. "Don't worry about it."

Gemma looks terrified for a moment, and I give her a halfhearted smile. I get up and walk toward the door.

"Malin," she says. I can't stand the pain in her voice. I know that I put it there. But it's for the greater good, Gemma is a sacrifice, I remind myself. She will recover.

"Yeah?" I say. I can't look at her.

"Why does nobody ever want me?"

My mind races for an answer. I know it has to be something sympathetic and reassuring, but I am tired of pretending today.

"Gemma," I say, standing over her, making sure she is looking at me. My voice stern. "You need to stop feeling sorry for yourself. Focus on yourself. Love yourself first. Stop worrying about what other people think. Stop whining. Sometimes life is hard. Dig yourself out of the hole and get on with your life. And stop getting so fucking drunk all the time, it's making you weak."

Gemma's eyes widen but she says nothing. If I've offended her, I don't care.

"I'm gonna go get ready, you good?" I ask her.

"Yeah, fine," she responds, finally breaking eye contact. She stares out the window. "Just going to sit here and plot my revenge."

She is joking, but there is something in her tone, something bitter and betrayed. She is hurt. I know that I should sit with her and make it all better, but I can't bring myself to do it. I think about Ruby, and I wonder where she is.

I should stay, but I don't. I fail Gemma in that moment, when I leave her alone.

But I'm distracted, and I need to prepare for Ruby's return. For the inevitable breakup that is coming our way. In the hallway, I pull out my phone and google *how to help a friend through a breakup.*

There is no way Ruby will stay with John after this. This is unforgivable. In my mind, it is so black and white, I don't understand the alternative. The other choice Ruby can make. I never even consider it.

CHAPTER TWENTY-ONE

Freshman Year

dated Charlie for a month. It was fine. I told myself I would hook up with him for four weeks. We never had sex; I only made out with him in public. I had to show everyone I was normal. So we made out at parties, and on dance floors, and, once, in the Grill at midnight. He was sweet. I didn't want to hurt him, but I could only take a month of being his girlfriend. He texted me all the time, always wanted to know what I was doing, when I wanted to hang out. He was so *dull*. All he talked about was soccer, or sporting events, or Cape Cod, where he was heading in the summer.

When our time was up, I told him I wasn't ready for a relationship, and I acted sad, and Ruby comforted me, and then it was finally over. And I could be by myself again.

I breathed a gulp of fresh mountain air, felt the cold wind whip against my nose and cheeks. I turned my gaze upward, watching my friends scrambling up the steep rock face to the top of the small hill. Ruby and Max were leading us up the steep incline to the Ledge. This was our second visit to the spot; we'd gone once in the fall, but it had started hailing so we gave up and returned to campus.

John was a few steps ahead of me, rocks crumbling down the path, hitting the tips of my sneakers. My shoelaces had become untied, and I'd been watching the laces dance around my sneakers, waiting to see if they would trip me or not. I liked being last in the line. It was easy to survey everyone this way.

I bent down to tie my shoelaces, and John turned around, noticing me stopping.

"You can keep going," I said. "I'll catch up."

"No worries," John said, stepping down toward me. "I could use a break."

The others got farther away, Gemma's pink shorts disappearing around a corner. John and I were alone.

"So, M," he said, putting one foot up on a rock, stretching his groin. I focused on my shoelace. "I feel like I still don't know you that well."

"Oh?" I said.

"Yeah, I mean, you're from Texas. You like to read. You're Ruby's best friend. Is there anything else?"

While someone else might have found that comment insulting, I found it annoying.

"I guess I'm not that interesting," I said.

"I'm not so sure about that," he said, pausing, taking his foot off the rock, and stepping toward me. I stared at his sneakers, a few streaks of mud against the red fabric. I stood up, only a few inches between our faces.

"I feel like I have to google you, or something, to get the full scoop," he said.

I knew he wouldn't find anything. Or would he? I did a few calculations in my head, wondering if those newspaper articles could have somehow made it onto the Internet.

"Go ahead," I replied. "Let me know if you find anything good."

John took a step toward me, and I swallowed. He brought a hand up to the stray hairs that had fallen out of my ponytail. I braced for his touch as he pushed the hair behind my ear, his fingers tracing against the skin on my neck.

"You're pretty," he whispered. "But we all know that already."

Before I could say anything, he stepped away and started back up the hill. I stayed still for a few minutes, processing what had just happened, waiting for him to round the corner.

By the time I caught up with everyone, it was as if the exchange had never happened. I eyed John, who ignored me, in the throes of a conversation with Khaled about a movie they wanted to watch.

I skipped past the two of them and caught up to Ruby and Max, taking my place at the front of the line. It was better with Max behind me, knowing there were other people between myself and John.

► ► ►

"You're being so otherwise," Ruby said to Gemma as she stepped up onto a boulder.

"Am not," retorted Gemma.

I looked up into the bright sky. We had reached the top, the path opening up to a small clearing and an outcrop of rocks. I glanced over my shoulder. I could see the top of the campus chapel and the glinting solar panels on the roof of the dining hall.

Gemma stopped and put a hand on her soft hip, heaving in gulps of air.

"I'm not—accustomed—to the altitude," Gemma said, her sentence broken by breaths.

"We're not that high," said Max.

"Speaking of," said Khaled. He pulled his one-hitter out of his pocket. "Anyone else?"

Khaled and John nestled themselves on the rocky ledge, their legs dangling over the steep decline. Their breath, and the weed, came out in puffs above their heads.

"It's still so cold," Gemma said. "Is it getting colder? It's supposed to be spring."

Ruby and I shot each other a look and held back smiles. Gemma had been complaining since we decided to make the climb at breakfast that morning. It wasn't even a hike; it was more like a steep, fifteen-minute walk up a hill. The Ledge was notorious at Hawthorne as the best place to smoke weed and day drink. Gemma wanted to stay in her dorm room and watch *Friends* reruns, but the fear of missing out drove her to join us.

"You'll be warmer if you keep moving," Ruby told her. "But, you know, it *is* spring. This is spring in New England, babe. Turns fifty degrees and everyone throws on their shorts and T-shirts. It's cool. Our paleness matches the snow."

"Did you guys hear about the body they found the other day? Over by Mill Street?" Max asked us.

"Ew, what?" Gemma replied.

"Yeah, so sad. That happened in Hanover a few times," Ruby said. "People get drunk during snowstorms and try to walk home from the bar, and they never make it. They freeze to death, and their bodies are found when the snow melts."

"That is so, so gross. In London, if you pass out walking home, you fall asleep on a bench or something. Fuck Maine. Fuck the cold."

Gemma had started doing jumping jacks, her arms pumping aggressively by her sides.

Shannon, who had tagged along for the hike, tiptoed out to the edge by Khaled and carefully sat herself down next to him, allowing only her ankles to stretch over the fall.

"They're kinda cute, I guess," Ruby said, dropping her voice to a whisper.

Max, Ruby, and I stood in a little semicircle, our view of the others right in front of us, and the trees below stretching for miles. Gemma huffed and puffed to the side, her eyes focused on the view.

I looked at Max. "Do you think he likes her back?"

After her comment earlier in the year, I had invited Shannon to hang out with us a few times. I wished she wasn't shy so I didn't have to facilitate so much conversation for her. I didn't think she had hooked up with Khaled, and I wasn't sure if she ever would.

Max shook his head. "She's not his type."

I looked over at the two of them sitting on the ledge, both appearing casual and relaxed with each other.

"I didn't even know he had a type," said Ruby, suppressing a laugh.

I thought back to when he had suggested we make out in the beginning of the year. I wasn't that different from Shannon. We were both thin and pale.

"And?" I asked him. "There has to be something else?"

"She's too quiet," Max replied.

"Max is being nice. What he wants to say is that she is boring," Gemma said, trying to whisper through her panting.

Ruby and I both stared at Shannon. Max was right. I knew this already, but I was hoping she would have opened up by now. I watched Shannon laugh at everything Khaled said, and since she had sat down, he had managed to put a large amount of space between them.

Ruby cocked her head. "Wow, now that you say it . . . she totally is. I mean, she always kind of annoyed me, but I never knew why."

"She just doesn't fit. With us, I mean," Gemma said. It seemed a little harsh, casting her off, back into the pool of friendless freshmen. "It's not a big deal. She'll find other friends."

Max shrugged and started unwrapping a granola bar. The three of us stood in silence, munching on snacks, the spring air fresh at our cheeks.

"That sucks," Ruby said. "I feel bad . . . but not bad enough."

"Yeah, right? I'm tired of forcing awkward conversations with her," Gemma added.

"I told him to say something to her. To get her to stop pursuing him," Max said.

"He's too nice," Ruby replied. "He'll never do it."

"But it's *not* nice, leading her on like that. He just hates confrontation."

Max was right. Khaled loved helping others but hated dealing with his own problems.

"Guys," Gemma said, her voice wobbly and high. She was inspecting something on her calf. "Ummmm."

We turned to her.

"What?" Ruby asked.

"I can't look," Gemma said, turning her head away from her left side. "I can't look. I think it's a tick, get it off, get it off. Oh, God, is it?"

Ruby and I tried not to laugh.

"It's not fucking funny," Gemma cried.

Max went over to her and bent toward her leg. "Tick season hasn't started yet," he said, looking from her leg to her face.

"Fuck off," Gemma said. "You sure?"

"Very," said Max. "But stay still, I'll check."

As Max, our future doctor, carefully inspected Gemma's fleshy calf, Ruby looked down at him, her face soft, adoring.

I recalled her recent diary entry, the words written in a hasty rush:

John has been so sweet recently. He even surprised me last weekend with a little getaway to a spa in Kennebunkport. He insisted I wear this weird piece of lingerie—there was a hole in the crotch, which wasn't very "me" but he seemed to enjoy it. How lucky am I? Sometimes I can't even believe it—that I get to date him. I hope it lasts. Is it bad that I think about marrying him? Sometimes I imagine our life. Living in Tribeca, spending weekends on the Vineyard, I could get a job in a gallery . . . there are so many in NYC. And John could work in private equity like he always talks about. But I don't let myself think about it too much. Because it's a dream. I don't want to jinx it. And . . . the sex is getting a little better. He keeps saying that I'll get used to it, but I don't know, it hasn't happened yet. There are other things in relationship other than sex, so it's not that big of a deal. Right?

Max stopped hooking up with Greta, thank God. Sure, she's pretty, but she's kind of a bitch. When she hangs out with us, she totally avoids eye contact with me, and I am OVERLY nice to her. Because, you know, I'm trying to be inclusive. Whatever. I don't even think Max liked her that much. He deserves better.

I watched Ruby take in the view, her face relaxed and fresh from the cold. She stood straight and tall, athletic, one foot up on a small rock. Invincible.

John, Khaled, and Shannon were laughing about something, their frames giggling in unison. Shannon kept stealing private glances at Khaled, but he wasn't reciprocating.

The situation was familiar. Like Ruby and Max. Two people who got along, respected each other, but whose relationship would never go any further. Shannon wanted more, but Khaled didn't. And Max was clearly in love with Ruby, which was a big, fat problem that none of us ever addressed. It lingered around like a bad cough.

I kicked a rock with my toe, and it flew off the ledge. John watched it fall and turned around to look at me. His face serious at first, then that smile he reserved only for me spread like wildfire.

CHAPTER TWENTY-TWO

TEXAS, 1997

Saturday was my favorite day of the week because my father took me, and only me, to get bagels. I liked that we left Levi at home, but I worried about him being alone with my mother.

At Bagel World, we ordered a bag of mixed bagels. We normally took them home right away, but my father asked me if I wanted to eat there. We chose a table by the window, and he handed me a blueberry bagel and a plastic container of cream cheese. He sat across the table, both his hands around his coffee, watching me.

"Happy girl?" he asked.

I smiled, my mouth full of bagel. He looked down at his coffee, angry or sad, I couldn't tell.

"How are things between you and your brother?" he asked.

I used my tongue to clean my teeth of doughy bagel, thinking of what to say. I didn't want to worry him.

"Okay," I replied.

My father nodded slowly, distracted.

"Does he make you feel unsafe?" he asked.

"Not really," I said. "He's annoying, that's all."

My father looked relieved, smiling almost.

"Good, good," he said.

"I'm more worried about Mom," I said, taking another bite of bagel. "He's really mean to her. Why is he mean to her?"

My father's face fell, and I regretted what I had said.

"Sorry," I said, stopping my chewing, realizing I had upset him.

"No, Malin, don't be sorry. You did the right thing telling me that," he said.

"Why doesn't she stick up for herself? She is always sad now. I liked it better when she was happy."

My father was quiet, thinking. "Sometimes when you love someone, like how your mother loves Levi, it can make things complicated. She wants him to be happy. Levi is probably going through a phase. And as a parent, you make sacrifices for your children, because you love them, and it's what parents do. You'll understand that one day. Does that make sense?"

I did not like the word *probably*. It made me think my father had doubts, and he was always certain about things, like when the car broke down on the highway, he knew which part was broken and fixed it. And when I saw my mother crying last week, when she was alone in the kitchen, he went to her, and knew what to say to make her better. And he was always fixing things at work, I heard him on the phone, telling people what to do. So I did not like this *probably* situation. None of it made sense to me. In my mind, it was very clear. Levi was mean. Our mother was not. He should be punished, or taught how to be nice. But I knew my father wanted me to understand, so I said nothing.

Our table was silent for a while, as I finished my bagel. Before we left, my father leaned in and took my face in his hands.

"I love you," he said. "Don't forget that."

I mustered a small smile.

"I love you, too," I replied.

And then we got in the car and went home, and never talked about Levi again.

Maybe if we had talked about him, maybe if my parents had addressed the issue the right way, he would still be alive.

CHAPTER TWENTY-THREE

Freshman Year

Freshman year was coming to an end. My flight was at noon the next day. I'd return home, work at my dad's law office, sit by the pool. I'd finally be alone. I never thought I'd be looking forward to going home. Free of everyone else's problems. There were only twenty-four hours left until I could breathe again. I'd made it through the first year, I got the best grades, I had friends. Everything would be easier now. I could go on autopilot for the summer.

Ruby and I were walking to the Greenhouse. We both had one last paper to finish before we could pack up our rooms and dedicate the rest of finals to partying.

"So I heard that Max has a show," Ruby said, cutting the silence. "I saw a poster with one of his photos. We should go."

"Sure," I said. I remembered his work, the tiny people in the land-scapes.

"But don't tell him; I think he's still embarrassed. Or something. I mean, he didn't exactly invite us."

I nodded, distracted. I kept thinking about Ruby's latest diary entry. My months-long dilemma had almost come to a close. I was leaning in a definite direction, and her words were pushing me to commit.

May 8

Quick update: I got the internship at the Museum of Fine Arts! THANK GOD. I don't have to go home. I am so relieved. Things with John are good. Really good. I'm really happy.

The sex is . . . well, it is what it is. Sometimes when he drinks too much, we don't even do it because he passes out before anything can happen. I am always relieved when that happens. I realize that is totally messed up, but whatever. Every relationship has weird things. This is our weird thing.

Anyways, he's going to live at his house on the Vineyard this summer, and he said I should come out every weekend. I told him that I should get to know the people in my program a little bit, you know, on the weekends, but he already bought a ferry pass for me, which is so nice. So of course I will go there every weekend. And the museum is providing student housing for me in Boston, so that works out. Dad wants me to come home for a week before the program starts, but I don't want to deal with him . . .

The phrase *shoot the messenger* kept playing on a loop in my head. I had been debating whether or not I should tell Ruby about what happened that night in February. Gemma had completely forgotten, and John hadn't acted any differently afterward. If he was worried Gemma would say something—though that would have been impossible—he didn't show it. Things went eerily back to normal. As if it had never happened. Like it was burned into my memory and nobody else's. I could carry it, but I wasn't sure if it was something Ruby should know. She *seemed* genuinely happy. She wrote it down herself.

What I knew was that John had been drunk. Gemma had been vulnerable, also drunk. And like Max said, John had a difficult childhood after his father went to jail and the divorce, although it pained me to say that since I'm sure he still spent every summer on the Vineyard and lived a very comfortable life with friends and family. Besides his transgression with Gemma, he treated Ruby like a queen. He complimented her, he bought her ferry tickets, he made her feel loved. So, it wasn't that bad. We were kids. Stupid, drunk kids. We were allowed to make mistakes.

Besides, how many college relationships actually lasted longer than a year? They'd probably break up sophomore year anyway. I didn't have to do anything. It would happen on its own.

The worst part was how selfish I was. I didn't want to be the messenger. I didn't want her to get mad at me for telling her. So I didn't.

▶ ▶ ▶

THE BIRDS FLITTED in the trees above us as we opened the doors to the art building. The days in the spring were long, sunset stretching out later and later. Gemma tagged along, chattering the whole way about how excited she was to go home for the summer. She said she was going to binge DVDs for at least three weeks, and eat tea and biscuits, and other British things she missed. She wouldn't need to get a job; her family was loaded. Her dad was in finance. Like everyone else's parents at Hawthorne.

"It's insane how bad some of these are," Gemma said as we strolled down the long hallway, looking at photos.

Ruby laughed. All three of us stopped to stare at an image of male genitalia, displayed in full on a leather tufted couch.

"Is this even allowed?" Gemma asked. "And who do you think that is? What if it's someone we know? Aren't you curious?"

Ruby gave her a look. "It's *art*."

"Well," Gemma said, "I don't know about you two, but I certainly wouldn't buy a dick and balls to hang above my fireplace."

We walked in unison toward the end, where Max's work had been hanging last semester.

"Here," Ruby said.

We stared at the first of Max's three photos. The first one had been taken during the winter—a solitary skier frozen in place, speeding down a soft white slope. The edges of the trail were thick with pine trees topped with powdery snow.

"He's an artiste," Gemma said with a French accent.

The next photo wasn't as focused on nature as the others were. It had been taken from far outside the dining hall at night, looking in. All the students were eating, studying, focused. The darkness of the night contrasted with the bright lights concealed within the tall glass walls.

"Interesting," I said. "He should stick to nature stuff."

"It's kind of neat. Look at how little we all look," Gemma said, amused.

Ruby was the first of us to step toward the last photograph. I watched her as she tilted her head to the side.

"Oh," Ruby said, her voice light with surprise. She brought a hand to her throat.

Gemma and I stood behind her, looking at the photo. Gemma gave me a look, lips pursed, slightly amused, slightly concerned. We were all quiet for moment, taking it in.

"Well, I'd say that's the best one," Gemma said. There was a flicker of teasing in her voice.

Ruby cleared her throat and shifted uncomfortably.

"When was that taken?" I asked.

"I didn't even know," Ruby replied. "I think it was early one morning. After the snow melted."

She paused, chewing at her lip. I watched her peel away a flake of dry skin and pull it into her mouth.

"We both had to get up early to study for a midterm. He said he'd bring me coffee in the Greenhouse, so we could at least study together. You know, misery loves company . . ."

Her voice trailed off.

"You look quite pretty," Gemma said, trying to lighten the mood.

Ruby gave her an embarrassed glance. She did look beautiful, perched on one of the couches, staring out at the frozen lake. She was always striving to appear perfect, so it was unusual to see her like this. She looked so sad. It was as if Max had invaded her privacy, revealing to the world that she did have problems. Problems she worked so hard at ignoring, denying certain truths. It was eerie and striking at the same time. He had captured something rare. A side of Ruby we still didn't know.

"Shall we?" Gemma asked, sensing we should leave. I felt it, too. It was as if we were staring at Ruby naked.

Ruby looked at me as we stepped away, silently urging me to leave it alone. To never speak of the photo. I gave her a knowing glance, and then we headed down the hall toward the exit.

We had a party to go to, far more important matters to attend to.

► ► ►

THE SIX OF us stood in a circle in the common room, packed tight together in a sweaty heap of freshmen. Khaled had made a histrionic toast to being sophomores, and we all took shots of vodka. I spit mine back into my cup without anyone noticing.

At one point, Shannon came over and stood next to Khaled. He greeted her as he always did, with a half-hug and a fist bump. She smiled, hesitant and awkward, letting him hug her, her cheeks lighting up. He was too flirty with her. I was starting to wonder when he would tell her he wasn't interested so she could move on with her life.

Gemma and Khaled were already drunk. They always got a little wobbly after a few drinks. Gemma swayed in place. I was standing next to Max, who still hadn't taken a sip from his beer. John and Ruby were curled around each other, John's hand a claw on Ruby's shoulder.

"Max," Gemma said, her words a tiny bit slurred, "youuuu are a greeeeeaaaat photographer."

Ruby shot her a glance, but Gemma missed it. She was too drunk.

"A photographer?" Khaled asked, giving Max a skeptical look.

"He used to carry a camera around when we were younger, remember that, Max?" John added, a hint of teasing in his voice. Not the nice kind of teasing.

Max stared at the floor. I wanted to tell him not to be so embarrassed, what was the big deal? He was good at it, why hide it?

"Kind of a girly hobby, if you ask me," John said. Only Khaled offered a quasi laugh, not wanting to hurt Max's feelings, but not wanting to let John's joke fall flat. Ruby cleared her throat, the grip on her cup slightly tighter, the red plastic denting inward.

"Seems Ruby is Max's *muse*," Gemma said.

Gemma, *no*. Her jealousy was manifesting into this vile, insecure *thing*. Jealous that Ruby so effortlessly gained all the attention, that everyone was in love with her, and not Gemma.

Shannon perked up. "Oh, I saw that. Max, it's beautiful, the way you captured her—"

"I'm not his muse," Ruby interrupted, aggressive and defensive, shutting down Shannon's comment.

Max looked at Ruby, his expression a mix of dejection and surprise. I watched Ruby's face burn a deep shade of crimson.

"Captured her what?" John asked Shannon, dropping his arm from Ruby's shoulders.

Shannon looked uncomfortable, undoubtedly feeling like an outsider now more than ever. The one time she decided to speak, she said the wrong thing.

Gemma noticed John's concern, her eyes brightening. She was exhilarated, pleased to continue. She opened her mouth to speak, but Max interrupted her.

"Actually," Max said firmly. Gemma looked annoyed, but she shut her mouth. In a more relaxed tone, he continued, "Ruby happened to get in the way of one of my shots in the Greenhouse, and my professor liked it, that's all."

Ruby was the one who looked hurt this time. She chewed her lip, glancing at the space by her shoulder previously occupied by John's arm.

"That's cool, man," Khaled said to Max, his voice light. I knew he was attempting to defuse the intensity. "I want to see your work."

"Thanks," Max replied. He actually smiled.

John looked at all of us, deciding to pretend he didn't care. I watched him calculate all the information he had learned, realizing that Max and Ruby spent time together without him, alone. Before anyone could say anything, a voice spoke from behind me, and I felt someone move me to the side to make the circle bigger.

"Oh, hey, guys, how's it going?" Amanda sang. I watched Ruby's eyes narrow.

"Amanda," Khaled said, giving her a fist bump. "What's up, girl?"

"Not much, just wanted to come say hey to your little clique before we all leave for the summer." She looked around at all of us, noticing the tension in the air.

"Looks like I'm interrupting something," she said.

"You're not," Ruby said.

"Nah," Khaled replied. "We're just talking about Max's photography. Kid's embarrassed or something, but sounds like he's really good."

Amanda swept her eyes over Max, head to toe, judging. She looked annoyed that she even had to talk about Max, let alone be in his presence. He wasn't good enough for her. His ladder wouldn't lead anywhere.

"That's not even that embarrassing," Gemma slurred. "I'll tell you what's embarrassing. I once jumped headfirst into a pile of leaves to impress a guy."

Ruby looked over at her. "What? Why would you ever do that?"

Gemma waved her hand in the air dismissively. "You know, I couldn't even tell you why I decided to do *that* particular thing. I think it might have been a dare. Yes, that sounds about right. But I had to wear a neck brace for a week. My cone of shame."

Khaled laughed. "Only you, Gems." He handed her a shot, and they both tipped their heads back and swallowed.

"You probably shouldn't tell people that story," Amanda said. "What about *you*, Ruby? Anything in your past that you're ashamed of?"

Ruby's face flushed.

"Oh, it looks like there is. Do *tell*," Amanda said. Gemma's eyes bobbled back and forth between the two of them, slowly registering that something interesting was unfolding.

"I have something," I said, suddenly all eyes on me. "One time I peed myself on the monkey bars at recess."

It was a lie; I had never done that. But a girl in my third grade class had. She was so embarrassed that she cried for the rest of the day.

Amanda wrinkled her nose. "Ew."

"When you gotta go, you gotta go," Khaled said, his voice awkward, air whistling between his teeth. He hated this conversation.

"Oh, you know, I've done that, too, now that I think about it. A few times, actually," Gemma said, now visibly swaying in place.

"I've never done anything embarrassing," John said, mostly joking, clearly unaware that Amanda was holding something over Ruby. I looked over at Max. He knew something had passed between Amanda and Ruby, but kept quiet.

"Of course not," Amanda said, looking up at him, making her eyes wide and innocent. "You're perfect."

"I'm going to get a drink," Ruby said, a little too loudly. "John, come with?"

"Actually, can you grab me a beer while you're over there?" he asked. He didn't look at her.

Ruby gave a forced smile. "Sure."

Amanda smiled at Ruby, being nice, trying to prove to us that she was the nice one, she had nothing to hide. I wanted to keep watching, but I noticed someone waving to me across the room. I squinted my eyes as the room cleared a little, spotting Hale in a group of seniors.

"I'll be right back," I said to Ruby. A part of me felt the need to stay and see if she was okay, but she gave me a feeble smile and headed toward the kitchen.

"Hey, you," Hale said as I approached. One rough hand nursed a beer. The other was hanging loose at his side.

"Hey," I said. "Hanging out with the cool kids again?"

He smiled halfway. "What? I'm not allowed to hang out with undergrads?"

Someone slapped him on the back, and some beer spilled at our feet. I looked down, relieved my sandals were spared, and then back up at Hale.

"Can I get you a drink? There's some soda in the fridge," he asked, looking at my empty hands.

"Oh, no, thanks," I said, noticing the slight sunburn on his cheeks. "Don't you get lonely here? Being an adult and all that?"

"I wasn't aware I'm an adult. But no, not really. I was a hall proctor for a while, so I know most of these hooligans. They're good people."

I guess it made sense. It seemed like he knew everyone, at least all the guys. They would clap him on the back, or shout his name from across the room, excited to be in his presence.

Another student, a junior, I think, bumped into him and sent him stumbling toward me. My face pressed into his shoulder, and I took a breath of his sweat and deodorant. I relaxed for a moment, letting him shelter me, making me feel safe in a place I was always on guard.

"Jesus," he said, his voice muffled then clear as he pulled away from me. "You kids get more wild every year. I saw coke at a party the other night. Coke! Never would've happened back in my day."

"Old Man Hale," I said. He smiled.

"Wanna come play twenty-one cup? I'd be honored to have you on my side," he said.

"Sure," I said and let him grab my hand and lead me over to a table in the center of the room. He guided me through the crowd. I stared at our hands, clasped together, and I felt aware of *it*. That thing. It was in my chest, warm, and in the space between our palms. My heart rate sped up. I yanked my hand away.

Hale looked back, a confused expression on his face.

"Sorry," I said, "I have to go."

"Sure?" he asked, his eyes worried, concerned. It made me cringe. I didn't want his feelings, I was fine.

I pressed back into the crowd, letting the party close around me. His face disappeared, and I exhaled when I was alone, regaining my composure as I tuned out the shouting and laughter, the room going cold and quiet and dark.

▶ ▶ ▶

AN HOUR LATER I sat on the toilet, scrolling through my phone. My mother had sent a text asking what I wanted for dinner tomorrow night. I still hadn't replied.

"Can you believe that ambulance?" a female voice flew through the bathroom door.

I lifted my feet up. The two girls entered the first stalls in the long row. Ruby's name flashed across my phone. She was probably calling to see where I'd gone. I sent her to voicemail.

"No, did you see who was in it?" Girl Two asked.

"I couldn't get close enough. So embarrassing. Getting sent to the ER on the last night," Girl One said.

There was a small silence as the girls began to pee.

"You know who I love?" Girl One asked.

"Who?" the other asked.

"Ruby Holland, the girl on the soccer team," Girl One said.

"*Who?*" Girl Two said again, more pointed.

"You know, the one dating John Wright."

"Oh! Yes, okay. He is so hot." She paused. "But you know who I think is cute? His cousin. Max. He's all dark and mysterious."

"Yeah and awkward as fuck."

They both giggled.

Girl One continued, "Anyways. Ruby. She is so nice. I kind of expected her to be a bitch because everyone is obsessed with her. But she's really not! We talked for like an hour about internships this summer."

"God, don't ditch me for her or anything."

The fear of losing our friends was still fresh in our minds, even though we had survived the first year.

"Shut up, you know I would never. Besides, she already has her clique."

"That Gemma girl, right? She's hilarious. And maybe an alcoholic? Did you see how shitfaced she was out there? I saw her dancing on a table a while ago. It was only ten."

"I think we're all alcoholics," Girl One said, laughing.

"Okay, but who's the other one? Ruby's other friend? The pretty blonde? Isn't she the one who's at the top of our class?" Girl Two asked.

"Yeah, Mary. Or Molly. Wait, no, it's Marin, I think, yes, Marin. She's kind of a no-add."

There was a slight pause as they flushed their toilets.

"A no-add?" Girl Two asked.

I heard the faucets turn on as they washed their hands.

"Yeah, like someone who is a complete no-add," Girl One explained. "Doesn't add anything to the conversation. Just is kinda *there*. Totally boring."

"I hope no one ever calls me a no-add," Girl Two said.

Girl One laughed as they pushed back out into the crowded hallway. I let my feet fall to the floor.

Boring. I appeared boring. I would take boring. I could play the no-add all day.

I held back a smile. My phone buzzed in my hand, a text from Ruby.

WHERE ARE YOU?

WE ARE AT THE ER @ ST. MARY'S.

PLEASE COME.

I sighed and stood up from the toilet, arching my neck to each side after being cramped for so long. It was probably Gemma. She had way too much to drink. I wondered if she had fallen, or broken a bone.

I checked to ensure the other girls were out of sight as I stepped out into the moody light of the party and made my way to the hospital.

Might as well end freshman year with a bang.

CHAPTER TWENTY-FOUR

Senior Day

The thing about my room, the reason why I know Ruby's secret, is the forgiving wall that stands between us. The upper floor of the Palace is divided into three rooms and a bathroom. Ruby's room and mine used to be one large room, but Khaled divided it into two, knowing we would each want a single. We have privacy, but share an intimate hall. Ruby lives in one corner of the house, I am in the middle, and Gemma is on my other side. The wall between Gemma and me is sturdy, a part of the house that has been there since it was built. But the one that Ruby and I share is flimsy, constructed of Sheetrock. She doesn't know this. I never make noise in my room, how could she know?

I know her secrets—the ones she doesn't even commit to the pages of her diary. The ones she locks inside her mind, the ones that have destroyed her over the last year. It has gotten worse—the things I hear on the other side of the wall.

When she finally returns, the wall rattles as she shuts her door. I am sitting on the edge of my bed. It is so quiet I can hear her pull up the top of the wicker laundry basket and then close it again. It is squeaky, a familiar sound now ruined by circumstance.

I consider my options.

A few minutes pass and I hear footsteps coming up the stairs. Heavy, resolute. John. Her door opens and shuts.

I can hear John's and Ruby's voices murmuring on the other side of the wall. I think about all the times I've heard them over the years.

Their fights. Sometimes, though more rarely these days, their shared laughs. And most unfortunate, the sex. I bought an extra pillow after sophomore year began, to block out Ruby's sex noises. They sounded unnatural.

I begin to pace, unable to sit still any longer. She will be breaking up with him soon, and I'll need to be there, to help her. I'll help her be strong.

There is a soft knock on my door, and then it swings open and Max slips inside.

"What are you doing?" I whisper, my voice on edge. I am aware that I no longer feel calm, confident. This has only happened to me once before.

"She's back?" he asks.

We both look at the wall, where the muffled conversation floats through the thin plaster.

Max's eyes widen. "You can hear them? Have you always been able to hear them?"

I look away, focusing on my desk. We are silent.

"You're not the only one who knows about how messed up they are," he says, keeping his voice low.

"It's not what you think," I say. I pull my towel from its plastic hook and add, "I'm about to hop in the shower, so."

Max doesn't look convinced. His eyebrows are knit together in furious determination.

The voices start to get sharper, the wall only slightly muffling the escalating cadence that surges next door.

"Just get out," I say at Max, getting so close to his face I could slap him. "Get *out*."

He backs away from me, his hand reaching for the doorknob.

"Fine, but this ends tonight," he says, his voice confident, resolute.

CHAPTER TWENTY-FIVE

Freshman Year

After receiving Ruby's texts and confirming they were at St. Mary's Hospital, I made my way through the common room toward the exit. The party was sloppy with intoxicated students. The men's rowing team was standing on a pool table, singing and kicking their legs in unison. They were wearing tight shirts that showed off their perfectly sculpted bodies. Their season was officially over, and they were drinking enough to make up for everything they had missed.

The hospital was only a mile from campus. I sprinted up to the glass doors and came to an awkward halt, waiting for them to open. I walked inside, the fluorescent light a stark contrast to the dark night. My sandals slapped against my heels as I followed the arrows to the ER.

I found Ruby, Max, and Khaled sitting on a couch in the waiting room, debating something.

"She's not going to get arrested," said Khaled. His eyes were bloodshot.

"Well, what about a strike?" Ruby asked.

"Nope," Khaled replied. "Look. I've read that handbook a thousand times. If a student goes to the hospital because they drank too much, they don't get in trouble. Administration would rather we go to the hospital than have a student die of alcohol poisoning."

"What's going on?" I asked as I approached. I was out of breath.

"Oh, good," said Ruby. She stood and gave me a hug. "Where were you? Did you see John?"

"No, I was in the bathroom."

"That whole time? I looked everywhere for you."

"Sorry," I said. She sat back down. She looked pissed. Or tired. I couldn't tell.

Khaled gave me a lazy high five. "Gemma's real fucked up," he said.

Ruby rubbed her eyes, and Max scratched the side of his head. Ruby and Khaled were fairly drunk. Max seemed a little buzzed, but nothing beyond that.

"Is she going to be okay?" I asked.

"Yeah, they're hooking her up to a banana bag," Max said.

"A what?"

"It's an IV. Fluids and minerals. Keeps her hydrated," Max replied.

"So, what happened?" I asked.

Ruby and Max looked at Khaled.

"It's not *my* fault," Khaled said, his hands in the air as if we were holding him at gunpoint.

"You kept giving her more shots," Max said pointedly.

"She asked for them!" Khaled said. "I'm not her fucking babysitter."

The air was tense. Summer should have started a week ago. We shouldn't have been allowed to stay a moment longer, everyone unraveling under the pressure of exams and summer plans.

"It doesn't matter," said Ruby. "She's going to be fine."

"You need to stop messing with people," Max said.

I wasn't sure who he was talking to at first, but then I saw him look at Khaled.

Khaled's body tensed. "Fucking Christ, man, chill out," he replied.

The two of them were quiet for a moment, and Ruby and I glanced at each other. She looked like she wanted to disappear into the gray hospital couch. Our eye contact decided we'd say nothing. Watch the car crash but do nothing about it.

Khaled stood up. "What does that even mean?"

Max looked strong. I knew he was athletic and built, in his shorter, slender way. Being a varsity athlete at Hawthorne meant you were in peak condition. But Max always lacked something. Something John had. Confidence. Max looked different now. Threatening almost. He stood up to match Khaled. Ruby and I looked from them to each other, still quiet. Staying out of it.

"We're here because you were feeding Gemma shots," Max argued. "You didn't care if she got sick. You never think about your actions. You do whatever you want."

I knew this comment would make Khaled angry.

"I care about her," Khaled said, his face turning a deep shade of purple. "Of course I fucking care."

"You're irresponsible," Max said.

"Dude, what is your problem?"

I'd never seen either of them in an argument before. The two of them were always playful with each other. Never serious. The boys were never serious. Everything was on the surface, and it never dipped below.

"Shannon," Max said. "You're leading her on. You're being a dick."

"Shannon? Seriously?"

"You don't give a shit about her; we all know that."

"That's not true."

Khaled looked at us to confirm. We avoided eye contact.

"You're not an idiot," Max continued. "You know she likes you. And you fuck with her, stringing her along, making her think you're going to change your mind. And you're not going to change your mind about her, are you?"

Max's voice was dark, laced with anger. Khaled was silent. He seemed to be considering something and glanced at Ruby.

"This isn't about Shannon, is it?" Khaled said.

Ruby looked like she wanted to throw up, her arms wrapped around her stomach. She leaned over, toward the tile floor.

Khaled looked smug. I noticed Max's chest rise and fall with his breath. I knew he was already regretting saying anything. Under normal circumstances, Max kept his opinions to himself. It was as if he had reached his boiling point, and everything from the past year was overflowing.

Max looked down at Ruby. When she didn't acknowledge his gaze, his face fell. He should have known better. She reserved that look for when they were alone, never in public, never with all of us around. Max grabbed his cellphone and wallet from the couch and disappeared down the hall.

Khaled sighed as he paced, running a hand through his dark hair. "Fuck."

Ruby groaned. "I think I'm gonna puke."

We watched her sprint to the bathroom, hand to her mouth. I knew Max was taking out his frustration on Khaled, cracking under the weight of his unrequited feelings for Ruby.

"What did I do to him?" Khaled asked me.

I was silent.

"Seriously. I didn't do *anything* to him."

I patted the seat beside me, and he sat down with a long sigh.

"He's tired," I said. "Everyone needs to go home. We need a break."

"Yeah, but what am I supposed to do? Just forget what happened?"

I thought about all the things I had forgotten.

"Yes," I said.

Khaled put his head in his hands, and we sat like that for a while, until Ruby returned, and the three of us were quiet together.

I was the only one awake when Gemma asked for us. Khaled and Ruby had fallen asleep on the hard, stained couches. I checked my watch: two a.m. The nurse led me to her room.

"Hey," Gemma said, her voice raspy.

"Hey," I said. I glanced at the bag of fluids attached to her arm.

Gemma followed my glance and rolled her eyes.

"You know British people are more susceptible to alcohol?" she said.

"Is that true?" I asked.

"No."

Gemma attempted a laugh, but seemed too tired to complete it. She flipped her hand over to open her palm. My neurons fired, but I placed my hand on hers.

"I think I'm acting out because I broke up with Liam," she said, looking away, a wistful glisten in her eye.

Mhmm.

"Oh, no. I'm sorry," I said, playing along.

Finally. I couldn't even believe her lie had lasted a whole school year and nobody noticed he wasn't really her boyfriend.

"Yeah," she said, her voice wobbling. "I decided it was time. So I think . . ." She paused with a deep, reflective sigh. "I think, I'm just a little emotional right now. And I got too drunk."

"I'm sure that's it; breakups are hard," I said.

We were silent. Hopefully Gemma was realizing her drinking was becoming a problem.

After a moment, she looked over at me, her eyes watery. "Sorry," she said.

I didn't know what she was apologizing for.

"For being so annoying all the time," she continued. "I like to make people laugh. I can't be the pretty one, or the smart one . . . so I guess I assumed the role of the funny one."

Her eyes were teary. For all her dramatic antics, crying was not her thing. This was real.

"Gemma the jester," she whispered. She looked so uncomfortable in her own skin. It seemed Ruby and I weren't the only ones pretending to be someone else. And Gemma had spent the year pretending for two. Herself and her fake boyfriend.

I didn't know why I was always the one to console. Why people always told me things. Maybe it was because I was a "no-add," and they could trust that I wouldn't tell anyone else.

I swallowed, not knowing what to say. I thought about what my mother would say. She was always so good at making things better when I was little.

"It's okay," I whispered. I squeezed her hand as one tear streaked her cheek. "Everything will be better in the morning."

We sat in silence, listening to the overhead light buzz. I waited until Gemma fell back asleep to make my escape.

▶ ▶ ▶

AFTER I LEFT the hospital, I made my way down the path toward the other end of campus. It was warm outside despite the early hour of the morning.

I passed a group of students, laughing and falling over one another. I kept my head bent to the ground until I felt someone pull hard on my wrist and my body was jerked backward.

"What the—" I said, turning around to see who it was.

John.

"Yeah?" I asked him.

"Where're you going so fast?" His voice playful, breathy. His shirt damp with sweat.

"My room," I replied.

His chipper demeanor faded. "Why?"

"Because I'm tired."

"You should stay out with me," he said. "And if you don't . . ."

"If I don't, what?"

"I'll tell everyone your secret."

We locked eyes. The curve of his mouth sloped upward. John took a step closer to me, and I could feel his breath, smell his smell. His blond hair had lightened recently, the spring sun acting as a highlighter.

"Oh, yeah," he whispered. "I know all about your family's dirty little secret."

I felt my body tense and took a breath, the air calming my lungs, relaxing my muscles. "Oh, and what secret is that?" How could he know about Levi? There was no way. It was impossible.

"Your great-grandfather. The Deerfield Hunter."

Oh, right. *That.*

"Yeah, so?" I asked. He looked so eager to ruffle my feathers, but I wouldn't give him what he wanted.

"It's kind of fucked up you never told us. Maybe that's why you're such a stone-cold fox."

"Maybe," I said.

"Just stay out a little longer, I know a good spot where we can go," he said. "I know you've thought about it. It'll be fun, I promise."

I felt his fingers at mine, rough and thick. His other hand was wrapped around my wrist, keeping me from leaving. My body braced, and I sucked in a quick breath. *Pretend.*

I smiled up at him.

"You promise?" I adjusted my tone to something he would like. Light and coy.

"Yeah," he said. "Promise."

I noticed his eyelids flutter. His breath smelled like vodka. The group was getting farther away, leaving us alone in the dark.

"Come on, you're killing me," he whispered in my ear. His breath hot on my skin. His other hand brushed my waist, his fingers pulling at my shirt.

When he pulled back, there was that grin. It was almost as if he was implying I should be grateful for his attention, like I should be glad he was interested. I did my best to smile back, my insides recoiling.

"I'm sorry," I said, hating that I had to utter those words to him. He should be the one apologizing to me. I stepped backward, his grip tightening around my wrist. "I have to get up early. Ruby and I are having breakfast together."

The mention of her name seemed to snap him out of it, if only for a moment. Long enough for me to make my escape.

"Fine," he said, his voice bitter. For a second I thought he might crack my wrist, but he released, letting my arm fall away. "I always knew you were a bitch."

He glared at me, challenging, but I turned fast and left him standing alone on the pathway, my feet light as I rounded a corner. Once I was in the clear, I began to run.

INSTEAD OF TURNING toward my dorm, I sprinted past the lake, past the art department where Max's photos hung, up the steps of the English department. I didn't want him to follow me, or go to my room.

The hallway was dark, comforting, as I peered out one of the windows. There was nothing. I put my hand on the door handle for the stairs that led to the bell tower.

A voice called out in the dark, "Malin?"

A surge of adrenaline spiked my veins. Hale stood down the hall, locking the TA's office.

"What are you doing here?" he asked.

I cleared my throat.

"I was at the hospital and I was on my way back, and, I thought maybe I should check if grades were out yet."

This was a semi-reasonable lie. There was a chance grades had already been released.

"Oh," he said, studying my face, not convinced. "Are you okay?"

"What?" I asked, feeling the distance in my voice. Maybe John's interaction had really thrown me off. "Yeah, I'm fine."

"You were at the hospital? Was that you? I saw the ambulance . . ."

"Oh," I said. "No, it was my friend, the one dancing on the table."

"Are they giving her fluids?"

"Yeah, she'll be fine," I replied.

A thought occurred to me, my pulse normalizing, blood returning to my cheeks.

"What are you doing here?" I asked. He seemed sober, and he was carrying his book bag.

He looked down at the bag. "Working on some stuff before summer starts. Get my best work done at night."

"You can study drunk?" I asked.

He laughed. "It takes a lot to get me drunk. I only had a few drinks."

I looked back out the window. It didn't seem like John had followed me.

"Okay," he said, starting toward me, following my gaze onto the lit pathways. "Seriously. What's up?"

I scanned the quad for John, hoping he had carried on with the pack of freshmen.

"Why don't you let me walk you home," Hale said, breaking my thoughts.

I snapped my head at him, knowing I looked cynical.

"As a friend," he said.

"Okay, fine," I replied. "Thank you."

I didn't like the idea of needing an escort, but I didn't want to risk running into John alone. I led the way down the hall and outside into the warm spring night. Hale walked with his hands in his pockets, and he matched my stride.

"Do you want to talk about it?" he asked. "Is it about the boyfriend?"

"Boyfriend?" I asked.

"Yeah, the one you . . . have been with."

Oh, right. Charlie. Our public make-outs.

"No, that's been over for a while."

I felt my cheeks get hot, and I realized I liked that he had seen me with Charlie.

"So what's wrong?" he asked.

I shrugged. "It's my friend Ruby. My best friend. It's *her* boyfriend."

It felt strange saying the words out loud, and somewhat relieving to tell someone.

"Ah," Hale said. "And was he being a creep tonight?"

I looked over at him, skeptical. "Yeah."

"I have sisters," he said, explaining. "Who have had the same look on their faces as you did back there."

"Oh," I replied. "Well, I'm fine, really."

I crossed my arms. We were silent for a moment.

"What are your sisters like?" I asked.

"I have two. Lauren and Corey. Lauren is older, married, kids, mature. Corey is younger. Crazy, senior in college, pretty typical youngest child, hysterical and reckless."

I obsessed over people's siblings. How they interacted with them, what they fought about, what they did together. Levi always in the back of my mind. My what-if.

"What about you?" Hale asked.

"I had a brother. He died." I figured it was easier to skip to the ending of our story rather than go through the whole *dead brother* conversation.

"I'm sorry," he said.

He didn't say anything else, and I was glad. I hated sympathy.

"Did you like the section on Tolstoy?" he asked.

We had finished *Anna Karenina* a few weeks ago. It had been one of the longer reading assignments, but I had finished it before everyone else.

"Yeah," I said, relieved he had changed the subject. "Good interior monologue. I was surprised by all the adultery. I didn't think it would be about that. It was heavy and depressing, but I liked it."

Hale laughed. When we got to the front door, he rustled around in his bag and pulled out a tattered book.

"Take this," he said. "Read it over the summer."

He handed me the paperback. It was an old copy of *White Fang*.

"It's a little less intense. But will still get you thinking. A good one to take your mind off all the miserable Russians."

I held the book in my hand, noticing the worn pages. It looked like my copy of *Walk Two Moons,* which was currently living under my pillow.

I felt my chest expand. I looked up at him, grateful. I realized I didn't want to say goodbye.

"Thanks," I said.

"Well, go inside then," he said. "I'll leave when the door closes."

I stepped inside, the smell of ramen wafting in the air. When I turned around, Hale was still standing there, eyes on me, hands shoved deep in his pockets. He gave me a nod and hopped down the steps two at a time.

► ► ►

As I was boarding the plane the next day, I got a text from Gemma.

Thanks for being there last night. Sorry I was soooo dramatic. That banana bag is a real treat though ;)

A minute passed before I got a second text.

PS—I've told everyone about Liam. Will spend the summer mending my broken heart. Some things aren't meant to be.

I rolled my eyes. I would never tell her I knew the truth. I put "Liam" in my back pocket. He might come in handy one day.

As the plane made its way up and out of the clouds, I thought about my friends. I wondered how things would be in the fall.

I spent most of the summer reading by the pool, poring over *White Fang*. The story was harsh and inspiring, and the message of redemption was at the forefront of my mind once I returned to campus in the fall. I was more determined than before to be a good friend, to listen to everyone, to try to understand the way they worked.

I thought about Ruby, and John, and the mess between them. I envisioned Ruby's written words in my mind—*I'm really happy, I'm really happy, I'm really happy.* Ruby was okay. It was not my business. They were the only two people who understood their relationship. I was an outsider. I shouldn't get involved. It was not worth losing her. She said it herself, she was happy.

Everything would be fine. And until senior year, it was.

PART TWO

SENIOR YEAR

When you spend your time lying to everyone else, you start lying to yourself. Pretending. Lying. I almost forgot who I was.

Sometimes I wake up two minutes before my alarm goes off. That was what senior year became. I was awake, but it wasn't time yet. I had two extra minutes. Graduation was so close. I could keep pretending and continue my life that way. Maybe I could be happy. Something close to happy. Or I could be myself, my true self. Would I keep lying, pretending the alarm hadn't gone off? Or would I get up and be the person I was supposed to be?

Everyone went static for a few years. The middle of college was a blur of monotony and schedule. Classes, parties, sporting events, fall, winter, spring, summer. During the day, our campus remained bucolic, lovely, innocent. We draped ourselves over the library couches and studied on the quad. We kicked our feet through dried leaves and piles of snow. But at night, our campus transformed into an inebriated mess, rich kids indulging in bacchanalian revelry. Inhibitions forgotten, the smallest desires exacerbated. Total fucking madness that I mostly avoided.

Then senior year happened. It was freshman year all over again. Our chaotic and exciting bookends. We were treated like we had somehow inherited a privilege. Professors looked at us like their little fledglings who were about to fly off into the world. We were full of promise and potential. Freshmen looked at us like we were adults. It made us cocky.

Except inside, everyone was frantic, trying to figure out what the next step actually was. We worked so hard for the ending. And now that we almost had it, we didn't want it. Among ourselves, we didn't talk about graduation.

The alarm was about to go off, and I knew it. I could sense it in my bones, but I pretended it wasn't happening. I closed my eyes, heavy with sleep and denial, and lived a life I could have had. A glimpse into this other person I was almost meant to be. It was nice, while it lasted.

CHAPTER TWENTY-SIX

SENIOR YEAR

The tip of my finger rested against Ruby's diary. It was one of those black leather ones, the kind that artsy kids bring to class and take notes in. It seemed like a waste of time to me, when we had the obvious efficiency of laptops.

I looked around the room, listening for noise in the hallway. Ruby's room was in chaos, bags still unpacked, books from the campus store piled next to her desk. She still had the same bedsheets since freshman year—pale blue with faded yellow daisies, thrown in a heap on the naked mattress. My room was already set up, textbooks organized by subject.

The pages of the diary were wrinkled, probably from getting spilled on or splashed with seawater. I pictured her sitting in a beach chair, curled over the diary, toes in the sand, while John played Frisbee with his cousins in the surf. *Summer on the Vineyard,* she had said to me, *it's just what we need.* So excited, bright-eyed, hopeful.

While Ruby sunned herself in Aquinnah, I worked at my father's law firm. Getting experience. Paying my dues. Being a good daughter. My hand was pale, white. No time for tanning, even in Texas.

Over the summer, I had decided I was done reading her diary. But now we were back on campus, and here it was. Calling me. I ran my finger down the cover, bringing my nail to the opening, ready to flip it open.

It was her fault, really. She left it out. She probably wanted me to read it. To read the words she couldn't say out loud. To save her.

I listened to the house. Silence, save for Gemma's hairdryer down the hall. Ruby would be in the bathroom for another five minutes, using the good lights to apply her makeup.

Just one more page.

It wouldn't hurt anyone.

CHAPTER TWENTY-SEVEN

SENIOR YEAR

The door swung open, and Ruby walked through, lips red, chestnut hair thick and wavy. Her presence brought a waft of hair spray into the small room. She looked at me, eyes narrowing for a brief second, flicking to the diary.

"What are you doing?"

"Reading your diary," I said, teasing. Testing. "While you spent a year in the bathroom."

I was calm. I was always calm. She wouldn't suspect anything.

"Very funny," she said, almost laughing.

Ruby walked over to me and added the diary to a stack of art history textbooks and stuffed it all in a drawer.

"We both know that if you wanted to read my diary," she said, smoothing out her dress, "you could've done that a long time ago."

I swallowed, watched her close the drawer, the diary disappearing from view.

"I'm guessing it's filled with *John this, John that, Malin is the bestest best friend in the whole world, oh and some stuff about art,*" I said, twisting my mouth into a smile.

"Oh, shut up," Ruby said. "Besides, you know I don't keep any secrets from you."

She was lying.

Ruby leaned in to the mirror to check her lipstick. She always made this face when she checked herself out. A slight pucker and eyebrow raise. It was endearing, seeing her care that much. I almost pitied her. But now I understood. You looked good when you wanted to impress someone.

"So, are you ready?" Ruby asked, adjusting her earrings. She turned to look at me, her eyes flitting up and down. "Dang, you look really pretty. Look at you!"

I smiled at her, confident. I was always confident, but over the summer I had started taking care of myself. Scrubbing the rough patches off my feet, brushing my hair and trimming the split ends. I went shopping with my mother, and she had helped pick out the dress I was now wearing. She had given me the head-to-toe in the dressing room, astonished, as if I were a new person. It seemed to please her, that her daughter was finally making an effort in her appearance. I even started to wear mascara, learned how to fill in my eyebrows, put on lip gloss when I remembered. It's not like I was a monster before, I had always been pretty, tall, and lanky. But now, I was beautiful. A brand-new daughter. It was a relief to see her that satisfied. I owed her, after everything.

"Come here," Ruby said, holding out her hand to me. I took it.

She pulled me close, so we were hip to hip in front of the mirror. She rested her head against my shoulder.

"We're so cute," she said, looking at the two of us in the reflection. "How are we seniors already?"

She said this as a fact more than a question. I saw myself smile at her, reassuring. We still had all year to be together, to bask in the glory of Hawthorne College's most respected rank: senior.

I glanced at a photo on her desk, taken freshman year on the quad. We were in the same position now. Me, arms crossed, tall and relaxed, and Ruby leaning on me, her eyes closed from laughing so hard. I tried to remember what she had been laughing about. Something about crabs. John and Khaled had made a joke about crabs, or herpes, I couldn't remember, and Ruby had thought it was the funniest thing in the world. Max had taken the photo. Our group photographer.

But the version of Ruby in the mirror looked smaller somehow. Everyone else had grown up, but she had gone backward. I thought about how she used to look, how she used to be, that apparent warmth that had now been replaced by something cold, remote, her spark gone.

"Let's go downstairs," she said, grabbing her keycard and phone. "The others are waiting."

As we walked down the stairs, I watched Ruby's hand sweeping the bannister. Small, delicate, breakable. I thought about her diary, tucked in her drawer. The things she wrote about. It set my stomach to steel, knowing her secrets.

CHAPTER TWENTY-EIGHT

SENIOR YEAR

I was hoping to walk to the cocktail hour with Ruby alone so I could talk to her about my situation. I didn't even know what to call it. *Situation* seemed like the right word. I wanted to tell her so that she would see me as someone normal, and I thought it could help us bond. I had been distant from her all summer, and I knew she would be excited to hear what I had to tell her. My plan didn't work, though, and Gemma decided to walk with us instead of the guys, who were a few yards behind us. Their pace was always too slow for me and Ruby, but just right for Gemma.

"Well, hello there," Gemma said, slapping Ruby's bottom as we headed toward the Greenhouse. Ruby winced and adjusted the back of her dress.

Gemma looked exactly the same as she did freshman year, her face forever embedded with those plush baby cheeks. She was wearing heels, on the verge of falling with every step.

"So," Gemma began, "do you think all the professors will want to fuck us tonight?"

I looked at Ruby, expecting her to give me a *trying not to laugh* face, her lips pursed with a smile, but her expression turned to stone. She crossed her arms over her chest, eyes narrowed.

"Seriously, Gemma?" Ruby asked.

"What?" Gemma scoffed. "I mean, they're all, like, *older* than us. And we look good. Like really good. They've never seen us like this before."

"It's gross. And you know that they have families?" Ruby asked. Her tone had changed fast, happy to irritated.

Gemma rolled her eyes. "So?"

Ruby didn't respond, jaw clenched tight. The tension settled on our skin. This was the dumbest fight, and the semester had only begun. Or almost-fight. Gemma gave a half-smile, toying with her expressions (what a good theater major, her advisor would be proud). She adjusted her posture, thrusting her chest out, shoulders back.

She continued, "I think we look straight fire. I wouldn't blame those naughty old men if their peckers got—"

Ruby interrupted, her tone out of character, "Stop."

I looked over at Gemma who rolled her eyes. Over the years, we had realized how to navigate around one another's pressure points. Retreating when we pushed buttons, all of us preferring to avoid conflict. Gemma was often the slowest to pick up on these cues. We rounded the corner onto the quad and fell in line with a few other groups of seniors heading to the Greenhouse.

"Guys," I said, interrupting their squabble. "Get it together."

Ruby and Gemma both took a breath, recognizing their argument was stupid, and let it go.

I would have to tell Ruby later. When we were alone, and Gemma was off drunk somewhere, too distracted to pay attention to us.

► ► ►

I SCANNED THE Greenhouse, eyes darting between students and professors. Everyone dressed up, mature. Having important discussions about politics or chemistry. The whole atrium had been converted into a cocktail party, couches replaced by bar tables and fancy flutes of champagne.

I stood with Gemma and Khaled. From across the room, I spotted Ruby and John out of the corner of my eye, noting how much closer they had gotten over the summer, how Ruby looked up at him in that adoring, sickening way. How she ignored me and clung to him. She studied John, deciding when he needed another drink. She laughed the hardest at all his idiotic jokes and commentary on life. The worst part was that when he was in her room at night, she would play his music. It was always this terrible techno. Long gone were the days of soft acoustic pop. His hobbies became her hobbies. Her life had become his. He had sucked her dry, draining her body of all life and personality. A robot was all that was left.

Somehow they had survived dating all four years at Hawthorne. I didn't think it was possible, but they had become the gold standard of college relationships. It seemed the longer they stayed together, the more unlikely they were to break up. They were called the "old married couple" behind their backs. If Ruby heard that, though, she would like it. She embraced the commitment, wore it as a badge of pride. John seemed to like it as well. He liked being the best at everything. Nothing could tear them apart.

"You know, Malin," Gemma said slowly, as if she was figuring something out for the first time, "I think you have resting bitch face."

"I what?" I asked, training my attention on Gemma. *Resting bitch face*. That didn't sound like a compliment.

Khaled studied me, nodding his head in agreement.

"Yeah, you know, Gems is right," he said.

I took a slow sip of champagne, the bubbles tangy against my tongue. I was allowing myself one glass tonight.

"It's because you don't smile, you know, when you're resting," Gemma said. "And your face falls into this, like, well, it looks like you hate everything."

She chugged the rest of her champagne. Her drinking had not slowed down over the years.

"But you're still super hot, don't worry," Khaled added.

"What a relief," I said, my voice flat. I tried to smile.

They both laughed. The skin on Khaled's face was soft and crinkled at the same time, his grin spreading over his face, teeth white and sparkly. He had somehow grown taller over the summer, and he looked adult in his suit and tie. I wondered how his internship at Mass General had gone.

"That's why I love you," Gemma said. She stood on her tiptoes to pull me in for a kiss on the cheek.

I found Hale from across the room, and the tiniest spit of adrenaline spiked through my chest. He was talking with a few other professors, a glass of what looked like whisky in his hand. The past few years had treated him well. He was still a sloppy dresser, but it had become an endearing trait rather than an annoying one. I watched him closely from a distance. He had taught a few of my classes over the years, and we'd spent time debating books and poets, but we never crossed any lines. How could we? I was still unsure of what I felt, which was why I needed to talk to Ruby.

I wanted to go over to him, but I stayed put. After a moment, he caught my eye and I looked away. I could feel his eyes linger on me and my dress, and I was glad, satisfied he had seen me looking like this.

► ► ►

"I'M GOING FOR a refill," I said to Khaled and Gemma. They were arguing about a television show; I wasn't paying attention, but they didn't seem to care that I was leaving.

I walked toward the balcony of the Greenhouse, which most of the students and professors had already abandoned, the wind pushing them indoors. A group of five were discussing economic theory, I recognized the students, but not the professors. They were off to my left as I leaned over the balcony and took a breath, noticing the drop. It reminded me of leaning over the edge of our treehouse, and then I saw Levi's face, and I stepped back, a little too fast, tripping in my heels.

I bumped into someone's chest and felt arms catch my near fall.

"Saved your life," Max said, grinning as I turned around. "Saw you come out here, thought I'd say hello." He looked handsome, tanned cheeks and freckles.

We'd started seeing less of Max toward the end of junior year. He became close with people from his pre-med study group, and soon I was only seeing him a few times a week. That house was so huge, and we were all so busy, sometimes we'd go days without seeing one another.

"How was Haiti?" I asked.

"Awesome. Going back next summer. Maybe the whole year."

"Really? Are you going to defer med school?"

"I think so," he said.

I pictured Max injecting little babies with needles, his vigilance protecting them, caring for them. Cracking jokes to calm a crying child, playing made-up games in his free time.

I wondered if being in Haiti made his anxiety better. Last spring, he got quiet, quieter than normal. Sometimes it looked like he wanted to run away. And he did, kind of, with his new friends.

"What are you thinking for next year?" he asked.

"Living alone," I said.

He laughed. "Sick of us?"

"You're one to talk," I replied. "You already made your escape."

His eyes were light with teasing. "Touché. It's surprising to hear from you, though. You're the most loyal one out of all of us."

Of course he would think that. He didn't know the truth, why I was such a loyal participant. I mean, where else would I be? With my other friends?

"But what about other stuff?" he asked.

Other stuff. We never said the word *job;* it was always very carefully avoided.

"Law school," I said.

"That makes sense. You've always been the studious one. And you've got that edge."

Edge. I didn't think anyone had noticed that before.

Max looked over the railing toward the lake. The trees hadn't turned yet, but they would soon.

"How's she doing?" he asked.

His face softened. It always did when he talked about Ruby.

I looked through the glass. She was holding champagne in one hand, her dress hanging from her frame. Too skinny. Max observed her, too, with a different kind of concern. The way he looked at her, I imagine that's how every girl wants to be seen.

"Fine," I said. "You know."

One night last spring, something had happened between the two of them. Ruby came back to the house, her face drawn. I asked her what was wrong, but she claimed she wasn't feeling well. I knew she was lying, but she didn't look like she wanted to talk. I looked in her diary, but all it said was, *can't be friends with Max*. And that was it. There was the date (*May 2*) and her handwriting, clearly rushed.

"You should try to make amends with her. I think she misses you," I said.

He perked up at this. I chewed the inside of my cheek. I shouldn't have said anything.

"Really?" he asked.

Shit.

"I mean," I said, thinking fast, "you guys were such good friends. What happened anyway?"

"Nothing really, just drifted apart," he said.

"Do you think she's happy?" I asked him.

Max looked at Ruby again and then down at his beer. "No, I don't."

"Shouldn't we do something about it?"

"Like what?"

"I don't know. An intervention?"

Max laughed. I was serious. "She's smart. Trust that she will make good decisions for herself. I've tried, but it's not a good idea with her. She's stubborn."

I deflated. He was wrong. So far, she hadn't made great decisions. She was still dating John.

I turned back toward the glass walls, scanning the room until I found Hale, who was leaning against the makeshift bar, talking to a professor. Max followed my gaze.

"Ah," he said, his tone lifting, teasing almost. "Look who it is."

I looked over at him, not sure what he meant. I had been so careful about whatever it was I had with Hale. Nobody knew. Not even Ruby.

"Come on," Max continued, "I'm not an idiot."

I resisted the urge to lie, and a part of me wanted to tell him. I wanted to tell him my secret because I realized, for the first time, that I was excited about it.

"You're not wrong," I said, hesitant.

"I know I'm not. He seems like a good guy. Maybe you should pursue it. It's only been what . . . three years of pining?"

"I don't pine."

Max smiled and shook his head. "Of course not."

I started to regret saying anything to him. I should have lied. Before I could cover my tracks, Max put a gentle hand on my arm.

"Don't worry," he said, "I won't tell anyone."

I looked over at him, sizing him up. He was telling the truth.

"Well," I said, taking a step toward the doors. "I'm gonna go get another drink."

Max sighed. "Classic Malin, always trying to escape."

I smiled back at him and clinked my glass to his.

▶ ▶ ▶

AT THE BAR, I requested a seltzer water with lemon. I felt someone brush my elbow. I knew who it was before I looked over at him. Hale grinned at me, leaning forward on the bar, his hair in that messy auburn tousle.

"Hey, senior," he said.

My lips twitched into a smile, and I cleared my throat.

"Hey."

"Guess who's your thesis advisor?"

Before the summer, Hale and I had met to discuss my literature thesis. I was writing two as a double major—one for pre-law and one for English literature. He was in his fourth year of the graduate program, which meant he got to take on more classes, and even advise a few students.

"Great," I said. "So, I can basically do whatever I want?"

"Nice try," he replied.

I didn't tell him I had been feeling torn between pursuing a more academic career or going to law school. I didn't want to get his hopes up, that he had succeeded in bringing me to the other side. I still had a year to decide. I would still apply to law schools, so at least the door was open.

"How was your summer?" he asked, trying to hide his smile. We had texted every day since we left campus in the spring. I wanted to wrap my arms around his back and press my face against his shoulder, inhaling his scent.

"Can we skip the small talk?" I asked, teasing.

He leaned in, his hand only centimeters away from mine. "You look nice," he whispered, so none of the professors around us could hear.

I straightened. "Watch yourself, Professor Adams."

"Not yet, kid. Still only assistant."

"Close enough," I said. My phone buzzed in my palm. Ruby. Back at the house. Where are you?

"I gotta go," I said, meeting his eyes.

"Come visit soon; glad you're back."

When he smiled, the lines around his eyes crinkled. It was my favorite part of his face. His voice was kind, genuine. It had become a comfort, something I could rely on to be good.

▶ ▶ ▶

I FOUND RUBY in the kitchen. Her head was bent down toward her phone, her expression focused and severe. She looked up as I made my way toward her, seemingly snapping out of a daze.

"Hey," she said, composing herself. "Where did you go?"

"I was with Max. And then I went to find snacks," I lied.

She laughed. She was in a good mood. "Of course you did." The screen on her phone lit up, and she paused to respond.

"Who are you texting?" I asked.

"My aunt," she said, flipping the phone upside down. If I had been paying better attention, I would've known she was lying.

I craned my neck into the living room to make sure nobody could hear us.

"Why are you acting weird?" she asked.

"I have to tell you something," I said, pulling her off the chair and leading her into the pantry. Her bones brittle under my grip.

"So cloak-and-dagger, I love it," she whispered. She stood in front of the shelf with our cereal and granola bars. "What's up?"

I took a breath. "I am hesitant to say this, because I'm not even sure if it's true. But I think I like someone."

Ruby's eyes widened. "Are you serious? Who?"

I knew she would be excited. I hadn't dated anyone since Charlie. I was too busy with schoolwork to focus on it ever again.

"Don't tell anyone," I said. "I'm serious."

Ruby held my hands. "You can trust me, M, you know that."

I looked over my shoulder, to make sure we were alone.

"It's Hale. You know, the TA," I said. She stared at me, her eyebrows furrowing, and I continued, hesitantly now, "You know, the guy in the PhD program? The one who's always at parties?"

Ruby's face fell; her eyes filled with the resigned judgment I had seen so many times before. She had looked at Gemma like that. But never at me. She let go of my hands.

"Yeah, I know who he is," she said.

"Are you mad?" I asked. I thought she would be excited I had found someone.

She stared at me, eyes calculating.

"Well, isn't he sort of a professor?" she finally said.

I stared at her. Smudged concealer gave way to purple-blue bags under her eyes. Her tone was cold, distant. I didn't know who she was anymore. I wanted to smash her to pieces and sift through the wreckage for the real Ruby. The one I met all those years ago. The fun, strong, smart Ruby.

"He's in the graduate program," I replied. "But yeah, he teaches."

"You shouldn't hook up with a professor," she said. "It's slutty."

"Okay, but he's not a professor, not yet," I said, not caring that I sounded angry.

Ruby kept looking at me, judging, her eyes hard and cold.

I wanted her to feel guilty for being such a jerk, so I forced my eyes to fill with tears. Ruby looked awkward, as I knew she would. I knew the tears would work, she had never seen me cry before.

She placed a sympathetic hand lightly against my forearm. "I'm sorry, I just, I feel very strongly about this."

I shrugged her off and didn't look back as I left her in the pantry. Upstairs in my room, I wiped the salty liquid off my face and sat at my desk, staring at a stack of books.

The thing is, I did what I wanted. Nobody had ever been able to stop me from that. Everything I did was self-serving. I was a selfish person. And I was fine with that. I owned it. I didn't need Ruby's approval, but I wanted her to be excited for me, like I always was for her, or at least pretended to be. Worse was that I didn't even know if it was true, about Hale. Or if it was something else. I had needed to ask for her advice.

There was something very wrong with her, and I needed to figure out what it was. So I planned to do what I always did when Ruby confused me. Read her diary.

CHAPTER TWENTY-NINE

SENIOR YEAR

A week passed, and I still hadn't gotten a chance to sneak into Ruby's room. She started locking her door after campus security sent out an email about a burglary in an off-campus house. Ruby was quiet, ignoring me when we ran into each other in the house.

I sat in class, focused on my laptop screen, pausing to look up at Hale and the words he wrote on the whiteboard. The class was filled with the drum of keyboards, and occasional comments from students or murmurs of thought and agreement.

Early Twentieth Century Literature was printed in italic font across the top of my document. I made sure each note was aligned, precise, and neat, and then flipped back to the Internet. I had started my applications for law school and spent the majority of my free time filling in the blank spaces. The forms kept me afloat, a distraction from my social life. I was almost done with the deal I'd made with my father, and I would finally have what I wanted. There was still that nagging in the back of my mind, about applying for the graduate program at Hawthorne. It was an option I had been ignoring. I typed my name into the blank field for Harvard Law. *Malin Ahlberg.*

I liked the sound of Boston. Hale had described the best restaurants in the South End, where he grew up, and how he liked to jog on the banks of the Charles River, watching the sailboats and kayakers. I listened to every word. I knew where the best burritos were (Anna's), and where I could get the best view of the city in the fall when the leaves would turn (on the Mass Ave bridge). I knew the entire city shut down for the marathon and that the sports fans were crude and aggressive, which only added to the game-watching "experience." He described how peaceful the city became in snowfall and how some people would cross-country ski through the streets. He made it sound like a place I could make home—a home miles away from Texas. And there was Harvard, of course. My trophy for all the long years at Hawthorne.

I looked up at Hale, catching his eye for a moment. I still hadn't gone in for office hours, not after what happened with Ruby. I knew what his glance said. He wanted to know why I hadn't visited him yet.

Hale turned to the whiteboard, and I noticed the space where his shirt tucked into his corduroys. I wanted to run the tips of my fingers along the grooves, to be close enough to reach out and touch him.

Frustration was burrowing into my thoughts, distracting me. Needling at my focus. I needed to go for a run.

► ► ►

I KNEW HALE'S address.

We were together in the Lit lounge during sophomore year, and he had gone to grab something in Professor Clarke's office. I was alone and saw an unopened letter sticking out of his bag, with the jagged scrawl typical of an older person, probably a grandparent. The letter was addressed to Hale Adams at 356 Pleasant Street.

I wasn't looking for the address, but once I had it, I couldn't stop thinking about it. I wondered if he lived in one of the industrial brick buildings that lined the tiny mill town, or a house in the suburbs behind campus. I needed to see it.

I took our house steps two at a time, my sneakers squeaking against the damp bricks. The light was golden on my spandex and hoodie, the sun sneaking behind the hills. I preferred to run in the dark, seeing into people's houses. Most of the homes near campus were old Victorians, like ours, and for the most part, boring inside. The rooms were too large for me to see anything good. I usually saw the tops of heads as people watched television or ate dinner. I wondered what they did that day, who they saw, who they talked to, what their secrets were. Who they loved. Who they didn't.

I ran the three miles fast. I grew up athletic, but never played group sports, much to the dismay of my parents. In gym tests, my agility far outweighed that of my peers, and I could always run farther and longer. But I never wanted to join a team, dreading the afternoon practices and unavoidable bonding I would have had to endure.

Nobody at Hawthorne knew this about me. When they asked if I wanted to join their intramural softball team, Ruby laughed, reporting I didn't do sports. She was right. But I would have been the best player on the team.

It was pitch black by the time I reached 356 Pleasant Street, his house lights the only guide in the dark. My heart raced, sweat beading at the base of my neck. The farmhouse sat back from the road, surrounded by fields and a weathered barn.

He was home, a shiny black truck tucked under the portico. I stepped behind a stone wall on the opposite side of the road. I could see my breath in the clear night air, and I zipped my hoodie up to my chin to stay warm. The house was still. I traced my eyes along the windows until I spotted him, sitting on the couch with his laptop. He wasn't doing anything interesting, but it was comforting, watching him.

I imagined the inside of his house was empty. Most graduate students lived on campus, but he had told me he liked the solitude, he needed it to get work done, there were too many distractions at Hawthorne. He probably had an old couch and hand-me-down furniture. The kitchen would be sparse, save for one set of dishware and a few pots and pans. I imagined his bed and quickly discarded the thought from my mind.

I didn't ask for this. I wasn't looking for it, either. But after that last night freshman year, I had started thinking about him before I went to sleep at night. I pictured him next to me in bed. I didn't understand it, the fixation on him, but I didn't push it away, either. I let it sit with me for just over two years. During that time, Hale didn't date anyone either, at least not that I knew of. There were a few women he could have dated in the graduate department, but I got the impression he wanted to stay single after his very public breakup. And maybe a part of him was waiting for me, like I was waiting for him. The feeling I had for him, or whatever it was, had failed to dissipate. I held it in my hand, watched it jump around, curious about its potential. Maybe it was my chance to be normal. And that was enough for me, so I held on tight.

I checked the time. I had two hours to get back, shower, and meet the others in the living room to walk to the Pub, our first legal drinking experience off-campus. I followed the stone wall far enough so I knew he wouldn't see me get back onto the road. Even if he did look out the window, I didn't think he would be able to make out my shape.

I started to run once I reached the end of the road.

▶ ▶ ▶

I WALKED WITH Khaled and Max to the Pub. Ruby, John, and Gemma were ahead of us, buzzed off multiple shots of tequila. Gemma shrieked about something, while John and Ruby doubled over with laughter.

We passed a group of freshmen on the quad. They looked nervous, carrying plastic bags with what I assumed was alcohol. One of them, a smaller boy, stared at us as we passed, probably thinking how cool we were, heading to the Pub. I tried to get excited, to be the person he thought I was—pretty, twenty-one, fun. But there was nothing.

Khaled talked about his parents. They were pressuring him to return home after graduation and get a job in the government, but he wanted to go to medical school in New York City.

"It's where I belong, I know it. There's always something going on. The city that never sleeps, right, guys?"

Max listened, quiet, as always. He was a good listener. I saw him reach into his pocket and pull out his phone, type a text to someone. He looked at the others ahead of us.

I wondered if the graduate students ever frequented the Pub. Maybe Hale would be there.

"That would be sick, right?" Khaled said.

I hadn't been paying attention. Both Max and Khaled looked at me.

I smiled. "Yeah, of course." I was used to filling in my responses with generic complacencies.

"We could live together again," Khaled continued. "Except you'd have to pay rent this time, pretty sure New York rent prices are a little steeper than Edleton."

I realized what they were talking about, but there was no way I was going to live with everyone again. Next year I would have my own apartment.

When I didn't say anything, Max side-eyed me, trying not to laugh.

"Nah," Max said. "She'll probably be at Harvard."

"Maybe," I said, silently thanking him for the cover.

When we reached the Pub, Khaled read the words on the sign outside.

"*Karaoke night?* Max, grab me a drink; I'll sign us up," he said, sounding excited as he bounced inside the loud bar.

"Karaoke. My favorite," I said, sarcastic. I pulled the door open. Max smiled at me again.

"Should I get you a water?" he asked.

When I didn't respond right away he said, "Don't worry, I won't tell anyone. I'll probably have one, too. Alcohol makes the anxiety worse."

"Fine," I said. "Thanks."

"Or should we get some fake shots, to really mess with people?"

I laughed. "Sure, let's."

► ► ►

AFTER I LEFT Max with his pre-med clique, I made my way to the end of the bar near the restrooms. I sat on one of the stools, pretending to be on my phone. The karaoke machine clicked over. The baseball team got up to the microphone and began an intriguing rendition of "Under the Sea."

I spotted John close-talking with a sophomore girl who must have snuck in with a fake ID. He caught my eye and straightened up, adjusting his posture, looking into the crowd, as if the girl was nobody significant. I pretended I hadn't seen anything and focused my gaze elsewhere. He wasn't my concern right now.

I waited twenty minutes until I got what I wanted. Girls always had to pee when they drank. I watched Amanda stumble to the swing-door and snagged her arm before she fell inside.

"The fuck?" Amanda sputtered as I pulled her over to a barstool. "Oh," she said, rolling her eyes. "What do you want, Malin?"

I turned on the charm.

"You look so cute tonight," I said with a smile. "Where did you get your top?"

"Okay, seriously, what do you want?" she asked.

I sighed. She knew I would never talk to her unless I had to. This wasn't going to work.

"Unless you're hitting on me," she continued. "I mean, Abigail finally came out, so maybe you are, too, and part of your plan is to tell me how in love with me you are."

"Don't flatter yourself," I said.

I looked over my shoulder. Ruby was standing with Gemma and a group of girls from our class. They were looking through the karaoke songs, deciding what to sing.

"Afraid she'll get pissed if she sees us talking?" Amanda said. She seemed somewhat excited by this.

"No," I replied, turning back to her. "Actually," I said, finding the right angle, "we are in a fight."

Amanda looked interested. "Really," she said, more of a statement than a question.

"Yeah. It's pretty bad. I don't know what to do."

"Well, well," she said. "Never thought you'd be the type to talk shit. You aren't as perfect as you seem."

"Neither is she," I replied, casting my line.

"Can you blame her?" Amanda waved her hand in the air.

Yes. *Tell me what it is you have on her.* Amanda had wanted to tell me about Ruby for years. This was her chance. I recalled the conversation we had when we first met, in front of the pizza bar during freshman year, the warning she gave me. I needed to know what Amanda had on her.

"Sucks about her dad," I said, hoping I would strike the right spot.

Amanda focused on me and then leaned in so we were nearly touching foreheads.

"If *my* father fucked his students, I would never speak to him again, that's for sure."

I blinked and looked over at Ruby. Something clicked into place. I guess that would explain a few things. Her aversion to sex. The reason she didn't want me to date Hale.

Amanda kept talking. "She doesn't even have a mother. Or siblings. Can you imagine the humiliation? Sitting at dinner with your dad, thinking about what student he was with that day? So awkward."

"Yes, super awkward," I said, still staring at Ruby. She stood next to Gemma, smiling at something another girl was saying. She looked up, and we locked eyes. Why didn't she tell me about her father?

Amanda kept talking, her words a faucet I had turned on. "That time I met her at summer camp, *everyone* knew about her dad. I kind of felt bad for her, you know. And she wanted to be friends with me. Ruby is sweet, I'll give her that. Until she's not."

Ruby had *wanted* to be Amanda's friend? I couldn't imagine it.

Amanda continued, "So we became close, for a few weeks. She was nice and did stuff for me. That's the sweet part I'm talking about. So we were friends. I had plenty of them; I didn't mind if she hitched along for the ride. The more the merrier. Whatever."

I sipped seltzer out of my glass, chewing on the straw.

"So one day, we go horseback riding, because that's my thing. Of course it became Ruby's thing too when we became friends. Anyway, there was this other girl, I think her name was Gigi . . . or Ginny or . . . whatever, let's just call her Gigi. So, Gigi strolls in, with her shiny, long blond hair and tries to ride Royale, who is *my* horse. I had been riding Royale every year for four summers and then Gigi shows up and steals him. She rode him *all* day. I was like, over my dead body. I see Ruby, watching me get angry, and she scrunches up her face all sweet and stupid, and I know she will do anything to please me. Literally, anything."

Oh, no. I knew where this was going. I had seen her like this with John. Doting on him, making sure he was happy, sacrificing herself for his benefit.

"I only *suggested* that Gigi should be naired. You know, Nair in the hair conditioner. I wasn't serious about it. It was a joke. Ruby was the one who went and actually did it. The next day, Gigi didn't even show to horseback riding. I did have Royale all to myself, so that was nice, but I saw her in the dining hall later, her eyes red and puffy, baseball hat and everything. She left camp the next day. It was sad, really."

Amanda paused, gauging my reaction. "See what I mean? Kind of messed up. Ruby's a freak, all I'm saying. I did warn you."

"Interesting," I said, trying to sound like I didn't care. Amanda looked annoyed that her story hadn't rocked my world. I needed to squeeze her for every drop she had. "That doesn't sound like Ruby."

Amanda straightened her posture and tossed some hair over her shoulder. "Well," she started, sounding very matter-of-fact. "Now she seems different, I'll give her that. She's done a fine job, playing the nice, fun, popular girl. College is great that way, you can really re-invent yourself. Of course, it doesn't work so well when somebody, like me, knows who you really are. And *Ruby* is a desperate social climber. I mean, you think she randomly chose you to be her BFF?"

I tried to keep a straight face but inside, Amanda had struck a chord. It was deep down, but it was there.

"Ah," she said. "You never thought about that, did you? She chose you for a reason."

I was the one who chose Ruby. Wasn't I?

Amanda continued, "You're pretty, but not as pretty as she is. You're nice, sure, but not as outgoing. She shines next to you. I don't think she liked being in my shadow at camp that summer. She didn't like being at the bottom of the totem pole. She plays the part well. The popular girl. She knows what to do; she's sneaky that way. I was good at it once, but it gets exhausting. Anyways, the only thing you're better at is academics, right? And she doesn't care about that because she's an art history major and wants to marry someone rich so she can own a gallery and prance around in Louis Vuittons all day."

Amanda put a hand on my wrist. "She *needs* to be better than you. Or you wouldn't be friends. I mean, why do you think she is still living with sloppy Gemma? Absolutely zero competition there. Ruby always wins."

Before she could say anything else, Becca lodged herself between Amanda and me, leaning drunk against the bar. She slapped her clutch on the wet surface.

"I need another a drink," Becca said, her words loud and long.

"No, you don't," Amanda said, taking Becca's clutch away. "Go puke now, before you get too sick. Boot and rally, baby."

Becca pouted and disappeared into the bathroom. Amanda rolled her eyes again, then turned to me, serious.

"Anyways," she said. "It's about time you two fought, and you saw that real side of Ruby. The desperate, pathetic, fake one. Because you know, she *is* a fake. How can you trust someone like that? Who hides who they really are? I am sorry that you had to find out. What are you fighting about, anyway?"

"Oh, um, it's nothing, really," I said.

"Well, I'm always here if you want to talk about it," she said. My stomach was in knots, because I knew she meant it. She actually thought Ruby was a bad person and that I might need to vent, or whatever it was people did to feel better.

The longer I processed what Amanda had said, the more I realized she had a point. About trusting someone who hides behind façades. I lived that life; I knew what she said was the truth. I couldn't be trusted. Neither could Ruby. Maybe Amanda was better than both of us. At least she was her true self; she didn't hide behind any walls.

I looked at Ruby. Did she even like me? Did she like any of us? Who was she, really? I wondered if Amanda was right, if Ruby liked me so much because I wasn't a threat. She was the popular one, and I wasn't. She was the one who got all the attention, and I could care less. Was that why she called me her best friend?

"Well, that was fun," Amanda said. "Let's do it again sometime."

She hopped off the barstool and leaned into the bathroom door, tipping her head back so that her red hair flailed behind her.

"And by the way," she said, pulling at her top. "It's from Zara."

CHAPTER THIRTY

SENIOR YEAR

I waited until everyone packed up their things and the classroom was quiet. I remained in control of my back corner seat all four years. I kept typing on my laptop. I used to run out of class as soon as it was over, but I now stayed seated until the whole room was empty. The emptiness helped me get work done.

It took me two hours to finish a paper on Shakespeare and his treatment of women, and then I stretched and slung my bag over my shoulder. The halls were silent. I traced a finger along the wall as I read a few of the posters there. Like freshman year, there was a photo of Ruby front and center on the varsity soccer poster. She was captain now, still commanding on the field. The only place John couldn't reach her.

At the end of the hall, I knocked my knuckles against the wooden door to the TA's office.

"Come on in," Hale said, voice loud and merry.

"You here to talk thesis?" he asked as I stepped inside. He was alone. I was relieved.

I sat, lifting my heavy bag onto my lap. Silence. I didn't even know what I was doing there.

"Everything okay?" he asked, not bothering to wait for me to speak.

I thought of Ruby.

"Remember that night freshman year?" I asked, hesitant. Maybe advice would help. "When you walked me to my dorm?"

"Yeah, creepy stalker dude. Best friend's boyfriend, right? He still bothering you?"

I considered lying, but I didn't want to lie to him. I wanted to get everything out. Maybe then I would stop thinking about it.

"Yeah, he's still dating my best friend. Ruby. And she's different, like he has her hypnotized. I don't know why I'm obsessing over it."

"Because you care," he said. "But you know, maybe she is changing; it happens. People change, and that's okay. As long as everyone changes for the better."

I continued, "But it's not for the better. And it's frustrating not being in control. And watching her make mistakes. I know how she should live her life, but it's not like I can say that to her. That's not how it works."

Hale seemed to be considering what I had said.

"There's something you can read, maybe it'll help," he said, getting up and walking over to the bookshelves. I let my eyes linger on his shoulders and lower back, and when he turned back around I shifted my gaze to the floor.

"It's a piece by Tsvetaeva. Actually we read it in your freshman seminar. Remember?"

"You mean the seminar where you made me stand up in front of the class?"

"You deserved it," he said, smiling, and then handed me the book, open to the page.

I read the poem while Hale settled back at his desk. It was vaguely familiar; I remembered noting it in an essay on our final exam. The poem was titled "I Know the Truth." It was about life and death. I didn't know what it had to do with Ruby, though.

"What do you think?" Hale asked.

"Um," I responded, reading the poem again. "Certainty. It's arguing there is certainty to life and death."

He didn't say anything, gave me that look like I needed to keep going.

"And . . ." I paused. "It's what you do while you're alive that matters."

"Yeah," he said. "It's also about how we treat others. Will we make others' lives worse or better? If someone is suffering, will we ease their pain or ignore it? At the end of life, there is only one truth, and it's yours alone. You must live a life that *you can live with,* at the end."

I thought about that. A life you can live with. I thought about Levi and the way he died.

"Maybe there is something you can do for Ruby; help her, don't help her, but think hard about how you want to go about it, because you're going to be the one who has to live with it," Hale added.

I stared at the poem, waiting for the words to guide me.

"You can borrow it, if you want," he said.

"Thanks."

I sank farther into the chair and re-read the poem.

I know the truth—give up all other truths!
No need for people anywhere on earth to struggle.
Look—it is evening, look, it is nearly night:
what do you speak of, poets, lovers, generals?

The wind is level now, the earth is wet with dew,
the storm of stars in the sky will turn to quiet.
And soon all of us will sleep under the earth, we
who never let each other sleep above it.

Hale leaned back in his chair with a pad of legal paper and put his feet on his desk. "You're a good friend, to care this much. When I was a senior, I felt like everyone was out for themselves."

"Am I? I don't think I'm a good friend," I said, not really caring about the answer. I looked at the floor.

"Yes, I think so," he said. "You're also one of the most confident people I know. You don't let anything get in your way. But sometimes, only very rarely, it's like you're trying to figure everything out. I watch you, trying to put the pieces together."

"I like to be good at things. Failure shouldn't be an option."

"You are definitely better at things than other people," he replied.

The compliment made me feel uncomfortable so I ignored it, pushing it aside.

"So, what do you do with the pieces?" I asked.

"Ah. I am the opposite of you. It's probably not the best plan of attack, but I do nothing. I let it be. I don't fight the wave, I let it drag me under and trust that eventually I'll come out the other side."

"Yeah, no thanks," I said.

Hale laughed. "That's why I love you."

The words fell out of his mouth, organic, like it was something he said to me every day. But it wasn't. When he realized what he'd said, his face went a deep crimson. I'd never seen him embarrassed before. I acted like what he said was nothing, just an offhanded comment.

"I'll figure it out," I said. "Let's talk about my thesis."

"Yup, yup. Let's." He avoided eye contact.

I didn't know what to do, or what to say. Talking about literature was what we did best, so I focused on that. I hoped he knew it was all I could give him in return for what he had said.

▶ ▶ ▶

I GOT BACK to the house later that night. Everyone was piled on the couch for family movie night. They were covered with fleece blankets Max's mother had provided for us, and the air smelled like weed and popcorn. I settled on the arm next to Gemma, and she looked up at me, sleepy and high.

"Hey, babe," she whispered, putting an arm around my waist. Max glanced my way, but the others focused on the screen. John had his arm wrapped around Ruby's upper half. He acknowledged my presence, his eyes meeting mine, and pulled Ruby closer to plant a kiss on her forehead.

Ruby and I still hadn't talked since the cocktail hour, weeks ago. I had briefly wondered if her seeing Amanda and me talk at the bar would make her jealous, force her to cave and apologize, the fear of losing me to the other side. But she hadn't confronted me at the Pub, and I walked home alone that night. Since my chat with Amanda, a shadow had been cast upon Ruby's flawless veneer. Had I really let her deceive me? Was she the person I thought she was, or was she faking her way through college? Not that I could judge her for that. But still. The potential deception ate at me and caused the rift between us to widen.

I still had some reading to do, so I got up and headed to the stairs.

"Night, guys," I said.

They mumbled a response, focused on the blare of the television. Ruby looked over at me, and we made eye contact before I started up the stairs, but she said nothing.

My room was neat and orderly, as it always was. I wondered if Ruby's door might be unlocked, but it was too risky to go in there while she was downstairs. I didn't turn on any music; I preferred silence. As I started to set myself up on my bed to finish studying, there was a knock on my door.

"Yeah?" I said.

Ruby's face appeared around the corner.

"Can we talk?" she said.

"Sure."

Ruby sat next to me on the bed, folding a leg under her. It was a habit of hers, subconsciously stretching at the same time. Her soccer practices were unyielding, and she often came home tired and sore. Ruby looked in my direction and chewed on her lip.

"So," she started. "You really like him? Hale?"

"I think so, I'm not really sure," I said.

"Have you hooked up?"

I shook my head.

"But you'll be careful, if you do?" she asked. "Like is that even allowed?"

"I don't think it's a big deal. But I doubt anything will happen," I said. As soon as I said it, my stomach dropped with disappointment. I *wanted* something to happen.

Ruby was quiet for a moment. I knew she was probably thinking about her dad and the students he slept with, or whatever he did. I wanted to tell her that I understood, but I couldn't tell her I had talked to Amanda. She would get mad again. So I was silent.

"I'm sorry I was a bitch about it," she said. "If you're happy, I'm happy. I promise."

I knew why she had been upset; it made sense. But I wished she would tell me about her father herself. She looked up at me, her eyes glossy.

"I missed you," she said. "I'm really, really sorry."

"I missed you, too," I said, and I let her hug me.

This was the real Ruby. This was her, I knew it. Amanda had to be wrong. She wasn't pretending with me. This was real.

I pulled back, looking her in the eyes. "I have a question, though," I said.

I tried to sit a little straighter, to compensate for the uncomfortable vulnerability I was about to experience.

"Yes, anything," she said.

"Okay," I started. "How do you know if someone likes you back?"

Ruby looked down. She was probably thinking of John. I really didn't want her to compare my thing to her thing, but I was desperate to hear her answer.

"I think you just know," she said. "It's like, if you're sitting next to them, or even looking at them, you can feel this excitement. And if they go out of their way to look at you, and talk to you, and do little things for you, then, well, that's confirmation they feel something, too."

"Is that how it is with John?" I asked.

She paused. "Yeah," she said, a slight hesitation. "In the beginning. Now it's so comfortable, I never question how he feels about me."

Before I could ask her more, there was another knock at my door and Max's head popped in.

"Oh," he said, surprised to see Ruby, and then looking over at me. "I wanted to see if you had done the philosophy paper yet."

I looked from him to her. I hadn't seen them speak since junior year.

"Not yet," I said.

Max nodded, as if he was trying to figure out what to do next. He looked at Ruby.

"Hey," he said.

"Hey," she replied. A broken smile.

Oh, Ruby. I wanted her to tell me everything so I could fix it. I looked at her, so pretty, so sad and full of secrets. I was so lost without her diary. I needed to find a way to get into her room, and fast.

CHAPTER THIRTY-ONE

SENIOR YEAR

But the days flew by, and I was busy with my honors thesis, spending most of my time in the library. I looked up one day and realized we were almost halfway through the semester.

My phone buzzed on the wooden desk, Ruby.

Wanna grab a coffee before I have practice?

I gathered my things in my bag and took the stairs from the top of the library. I preferred to study in the quiet corner where the windows surveyed the quad. I liked how small and far away everyone seemed from up there. A few slacklines were hung between trees, and some students balanced precariously on top of them, bundled in their fleece-lined jackets and wool hats. As I made my way across the grassy expanse, I wondered what Hale was doing.

Ruby was sitting alone when I got to the Grill. She smiled at me as I approached. I was relieved to see it was one of her real smiles, the one she used to give me all the time.

"Guess what?" she said.

"What?" I sat down next to her and started unbuttoning my coat. She pushed a coffee toward me, black.

"I applied for the Getty grant today."

Ruby's dream for the past three years was getting a job at the Getty Museum and moving to Los Angeles after graduation.

"That's awesome, I'm sure you'll get it," I said. "So you'd go to L.A.?"

Ruby took a sip of coffee. She was dressed in her practice shorts and sweatshirt. Her tanned skin was fading, and the tendons on her hands stood out like mountain ranges on her skin.

"No, actually," she explained, "it's a grant to go to Scotland and prepare a conservation plan for this old estate that is falling apart. I've been working on it with my advisor."

"Wow," I said, surprised she would want to go so far. "I didn't know you'd be leaving the country."

"Yeah," she said, picking at the recyclable cardboard cup. "Anyways, what's up with you? I haven't seen you in forever. How does that even happen? We live together."

"Well, I've been living in the library, so."

"God, you need to get out of there," she said. "Did you hear about the Portland night thing? In November?"

"No, what is it?" I took a sip of the coffee, eager for the caffeine.

"Hawthorne is busing us to Portland for the night, to go out and stuff. As like a *good job being seniors* type thing." She paused. "They really like getting us drunk, don't they?"

We laughed.

"Or maybe they're hoping we'll finally act like adults and drink an appropriate amount," I said.

"It's not like adults are any better."

"True," I said.

"Anyways, you'll come, right? It'll be fun, you should," Ruby said. She didn't really sound convinced herself.

"Um, yeah, definitely," I replied. Maybe that's when I could ask her about what was going on, when she was slightly intoxicated, in a sharing mood.

"Okay, good," she said. "So has anything happened?"

"With what?"

I didn't know why I was playing dumb, manipulating her.

"With Hale," she whispered.

"Oh, nothing. I see him a lot, but that's it."

She looked relieved. I wished she didn't.

"How are things with John?" I asked, changing the subject.

"Fine. The same. I feel like he's trying to soak up as much bro time as possible before graduation. I'm kind of on the back burner. But it's fine."

I watched the pulse on her neck quicken. Fake smile, tightened grip on the cup.

This was my chance. "What's going on with you and Max?"

She looked up, eyes sharp. "Nothing." She paused, knowing she had to say something. It was obvious they weren't talking. "He got all weird last semester. I couldn't deal."

"Maybe if you tried to talk to him, things could go back to normal," I said.

She shook her head. "It's complicated."

She said it as if I was too dumb to understand. I wanted to scream at her that I wasn't, that she could tell me. But I also didn't want to beg her. Or give her the smug satisfaction that I had to know. I'd find out on my own anyway.

"Okay. Well, tell me more about Scotland."

Ruby began to explain all the intricacies of the dilapidated house where a guy named James and his family used to reside hundreds of years ago. I expected to see that spark she used to get when she talked about art, but it was long gone. It was almost as if she was sad to talk about it, like she didn't really want to go.

► ► ►

"Max?"

I knocked on his door. Silence. I almost started toward the stairs but I heard something fall inside the room. I considered ignoring it; maybe he wanted his privacy. I thought about the things he did when he was alone, what most guys did when they were alone, and decided to walk away. But then I heard a loud thump, as if something heavy had fallen to the ground.

When I opened the door, Max was on the floor, trying to get his back against the desk, struggling to sit up. He was shirtless, and his hair damp—he must have been getting changed after a shower. He looked up at me, a wounded animal.

I didn't move toward him, my body flaring with the sense to run. I hated hospitals, all the bodies weak and vulnerable. On display. This was the same way.

He opened his mouth to talk, but nothing came out. I hoped he would say he was fine, thank you, and then I could leave.

"Panic attack," he said, his voice choked.

Shit. I looked out into the living room for Khaled or Gemma. Or even Ruby. Anyone but me. I wasn't the right person for this.

He seemed to be struggling for air. He looked up at me again.

"Okay," I said. I couldn't leave him like this. I took a deep breath and stepped toward him. I kneeled on the ground in front of his feet. I remembered what my father used to say to my mother when she had her anxiety spells.

"Let's do some math," I said.

Max took a reassuring breath, as if he had done this before.

"Four times six," I said.

In between raspy breaths he sputtered, "Twenty-four."

"Five times five."

"Twenty-five."

We went on like this for a while until his breath returned to normal. I figured I could leave since he seemed to be recovering.

"All right," I said. "Well, I should go."

He grabbed my wrist. "Stay."

I looked down at his hand on my arm. His skin was cold to touch. He followed my gaze.

"I can't feel my hands yet," he said. "Or legs."

What a mess. I couldn't believe he had done this to himself.

"I realize," he said, "that I am being very needy right now."

I knew he wanted me to laugh, so I smiled. My ankles started to hurt, and I lowered myself to the floor. From what I knew, anxiety was an imbalance in the brain, or the result of some sort of trauma. I didn't know if he had been through something damaging, or if he was born this way. I thought about myself, the problems I buried inside. For a second, the wires crossed, the words *you're broken* screamed through my synapses. I shook my head, chasing the thought away.

Max stared at me, blinking heavy and slow.

"Maybe you shouldn't put so much pressure on yourself," I said.

"I've tried that," he said, his words slow. "I've been like this for so long, I don't know what to do anymore. I eat healthy, barely drink, exercise. I even tried to meditate."

I wondered if this was what Ruby was talking about. The weirdness she was referring to. Maybe she had attended to one too many panic attacks and decided she had had enough.

"What about medication?" I asked.

"No. No way."

"Why not?"

"Because."

"Well. It would be better than this," I said.

"No," he said. "It would be better if there was something wrong with you, too," he said. I gave him a confused look. "Selfishly," he added. "So I wasn't the only mess in the room."

"I have things," I said. The words had escaped my lips before I could stop them.

Max looked up at me, a soft look in his eyes. I could probably tell him the truth, and he wouldn't tell a soul. But it wasn't worth the risk. I could lose everything.

"What kind of things?" he asked.

I tried to think of something that would satisfy the situation. I looked down at my hands, the scars. Max followed my gaze.

"Does it have to do with those?" he asked. His voice calm, quieter.

"No," I said, a long breath exhaling from my lips. A recited lie. "That was an accident. I fell through a glass table." How many times had I repeated that line over the years?

"But, I was bullied," I continued, trying to find the right words, "for a few years."

"I'm sorry," he said. "At school?"

I hesitated. I couldn't say his name. I hadn't spoken it since the day he died.

"Yes, at school. One girl hated me. She made life very hard," I lied.

We were quiet for a moment; he looked over at me, sizing me up. I knew I didn't come off as someone who could be bullied, so I tried to look sad. I leaned an elbow against my knee and let my chin fall into my hand.

"I didn't know that about you," he said.

"Surprise," I said.

Max almost laughed, then sighed, leaning back against the desk, closing his eyes. He opened his hands a few times, as if he was coaxing the blood to run through them, allowing the feeling to return.

"How are those extremities doing?" I asked.

"Better," he said.

He looked guilty and sad.

"It's fine, really, don't worry," I said. "I don't mind staying here."

He looked at me, his eyes sweet and understanding, and started to stand up. He lifted himself up onto the desk and steadied himself.

"But put a shirt on," I said. "Your six-pack is burning my eyes."

He cracked a grin. Back to normal. He pulled the shirt over his thick tuft of hair.

"Did you need something?" he asked me, looking at the door. "You knocked, remember?"

"Oh, yeah," I replied. "Wanted to see if you'd studied for the quiz yet."

Our philosophy quiz was tomorrow afternoon. Our class was Contemporary Moral Disputes. Max had to take it for his pre-med major, and Hale recommended I take a philosophy class to bolster my law school application.

"I haven't," he said. "Want to study together?"

"Sure," I told him, standing up and heading into the living room. I turned on one of the lamps, preferring the dusky light to the bright overheads. Khaled must have been at the library, but I had no idea where the other three were. Gemma was probably in the theater. I made a mental note to keep in touch with Gemma and Ruby more. It would be good to know their whereabouts. John often disappeared around this time of day, either to the gym or the econ lounge. I made myself comfortable on the couch and bit into a fresh apple from the local orchard. The sour juice plucked at my tongue.

Max sat down in one of the love seats across from me with his notebook.

"Ready?" he said.

"Yup."

I was relieved to see some color back in his cheeks, his voice returning to its low, steady cadence.

"You know," I said, "I eventually stood up for myself, with that girl. If you have a problem, like the anxiety, the panic attacks . . . you can change it."

"Thanks, Malin," Max said, looking surprised. A flash of confidence swept his demeanor.

It made me powerful, being able to fix Max. There was one more thing I needed to do for him, before he was fully fixed. But it would have to wait until the morning.

► ► ►

THE CAMPUS HEALTH center was a joke. I think most of the time they handed students packets of ibuprofen for any pain they were experiencing, and then sent them on their merry way. A guy in my literature class suffered through appendicitis for three days before a nurse realized he should be sent to the hospital.

The mental health department, however, was more than efficient. A student had committed suicide a few years back, and the administration was on high alert.

My breath unfurled in the morning fog as I strolled down the path, a kick in my step. Before I entered the building, I slackened my shoulders and steadied my expression. I rubbed my eyes a little, smudging the mascara. My boots were damp with dew as I pulled open the door.

At the front desk, I was greeted by a woman, probably in her forties. Her eyes were sleepy and heavy, a steaming cup of coffee next to her mouse pad.

"Hello there," she said through a yawn. "Flu?"

"Um, no," I said, sniffling, eyes watering. "I was wondering if I could talk to someone?"

"To one of the psychologists?" she asked, glancing up at me, her hand already maneuvering the mouse on the screen.

"Yes, please," I whispered.

"Okay, hon, let me see when the next available appointment is." Her finger clicked heavily, with purpose. "Could you do—"

I cut her off. "I think I need to see someone now." I widened my eyes, illustrating the panic in them.

She paused, her finger hovering, scanning my face. "Is this an emergency?"

I nodded.

You would have thought I told her I was carrying a bomb by the way she dialed the phone and talked to someone on the other end. Her tone hurried, hushed.

"Come with me, dear," she said, standing up. "You're lucky; he's in early."

Oh, goody.

The nurse led me into a room that looked more like a living room than a doctor's office. There was art on the walls, and it was decorated with soothing colors and furniture. I sat on one of the oversized chairs and waited. I adjusted my posture to look weak, vulnerable. I closed my eyes and thought of Levi, Bo.

There were some whispers in the hallway, and the door swung open.

"Hello, Malin, is it? I'm Dr. Vonn." He had a kind smile.

"Hi," I squeaked. I spoke so softly I could barely hear myself.

"How are we doing?" he asked, sitting in one of the other chairs. He had a clipboard in his lap with a blank sheet of paper.

I didn't know why he said "we." It irked me, but I pushed the annoyance aside. I started sniffling and forced a few fat tears to roll down my cheeks. I took a sharp breath for effect.

"I'm sorry," I said.

"Oh, don't apologize, please. Here," he said and got up to hand me some tissues.

"Thanks," I whispered, wiping away the mascara streaks and snot.

"Why don't we start by telling me what's going on, why you've come in today," he said, encouraging.

"Well," I started. Paused for a few deep breaths. "I'm an only child. I love my parents. But I feel a lot of pressure . . . to get good grades, and stuff."

"Yes, pressure can cause us to feel many bad things." He started writing on his notepad. "What are your parents' names?"

"Celia and George."

I didn't think we would be going over this many details. I checked the time: seven thirty A.M. I needed to get to class within twenty minutes. I would need to move quickly.

"They're not the problem," I said. It came out too sharp so I adjusted.

"Oh?" he said. I couldn't tell if he had noticed my urgency.

I continued, "Well, I had a brother. I think it's about him." More tears.

"What happened to your brother?"

"He died when I was eight, right in front of me," I said.

"That must have been really hard," he said.

"Yeah," I said. I slowed down my voice, worried I was talking too fast. "It changed everything. Sometimes I wonder what my life would be like if he was still alive, you know, if things were different."

I was surprised the words tumbled out of my mouth, and I stopped myself before saying anything else.

"What do you mean by that?" he asked.

Shit.

"Oh. I don't know. My parents have never been the same since he died."

I picked at the balled-up tissue in my hand. Dr. Vonn was quiet, waiting for me to speak. Patient. A good quality in a therapist.

"Anyways," I said, steering the conversation away. "I've been having panic attacks. They're controlling my life. Sometimes they come out of nowhere. I feel like I've tried everything—meditating, eating right, exercising . . ."

Dr. Vonn looked like he wanted to talk more about my family. I hoped he would let it go. I glanced at his wedding ring. He looked like a dad, scruffy beard, plaid button-up, gentle, crinkled eyes. I wondered how many kids he had. If he was good to them.

"Panic attacks can be very scary," he empathized. "Can you describe them for me? How long do they last?"

I took a deep breath, tucked a strand of hair behind my ear. "Okay, sure." I pictured Max on the floor, his tensed body and that scared, wild look in his eyes. "It's like my whole body freezes up. My hands go numb, and I feel like I can't breathe, and I get scared I'm going to die. Sometimes I think I'm going to throw up."

I thought of Levi, and my heart ticked up a beat.

"And then my heart beats really fast, and I start to see black. Black blotchy stars."

Levi standing in the yard, staring at me. The baby bird at his feet. I pressed my thumb along the pressure point in my other hand.

"They last about twenty minutes sometimes. I usually have to go for a run to get out of it. It's when I'm in class that's the worst, because I'm just stuck there, and I can't focus. My professor starts to sound underwater."

I looked up at Dr. Vonn with teary eyes. He thought for a moment.

"Running is a great distraction," he started. "But I see what you're saying. We can't have you running out of class all the time, can we?"

I felt myself give a small smile.

He leaned back in his chair, hooking the pen into his clipboard, which he placed on the desk.

"We can do cognitive behavior therapy," he said.

"What is that?" I asked. "I'll try anything."

"Well, it'll retrain your brain, and should help you feel better. You can learn to control the anxiety."

"Okay, that sounds good, I could at least try it," I said.

I balled the tissue up tighter, squeezing it in my hand.

"I'm just so scared all the time," I said. "I know I'm going to be sitting in class later today, and I will start to panic. The adrenaline is the worst part. What do I do then?"

"Well . . ." He paused. I stared him down. *Come on, come on.* "Have you considered medication?"

Finally.

"I don't know," I said. "I don't want to have to use drugs. I heard it can have side effects and mess up your personality."

Dr. Vonn nodded, his eyes sympathetic. "I understand your concerns. Usually when someone describes the symptoms you've shared with me, I like to get a sense of their thoughts on it. And just so you know, the medication would not affect your personality."

I looked down, took a deep breath.

"Well, maybe," I said slowly. "If you think it would help."

"It's not a life sentence," he added. "We can discuss it as you continue treatment. I think there would be benefits in your case."

"Maybe if it's a backup, like a security blanket, maybe it will make me feel better to have it, just in case."

"Of course. I think that sounds like a good idea," he said. He made some notes on his computer and then faced me again. "Let's talk a little about CBT, and what our goals will be. We can also discuss your family, if you think that would help."

I listened to him talk about training my thoughts, and zoned out, watching students walk to class. There was no way I was going to train my thoughts. They were how I survived.

I heard the clock ticking on the wall and gave in, realizing I would be late to class. It would be worth it.

At the end of our session, Dr. Vonn wrote out a prescription. "I'll give this to you, and you can use it if you need to."

When he handed it to me, I folded it up and held it with the tissue.

"Should we schedule a time for your next appointment?" he asked.

"Um," I said, searching for an excuse, rummaging through my

bag. "Shoot. Is it okay if I call later today? I need to check my planner. I'm so stupid, I forgot it in my room." I made it look like I was going to cry again.

"Yes, of course," he said. "Not to worry. And please come in anytime if you need to talk to someone—anytime, there is always someone here."

I paused for a moment, considering his words. A very small part of me wanted to tell him everything.

I thought about my father, my family. No, he couldn't fix me. I couldn't tell him what happened. That was not an option.

"Thank you," I said, standing up.

"We'll see you soon."

No, you won't. If they called to follow up, I'd say I was doing great, that I had tried one of the pills and it made me feel much better, thank you very much.

SENIOR YEAR WAS almost halfway over. I could help Max feel better, take the burden of his anxiety away. It was so simple. Drugs would make him normal.

I picked up the prescription after class and carried it home in a white paper bag. After making sure the house was empty, I put one pill on the counter, wrapped it in a paper towel and crushed it with a hammer. I scrubbed clean two of the coffee-encrusted travel mugs in the sink and filled them with hot chocolate. One for me. One for Max. I mixed the white powder into his mug, watching it dissolve, and made sure to carry his in my right hand as I made my way to Contemporary Moral Disputes.

CHAPTER THIRTY-TWO

SENIOR YEAR

The night before we were supposed to go to Portland, I ended up alone with John.

Avoiding him had become second nature. I sat farthest away from him in the dining hall and always waited for him to be distracted before I left a room or party. I locked the door to my room at night. I didn't expect to see him in the middle of campus in the early hours of a Thursday morning.

I had lost track of time in Hale's office. We were both working, barely talking. He was focused on a paper, and I had been studying for a test. I went in right after dinner and found myself yawning around one A.M., long past the time he had stretched, touched my shoulder, and said he was heading out.

Campus was deserted, everyone tucked away inside their warm dorms and houses. It was a weekday; nobody was out tonight. I looked up at the stars blazed across the sky.

"Fancy seeing you here," a voice called out to my right.

I stopped in my tracks and peered into the dark. I saw Levi in the shadows and felt my breath catch in my chest. *No.* He was dead. He died, I reminded myself.

John descended the stairs of one of the freshman dorms and came into the light of the lamppost. I didn't know what he was doing out so late, and by himself, especially since I knew Ruby went to bed hours ago.

"Where are you coming from?" I asked.

"You know." He grinned. "Here and there."

He didn't care about anything except himself. He was reckless, and I didn't want to get stuck in his wake. I kept walking, leaving him behind.

"Where are *you* coming from?" he asked.

I picked up my pace, my boots scraping against the brick pathway.

"You know, we live in the same house," he said. "It will be awkward if you don't walk with me."

I slowed my pace with gritted teeth.

He looked behind me, toward the English department.

"Oh, right," he said. "I heard about your little crush."

Ruby must have told him. I told her to keep it a secret. I didn't respond and tightened my grip on my bag.

"You know," John continued, "I'm surprised you would do that to Ruby."

And she had told him about her father. She told him and not me.

"She's fine with it," I said.

John smirked. "She didn't tell you, did she? About what happened this summer? With her dad? I guess she doesn't tell you everything."

I had no idea what he was talking about.

He clapped me on the back. "Oh, don't freak out. She still worships you."

He sidled up closer to me, and I felt my bones brace. "Why do you hate me so much?" he asked.

"I don't," I said, trying to walk faster. We turned the corner of our street.

"You never talk to me, or even look at me. You talk to Max. I don't really get that, but if it's what you're into . . ."

I didn't say anything.

"Seriously, though, what did I do to you?" he said, relentless. "I'm sorry, for whatever I did."

He was so loose with his apologies. It only made me dislike him more.

"I don't hate you," I said again.

"Maybe it's because I have you all figured out, and it makes you jumpy."

He shouted *jumpy* into my ear and laughed, trying to be funny. I kept walking, unaffected by his attempts to throw me off guard.

"Yes," I said as we finally reached the house. "That must be it. You know me so well, and I'm all freaked out by it, poor me, I can't stand it."

He looked put out, as if I was ruining some game he was trying to play.

"Jesus, you're always such a buzzkill," he said. He crossed his arms over his chest, resolute in his judgment.

Once we were inside the dark hall, I started up the stairs, leaving him behind in the entryway.

"You should be grateful," he called out, "that I never told anyone about your grandfather, or whoever it was. The one that killed all those people."

I stared at John, Levi's face blending with his. Bo in my arms. My mother's limp hand, clasped with Levi's. The tears that stung my cheeks in the driveway that day, the pain I had suffered. I needed Levi's story to stay a secret. His truth would destroy what I had worked so hard for, exhausting myself pretending all these years. John was not going to fuck everything up. There was only one way to get him off my back.

"I don't care if you tell anyone." I turned around. "Go ahead, tell the whole campus."

I could bluff, but there needed to be more. I knew what I had to do.

John let out a breath of frustration. "Why don't you like me? Just tell me why."

I stopped on the stairs, looking down at him. I wanted to tell him the truth. There were so many things I wanted to say to him about why I didn't like him, but I knew better than that. I knew I needed to be patient.

I tried to relax the muscles on my face, so my next words would be believable. "You know why," I said softly, trying to look sad, sympathetic. "I can't like you because of Ruby; it's not right."

I knew the melodramatic statement would be enough to satiate his ego. He didn't say anything, but I could tell he was pleased with my answer.

"Can I go now? I need to be alone," I said, still trying to sound sad and pathetic.

"You know, we can still be friends," he called out.

There was no fucking way I would ever be his friend. I gave him a long, drawn-out look, and then continued up the stairs and made my way to my room where I locked the door and sat in the reassuring silence.

It was time to break into Ruby's room. Tomorrow. It had to be tomorrow.

► ► ►

PORTLAND WELCOMED US with gale-force winds and sheets of rain. We arrived in a yellow school bus, all of us pouring out onto the streets of the big city, delighted for a night out of Edleton. I timed the drive on the way in, about thirty-five minutes.

Gemma, Ruby, and I clung to one another as the rain pelted us in the face. It was coming down sideways, somehow working its way up my skirt and in between my legs. We were drenched by the time we got to the bar.

"Yuck," Gemma whined. "How's my mascara? Still there?"

Ruby inspected her face. "Yes, mine?"

Gemma ran her thumb under Ruby's eyes. "All good."

The three of us had decided we would do a girls' dinner first, and then meet up with everyone else afterward. It seemed as though we were too late; everyone was already loud and sloppy. Gemma and Ruby were buzzed, but nothing compared to what we were walking into. We were pushed inside the hot bar, the music blaring in our ears, walls covered with New England sports paraphernalia. The room opened up to a hall filled with foosball and pool tables.

"Oh crap. Not games," Gemma started. "I loathe games. Do we have to?"

"Gems, yes," Ruby said, "Our whole class is here."

The three of us surveyed our classmates screeching and laughing in their contented drunkenness. I spotted Shannon with her group of friends, her arms around her boyfriend's neck, nuzzling into his shirt collar. I hadn't spoken much to her since freshman year, only in a few classes we shared. I was relieved she seemed happy, finally having found a place to belong.

"Do you see the guys?" Ruby asked, scanning the crowd. She was holding her clutch tight against her chest, her leather jacket slick with rain.

"Over there," Gemma shouted, and we made our way over to Khaled and John, who were stacking a life-sized Jenga tower with a few of the guys from the soccer team.

We passed a group of pre-med students playing pool, and I spotted Max laughing with two guys and a girl. I think he had hooked up with her one year. Sophomore? Junior? I didn't know, I couldn't keep up with the many hookups. They all blurred together.

I watched Ruby's eyes trail toward Max, her face dissolving into some sort of regret. Max watched her, too, but he didn't leave his post. I looked at him as we passed, and he gave me a small wave.

Gemma shouted at the two of us. "Do you think Max will hook up with that chick again?"

Ruby was quiet.

"Who cares?" I said. "Let's go."

"You're no fun," Gemma replied.

"So I've heard," I said.

"Hey, guys," John said as we approached, pulling Ruby in for a kiss. He wrapped his arm around her tiny waist, telling her she looked beautiful. His face was sweaty and flushed, the heat radiating off his damp skin.

"Can you grab me a drink?" Ruby asked him, her words loose and loud. She pawed at his beer.

John hesitated, pulling the glass back. "I think you've had enough, babe."

Ruby looked at me; I was the only one paying attention. I forced a smile and turned my gaze to Gemma and Khaled.

"Did you get goodies for me?" Gemma asked Khaled, clearly over her disappointment in the choice of bar.

"I did," Khaled said, looking around us. When he decided there was no threat, he pulled out a small plastic bag filled with white powder. I watched their faces light up and tried to look excited.

"I fucking love you," Gemma said, planting a wet kiss on Khaled's mouth. They did that sometimes, and I still found it strange.

Khaled bent his head down and opened the packet. We formed a tight semicircle around him to block any bartenders' potential view. The bar was so packed though; there was no way he would get caught.

"Ladies first," he said, handing the packet to Gemma.

Gemma poked a pinky finger in the bag and brought it to her mouth first, as if she was tasting it. I knew nothing about drugs. I never felt compelled to use them.

"Wait a sec," she said. She squinted her eyes, focused, and then started laughing. "Oh my God, oh my God, you are such an idiot."

Gemma dissolved into laughter as Khaled grabbed the packet and tasted the powder. We all watched.

"Shit," he said, taking a step back. "It's powdered sugar."

I breathed a sigh of relief. We played Jenga until everyone was slurring their words, swaying, and hanging off one another. Ruby managed to procure some tequila. She and Gemma threw shots back, laughing and stumbling together, falling into the Jenga, scattering the wood blocks across the floor.

I spotted Ruby's clutch under her chair. Nobody even noticed me leave.

► ► ►

WHEN I WAS outside the bar, I sprinted a few blocks away to an aw-ning, sheltering myself from the rain. I leaned against the brick wall and pulled out my phone. I took a deep breath.

The phone rang twice before Hale picked up.

"Malin?"

"Yeah, um," I said, saying the words I had already planned out, "hi."

"Are you okay?"

"Yeah. Well. I don't know."

"What's going on?"

I liked how worried he sounded.

"I'm at that thing, for seniors. In Portland." I felt the wind at my back, rain soaking through my jacket. "I'm sorry to ask this, but is there any way you could come pick me up?"

He didn't hesitate; I knew he wouldn't.

"Where are you?" I heard the jingle of keys and a shutting door.

I craned my neck to read the street signs. "Corner of Fore and Franklin."

"Give me thirty," he said.

"Okay," I replied. "Thank you."

"Call back if you need anything."

I hung up the phone and leaned against the brick. I knew I couldn't take the bus back, not with everyone else. I had to get to the house before they did. It was ten forty-five P.M. The school buses were scheduled to leave Portland at midnight. I would have ample time to get into Ruby's room.

I sat down on the stoop, my skirt instantly soaked.

Ruby's clutch smelled of leather, expensive. I unhooked the clasp and rooted around, finding the key to her room. I felt something heavy at the bottom of the bag, rectangular and hard. Her phone. It buzzed in my hand. Ruby didn't have a password on her phone. Typ-ical of her, to lock her room but not her phone.

A message popped up on the screen.

Where are you?

Another.

I thought we were going to talk tonight?

I miss you.

I looked at the sender. Max.

I opened the text thread between Max and Ruby. My thumb tried to scroll upward, but the only texts were from Max, tonight. She must have deleted the others, if there were any.

Another buzz.

Ruby. Please.

What was going on? I didn't know they had been texting, but I guess it made sense. They had been acting shady with their phones for a while now. I hated that I hadn't picked up on it.

There were only those three messages, and then the buzzing stopped. I remembered seeing Ruby hide her phone from me when I asked who she was texting after the senior cocktail party. And Max typing out texts, facing the screen away from me in class. Always making sure I didn't see.

Two figures made their way down the street, their arms wrapped around each other. I looked down, focused on the phone, not even thinking they could be Hawthorne students.

After I put the phone back in Ruby's bag, I looked up to find John staring at me, both of us caught, a girl from the lacrosse team hanging off his shoulder.

"Where's Ruby?" I asked him. The girl he was with began retching in a bush.

"I thought she was with you," he said, taking a few steps toward me. I jumped up, out of the confined space of the stoop.

"What are you doing out here?" John asked, skeptical, prying. His hand reached for my arm, his eyes on Ruby's clutch. I watched in slow motion as he made contact with my jacket.

I jerked back. "Don't fucking touch me," I said. My real voice.

He recoiled, surprised by my aggressive reflex. "Jesus, chill out, M," he said.

I took a breath, composing myself. I saw John looking at Ruby's clutch, thoughts forming in his mind.

"What are you doing with that?" he asked.

"I found it on the floor when I left the bar, holding on to it for her."

He narrowed his eyes. He didn't believe me.

"Well, give it to me. I'll take it to her."

I eyed the girl behind him, relieved. "I think you're a little busy, don't you?"

I had won this time, but only by a small margin.

John lowered his eyes, taking a step closer to me. I could feel his breath on my face, smell the alcohol on his lips. "I'll keep your secret if you keep mine."

Hale's truck came around the corner and splashed toward us, bobbing back and forth on the cobblestones. I stepped off the sidewalk, holding up my hand to flag him down. I didn't say anything to John as I yanked on the slick door handle and climbed inside.

I looked over at Hale. "Let's go. Please."

► ► ►

"THAT KID'S A troublemaker, huh?" Hale said, eyeing John in his rearview mirror.

I didn't say anything. I used my sleeve to wipe the rain off my face. I held tight to Ruby's clutch, my nails clawing the soft leather.

We sat in silence for a few minutes, listening to the radio.

"Can I ask why I'm picking you up?" he asked.

"I wasn't feeling it," I said. I watched the windshield wipers, tick, tick, tick. Once we were on 95, the trees disappeared into a dark smudge.

His eyebrows furrowed. Deep in thought, protective.

"Did something happen?" he asked.

"I wanted to get out of there, so I called you."

He looked over at me and then back at the road. "I'm glad you did."

The car jostled with the wind as we made our way north. Ruby's clutch sat against my foot, the phone quiet. The texts from Max had stopped.

"Tell me something," I said, eager to think about anything else.

"About what?" he asked.

"Um. About your sisters. How are they doing?"

He smiled. "Well, Corey just got engaged. And Lauren went back to work actually. She's at an architecture firm in the city. They're both happy."

I didn't say anything. He must have one of those families that clicks, the gears grinding in an ever-present happy melody. Their problems probably involved Mom worrying too much, or Dad retiring and needing a hobby.

Hale's smile faded. "Do you miss your brother?" he asked.

"I don't know. It was so long ago, I barely remember him," I said, lying.

Hale was quiet. He focused on the road.

"It was my fault," I said. "That he died."

I had never said the words out loud. I felt like a heavy piece of me was floating away, and I watched it fade. I wanted to remove that part of me, forget it forever. Maybe Hale could box it up and throw it away for me.

"One minute he was there with me, and he was alive, and the next, he was gone."

"You can't blame yourself," Hale finally said. "You were only a kid."

Only a kid. I had heard that phrase so many times from my parents, about Levi. Their arguments got more and more heated as Levi caused more pain and destruction. My mother pleading with my father not to send him away to get help. *He's only a kid.*

"It's no excuse," I replied.

After the accident, nobody asked me what happened. It was an accident, they said. I couldn't remember much, everything was blurry, except his face, his eyes wide, more out of shock than fear. Levi was afraid of nothing, not even death.

"Sometimes I think his death broke me," I said.

"Death does that to people," he said. "You don't have to fight it."

We sat in silence the rest of the way, the rain streaking the windows, cocooning us in our own thoughts.

▶ ▶ ▶

WE PARKED AT the bottom of the hill. I looked up at the house. I needed to go inside, to unlock Ruby's door and find her diary, but I didn't want to leave the car.

Hale looked at me. He was so good. I didn't want to damage him, but I didn't want to be away from him, either. I could at least try this life. I could try to be someone else. Maybe it would be okay.

"Malin," he began, his voice barely a whisper. A warning tone, but it was so watered down, I could barely hear it. "Whatever it is you're trying to figure out right now, let it go. It'll be okay."

I wondered what he saw, looking at me. Damp clothes, wet, un-kempt hair. Green eyes. The same eyes I shared with Levi.

Hale was closer than ever to seeing the real me. After what I had told him, he was almost there. If I told him the truth, would he still look at me like that?

Rain drummed on the roof of the truck, the windshield wipers rhythmic in my ears. *Now, now, now,* they whispered.

I put a hand on his. It was the second time in three years we had touched each other like this. Intentionally. The first time at the party freshman year, hands clasped in the crowded room. I felt energy there, existing between our hands. And then I leaned in, and my lips were on his, soft, warm, and our hands pulled at our clothes, and I scrambled on top of him so that we were skin to skin, and it was a rush, a thrill, urgent. And it was right.

THE RAIN STOPPED as I walked on rivers up to the dark house. I turned before I stepped inside, Hale watching from the truck, one hand on the steering wheel. He flipped the lights on, twice, as if to say goodbye. I knew he wouldn't leave until I was inside, so I opened the door and stood in the entryway for a long time, before I remembered why I was holding Ruby's clutch, and why I was here all alone.

CHAPTER THIRTY-THREE

SENIOR YEAR

After I unlocked Ruby's door, I hitched it open with a shoe. I took her clutch out into the woods behind our house and buried it under a pile of wet leaves.

Ruby's room was organized and neat, except for the dank soccer cleats hanging on the back of the door, the grass still damp from morning practice. I wrinkled my nose, making my way over to her desk where I opened the drawer and pulled out her diary. It was always in the same place. Ruby was a creature of habit.

I knew reading her diary was wrong. It was a fucked up, creepy secret of mine. I knew if she found out she'd call me a freak. She'd never talk to me again.

I didn't have time to sift through the bullshit. I wasn't a mind reader. This was what made me such a good friend to her. She would have been grateful, if she knew how helpful it was. I flipped to the most recent entry, from last night, and read.

November 10

John got angry again tonight (thank God Malin was at the library, she would have heard everything, and then what?). He stormed out afterward, and who knows where he is now . . . I can't even think about it. I hope he doesn't drink. Or do anything stupid. I worry about him when he's in moods like this. It's probably because he is stressed out about graduation and next year and everything. I am being supportive, but it's hard because I know what I want. Although now, I'm reconsidering Scotland. I think John needs me here on the East Coast. I can spend the summer with him on the Vineyard, and we can figure this out together. I literally feel like my brain is melting I am so exhausted. Fighting is so tiring. This is how it started tonight: my advisor gave me this amazing print of White Sands at sunset. It is really stunning. The photographer is incredible—the way he captured all the white and pink and orange. I had been lusting after it for months; it was so sweet of Anita to give it to me. I even talked about it to John like a MILLION times. So I put it on my desk for safekeeping until I could hang it up. But when I got home last night I saw that John had left a beer on top of it. A SWEATY beer. It left a ring. The print is completely ruined. I am so mad. Even more mad that he didn't seem to feel bad about it at all. He doesn't understand how to take care of things. Probably because he can BUY a new one if it gets ruined or breaks. How can you learn to take care of things when you are super rich and it doesn't matter if they break? When I asked him why he did that, he said it was my fault for leaving expensive things out and that I should be more careful. I told him that was absurd, since it was clearly his fault. But then he told me to fuck off. Because that is super helpful in an argument . . . And why the hell was it even an argument? Shouldn't he have apologized for ruining the print? He said if I didn't stop acting like such a complainer that he was going to cancel our trip to New York over winter break. So then I started crying. I asked him not to yell or cancel the trip (we've been looking forward to it for sooooo long). I literally got on the floor onto my knees and I begged. He looked at me like I was a piece of trash and left the room.

There has to be a way for me to fix it. I want to be a better girlfriend; maybe if I'm better, this won't happen. Then again, there is that other part of me, that wants him to hurt the way I hurt. I want him to feel real pain. Isn't that terrible of me? I've never felt that way about anybody before. Wanting to inflict pain. Maybe if he understood how terrible it is, he would stop.

Sometimes I wonder where the line is. Between right and wrong in a relationship. How much does one person put up with? I'm sure most people would not put up with him. Sure, he could get another girlfriend in a second—he is rich, popular, handsome, charming—but would THEY stay? Probably not. I always stay; I always end up apologizing. Sometimes I don't even know what for. I laughed the other day, in the middle of one of our fights, because I couldn't even remember what I was apologizing for. That just made John more angry, so I shut up. But it's still funny, now that I'm thinking about it again. Anyways, I stop caring about these things after a day, so it doesn't bother me too much. Right? I don't think it bothers me. I'm not sure. I'm not sure of anything anymore, to be honest. There's that voice in the back of my mind . . . What if he does something worse next time? What if he hurts me? He wouldn't. Would he? I honestly don't know the answer to that question.

On top of all that . . . there is the other thing. I can't even write it down, that's how pathetic I have become. And then I end up thinking about home. It makes me sick to my stomach.

Sometimes I wish I could talk to someone about all this. But how do you say: "Hey, my boyfriend is an asshole to me, but I'm staying with him anyways"? It doesn't exactly roll off the tongue.

I think the worst part is that I used to be so strong. I used to be happy and fun. Sometimes I'm so tired. I know I come off as a bitch. My whole face hurts from smiling. I'll be in the middle of a conversation and I'll think, Wouldn't it be nice to frown right now? I'm so tired of pretending. I feel like I'm the only one who has to fight so hard to be normal. It makes me feel so alone. And tired. Did I mention how tired I am? Ha.

I need to stay positive. Every couple goes through a tough time. John is stressed, that's all. It will seriously be fine!! Couples have problems. It's normal. I need to stop being so bitchy and get over it.

I skimmed back, electrified by having the diary in my hands again. I flipped to last spring. Nothing. How could there be nothing? That was when she fought with Max, or whatever happened. But there was a gap between winter and summer. Her updates were short and sporadic.

Then, finally, I spotted Max's name on July 5.

Max texted me last night. It was so out of the blue. John and I were at a bonfire on the beach. I didn't think I'd hear from him all summer, especially since he's in Haiti, but there was his name on my phone. I felt excited at first, so happy. But John saw it, and the look on his face . . . He threw the phone into the ocean. Today he apologized, but he says it's for the best, since he will buy me a new one, and it will be better than the old one.

John said I can't talk to Max anymore. He said it's not good for our relationship, that if I want us to stay together, I can't be friends with Max. It hurts my chest to think of not talking to Max when we get back to school, but I love John. I want to be with John. It's for the best. Right?

Is that what John was talking about? Something had happened last summer, was this it? I didn't understand what it had to do with Ruby and her dad. I skimmed a few more pages, my fingers searching the words, but there was nothing.

I let the diary shut in my hand, the pages heavy with Ruby's thoughts. I recalled this morning. The six of us at our table. My coffee and bowl of oatmeal with berries, working on my thesis. Max was to my right, reading something, I don't remember. Gemma and Khaled were complaining about how the dining hall had stopped ordering Lucky Charms, and now the cereal options were too healthy, not sugary enough for them.

Ruby and John.

I scoured my memory, searching for inconsistencies. A worried glance, unease, disappointment, fear. But there was none of that. Across from me, acting normal. His arm slung across the back of her chair, her upper body leaned in toward him. Reading the newspaper together, smiling softly at the cartoons. Her hair wet from showering after practice, his sweater rolled at the sleeves. Her head resting so often against his shoulder, her eyes warm with adoration.

Hale's voice. The poem.

Will we make others' lives worse or better? If someone is suffering, will we ease their pain or ignore it?

CHAPTER THIRTY-FOUR

SENIOR YEAR

I watched Ruby and John. Calculating his movements, reading her face. Trying to understand why they were even together. I became their shadow. I listened through the wall when she thought I wasn't there. The arguments got worse, always ending in John calling her names, Ruby crying, her tears muffled on the bed. I tried to distract myself with work, with class.

John and I did a good job of avoiding each other after Portland. Our brief eye contact was threatening. We were playing a dangerous game. I knew he was calculating his risks, wondering what my next move would be. I wondered if he would tell the others about my great-grandfather, but I also knew John didn't want me to get any more attention. He wanted them, and Ruby, all to himself. Besides, I think he liked knowing something about me that nobody else knew. It made him feel powerful.

Ruby never found her clutch. She had ended up with John at the end of the night, of course. I watched her standing in the hall the next morning, a locksmith getting her into her room. She had been chewing her lip, wearing a pair of John's sweats and a T-shirt, a worried look on her face. At lunch, she asked us if we had seen her clutch, did she leave it at the bar? Did she drop it on the street? Or maybe it was in her room? John looked at me, his mouth cocked to one side, eyes excited. But he said nothing. We each held tight to our end of the rope, hoping the other would become weak and let go. He should have known better than to challenge me.

I spent more time with Hale, at his house, inside instead of outside. I explored his kitchen, living room, bedroom. Read the stacks of books on the floor, ate takeout with him on the couch, slept with him in his bed. I liked his lightness, the way he laughed at everything, how he was content and settled. He talked about the future sometimes. Our future. How he could move with me to Boston, if that was where I would go to law school. I was waiting for the right moment to tell him that I wanted to stay in Edleton; I wanted to do the graduate program while he became a full-time professor. I wanted to live in that house with him and read and write together. I wanted to be normal with him. I had a chance. I was going to take it.

He said he felt more himself with me than anyone else. There were so many things I should have told him, but didn't.

I liked that it was our secret. I didn't have to talk to anyone about Hale. I wanted it to stay private, ours.

In my spare time, I tried to figure out what to do about Ruby.

I went for hour-long runs to think, the rhythm of the pavement a relief. No one else seemed to know about the abuse. I pressed Gemma and Khaled with seemingly odd questions.

John and Ruby are cute, right?

Do you think John and Ruby will get engaged after we graduate?

Ruby looks happy, right?

They responded to my questions with shrugs and vague answers. Not caring, not noticing.

Ruby grew quiet. Attached to nothing. Floating through the semester. The farther up she got, the more my concern grew. I tried to pull her back down. It felt like scrambling up a cliff, but I couldn't get ahold of anything and by winter break, our friendship was dull, our conversations tired and worn. I didn't know what to say, which left me with silence. It bothered her, the awkwardness I had created.

I knew it was wrong. Its wrongness stung my bones. He wasn't physically hitting her, at least, not yet. But it was almost crueler—the way he used his words to bend her will, manipulate her, beat her into submission. He was breaking her.

Max knew something was off, but we didn't talk about it. We

never admitted to knowing the same thing. He was quiet when I asked my questions.

I knew he couldn't help, not if he wanted to. Nobody was as strong as me, I was the only one who could handle carrying this around.

I DREAMED I was a wolf. I wandered the woods surrounding Hawthorne. I fed off basic instincts. I was at my best when I was alone. It was about my needs, and my needs only. Survival.

But then there was Hale, saying my name. "Malin."

I looked up at him, through my wolf eyes.

"I've been saying your name," he said.

"I didn't hear you," I said.

"What's going on?"

"I'm reading."

"Reading what?"

I looked down, but my hands were gnarled and matted, transformed into paws. *White Fang* was on the ground in front of me.

"Have you studied for the final?" he asked.

"Yes."

"Did you reread the Tsvetaeva poem? It's on the exam."

"No."

"Do you remember what it's about?"

"Yes."

"What are you going to do?"

He got down and crouched in front of me. I liked him there. I wanted him there. I pressed my head to his chest. He was so close, his face inches from my own. I watched his lips as he spoke, but nothing came out. His lips were moving but I couldn't hear him.

"What?" I asked. "I can't hear you."

He began to shout, but I still couldn't hear him. I shouted back, "I CAN'T HEAR YOU."

And then, as if the volume had been switched on, his voice screamed in my ear.

"WHAT ARE YOU GOING TO DO?"

. . .

ANOTHER DREAM.

At home. Sitting on the front lawn with Bo, running my fingers over his silky ears. He nuzzled into my palm, licking the base of my thumb.

I heard Ruby's voice, so I got up and looked around, but there was nobody. No neighbors, no cars driving past. I heard that stifled sob, the one she makes when I know she is burying her head in a pillow, and it sounded like it was coming from the tree by the driveway. I walked over to it, Bo at my feet. The tree was covered in cicada shells, their transparent casings littering the trunk. I moved closer, and the cries became louder. Ruby was inside the tree. Or was it my mother? I couldn't tell. I could hear both their voices, making excuses about something, but I couldn't make out the words. I pressed my ear to the rough bark. And then my feet glued to the grass, and I couldn't walk away. I was forced to stay, listening to their muffled voices. I looked down, but Bo was gone, and something cracked and bent inside me, and that's when the alarm clock went off.

And once it started, I couldn't stop it.

PART THREE

WE ALL
FALL DOWN

CHAPTER THIRTY-FIVE

TEXAS, 1997

Levi was being unusually nice that morning. He hadn't been nice for so long, and I was relieved to have my brother back. I was also skeptical, so I kept a watchful eye on him. We ate our waffles together, and when I asked my mother for syrup, Levi was the one who got up and retrieved it from the fridge. That is the detail I remember most from that morning. The sticky syrup on my fingers, and the sweetness caked in the corners of my mouth.

Mom rushed around; she was late. She was always late. She couldn't find her keys, and she muttered something under her breath as we ate in silence.

"Babies," Mom asked us, "have you seen my keys?"

"No, sorry," I replied.

Levi smiled at her sweetly and shook his head.

"More juice?" Levi asked me.

As he filled my cup, he gave a sly grin as if he had a secret to tell me. I was still mad at him for talking to our mother the way he did, for making her so upset, so I didn't ask him what it was even though I wanted to know what he was thinking.

"Well," my mother said, "I guess I'll call a cab."

She stood with her hands on her hips, surveying the countertops and kitchen table.

"Good idea," Levi said, getting up to wash his plate. He never did the dishes.

I spent the morning avoiding Levi. Bo and I swam in the pool while Lane sunned herself in a lawn chair.

Around noon, I retreated to the cool kitchen for a Popsicle. I opened the freezer and rooted around for my favorite flavor: strawberry. I sat on the floor with Bo as I pushed the frozen sugar to the opening in the plastic, careful not to sink my teeth in.

Levi appeared in the doorway. "Guess what I found?" he asked.

He had that grin on his face again. I didn't like it. I ignored him, but he didn't care. He held something up in my face. I looked at what he was holding in his hands. The silver key dangled from a miniature Eiffel Tower. We went to Paris last summer for a family trip, which was mostly spent making sure Levi was happy. He didn't like being away from home.

"Where'd you find those?" I asked.

"In the entryway," he said, throwing them onto the counter.

"But we never go in the entryway."

We always used the garage door. The entryway was in a weird part of the house, the formal part of the house that only guests entered and exited through.

"I dunno," he said. "But she'll be so glad when she hears I found them for her."

I lowered the Popsicle by my knee, and it started to drip onto the floor. I studied Levi—his deliberate movements and overwhelming sense of confidence. Something was wrong. He was too pleased with himself.

"You hid them, didn't you?" I asked.

Levi snapped his head in my direction. He always thought I was so dumb, never smart enough to keep up with him. Baby sister, always in his shadow.

"Finish your Popsicle," he said. His voice spiteful, off-kilter.

"I'm going to tell Mom," I said. "You made her late for work."

Bo nestled closer to my thigh, and I saw him eyeing the Popsicle in my other hand. His soft brown eyes kept darting back and forth between me and the Popsicle. I loved when the whites of his eyes showed, so innocent and sweet. I shot him a warning glance; dogs weren't supposed to have dessert. He sighed loudly and settled onto my knee, content with cozying up for a nap.

"If you tell her," Levi started.

"What? You'll tell on me?" I stared him down, unflinching from my post on the floor. "I didn't do anything wrong."

Levi turned red and for a minute I thought he was going to say more, but he stalked out of the room. I heard him run his hand along the wall, scratching the paint with his nails.

I WISH I had never said anything. It would have been better that way. He was always scheming his next attack. I should have known better. I should have known that he wouldn't let this go. But I missed the signs, and then it was too late.

CHAPTER THIRTY-SIX

Senior Day

I have a plan, and it's a good one. It took me a day over winter break to put the pieces together, figure out how I would make it work.

I stare at the blue paint encrusted in my nails as I listen to Max disappear down the staircase. Good. I will deal with him later.

Ruby and John are next door. I imagine John is sitting at her desk, leaning back in the chair. She is probably thinking about what she's going to say to him. About how she knows he was with Gemma in the shower, and how they have to break up. I wonder if we will still go to Last Chance. Maybe Ruby would prefer to stay home. That would be okay with me. I will help her get through this; she just has to break up with John.

Gemma was easy. She always is. I remembered Liam, how desperate she was to look wanted. All she needed was the suggestion that something was amiss between Ruby and John and she got sucked right in. She has always been obsessed with John. She hooked up with him before, I knew she would do it again if she was drunk enough. Encouraged enough.

Ruby is buried inside her shell, but she's still there. Maybe they are only pieces, but it's enough. There is no way she will stay with John after this. After he cheated on her. I knew she needed to see it, too. It couldn't be something she heard from one of us. She needed to witness his filth and feel the pain. My plan worked perfectly. She only had to see Gemma and John flirting, bonus points if they were hooking up, which they were. I needed to plant that seed of doubt in her mind.

She is strong enough to make the right decision. She will struggle at first, but I will help her, and she will be better. And if she needs to date someone, let it be Max. Max, who loves her the way she should be loved. And then our group will be healthy, whole. Without John, everything will be better.

I press my ear to the wall, and the voices become clear through the drywall. My cheek and face act like a seashell, canceling out the noise of the house. I hold my breath.

"Babe," John says. His voice on the rise. Warning. "What's up with you?"

"Nothing," Ruby says. She sounds strong. I am relieved.

"Fine," John says. "Well, you're acting kind of bitchy. I walk in here, excited to see you after this long day, after I saved Becca, and you won't even look at me. Don't tell me you are jealous."

John pauses; I feel his footsteps through the wall. He does not tread lightly.

Ruby's voice. "This is about you. Not me."

John is quiet. They are both quiet. I hear Ruby's laundry basket open. She cleans when she is nervous, when she doesn't know what to do with her hands.

"What did I do this time?" John again.

Ruby is quiet. I know she is deciding what to do. *Do the right thing.*

"I saw you with Gemma," she says.

Her words are clear, strong, confident. There is no he said–she said, as I planned. She saw it with her own eyes. There is no defense for John. He can't weasel his way out of this.

"So?" he asks, incredulous. "We were together all day, of course you saw me with Gemma."

"Are you denying that you hooked up with her?"

Silence.

Ruby again. "You're really trying to deny that you cheated on me with my friend? I saw you, with my own eyes."

"Clearly she's not that good of a friend."

"Stop trying to work around this," Ruby says. Steady. "I saw you. There is nothing you can say to manipulate the situation so don't even try."

I know that Ruby is trying to stay calm. She wants to cry and yell but she won't. Her latest diary entry told me so. *I can't let my emotions get the better of me, he only uses it against me later. I have to be the bigger person. It is the only way to win.*

John says something but I can't hear it because I shift positions and their words become slurred.

"Wait, what?" Ruby asks. Shocked and offended.

"Max."

"This isn't about him," Ruby says. "He has nothing to do with this."

They are quiet for a moment. And then I hear John say the word, "Slut."

John uses this tone for his nastiest remarks. I had heard it before, freshman year, after the officer pulled us aside, John's comments to Max.

"You're joking. You have to be joking," Ruby says. "This isn't about me and Max. This is about you; stop trying to blame me for something I didn't do."

"I saw him pull you out from the lake." I must have missed this, when I was still underwater. "You looked at each other like you wanted to fuck."

"You are pulling things out of thin air," Ruby says.

"I know you text him all the time," John says. "You go cry to him. Shit, you two probably cry together all the time, about what a hard world you live in. You poor thing. You better run to him right now."

John is breathing hard. He is caged. A wild animal without a hole to wriggle out of.

"How could you do this to us?" Ruby asks. Still strong. "And Gemma. How am I supposed to be friends with her now?"

"She fucking attacked me. I told her to get off, but she wouldn't. You know how desperate she is."

"So you didn't mean to press her up against a wall in a shower and suck on her neck? She forced you to do that all on her own? If she really, what were your words? *Attacked you?* You must have led her on. She wouldn't do that out of the blue."

John must be pacing because I can hear the walls rattling.

"I wouldn't have done anything if I hadn't seen you texting Max," he said.

"So this is my fault? If I wasn't such a slut, this would have never happened? I deserve you cheating on me? Is that what you are really trying to argue right now? What is wrong with you? Stop trying to make this about me! This is about you cheating on me with Gemma."

Her voice is high and shrill, violent. Screaming. She is breaking. This is his will. His nasty, puppet-master way. He breaks her, every time. She will never win.

"You need to chill out," he says. "You're acting crazy."

His voice so calm, regulated. A predator calculating his prey before he lunges.

"I'm crazy? I fucking saw you and you won't admit it and now you won't even apologize."

"Look at yourself, you're losing it. You're mental," he says.

I hear Ruby begin to cry, heaps of sobs. They rack her chest. Surges in a storm.

"And now you're crying," John continues. "See? I told you, you're nuts."

I hear something slam into the wall on the other side of me and back away for a moment. I hear scuffles. My ear is against the wall.

"You're trying to hit me?" John asks.

Ruby is still crying. The sounds from her body make me wince.

"You need to stop crying, Ruby. Stop crying. Stop crying."

Another item, it sounds like a book from the way it hits the floor, the pages fluttering back to their places.

"You think you can hurt me?" John says. I can tell he is in her face, because his voice is quiet. Ruby makes a noise like she is struggling. I am enraged, and I want to tear through the wall. But I don't. She can't know I'm listening. She can't know I have anything to do with this. She will break up with him. It has to happen. Now.

I hear his fist hit something soft, and then a gulping sound from Ruby. The sound someone makes when they are plunged in cold water.

Again.

This is a new sound that I hear through the wall. Something physical.

Everything is silent for a moment, and then I hear John talking again.

"Jesus, fuck, I'm sorry," he says. "Ruby, I'm sorry."

And then I hear the door open and close, John's footsteps down the stairs, and then silence.

THE LOSS OF precious life is not a part of my plan. Everyone is on edge, out of control. I am only focused on Ruby, and everything falls apart before I have time to put it back together again.

CHAPTER THIRTY-SEVEN

TEXAS, 1997

On the same day Levi hid the keys, I waited patiently for our mother to come home. When she finally did, I sat on her bed and watched her get undressed. She transformed into the version I knew her to be, taking off her earrings and rings as they clinked into the ceramic dish on her bureau. The consistency of her post-work routine was calming and precise.

"How was your day, baby girl?" she asked.

She untied her blue work pants, and they fell to the ground. I liked the way she said *baby girl*. She sang it, the two words unfurling with comfort and familiarity. When she said it, everything was good.

"It was okay," I said. "Bo and I swam and then I read a book."

"A whole book?" She was impressed. I liked making her happy. "Which one?"

"The babysitter club one," I replied.

My mother took off her shirt and threw it into the basket on the floor. There were clothes piled next to it, too, and I thought about how I was almost out of clean clothes. I made a note to ask my father how to use the washing machine. My mother was too distracted recently, focusing her energy on Levi. She didn't have time to take care of all of us.

"That's amazing," she said. "You're my amazing daughter, how lucky am I?"

"Pretty lucky," I said.

I heard Bo's dog tags chiming down the hall. He leapt on the bench at the end of the bed and then onto the duvet, where he settled on my knee.

"Not on the bed," my mother said, and he jumped down.

Bo looked at me, expectant. "Good boy, Bo," I told him. He panted, eager and content.

My mother looked out the window at the lawn and pool.

"Hot out there, huh?" she asked. She does this with the weather when she is really thinking about something else.

"How was your brother today?" my mother asked.

I felt her tense, so I looked down at the duvet, not wanting to make eye contact, not wanting to see her hurt. She pulled a gray T-shirt over her head and looped her hair back into a ponytail.

"It's okay, sweetie," she said. Her voice tried to be calm. "You can tell me."

I thought about telling her, and not telling her. I considered Levi's threat.

"I don't want to tell on him," I said.

My mother sat next to me on the bed, and the duvet wrinkled between us. I tried to smooth it out with my hand, desperate to make it perfect again.

"Levi is going through a hard time right now. If he's done something bad, it's better that I know about it, so we can help him. You want him to get better, right?"

"Yeah," I said. I was still staring at the bed.

She began to rub my back, my apprehension lessening. She and my father were the only people who could touch me and it didn't bother me.

I was quiet for a while, focusing on Bo's breathing, and then told her, "He hid your keys this morning."

She stopped rubbing my back and stared at the floor, a few strands of her hair falling around her cheeks.

"When I thought I lost them?" Her voice was steady, but I could make out a slight crack, somewhere deep inside her throat.

I nodded, and she hugged me.

"Thanks for telling me. I know that wasn't easy," she whispered.

"Levi will be all better soon. He's not himself right now. He's still your brother. We have to keep helping him, keep loving him, and he'll get better."

I decided not to tell her about his threat. If I told her about that, the crack might become bigger.

AFTER I WAS tucked in that night, my stuffed animals lined up in order of size at the bottom of my bed, I heard the door open. I lifted up onto my elbows and peered into the dark.

"You told Mom?" Levi asked, his voice low and quiet.

I said nothing.

After a moment he whispered, "Wrong move, baby girl."

CHAPTER THIRTY-EIGHT

Senior Day

I don't bother knocking on Ruby's door. I hold my hand up against the wall for a moment and listen inside.

Ruby is on her bed, in fetal position. From what I heard through the wall, it didn't sound like he hit her face. The sounds of the punches were muffled, and the way Ruby had sucked in breath made me think it was her stomach. I step across the room carefully, Tutu in a heap by the corner of her bed, wet and bedraggled.

I sit on the end of the bed. "Hey," I say, my voice barely above a whisper. Her sweatpants are pushed up around her calves. "You okay?"

Ruby's eyes are open but she is staring intently at a vintage poster of New York City. John got it for her sophomore year when they visited the city over the holidays. It was the first of many trips they took there, staying in lavish hotel rooms with views of the metallic landscape. I used to wonder what they talked about when they were alone.

"Can I do anything?" I ask. I want to say *let's go, you need help,* but the words are stuck in my throat. The reality so thinly veiled, as it always is with Ruby, I'm not sure if she's aware why I am there.

I hear a door shut downstairs. I wonder if we will still go to Last Chance. It seems so unimportant now, more than before.

Ruby gets up on an elbow and moves her body to stand. I go to help her but she shakes her head. She walks over to her desk and pulls out a hair straightener.

"What are you doing?" I ask.

"Getting ready." Her voice is regular, nonchalant.

"Should we get help?"

"Why?"

"Because John hit you, didn't he?"

She doesn't skip a beat before responding. "It was nothing."

Ruby holds the plug and lets the straightener unfurl to the ground, where it clatters against the wood floorboards. As she moves toward her closet, she winces and then clears her throat, not wanting me to hear her pain.

"What should I wear tonight?" she asks, but her voice feels far away. She opens her closet and pulls out two dresses—one black and beaded, the other structured and red. "They're so different. I can't decide."

"Ruby," I say. I think carefully about my words. "Is your stomach okay? I heard him hit you."

"I'm fine," she replies. "We have to be ready soon."

"Last Chance doesn't matter. You're hurt."

I don't understand why she is acting this way. I want her to snap out of it.

"Let it go," she says, warning.

Steam rises from the straightener as Ruby pulls her fingers through tangled knots.

"Okay, look," I say, pleading with her, "you can't date someone who hits you, and yells at you, and treats you the way he does. He cheated on you with Gemma, doesn't that upset you?"

She looks over at me, so calm. "You think I don't know he cheats?"

I am quiet.

She looks back at her reflection, catching my eye in the glass. "Every relationship is different."

This is not how I thought this would go.

"You don't get it." She keeps talking, her hair getting smoother with the iron. "He had a difficult childhood; he can't help it. His dad is fucked up and MIA. I mean, if anyone can understand that, it's me. Who knows where my mother is. So I get it."

I don't feel bad for John. He could use what he went through with his father to be a better person. It's not like Ruby is destructive. Well. She is, only toward herself.

"You don't have a mom, and you don't go around punching people. I don't think you can use his dad as an excuse. You're breaking up with him, right?" I ask.

She has to break up with him. I orchestrated this whole thing so she would end the relationship. We look at each other, our eyes clear and focused. She takes a second and then looks away.

"Ruby," I say. I am firm. "Ruby. No. You have to break up with him. His childhood is not an excuse. If anything, he should know that what he is doing is wrong. This is ridiculous; stand up for yourself."

"I can't break up with him." Her voice now stressed and muddled.

I walk over to her, shut off the straightener, and take it from her hands. I stand in front of her, so she can't avoid me.

"It's simple," I say. "You go downstairs, you tell him it's over, then you come back upstairs, and you get on with your life. I will help you."

"Everything is so black and white for you," she says, sitting back down on the bed. "You are so regimented. You follow a set of rules, what the rules are, exactly, I'm not sure, but not everyone else has to color in your lines. This isn't your life, M. This is my life."

"Why would you want to stay with him? He is terrible to you. And you know it, you have to know that."

Ruby sighs. She is tired and frustrated. She won't look me in the eye.

"Tell me. Explain it. You need to tell me everything," I say.

Ruby frowns. "Fine. Okay. I don't have money like you do. Or Gemma, or Khaled, or Max . . . or John. I am here on a scholarship. You know that, right?"

"Yeah." I don't understand what this has to do with John. "But your dad is a professor, that's a really good job. Anyways, nobody cares about that. The money stuff doesn't matter."

"That's exactly why you don't get it."

I am quiet.

She continues, "You don't need money. Your parents pay for everything, but I need money. So it matters."

She's right.

"I still don't understand why you have to be with John," I say.

Ruby is silent. Her nostrils flare, and her cheeks flush red. "My dad got fired."

"Oh," I say, not sure how to continue.

She considers something, then says, "I caught him . . . with one of his students when I was ten. I walked into his office and saw everything. And he knew I saw him, but he didn't say anything. I couldn't look at him for months. When I was in middle school, he received a 'warning' from the college. He didn't tell me why, but I heard everyone whispering at camp. Our town is so small. It was impossible to escape the rumors. I heard how he had been caught again, this time by another professor."

"Ruby, I'm sorry," I say. I can't imagine dealing with that with my own father. It makes me nauseous.

Ruby continues, "It's not like the warning did anything. This time, he *fell in love* with one of his students. So fucking stupid. So, he got fired this time. And without his salary, I couldn't afford school. I mean, I had some money, but not enough."

"What about the scholarship?"

"It's only partial coverage of tuition," she said. "And you know what it's like here. I couldn't not go out to dinner with you guys, and not buy drinks at the bar, not go on ski trips. Even the books for my classes are like fifty dollars each. So, John, he offered to pay for everything."

I stop pacing and put my hands on my hips and focus on a pile of dirty clothes. It was so John. Swooping in to save the day, to feel good about himself. To compensate for his filthy habits. He loved to be loved, the hero.

"If you needed money, why didn't you come to me? I would have helped you; I will still help you."

"Because he's my boyfriend. Those are the things you tell your boyfriend. And when he offered to pay, well, I said no at first. I worked hard all summer waitressing on the Vineyard. But it wasn't enough. I had no other option."

So John owns Ruby. He can do whatever he wants with her, and he knows she won't do anything about it.

"I'll pay him back whatever it is you owe, and then you'll be free," I say. I quickly calculate what is in my savings account, given to me by my parents. I haven't had to access it before, but this is an emergency.

Ruby shakes her head.

"Ruby, this will go on forever if you don't end it."

She looks out the window. Her eyes are shadows of what they once were, the joy depleted. The image of my mother looking at me in the hospital. That helpless, lost look.

"Thank you, but no. I'm going to stay with him. Just stop, please. I swear I'm okay. He will probably come in here in an hour and apologize. He always does. And I'm going to marry him one day. I love him. I know it sounds crazy. But he takes care of me, and he's trying to change. When he's not, well, awful, he's the complete opposite. The love of my life."

"Marry him?" I ask. It's the only thing I hear.

Ruby looks back at me. Her skin is pale and tight against her cheekbones, her freckles weathered by the winter.

"You still don't get it, do you? I want that life. I want to be wealthy, like you. You don't have to worry about anything. It's not like I'm going to make a ton of money working at a museum or gallery. If John is my ticket to that life, then I'll take it. Please don't say anything. Okay? You have to promise me. This is important to me."

"This is crazy," I say. I can't help myself. "He is crazy, Ruby. He could kill you."

"He won't."

She glances down at her stomach, the skin covered by her sweatshirt.

I sit down next to her on the bed. Maybe if I touch her, she will see the truth, she will listen to me.

I try to sound gentle, but it comes out harsh and quick. "You could have internal bleeding."

She doesn't say anything.

"I wish you could be stronger," I say.

Ruby looks at me, her eyes lit with a fire I haven't seen before. "This is me being strong. Just because you see being strong as one thing, doesn't mean it can't exist in another way. I am doing this for me; let it go. I am fine, okay?"

I still think she's wrong. She's not admitting that John isn't the person for her. She's in complete denial about who she really is. And then I ask the question I know she doesn't want to answer.

"What about Max?"

"I don't know," she says.

"What happened between you two?" I ask.

"He kissed me last year. We were walking back from the library one night, and it was one of those early spring days where you're stupid happy all the time because it's finally warm out. You know?"

I don't. I hate the heat.

"And, well," she continues, "there's always been something there. It was nice. I couldn't stop thinking about him after that. He said he would wait for me, that I could take as much time as I needed. It's fucked up, I know."

She stares at the floor, avoiding eye contact.

"And then the whole thing with my dad happened, and I decided it would be better if Max and I weren't close anymore, and here we are."

You mean John decided it would be better if you weren't close anymore. I let out a breath and decide to let it go.

"I need to ask you one more thing," I say.

"Sure, what?"

"Did you choose me to be your friend because you didn't see me as competition?"

Ruby looks confused. "What are you even talking about?"

"I talked to Amanda. I know about what happened when you were at camp. With Gigi?"

"So you know. I'm not surprised she told you. She has loved watching me squirm, threatening to tell people about it. Well, yes, it's true. I am mortified by it, still. It's this thing I am so ashamed of, and I wish I could find her to apologize, but I'm too much of a coward."

I stare at the floor.

She sucks in a breath, contemplating something. "But what does that have to do with me being friends with you?"

"Amanda implied that . . . well, you want to be the best, and I mean you did admit that you want to be popular and rich."

Ruby's eyes crinkle, and she puts a hand on mine. "You think I'm just using you?"

I stiffen.

Ruby is serious. "M, no. You are my dear, dear friend. I didn't 'choose' you. It just fit. I liked being around you. And you're the only one who is always there for me. I'm not a monster; I would never fake my friendship with you, or use you, or whatever it was Amanda was implying. Maybe what I did with Gigi makes me a monster, but I've been trying to atone for it ever since."

I decide to believe her. The other option means I've been deceived for four yours, and I can't tolerate entertaining that idea. And there is something in her voice that makes me think she is telling the truth. I have seen her kindness. She may be desperate for a different life, but I don't think she will sacrifice someone else for her benefit ever again. If she's going to sacrifice anyone, it's herself.

We stay there for a long time, sitting with each other in the dimly lit quarters of her room. While she thinks about her future with John, I make a new plan. One that will work.

CHAPTER THIRTY-NINE

TEXAS, 1997

The events of this day replay in my mind when I dream. The screams crowd my skull, pulling at my bloody hands, my nerves rewired to remind me of what happened. Despite all the years that have passed, the feeling of that particular moment does not fade.

I woke up later than usual, which was odd. Through heavy lids, the clock read 8:53 in fluorescent red. The house was quiet, the hum of the air conditioner stirring outside my window. I worked my legs to the spot where Bo slept, but the sheets were loose against my legs.

When my grogginess passed, I sat up. My mother always woke me before she left for work, the scent of her shampoo lingering on my pillows after she planted a kiss on my forehead. My father did the same, but it was always so early that I didn't register his presence.

My toes pressed into the carpet, and I made my way to the kitchen, passing through our long hallway. It was lined with framed photographs leaning against the wall, my parents too busy to hang them. They had been like that for over a year.

Levi was at the table eating cereal, teeth crunching, milk sloshing his tongue.

"Where's Mom?" I asked.

"Left early," he replied, not looking up. He was reading a magazine, the one my father ordered for him about machines. He was so smart already, a genius in the making. I eyed him carefully.

"Why didn't you wake me up?" I asked.

"Didn't want to disrupt your beauty sleep," Levi said. His voice was not kind. I was young, but I already knew the difference in tone. Levi started using sarcasm at a young age. I didn't know the definition for it yet, but when I would learn it later, I would think of him.

I didn't want to be alone with him.

"Is Lane here?" I asked, looking through the glass doors into the backyard. She was already set up on her chair, headphones in place, eyes closed to the sun, ice coffee at her side. Levi watched me notice her, and then went back to his magazine.

I got on a stool and reached into the cabinet, pulling down a box of English muffins. I rustled the plastic, twisting the bag open, and realized Bo wasn't at my feet where he usually was.

"It's real hot out today," Levi said, casual.

I looked outside at the glistening pool and then back down at the floor. Bo always came running when he heard the plastic, knowing I saved the last bite of muffin for him.

"Bo?" I called into the kitchen.

I got down from the stool, left the muffins on the counter.

"Bo?" I said again, peering around the corner to the living room. Empty silence. He was not in his usual spot on the couch licking his paws, or on the floor by the glass door, wet nose pressed up against it.

I checked my parents' room. Empty. Levi's room, not that Bo ever went in there anyway. Empty. My room. Empty. Guest room. Empty. All the rooms, empty. I walked back into the kitchen, a slight panic on my heels.

"Levi," I said, "where's Bo?" I tried to sound as nice as possible, my eyes pleading.

Levi looked at me and began to smile. He stopped, as if he wanted to hide something. He looked outside. "Toasty out there, huh?"

My heart began to beat wildly in my chest. My tongue went stiff, and my teeth locked together. Levi watched me and stifled a laugh, resisting his smile.

Something in the back of my mind told me to check the garage. The look on Levi's face. Something was wrong. *Real hot out today.*

The warnings my mother had been giving us, her paranoia at leaving us in the car without the windows down, the AC blasting in our faces.

I turned on my heels and ran to the garage door. I opened it. Nothing. No car, no Bo. I stepped inside, the concrete floor cool, the dust and dirt sticking to my feet. Levi was watching me, a curious look on his face.

"Mom had a meeting downtown. She took a cab. Her car is outside, remember?" he said, so matter-of-fact, annoyed that I hadn't pieced it together yet.

If her car wasn't in the garage, she would have parked it under the basketball hoop.

Real hot out today.

I looked to my left, where the faded garage door button waited for me. My hands were ice cold as I pressed it. The garage door jolted and clanked open, slow and revealing. When the space between the door and cement floor was large enough, I crawled under it and into the hot sun. The heat was overwhelming even in the morning hours. It stifled my lungs, and the humidity clung to my pajamas as I stood up.

My mother's car, baking in the driveway. The sun reflected off the bright blue surface. Something inside me broke. I felt it happen. It was as light as a heel stepping onto a twig.

I ran to the car and pressed my face against the warm glass. My feet blistered on the driveway, but I didn't notice the burns until later.

Bo was panting, quick and light. He was lying on the fabric seat. His chest worked fast, up down up down up down.

His eyes locked on mine. He tried to wag his tail, but he was already weak, exhausted. His eyes closed and opened slow, steady.

I pulled at the handle, but the car was locked. I pounded on the windows, screamed his name.

I needed the keys.

I turned around, but I knew it was too late. Levi leaned against the garage door, watching. He shook his head, his hands in his pockets.

"You'll never find them," he said.

He smiled. Triumphant.

. . .

BY THE TIME our neighbor found me, my hands were mangled and broken. The window smeared with blood. The police arrived shortly after. The neighbor who heard my screams, a plump grandmother in her sixties, clutched me to her stomach as the police took over. She smelled of baby powder and burned coffee. I didn't even care that she was touching me.

The police broke the window, did what my fists couldn't, what my mind didn't register. Now, whenever I see a sizable rock, one that a child could pick up above her head and smash into a window, I am reminded of what I should have done, and I bite the inside of my mouth to feel the pain and taste the blood.

I wriggled free and ran to the window, darting between the officers. I don't think they expected me to do what I did, to try to climb through the window. They grabbed ahold of my waist, but I clung to the broken glass, scrambling to help Bo. I didn't even feel the pain as the officers pulled me away, the glass edges dragging against my palms. One of the men held me back as another pulled Bo from the car and placed him on the ground.

He wasn't moving. They dowsed him with water from our hose, his body still and quiet. His dark fur wet, the curls tight against his pink skin. The police shook their heads, a grim look on their faces. The one holding me let go, cautious. I sat next to Bo, placing a bloody hand on his chest. Nothing. Lane was pacing at the end of the driveway, crying, claiming the headphones had blocked out my screams.

I picked Bo up off the asphalt and cradled him in my arms. *Please wake up, please wake up, wake up, wake up.* We were so small together. His eyes were closed, like he was sleeping. I pressed my face to his, nose to nose, and held him there, my face wet from his fur. An ambulance sounded in the distance as the glass embedded in my palms began to sting.

I LATER LEARNED that Levi was found sitting at the kitchen table, reading his magazine. He claimed he didn't hear what happened outside, the noise from the air conditioner too loud.

My mother met us at the hospital as the finishing touches were put on my bandages. The sterile room was silent as all four of us sat together. I still hadn't spoken, the doctor told my parents it was shock. Of course, my mother was a doctor; she probably figured that out for herself.

She was too weak to do anything, her years of schooling thrown wayside in the shadow of her son. She was consumed by him. She didn't even ask how Bo got in the car, how he got *locked inside* the car. She didn't know what to do, trapped by her own motherly instinct. She couldn't protect both of us.

My father eyed Levi. Skeptical. Afraid.

Levi smiled at my mother, held her hand as we left the hospital. His grip was strong against hers, which had weakened and now looked so limp and tired in his.

We all knew what he did. I watched my parents throw worried glances at each other. A son lost in his own mind.

WHEN WE GOT home from the hospital that day, I went straight to my room. I wanted to bury my face in Bo's spot. I wanted to smell his smell and forget, wanted to feel his body against the crook of my knees. My hands were wrapped tight in bandages and my arms felt detached, like they were still outside holding his body.

Before I collapsed on the bed, I saw something glinting in the corner of my eye.

Car keys on my pillow.

CHAPTER FORTY

Senior Day

Everyone is back in the house now, doors shut.

I hear *Friends* playing in Gemma's room as I pass her door. She is probably getting ready, putting on her stockings and dress, and straightening her blue hair. Calming herself down, telling herself she didn't mean to hurt Ruby.

At the bottom of the stairs, Khaled's door is shut. He is playing loud music with a vibrating beat. Not a surprise that I am the only one who hears things in this house. I walk through the living room, passing Denise on the couch. Her black-lined eyes follow me to the other side of the room. I wonder about the things she has seen. I press my ear to the door and listen, but the space behind Max's door is quiet.

Back in the front of the house, I lace up my sneakers and throw on my down jacket. Outside, my legs stay warm in my fleece leggings. I hop down the stairs, making sure to step on the salty patches, where the ice can't trip me up. It is so dark outside, but I am used to running in the dark.

The cold air burns my lungs as I sprint toward 356 Pleasant Street. I know he'll be home, waiting for me to text him back.

When I get there, the lights are on, that warm glow inviting me inside. Except I don't walk up the driveway, don't knock on his door. I hop over the stone wall and go to my spot. For the first time in months, I watch from the outside.

I want to watch one more time, since this will be our ending.

CHAPTER FORTY-ONE

TEXAS, 1997

My father's hand rested on my shoulder. His touch burned through my T-shirt, my nerves like knives beneath my skin. I leaned down to pat the new grass firm into the ground. The blades took the shape of my bandaged hand, and I watched as they unfurled and bent back into their upright position. The two of us buried Bo, and I thought of his body deep beneath the surface of the backyard, alone and dark, packed tight in the sandy earth. It was not where he belonged. He was supposed to be next to me, wet nose grazing against my kneecaps.

"I'm sorry, Malin. I know how much he meant to you."

I said nothing. He was apologizing for the wrong thing. He should have said, *I'm sorry for letting your brother kill your dog.* But I didn't want him to know that I knew about Bo. Something told me to keep quiet about it, in case I needed to use it later. If I wanted to survive Levi, I needed to be careful.

My father leaned down in front of me, knowing better than to touch me this time.

"Malin," he began, "I am always here, if you need to talk to someone."

Except he wasn't. He could never be on my side. He was Levi's father, too.

Without Bo, I was alone.

. . .

THE FOUR OF us sat at dinner, quiet. My father made King Ranch chicken, each bite felt like glue in my mouth. I wasn't hungry. I eyed Levi out of the corner of my eye. He had almost finished his meal and had begun to scrape the edge of his fork against the plate. The scraping echoed against the tile floor and glass windows.

"Not hungry?" my mother asked me.

I shook my head.

"You should eat something, sweetie, you'll be hungry later."

"I'm okay," I said.

Levi finished his meal and leaned back in his chair. He watched my mother looking at me, the concerned look flitting in her eyes. Levi hated when she gave me attention. I tensed, bracing for whatever he was about to say.

"I heard Daddy and Malin talking about me today," he said, gazing down at his plate, slumping his shoulders.

My father looked at me, confused. I wasn't confused. I knew exactly what Levi was about to do.

"They said I need to be sent away." He began to cry. He looked at my mother, pleading.

"We said no such thing," my father said, putting down his fork. He had his serious voice on, the one that he used when one of us (usually Levi) was in trouble. "His name never even came up."

"Mommy," Levi said, turning to our mother, eyes brimming with fake tears. "Tell him I'm not going anywhere."

My mother looked at my father. The look in her eyes said she believed Levi.

"Don't worry, honey, you're staying here. Of course. With your family," my mother cooed, reaching for Levi's hand.

My father and I looked at each other. I knew he didn't want me to get involved; he wanted to protect me. But I didn't want my mother to be mad at him.

"He's lying," I said, staring down at my plate, rice now cold and hard. Everything drained of color, the chicken gray.

"No, I'm not!" Levi cried. He ignored me, staring at my mother. "She hates me; she wants me to leave."

"That's enough," my father said, his voice thunder. "Both of you, go to your rooms."

I knew he wasn't mad at me. He was mad at Levi. I got up and walked down the cool hallway, stopping at my doorway. I waited for Levi, who was following me, straightening as soon as we were out of sight.

"Why did you do that?" I asked him. We both knew he was lying.

He shrugged. "I was bored. Dinner is *so* boring." He paused, glancing out the window, the sun beginning to set behind the trees. The walls beginning to splash in golden light. "Wanna go play in the treehouse?"

"I thought you hated me?" I asked.

He twisted his mouth. "So?"

"No, thanks," I said. I felt like every word had to be chosen carefully, not sure what I was supposed to say or do, or how to act, in case I made the wrong move. "I'm going to read."

Levi sighed. "You're such a loser," and then disappeared inside his room, leaving me paused outside mine, hand on the doorknob, doing the math on how many more years we would have to live in this house together.

MUCH LATER THAT night, I waited for the house to settle into darkness.

I pretended to be asleep when my mother cracked the door open, letting the yellow glow splash against my face. I breathed even and slow, leaving my eyes half-open. My parents joked that they knew I was in a deep sleep when my eyelids fluttered, the whites beneath my eyes flickering. They said I was their weird little sleeper.

I waited thirty minutes before I pushed back the blanket.

My parents had their hidden talks when they thought Levi and I were asleep. I'd discovered this a few months prior when I had to pee in the middle of the night, and I heard their voices hushed and muffled behind their door. I was too tired, and didn't care, to listen at the time. But things were different now. We all tiptoed around Levi like he was important and breakable. I wanted to know what my parents were going to do about it. They had to do something.

I huddled under the credenza outside their bedroom door.

My parents were terrible at whispering. I didn't try hard to listen, to make out their hushed words. Sometimes I wished they were better at it. I wished I didn't have to pick up on their lowered tones, wished I didn't even have to think to listen.

It took me a couple seconds to tune in to their exact words. I heard my mother first.

"How am I supposed to know which one of you is lying?" she asked, her voice pointed and accusing.

"Seriously? I am your husband. He is a kid."

I knew this was what Levi wanted. He wanted our parents to fight. I envisioned my mother standing in front of my father, arms crossed, eyes glaring, probably filling with tears. She cried at everything, but sometimes it wasn't because she was sad. Sometimes it was because she felt things too much, I think. She used to cry when she would read me *The Giving Tree* before bedtime. I'd grab a tissue and hand it to her, puzzled by her emotion.

"I'm not lying to you," my father said, his voice more patient this time. "Malin and I were burying the dog. We didn't mention Levi."

"So, what does that mean? He made that up, for what? Fun? Why would he do that?"

My father sighed. "Celia, you know why. We need to face reality."

"No," my mother said, as if whatever my father was suggesting was impossible. "He is our baby. I can't give up on him."

"He is affecting our family. Bo is dead. The house is a mess. We are a mess. I can't even focus on Malin because I'm trying to protect her from him. He needs help, serious help; we need to send him somewhere. He can't be around her anymore."

"No," my mother's voice again. "He is our *son*. We can help him ourselves. I am a doctor. We are the only ones who can fix him; give me more time. Please."

"This isn't a problem you can solve. He needs professional help. Psychological help. He needs to go somewhere."

There was silence for a minute and then my mother spoke, "What if we send Malin to your mother?"

"What?" my father said, sounding offended.

"It's summer. School's not in session anyway. She'll love it up there."

"Wait. You want to send *Malin* away? She hasn't done anything wrong. Her dog died and you want to send her away? What kind of message does that send to Levi? To Malin?"

"Levi needs us more. She is so independent. I feel like she never needs me."

"She does need you. You're her mother. And you really want to send her up there? After everything that happened? I told you about my family."

"That was years ago; it's fine. Right?"

My father didn't answer.

"Please, George, at least if she's gone, she's safe."

I wanted my father to fight her, but he didn't. I didn't want to go to Massachusetts. This was my home. I didn't want to leave Bo. Levi was the one who messed everything up, *he* should be the one who had to leave. He should go to the hospital, or a doctor, or something. *He is the problem,* I wanted to scream. *Not me.*

"Sometimes I worry. That if she stays here, with him . . . and something happens . . ." my mother said, so soft I barely heard her, her voice tainted with panic. "What if something happens, and she's just like him? What if it's genetic? There's your family, and the way he's acting, and she's so quiet all the time. The thought—it's there—in the back of my mind. I want her away from this place."

They were quiet for a long time.

My father must have pulled my mother close, because I could hear her sobbing into his chest while he said to her, "It'll be okay."

My mother used to be strong and colorful. She smiled all the time and kissed my cheeks and sang loud annoying songs while she folded laundry. She was excited to go to work every day, and help people feel better, and then tell us about it when she got home. Some kids in my grade would complain about their mothers, how angry they could get, or how annoying they'd be about chores. But my mother and I weren't like that. She asked me to do the dishes, or tidy my room, and

I did it. I didn't mind. It was my job, and she always said *thank you, what a helpful daughter you are. Sweet baby girl.* And she never got angry. She was patient and kind. Where did that version of her go? Was she gone forever? Levi had stolen my mother, and I wasn't sure if she'd ever come back.

That night was the first time I fell asleep to the screams in my head. My screams.

CHAPTER FORTY-TWO

Senior Day

Back at the house, I knock on Max's door.

"Yeah?" he says.

"Hey," I say, walking inside, closing the door behind me.

"You look nice," he says.

I look down at my dress—navy, simple.

"Oh," I say, distracted, "thanks."

Max looks back at the mirror and finishes adjusting his tie. I look around his room. I like how neat he is, books stacked on the table, poster edges flush with the wall.

"Do you want some help?" I ask him as he unfurls the tie and begins again.

I walk over to him, and our eyes meet at the same level. I think of a study I once read about how taller people are more likely to succeed at work. I think about Max in his scrubs and white coat one day, and all the people he will heal, and how this rule will not apply to him. The silk slips through my fingers as I place the wide end over the skinny end.

"Do you think they'll break up?" he asks.

"I don't know," I reply.

We are quiet, and I remember something.

"How did you know something was wrong with them?" I ask.

Max pauses for a moment before replying, as if he isn't even sure of the answer. "You know how I told you about that time at soccer camp?"

I remember, looping the tie.

"After that, especially after my uncle went to jail, John kept changing," Max continues. "He used to be fun; he was normal when we were younger. But then he started to tear into me every chance he got. Only me. Never anyone else. He likes to be liked, so he couldn't take it out on anyone else. I think he knew I wouldn't fight back. I wanted us to go to different schools; I was relieved I wouldn't have to see him. I got in early decision here. And then when he got in that spring, he announced he was going, too. I tried to be positive about it. I thought maybe we could start over here, be friends even. I put in the effort. I hung out with him all the time. I thought maybe he could reinvent himself. That didn't happen. He was still a dick to me here. And then by sophomore year, it got a little better. I wasn't his only target anymore. Someone had to be, so I assumed it was Ruby."

I adjust the final knot of his tie and step back, crossing my arms.

"Is that why you're so anxious? Because he bullied you?" I ask.

"Maybe." He sighs, pulling on his suit jacket. "Yes. Probably. It's like having an illness you can't shake. He's there, this thing weighing me down. Makes me feel trapped. I didn't even notice it for the longest time when I was younger. It was what I grew up with; I didn't know any better. And he's my cousin, he's blood, my mom always made such a big deal about that, wanting us to be friends. I was always uneasy around him, but I didn't know why. Obviously now I do."

Max is a ticking time bomb. He doesn't know about the violence, and I don't tell him. I don't know what he will do to John if he finds out about that part, and I don't want any distractions tonight.

► ► ►

AT NINE P.M. we find ourselves in the living room. All six of us. The guys are dressed in their suits and ties. Gemma is wearing a tight red dress, and Ruby is in the black dress. The beading glimmers as she moves, making her look like a movie star. I realize John must have bought it for her.

We all share awkward exchanges, not sure of what to say or how to act. Ruby is uncomfortable, and she winces when Khaled gives her a hug.

Ruby refuses to look at Gemma. John ignores Max and puts an arm around Ruby's shoulders. She looks at him like she always does, and then catches my eye, a warning glance.

Khaled cracks a few jokes about how hungover we are already, and how we should start drinking more. I think he can sense the tense air, and he's trying to defuse it. Maybe he knows something bad is going to happen.

"Should we take a photo?" Khaled asks.

Ruby smiles politely, and Max goes to get his camera. We arrange ourselves in front of the staircase as Max sets up his tripod. Somehow I end up between John and Max. I feel John's palm rest on my hip and bile pools in the back of my throat.

"Wait, don't forget Denise!" Khaled says, grabbing her from the couch. I think he expects all of us to laugh, but nobody does.

"Can we not?" Gemma asks, her voice brittle, on edge. "She's a sex doll for fuck's sake."

Khaled drops his eyes and pushes Denise back onto the couch. He doesn't say anything and lines up for the photo. He looks at me for reassurance that everything is good. But it's not. I am tired of pretending. I don't acknowledge his glance and turn away.

Our group dynamic is officially shattered.

"Okay," Max says, settling into place next to me, his presence a surprising comfort. "Three, two, one."

The camera flashes, and we all give our best fake smiles. It will be the last photo taken of all of us together.

We gather our scarves and hats, and bundle up in our warmest wool coats. Khaled leads the way down the path, and I look up at the sky, waiting for that snow.

My backup plan. My perfect, beautiful snow.

CHAPTER FORTY-THREE

TEXAS, 1997

It was another hot day in Texas. I watched the street from the dining room window. The entire front of our house was made of windows, designed in the mid-century modern appeal my mother loved so much.

A couple girls my age bicycled past, laughing with each other. I knew their names, we met so long ago, but I wasn't interested in being a part of their group. My parents had long ago stopped suggesting I *go play* with them.

I sat cross-legged, a paperback in my lap. I stole it off my parents' bookshelf. I'm not supposed to read their books without permission, but I woke up off-kilter, not bothering to follow the rules today. The book is about a boy who went exploring in the wilderness, got lost, and died from eating poisonous berries. I knew this because I always read the last page of a book first. I flipped a page, letting the paper lightly slice at my finger.

I wasn't paying attention to the words on the page. I couldn't focus. My forehead rested against the glass, the surface cool on my skin. The urge to reach down and pet Bo came and went, each day the mechanical movement becoming less frequent. We didn't talk about him. Since the *accident*, it was as if he never existed, his name erased.

The next day I was supposed to leave for my grandmother's house in Deerfield. My parents had told me I'd have fun, go swimming in the river and ride horses at the farm. They acted excited, so I faked a smile, even though my insides twisted.

Last night at dinner, as the four of us sat together, my mother told us that we were going to spend the summer working on our family. I wasn't sure how I was going to contribute to that since I wouldn't be around. My father wouldn't make eye contact with me, and I knew he was done standing up for me. I looked over at Levi when they said the word *family,* and he gave me a grin when my parents weren't looking. My mother put a hand on his shoulder, and he looked at her in a sweet, syrupy way that made me want to scream.

He would never change. My parents were blind. I understood it was because they brought him into the world; he was theirs. So they thought they could fix him. I understood why they couldn't *really* fix him, couldn't send him somewhere with professionals. My mother was afraid of losing her baby, and that fear made her weak and vulnerable. Levi knew it. He took advantage of her love. I think my father knew he was beyond repair, but he wanted to make my mother happy. It was a mistake he shouldn't have made.

Levi was bad. It was simple. Black and white. I could see it, when nobody else could. There wasn't anything to be fixed with my brother, because whatever it was inside him was there to stay. I knew this for one reason, but I couldn't tell anyone. It was my secret.

My parents might have been blind, but I wasn't. They taught me that when you love someone, like a parent loves a child, you can choose to ignore bad things, which causes you to make bad decisions. But I didn't love Levi. I was the only one who could make things better.

We had a new babysitter. Lane had been "let go" as my mother told me. Our new babysitter was a round Hispanic lady named Sonia. She was nice; she braided my hair and spoke to me in Spanish, and made us quesadillas for lunch. I could hear her vacuuming in my parents' bedroom.

I looked over my shoulder, gazing through the other side of the dining room, and out the backyard-facing windows. Our glass house, breakable. I spied Levi out of the corner of my eye, carrying a stick. He was whacking it against the base of our tree. I heard my father's hushed words to my mother. *The idle time isn't good for him; he needs to be occupied. Challenged.*

I looked over at the microwave, 4:37 P.M. My mother would be home by five P.M. I was glad she would be happy soon, back to her regular self. Soon, everything would be okay. I closed the book and left it on the floor.

When I stepped outside I heard the cicadas humming, calling out to each other in the humidity. I walked out to where the stone patio met grass and pressed my toes into the dry earth. I scanned the lawn, which was dotted with groupings of palm fronds and ceramic planters. My father spent the most time out here, maintaining the plants, making sure the backyard looked nice. I made my way toward the large tree in the back corner, where Levi was breaking the stick into tiny pieces.

"Want to play?" I asked.

He looked up at me as if I'd interrupted him from some deep place in his own mind.

"Play?" he asked.

I realized this was out the ordinary for us. We hadn't played together in so long. I didn't want him to catch on to anything.

"Let's go in the treehouse," I suggested. "Play spy."

This was one of Levi's favorite activities. From the vantage point in our treehouse, we had access to three other backyards. Levi used to throw pebbles at people and pets, until my father caught him and ordered him to stop. We had a notebook tucked away in one of the eaves of the treehouse, where we documented our neighbors' habits, detailing their every move. It had been months, maybe a year, since we'd done this together.

Levi looked at me and didn't answer right away. He liked to leave me hanging, another one of his pastimes. He thought it made me feel awkward to be left unanswered, but I'd never minded the silence.

After a minute he responded, "Okay."

I followed him up the wooden ladder, careful to avoid splinters in my hands and feet. In the spots where sun reflected, the wood was warm against my exposed skin.

Levi leaned out over the short railing. He was getting bigger, his small muscles protruding from his T-shirt and shorts. His tan was darker than mine; my skin was fair like our mother's, his like our father's. I noticed Levi's hands, and the raw edge around the fingertips where he chewed the nails away. I thought about how the girls at school always told me how cute my older brother was. I didn't see it. All I saw was ugly. I wished he didn't look so much like my father. Levi wasn't deserving of his looks.

"There's nobody out," he said scanning the view, "too hot."

He looked at me with a jaded grin, and we both remembered the last time we discussed the weather.

"Okay, whatever, then leave," I said.

"You must be really bored, to want to hang out with me," Levi said.

I didn't answer him and looked into our neighbor's yard. There was a cat snoozing in one of the shaded lawn chairs. I thought about how Bo used to stare at that cat for hours, endlessly entertained by the uneven flick of its tail. I hoped Levi wouldn't see the cat, knowing he would want to throw rocks at it.

I hadn't cried since the accident. I felt nothing except an overwhelming need to protect my parents. I wanted them to be able to talk about television shows and their workdays, where we should go for vacation. The stuff they used to discuss, before everything with Levi started.

I looked over at him, at his boyishness, the warmth of his golden hair parted on the right side. I wondered if he had always been like this, spoiled like a peach that has been left on the counter too long, and if I just never noticed before.

"Do you love Mom and Dad?" I asked.

Levi smiled. "No."

"Do you love me?" I made my voice small and weak.

"No."

He narrowed his eyes. "Haven't you heard?"

"Heard what?" I asked.

"I'm sick," he whispered. "A freak."

I cocked my head, the faint hum of my mother's car in the driveway, a door shutting. I knew I needed to move quicker if I didn't want our mother to see us, but I stayed calm.

Levi laughed. "Don't worry, baby girl, you're as normal and boring as they come."

Levi started toward the ladder, where the gap showed off a view of our pool and glass windows. I watched him stop before he descended, and I stepped toward him.

"Don't look like such a wimp," he said. "You want to know what's wrong with me?"

I didn't say anything. We were close, and I could smell his prepubescent body odor, still untamed by deodorant.

"I feel nothing," he said. "I can do whatever I want."

Levi grinned, wide and wicked. This time, I gave him a soft smile in return, and he looked confused for a small moment. His hands were loose on the ladder. He was exactly where I wanted him.

I moved forward in a flash, before he could realize what was happening. I gave him one hard shove against his chest and backed away, swift and neat. He sharply sucked in air where I knocked it out of him. I knew he would try to grab at me, to pull me down with him, so I made sure to tuck into one of the far corners of the treehouse.

I will never forget the look on his face, the shock, surprise.

He fell fast. There was a quick and sudden thud, and then the heavy buzz of cicadas in the afternoon air.

I only had one thought as I sat with my back to the treehouse, my breath calm and satisfied, listening to my mother's screams. I realized something that would gnaw at me as I grew older. It wasn't that Levi was dead, but that he was wrong about me. I felt nothing, too, except maybe relief.

I was just like him.

▶ ▶ ▶

I CAN'T REMEMBER the specific moment when I knew I was born broken. A crack ran through me, indistinguishable at first. Levi was the one who pried it open, making sure I became like him, solidifying the sociopathic nature of my brain. I hate that word. I don't think I can be lumped into a group so easily. There are shades of gray. But there it sits, bouncing around my brain, always there, following me. I am tired of pretending that I'm not broken.

It was something I started to realize slowly, the dawning of my indifference a tide that crept in over my childhood. It's not that I lack feelings completely, though. I care for a select few. My parents, Bo. I did care for Levi at one point, maybe even loved him. Love is something that I may never fully understand, but I've seen glimpses of it.

In elementary school, I watched my peers. It didn't take me long to realize I wasn't like everyone else. While they happily drew with crayons and played games, I sat by myself, bored and uninterested. The more I grew, the more I knew something was wrong with me.

The class bully made me his target for a few weeks. After some annoying rounds of hair-pulling and name-calling, he had become comparable to a fly that buzzes when you're trying to take a nap. One time the teacher scolded him, and then later told me it was because he had a crush on me. She gave me a wink, like it was a good thing he was pulling my hair. Later, the boy stomped on my toe at recess after I wouldn't let him cut me in line for the swings. I didn't scream or cry, and his fat face got all red and frustrated. He demanded that I get out of line, or he would stomp on my other toe. I shrugged, not actually caring if I got to go on the swing, since I was only in line because everyone else was. I was doing what I was supposed to do. I must have been a boring subject because he didn't bother me again.

My mother's mother died when we were very young. The memory of her is blurry, but I remember her loose, translucent skin, the veins highlighted by blue. Our parents sat Levi and me down to explain the concept of death. We shrugged our shoulders, like it wasn't a big deal. We didn't understand the point of a funeral, why everyone was so upset. All I wanted to do was get home and finish my book.

At some point, our tendencies veered in sharp and opposite directions. Where Levi preferred destruction, I chose silence, making my way through the day like a ghost, avoiding human interaction.

One Christmas, my parents brought home a wriggly puppy. They looked so excited and expectant, like my brother and I would snap out of our hazy fortresses if we were distracted by a bundle of dark fluff. His warm body pressed up against my chest, and he licked my face, and I laughed, a new warmth replacing the emptiness. There was hope for me. Levi reacted with a wrinkled face, his disgust at the puppy apparent from the very first moment.

I named him Bo. "Like on a present," I told my parents.

My mother had looked at my father, their faces plastered with relief.

Bo was always mine. He was my only friend, my sweet companion, and I cared for him. I loved him, I know it; the feeling wasn't lost on me.

I probably would have turned out somewhat normal, if it wasn't for Levi. He ruined me, molding my life with chaos and cruelty.

MY MOTHER MUST have seen us that day in the treehouse; it was my only mistake, my only regret. She would have seen him standing in the gap, a stretch of anxiety tied in her stomach, but her logic telling her not to worry. There was no way she didn't see my small arms dart out to his stomach, push him backward and out of the tree.

We never discussed what happened. I said he fell, that it was an accident, and they never questioned it. I didn't expect my parents would be so upset about Levi's death. I thought everyone would feel how I did. Relieved. They separated for a while, only to find themselves back in each other's arms a few months later.

I told myself to make it up to them, make them feel like they had one child who would succeed at life. They'd never have to worry about me; I'd help them forget about Levi.

"It's in your blood, your *father's* blood, not mine," my mother had said after swallowing her pills one night.

She spat the words at me like I was a dirty stranger she wanted to rid herself of. She eyed me cautiously from across the dinner table, and I did my best to appear normal. I didn't want my parents to worry about me. I faked smiles in an attempt to comfort my mother, but she saw through my feeble efforts and drifted away from me.

Baby girl was left behind, buried somewhere in my mother's bureau, beneath the scrubs she never wore again. She spent her days reading magazines in the air-conditioned house, watching me play outside, hiding herself behind the glass walls, her trust of babysitters a thing of the past. She checked out of life, leaving my father and me behind in a wash of memories and disappointment.

My father was the only one who understood. When I was fifteen, he explained how he lacked empathy, not completely, but it was a problem for him and the people who cared about him. When he met my mother, he fell in love, and he knew he had to learn how to empathize if he wanted to be with her. He had to pretend to be thoughtful and caring because it was the right thing to do. *Pretend.* The mantra was stuffed down my throat, and I held it tight; not wanting to disappoint him, I would pretend, too.

It was the first time I had clarity into who I was. My father and I were the same, except he grew up in a safe, loving home. He didn't have a tormentor. For me, empathy seemed to manifest in protection. I don't like seeing the weak suffer at the hands of others. I have Levi to thank for that.

My father told me about my great-grandfather, Martin Ahlberg. He said he didn't know much, since his mother refused to talk about it, but he did know that his grandfather had been a serial killer. It was so long ago, and there were only a few newspaper articles about it. Journalists at the time had dubbed him the Deerfield Hunter—as John had discovered. At first it only made local news, but eventually it spread after they realized the victims were from all over New England. It was after my father told me about him, and I needed to understand who my great-grandfather was, and why he did what he did. I found his name in a psychology profiling book. Martin Ahlberg was an enigma apparently, since the police could not find a tie between the victims. It was seemingly random, though he was a highly organized killer. I couldn't find much else, since there have been far more popular serial killers since his time.

Before he was caught, my great-grandfather spent ten years kidnapping people and letting them loose on his property, which spanned almost a hundred acres. He would tell them to run for their lives, hunt them down, shoot them with a rifle, and then bury them in the cow pasture. It took the police almost a year to uncover all the bodies. I've seen the grainy, brown photographs of men shoveling out the field. I always wondered who the victims were, why my great-grandfather killed them.

My father explained that the part of the brain lacking empathy can be genetic. The *serial killer gene,* he called it. It can lie dormant though, only brought on by childhood trauma. Abusive parents, that sort of thing. With the right upbringing, it could be managed. His mother, the hunter's daughter, kept a close eye on my father. She was a single mother, in a time when single mothers were rare, so she worked overtime to make sure her only son would be healthy, happy. I think being raised with an absent father made my dad even more aware of the importance of parenting, made him more present with me and Levi. My grandmother was the one who taught him how to interact with others, showed him love and compassion, did everything she could to make sure that even if he did inherit anything, he could still be a good person. He could live as a normal member of society. And she succeeded.

My father must have seen the hints with Levi. His behavior. How he manipulated my mother and killed Bo. It would have only been the beginning. My mother was so insistent that it was a phase, but she was wrong. They didn't help him the way he needed, not in time.

My father saw potential in me, so he taught me how to be *normal.* I don't think he realized it made me more dangerous, to know how to appear like I cared. There was no way for anyone to know about my potential, I worked so hard to hide it.

I chose Hawthorne because it wasn't Texas. I couldn't stand to live in the heat any longer, couldn't bear to face my mother's disappointment in me. I was rejected from the Ivy League schools I applied to. Yale, my first choice, Harvard my second, Princeton my third. None of them wanted me because I lacked *extracurriculars* and *community interests*. It didn't matter that I was top of my class, perfect SAT scores. None of it mattered. My résumé, devoid of school activities, acted as a warning to admissions officers. Hawthorne must have missed it, my acute lack of interest in others lost in the shuffle of papers on decision day. I had to take what I could get. Hawthorne College, one of the *mini Ivies,* was my only option.

In the beginning of my life at Hawthorne, everything was covered in a frothy film. Friends, classes, events, parties. I took what I could find and stuck with it. I didn't mean to start actually caring about Ruby. It was easy getting her to be my friend. Amanda did all the work for me that day in the dining hall, sending Ruby into a vulnerable state. I rescued her, put her back together again. It was perfect, really. I was Ruby's best friend after that, her most trusted ally. I didn't have to work very hard to keep her tied to me. She did all the work, she texted me, asked me to hang out. Left her diary open like it was a magazine in a waiting room, eager to be read and dissected. It was easier than I thought, making friends.

I made some questionable decisions with those friends, because if I didn't, their problems would only get worse. I read Ruby's diary to know her, *really* know her. If I hadn't, I might have never figured out about John's abusive side. I'd be in the dark, like the others. And if I hadn't secured a prescription for anti-anxiety meds during our fall semester senior year, Max could have spiraled into some sort of crazed permanent panic attack. He was going to explode from trying to keep everything inside—his love for Ruby, hatred for John . . . It was for them, I did it all for their benefit. They should thank me for helping them.

I think if Ruby hadn't reminded me of my mother, and if John hadn't appeared so eerily similar to Levi, I wouldn't have needed to do what I did. Ruby would have continued to disappear into herself, allowing the abuse to continue. John would have gotten stronger, stealing her light and strength for himself. He was just getting started. I saw his potential to hurt. To be someone like Levi. I was nipping it in the bud, as they say.

I didn't kill Levi because I wanted to, I killed because it was necessary.

I was a protector, not a murderer.

CHAPTER FORTY-FOUR

Senior Day

*P*retend.

  I am dancing at Last Chance, my arms in the air, jumping to the beat. I learned this dance from a girl I watched freshman year at a party. It was endearing, not slutty or try-hard. I copied it flawlessly. I make sure to smile, to look like I am having fun. Look at me, I'm so normal, so happy. A regular college student, living it up, soaking in the goodness of being a senior. Totally completely carefree.

It's late at night. I don't know what time.

Everyone is having the best time ever. We are all pretending. And we are good at it.

When Ruby leaves, she runs into Max, the two of them pulled together by some random circumstance. They talk about something, she smiles, and there's that way they look at each other. Everything real exists in those glances. In those in-between moments. That's when you see who they really are, what they really want. When they think nobody is watching. But I am. I am always watching.

I MAKE SURE to stumble, like I am drunk, and I fall into Khaled, who is next to me. He smiles and we are dancing, and Gemma is there, her eyes rolling back and forth, loaded with glances at John, who is on my other side. I need them to think I am wasted.

If you're not looking for the rot between us, we all look so happy. Our happiness is contagious. Don't get too close or you'll catch it.

The song changes, and we fix our bodies to the beat, our expressions drunk and focused. Someone pushes me from behind and I fall into John, and he gives me that slick smile.

SOMETIME LATER, I am alone, watching John on the dwindling dance floor. He is so drunk, oblivious, his tongue is out and he is with a group of his soccer teammates. They are spraying one another with beer. They are happy, a pile of sweat-laced boys living the dream.

In the beginning, I used to like to watch my friends from a distance, laughing and light. Without complications, problems, drama. Now I see all the strings that tie us together, how they are knotted and furled around us in a complex netting. I see everyone's stink, who they really are.

Gemma disappears with a guy from my English classes. He appears sober, holding her limp body up with one hand. He practically drags her off the dance floor. I don't worry because I know he is the kind of guy who will make sure she gets home safe. He'll put her on her side in case she vomits and cover her with a light sheet. It's always been clear to me. The good versus the bad.

Khaled is gone, too. I watch him walk into the dark of the locker rooms with a petite dark-haired girl, his hand pressed lightly against her back. They were giving each other that look I so often see at events like this. That *let's fuck* glance that gets tossed around between sweaty bodies.

Around midnight, I take a moment to collect myself. I'm ready. I start to walk over to John, who is now dancing with a girl I recognize as a freshman. She must have snuck in, desperate for attention from an older boy. John is pressing her front tight against his crotch, grinding back and forth. His lips are furled, teeth bared. I can't help but grimace at the look in his eyes, the disgusting lust he can't avoid.

I give the freshman a look as I separate them, and she dance-hops in another direction, careless and oblivious. I give a quick scan of the people around us. Nobody we know particularly well, and even if there was, everyone is blackout drunk, they will never remember seeing us like this. Besides, our group of friends dances together all the time. It wouldn't be out of the ordinary for John and me to be together.

"Hey there, M," John says into my ear. He puts both hands on my waist, and I smile up at him. "Finally realize who the better cousin is?"

I smell the bourbon breath, his eyes not quite steady, pupils dilated. I see Levi in the sly grin and blond hair, and for a brief moment I wonder if this is what he would have looked like so many years later. If he had lived, he would have graduated from college, living on his own somewhere. Would he be like John? Would his tendencies have gotten him into trouble by now? I almost pull away but temper myself, remembering why I am here, why I am doing this.

John leans his head down toward mine, and we are looking at each other, and I smile again, coy and charged. I put two fingers on his chin and bring his face down to mine and speak into his ear. "I've always known."

He pulls back quick, grinning. "Known what?" he says. His hips dig into me, needling his thigh in between my legs.

"Who the better cousin is," I reply, pressing into him, dragging my fingertips up the back of his waist. His skin is damp and warm, the shirt clinging with sweat.

I hand him the flask from my back pocket, and he takes it eagerly, thirsty for more alcohol. He hands it back to me, and I pretend to drink, as I always do.

"About time," he replies, his voice thick with appetite, the promise of sex. I smile toward the high ceiling, arching my back toward his pelvis. His eyelids flutter. I am almost bored by how predictable he is. He is used to being wanted, being the star. Girls throw themselves at him, and he accepts it, never questioning their motives. He should have questioned mine.

"Let's go," I say, nodding toward the back exit, toward the woods.

Convincing people to do things has always been a talent of mine. I watched Levi do it when we were young, watched him manipulate my mother, inch by inch, until she lost herself in his web.

Unlike my brother, I didn't want to hurt anyone. The urge to kill, or maim, or deceive was not in my nature. It only arose after what happened with Bo. An instinct took hold of me; it was so strong it was all I felt. The urge to protect myself, my parents. And now Ruby.

I clasp John's hand, guide him behind me. He is a pig being led to slaughter. It is the only solace I have as I let him grasp at me, cupping my ass in his large hands.

IN THE COLD air outside, the beat of the music dims, and my ears ring with white noise.

"You're hot," he says from behind me. His words sound awkward and heavy. I wonder if this works on other girls.

I begin to walk toward the stretch of road that will take us to the path, the snow beginning to fall, the dark earth speckled with white flakes.

"Are we going to the Ledge?" he asks, skeptical.

I turn my head over my shoulder. "Scared?"

He hesitates for a moment, but I know he will follow.

"Nope." John jogs to catch up with me, follows close behind. His movements are getting slower, the alcohol messing with his nervous system and brain.

I am only wearing my dress, but the cold is where I belong, where I feel at ease. When we get outside, I take a few sips of whisky to keep warm. We turn off the road and onto the narrow dirt path. The ground is frozen, the soil compact and hard beneath my feet. I am strong, confident. John likes it. He keeps trying to pull me in for a kiss but I dodge him, smiling, leading him up to the Ledge.

"I've never been up here at night." He is breathy, intoxicated. He stumbles over roots and rocks, giving himself bruises. His hand pulls at mine.

"A little farther," I reply, singsong and sweet.

When we reach our destination, I look up at the sky. No starlight tonight, shadowed by clouds. The snow scatters on the ground, whipping in the wind. I know I have to leave before my footsteps show, but the forecast promised at least two feet, so I'm not worried.

I face John. I have to do something I really don't want to do, but it will be worth it. I touch his face and bring his mouth to mine. He is excited, I can feel his anticipation press into my stomach. He's a bad kisser. His tongue reminds me of that cold, dead lobster from the freshman picnic.

I bite his lip to shut him up and push him backward.

"Get down," I demand.

He likes being bossed around. I watch him brace himself against the dirt, not bothering to wince against the cold.

I get on top of him, straddle his torso, bend down to his mouth.

"Let's drink a little more," I say.

He doesn't want to, he shakes his head, his eyes are delirious with eagerness for something else, for me. I press my flask to my lips and pretend to gulp down the whisky, then pass it to John. He doesn't want to look weak, so he takes a few long sips.

"Fuck," he says as he falls back on his elbows, letting his head hit the ground. I continue to make out with him, letting our tongues do most of the work. He starts to get tired and unbuttons his pants.

"Wait," I say, trying my best to sound sleepy and drunk. "Let's wait. It'll be better. Let's lie here for a minute."

John protests but I convince him this is the best he's going to get from me, and so he settles down and closes his eyes. He is passed out within a minute, his breath even and slow. I get up and brush the dirt from my knees and backside. I whistle a little, nudge him with my shoe, to see if he is truly out. His body is still.

It is the easiest thing in the world, letting him die.

I stand above him, alone in the silence. The wind whirls icy flakes around us in a warm, satisfied hug. And then I look down at him. I think of Ruby, how she won't get hurt anymore. And Max, who is finally free of his tormentor.

The heaviest part of the storm rolls in over the southern hills of Maine. My perfect snowstorm. John will freeze to death, and it will be ruled an accident. It happens all the time up here. I turn around and start down the path. I pick up my pace, I need to get out of the woods before the snow begins to pile, I can't leave tracks. I don't bother looking back at his body. I know he isn't going anywhere. A welcome rush of fresh blood to my cheeks.

Our world is better off without him.

As I MAKE my way down the steep path, and I am almost to the road, I hear something in front of me. Fast steps against the packed dirt path.

"Malin?"

A figure appears in the dark, and suddenly I can't breathe. Throat constricting. Chest tightening. It must be panic. This isn't a part of the plan.

CHAPTER FORTY-FIVE

Senior Day

M ax stands in front of me on the darkened path, looking at me with those concerned and sweet eyes.

"Where's John?" he asks. He looks past me to the space he thinks John might be inhabiting.

"I don't know," I say. "I'm alone."

I think fast: How can I get Max away from the Ledge? I brush by him, starting back toward campus. Hoping he will follow, that he will not say a word.

"What are you doing? I saw you leave together."

"Can we walk?" I say, making sure to stick to the side of the road. The road is already icy in patches. I wonder when the salt trucks will start dusting the roads with sharp crystals.

"Seriously, where is he?" he asks again.

My throat begins to constrict in an unusual way; my heart beats wild in my chest. John's body will be found eventually. Max will piece it together. He'll know what happened.

"Why are you here? Why did you follow me?" My voice comes out shrill.

"To make sure you're okay. Because you're my best friend, and he's, well, he's John," he says, quick on my heels.

Max cuts in front of me, making me stop in my tracks. He puts his hands on my shoulders. The road is quiet, empty, the snow getting heavy. "Malin, where is John?"

I feel like I am choking. This is not a part of the plan. He keeps his gaze steady. I wish he would give up, leave it be. I wish he didn't care so much. In the distance, I hear the familiar rattle of a logging truck making its way down the road. I know what I have to do. Max is too pure, too good, and because of that, his fate is decided.

"He's up there, isn't he? What did you do?" he asks.

"Ruby will keep getting hurt," I say.

"Malin," Max says. He is pleading with me.

I want to erase the last hour. I want to go back to the gym and look for Max. Why didn't I look for him? I knew he was watching; he always wants to keep Ruby and me safe. Why didn't I make sure he was gone? A mistake. I don't like making mistakes. The air constricts in my throat.

"You're killing her," I am shouting now. "You're killing Ruby by not killing him. He hurts her. You didn't know that, did you?"

Max looks like I have slapped him. He processes the information, and for a second I think he will understand what I am doing, why John needs to die.

"That doesn't mean you can kill him. What did you do?"

When I don't answer, Max drops his arms and starts back toward the beginning of the trail. He is going to get John, he is going to ruin my plan, he is going to tell the police.

"Stop," I say, catching his arm. "*Please.*"

He shrugs me off. "I'm not a murderer, you're not a murderer, this is insane, Malin."

And then the logging truck comes barreling down the hill, and there are only seconds left to make a decision. I grab Max's hand and pull him toward me.

"Wait," I say.

He is so heavy, resistant, but there is that concern in him that allows him to give me another chance. I see it in his eyes. He is anxious, but he loves me. I am his friend. He wants to believe I am good, that I would never hurt anyone.

He steps so close to me, his natural instinct to shield us from the spray of dirt and snow. He doesn't even see me raise my arms.

I want to tell him I'm sorry. I open my mouth but nothing comes

out. His back is to the truck as it hurries toward us. There is no time
left.

I lunge at his chest, push him. It's not hard to knock him backward. He's thin, much lighter than John. The space he occupied a
second before is now empty. He's staring at me, confused, and I look
away as his body makes contact with the front of the logging truck.
It is a horrible sound. A cracking thud, followed by the jagged rhythm
of the truck as it continues down the road.

CHAPTER FORTY-SIX

Senior Day

I wake early and trudge across the quad, postholing in the foot of snow that fell overnight. Hawthorne's canvas blank in the heavy snowfall. I follow footsteps in front of me, keep my head to the ground. By the time I get to the dining hall, I am covered in snowflakes. I stomp my boots on the floor and shake my head. In the warmth, the snow melts off my jacket and drips to the floor.

Sundays are slow in the dining hall. I show up first, everyone else still sleeping when I sneak out and down the stairs. I bring my laptop and set myself up at our table, coffee and oatmeal to my right. I'm not hungry but I force myself to eat, make sure everything appears normal. I stare at my half-written thesis.

I think about Hale. I want to read next to him, and then disappear into the folds of his arms. He's texted me all night and into the morning.

You okay?

Call if you need anything.

Let me know you're all right.

I don't respond.

Gemma arrives first. She is more quiet than normal, placing her jacket neatly on the chair before disappearing to the cereal bar. Gemma is not a quiet person. She always crashes her bag and coat onto the table, the books thumping, making her presence known.

While Gemma and I sit in silence, I spot Khaled and Ruby swiping their keycards at the front door. Ruby and I make eye contact, but she doesn't say anything. She doesn't have any makeup on, her skin transparent and pale.

After five minutes, the four of us are all seated, quietly processing the morning light. Khaled moans beside me, shoving his food away, hungover. He leans his forehead down on his arm.

I hear a couple behind me talking about Becca, how she almost died, but John saved her. *John the hero.* How convenient for the newspaper headlines that are still to come.

We all hear his name and look at one another.

John.

Khaled lifts his head. One of his thick eyebrows furrows. "Where's John?" he asks, looking at Ruby. "And Max?"

"I thought John was with you?" Ruby says. "I haven't seen him since the dance."

"We didn't lift this morning," Khaled replies. "I checked their rooms before I left the house. I assumed they were here."

We all check our phones. Nothing. I lock eyes with Ruby, her face already the color of ash. She presses John's number on her phone.

"Straight to voicemail," she says.

I know she wants to call Max, too, but she doesn't.

"Call Max," Gemma says, still not looking at Ruby.

Ruby presses his name.

"It's dead," she says, voice quiet, eyes glassy. She looks out at the snow.

And then I see Gemma and Ruby shift their attention to something behind me, relief flooding both their faces, and I feel heavy hands upon my shoulders.

No. *No.* I think my teeth might crack from the pressure. I try to stay calm, but his hands squeeze my shoulders harder. I think my whole body may break in half. The anger turns acidic in my throat and I wonder if I can still breathe, or if I'm just imagining the air being sucked from my lungs.

I glance up to see John standing behind me, leaning hard on me, smiling at the others. I tell my face to remain neutral as I bury the rage beneath my feet and shove it into the carpeted floor.

"Guess what happened to me last night?" he says, his smile fading into a sick grin as he looks from the others to me. "Woke up on the Ledge freezing my ass off. Completely blacked out, no idea how I got there. Somehow I made it back to the gym and passed out on a pile of coats. What a night, am I right?"

I look up at him, reading his face, looking for signs of recognition.

I stare at my laptop, static in my ears, thinking of Max, of our last exchange.

How it was all for nothing.

CHAPTER FORTY-SEVEN

Senior Day

"But where's Max?" Ruby asks, after John has seated himself next to her. We all sense the strain in her voice.

John shrugs, stealing a bite of her toast. "I dunno, I didn't see him all night. Then again, I don't remember a thing."

I don't look at anyone. My body wants to run, but I stay still. I am calm, normal.

A group of freshmen walk by, their faces concerned, voices scared. We overhear something about a hit-and-run over on Route 26. The words *ambulance* and *student*.

Ruby is the first one out of her chair, not bothering to pull on her jacket and hat. The rest of us follow her out to the corner with the flashing lights, where the far side of campus meets the path to the Ledge. We push our way to the front of the crowd that has formed, Ruby cutting in front of everyone else. I wait in the back. I can't look at her, watch their reactions.

MAX WAS FOUND by a plow truck earlier that morning. He had been covered by snowfall, but the driver noticed the color of his winter coat sticking out on the road.

Max died upon impact with the logging truck. In the official autopsy report, cause of death will read *blunt force trauma*. Everyone will ask why Max was out there so late, wandering the road by himself, but nobody will have an answer.

Khaled will turn to John, while we are standing there on the side of the road, and ask the question, "Were you there? You were at the Ledge, right? Did you see it happen?" John's face will be white, drained of blood, staring at the back of the ambulance driving away with his cousin's body. Maybe he is questioning if he did it, if he pushed Max into the road, and he doesn't remember. Maybe he is wondering if it was supposed to be him instead. I don't know what he's thinking anymore. I don't know what he knows.

CHAPTER FORTY-EIGHT

Commencement

Beads of sweat pile under my knees, in sneaky folds of skin. I curse whoever thought to adorn seniors in synthetic gowns in the middle of the day, outside under the baking sun. I wait for the next breeze to roll through campus, praying it comes before I have to walk onstage.

The speaker is an actor, someone who went to Hawthorne twenty years ago. He cracks a joke about the record-breaking bong from his old dorm, which spanned the staircase from basement to top floor, and how it was featured in *Playboy*. How times have changed, he jokes. The students laugh, while the older professors grimace and will undoubtedly complain about the comment later. I think this actor was in a popular movie, but I can't be certain. I am bad at watching movies, I move too much to sit for that long. I start to zone out, wondering where my parents are sitting, how the heat must be comforting to them.

The president of the college stands after the actor takes his seat, and begins to talk about change, and progress, and how impressive our class is.

"We are blessed to educate these well-rounded individuals, excited to see what they have in store for them after they leave our campus and make their way in the world. Of course, I cannot stand in front of all of you and fail to mention the passing of Max Frasier. He was a talented student in the biology department, and spent every

Thursday afternoon at the Senior Care Living in Edleton. I believe a few of his biggest fans are in the audience."

I look to the right of the podium, where a small gathering of elderly men and women are sitting in the shade. A few of them have tissues in their hands, others hold their chins high, proud, saddened, to be included in the event.

"As most of you know, he was a wonderfully talented photographer. We've placed some of his most impressive photographs on the stage to honor his memory. Please allow for a moment of silence," she says, holding up a hand to her right, where five prints are on display. There is one I haven't seen before.

I squint to get a better look at the photo. I recognize the quad, aflame in fall colors. There's a person walking away from the camera, walking away from the tree Max always sat at. Blond ponytail, the profile of a girl. I make out the backpack I used freshman year, and I know it's me. I remember what day that was, the first time Max and I spoke, just us. I inhale through my nose, hold back the vomit in my throat. The crowd is mournful. A breeze ripples through our robes.

I glance behind me, the printed paper creasing in my fingers. I look for the row of H students, searching each of their faces. I find Ruby sitting on the end near the audience. Her hands are clasped in front of her, and she stares at the stage, a blank expression on her face.

The president of the college begins to finish up her remarks.

"I'm so happy to introduce our outstanding valedictorian, a student who has surpassed our expectations. Ladies and gentlemen, I'd like to proudly introduce Malin Ahlberg."

Sweat rolls down my legs as I stand, and I give the gown a slight tug to pull it off my perspiring torso. I walk to the podium among a sea of claps and a few cheers. I recognize Khaled's whistle, sitting with the B section; he sounds close by.

I stand on the stage, looking at the students, professors, parents. I find my own parents sitting near the stage, in their reserved seats, looking proud. My father gives me a nod, we lock eyes, he smiles. I've accomplished our goal. I've made it through college, I found a group of friends, I worked hard, and I am the best in my class.

I think about the conversation I had with my father the night before my parents dropped me off at Hawthorne. We stayed at a quaint bed-and-breakfast on the coast of Maine, the car packed with my belongings. My mother went to sleep while my father and I stayed out on the porch, listening to the waves roll over the gray pebbles. *You have to make friends. It's the most important thing. You will never succeed without them. Pretend, Malin. Pretend to be normal. A person without friends is a person without power. You want to be successful one day? Surround yourself with an army, be beloved and respected, and you will succeed.*

I listened to his every word; I always did. I wanted to make my parents proud, I owed them that.

Now, though, as I think back on it, I realize my father was wrong. He shouldn't have listened to my mother when she was fighting for Levi. He shouldn't have tried to embrace empathy, or any of that *love will conquer all* bullshit. He should have sent Levi away. My father pretended and lost. I trusted him, and I listened to him, because he is my father, and I respect him. But I know better now.

I think of Levi, where he would be if he were alive. Prison, probably. Locked away somewhere. I am glad he is dead.

I was afraid for so long that we were the same, Levi and I. But we're not. I am smarter. I am the survivor. I do care for others. I have the ability to love; I know it exists, even though I can't do it anymore.

When the crowd is silent, the sea of caps and gowns growing hotter in the summer heat, I begin my speech.

► ► ►

I TALK WITH my parents after all the diplomas are handed out. We stand on the quad under the shade of a tree while my mother fans herself with a program, looking at all the other students. Looking for Levi, like she always does.

I see Ruby out of the corner of my eye as she makes her way toward the biggest tree on campus. I know where she is going. I tell my parents I have to take care of a couple things before we leave.

My father gives me a strong two-pat on the shoulder, and my mother leans in close to my cheek. A brush of a kiss, the comforting scent of her shampoo. Home. She whispers so soft I can barely hear.

"Proud of you," she says, stepping back. She gives me a small smile, a real smile, the most cherished gift, and I want to pull her back to me and hold her tight. "I guess next year we will be visiting you in Boston."

She's right. Harvard Law starts in September. I will begin this process all over again, but I will do it much differently. I don't tell them about my new career track, to become a judge. I'll make sure people like John and Levi don't get away with their abuse.

► ► ►

"Malin," a voice calls to me. I turn around; Amanda pulls away from what I assume are her parents. They seem nice, smiling at their daughter. I stop and wait for her to catch up to me.

"Hey," I say as she matches my stride.

"Hey, I know we haven't talked since that karaoke night at the Pub—God, that seems like forever ago—but I wanted to say sorry, before we leave. About Max. I'm not good with death stuff, so yeah . . . But I do feel bad. I know you two were tight. He was kind of weird, but—"

She starts rambling, as she does, so I cut her off. "I know. It's okay, thanks."

We stop walking and I look at her, knowing she is trying to mean well. I can't talk about him, though. I haven't, and I won't.

Amanda takes off her cap and fans out her gown, waving herself in the heat. I can tell she has something else to say so I wait for her to speak.

"It's kind of a bummer," she says, "that we weren't allowed to be friends. I think it could have been fun."

I still wonder how things would have turned out if I hadn't met Gemma that day at orientation. Maybe if I had met Amanda first, I would still be playing at the game. Maybe she would have made it easier for me, easier to be myself.

"PS," she says, suddenly coy. She lowers her voice. "I called it, freshman year. With Hale."

I haven't spoken to Hale in months. She must read the look of confusion on my face.

"I saw you guys once, in the TA lounge. I figured it was a secret, so I didn't say anything. Told you, though. Just had to tell you. Because I was right."

I give her a smile. "Yes, Amanda, you were right."

"Well," she says, sighing and searching the crowd, "I gotta go find Becca and Abigail. Have a good summer. I mean life. Have a good life."

"You, too," I say, and I watch as she strides away, full of confidence and ease.

I MEET UP with Ruby, John, Khaled, and Gemma by the tree.

Khaled envelops me in a hug, Gemma on his other side.

"Ready?" Ruby says. We all look at her. Somehow, she is strong again. As if Max's death plunged her back into the world, reminded her to live. She pulls the framed photo out of the bag and places it at the roots.

Everyone looks at the photo, the one we took on Senior Day. Max's face frozen forever as a college senior.

"It's a good one," Khaled says. "I'm actually glad Denise isn't in it. You were right, Gems."

Gemma shakes her head. "I dunno. I kind of miss her."

Denise was the *before*. Khaled threw her out the day Max's body was discovered. As if we could no longer joke or have fun. The house would be devoid of anything light, happy until we graduated. In the *after*, we couldn't be happy without Max, we didn't allow ourselves, and so everyone shut their doors and mourned alone in silence.

We stand in a semicircle, Khaled the first one to take a step forward. The night before, we gathered in the kitchen and silently painted Max's initials on the tops of our caps, the white paint bright against the black. We all take our caps off and place them at the base of the tree, our guilt weighing us down.

After a few moments, Khaled speaks first. "If you guys are ever in New York, call me," he says. "Stay with me. Anytime. Please."

His words almost sound desperate, as if he can't stand the idea of living in his high-rise alone. We all promise to come visit him, although I doubt we will. We have already been seeing less of each other, the loss of Max dampening a piece of the spark that once held us all together.

A few weeks ago, Khaled pulled me aside in the library. We had all been avoiding each other. He had looked at me with wild, sad eyes. *I'm sleeping better,* he had said, blurting it out like a confession. The bad thing had happened. I had reassured him that he was dealing with grief, and he would be fine. He shook his head and walked away, still in a daze. I hadn't spoken to him since.

Gemma clears her throat, looking at Khaled. "I'll go with you," she says. "My flight."

She hugs me, squeezing extra tight and planting a kiss on my cheek. "Bye, love."

She looks at both Ruby and John, and then she and Khaled begin the walk back to the house. Gemma was going home, to a theater program in London. Since Senior Day, she had spent all her time in the theater department, and I had only seen her when we crossed paths at the Palace. She was always with the drama students, keeping her distance.

John doesn't say anything. He has said nothing about Max since the accident. He went home for a couple weeks afterward, to be with his family. Max's family. I couldn't tell what he was thinking anymore.

Ruby looks up at him. "Can you give us a moment?"

John looks up at me, his face drawn. There is something about the way he looks at me, a suggestion in his glance. I hold his gaze until he looks away.

"Sure," he says as he turns to leave.

Ruby and I stand alone. Our necks bend to the tree, staring at the shiny new plaque on the trunk.

She speaks first. "Remember how I used to give him so much shit for sitting out here, even when it was thirty degrees?"

She tucks a strand of hair behind her ear.

"I never told you this," she begins, "but I ran into him when I was leaving Last Chance. And I thought he would still be mad at me, but he wasn't. He looked at me and asked if I wanted to dance."

I look at the plaque, that choking sensation in my throat.

Ruby continues, "But I told him I had to go. I couldn't be around people anymore that night, pretending to be happy when I wasn't. I wanted to tell him . . . but I didn't."

"Tell him what?" I ask.

"That I loved him, too. And I was sorry."

I grit my teeth as hard as I can, blood running from my gums into my throat. Ruby crosses her arms over her chest and lifts her chin.

"I think it's time I stop caring so much about what other people think, and stop fighting who I really am. I'm gonna take things slow. I decided to go to Scotland, by the way," she says, and I see a flicker of that girl from the freshman picnic, that shining face full of potential and strength. "I'm leaving tomorrow, so this is goodbye."

▶ ▶ ▶

MY LAST STOP at Hawthorne is Hale. He stopped texting me a few months ago, giving up after I failed to reply. I did a good job avoiding him around campus, letting my eyes fall to the ground when we ran into each other in the English department. After I switched advisors, I deleted him from my life.

He is standing with a few graduate students, but I catch his eye as he excuses himself.

"Hey," he says. "Good speech."

The leaves on the tree move with the breeze, and the light dapples on his face and chest.

He smiles, but there is resignation in there. Bitterness.

"Thanks," I say. I hold my gown in my arm, the wind a relief against my white dress.

"What's up?" he asks. I like this about him; I always have. He gets to the point, cuts through the bullshit.

I have rehearsed the words I have to say to him, rolling them around in my mind until they are smooth.

"I'm sorry," I say. "For not responding to you."

"You've done a fine job of avoiding me," he says, almost smiling. "And you switched advisors?"

He doesn't sound angry, but he's hurt.

"Yeah, sorry."

I don't know what to say.

"Malin," he says, stepping toward me, taking my wrist in his hand, gentle and light. I don't like the desperate edge in his voice. I've broken him, too. "I know it has to do with what happened that night."

I hear the thud and crack of breaking bones and look over at the quad, where a group of girls in white dresses are hugging each other tight.

He is so close now; there are only a few inches between us. "And I know you feel something, and that we had something good. It was real, wasn't it?"

"That's the thing," I say, snapping back to attention, interrupting him, remembering what I have to do. "I don't feel anything."

"What does that even mean?"

"You can't understand because you're normal."

"Normal? Who wants to be normal? Normal is boring," he says, persistent. Confident. "Why did you push me away?"

"Because I don't care," I say. There is a sharp edge in my voice. It reassures me. "About you."

I cross my arms and look around us, hoping he will give up and walk away.

After a few moments, I can tell he is done with me. He leans in and kisses me on the cheek, and then releases my wrist and walks away. This is the last time I will see him. There is still that thing, that energy, whatever it is, but I don't want it.

By the time I am forty, I will have killed five people. Only one of them will haunt me.

Max was too good. John hated that about him, hated that he had that moral compass. Max had the happy home life, supportive parents, loving sister. An artistic talent. Ruby's attention. My attention. John wanted to be Max, he wanted to be cherished and revered, but it wasn't in his nature. He tried to cover up his true self, and did a pretty good job with everyone else, but I saw right through it that very first day. You can't hide malevolence. Not from me.

My guess is that John's potential to be a decent human was ruined by his father. I know that a bad childhood can really fuck things up. Some of us escape it, others don't. John was ruined. Max wasn't. The stronger Max became over our years at Hawthorne, and the more he distanced himself from John, the more confident he became. John couldn't control him anymore, and it drove him crazy. The anger and resentment were transferred to Ruby. He hurt those he was closest to because he knew they would forgive him.

I wish Max hadn't cared so much. That compass became a weakness, and it got him killed. I didn't need protecting, but he didn't know that. It wasn't his fault. Max lived in the shadows, like I did. We thrived out of the spotlight, it's where we could be ourselves. Our friendship was behind the scenes.

He was my one friend, the person who cared about me, even when I was at my worst. I always thought it was Ruby, the person I was looking for. My *best friend*. Yes, I was always there for her. But she wasn't there for me. Max was. He was my true friend.

The others who die because of me, they deserve it, like John. I didn't make mistakes after him. I learned. I got better.

I am done caring. After a minute or two I walk away, back toward the house, toward my parents, to pack up my old life and move into the new. And I feel nothing, except maybe annoyance at all the people who think they know me, who are always telling me who I am, why I should care what they think.

Nobody knows who I am, except me.

Acknowledgments

ROSS: My best friend and husband. For encouraging me to *write the book,* for celebrating every step along the way, and, most important, for always making sure I am well fed.

MOM & DAD: For the adventures, for cheering me on. For listening to my anxieties and fears, and telling me to *put that active imagination to good use.* I finally took your advice. I love you both very much.

LORI: My rockstar agent; for reading and re-reading, and helping make this book what it is now. And for bringing LANE on to help get this book into good hands. Thank you.

KARA: My brilliant and thoughtful editor; I love working with you. Thank you for having faith in Malin and the crew.

LAUREN W: For always being there, no matter what country you are in.

JANICE: The best mother-in-law. You can read the book now. Please skip the hookup scenes.

My earliest readers: CHAR, COREY, CHLOE. Charlotte, who put me in touch with Lori. Corey, who provided such thoughtful insight. And Chloe, for always loving to talk books, and for your therapy lingo and advice.

HANNAH L: For taking care of Warren and Olive while I finished writing.

BATES COLLEGE: For your inspiration. What a sweet four years it was.

The team at BALLANTINE: For making the book magic happen—Kara W., Kim, Jennifer, Karen, Jen, Debbie, Scott, Steve, Madeline, Taylor, and Jesse.

AEVITAS: For working so hard to get this book out into the world. CHELSEY H.: You are wonderful, thank you.

To EVERYONE who asked how the book was going, and checked in on it, thank you.

WARREN: You were only five weeks old when this book was picked up by a publisher. I wore you in a wrap while I took editor calls (you snored through a few) and nursed you while I thought out plotlines. I've only known you nine months, but it feels like you've been with me forever. I love you, baby boy.

Lastly, LO, LAUREN McALLISTER: My strong, beautiful, hilarious, smart, kind friend; a true gem on this earth. Thank you for believing in this before it ever existed, for always saying *put this in your book one day*. This one's for you.

TELL ME
EVERYTHING

CAMBRIA BROCKMAN

A BOOK CLUB GUIDE

QUESTIONS AND TOPICS FOR DISCUSSION

1. In *Tell Me Everything*, the characters go to extraordinary lengths to conceal, deceive, and maintain appearances. Why do you think Cambria Brockman chose to title her novel in this way?

2. In the beginning, the six friends get up to your average freshman shenanigans. When do you think you begin to see the cracks in their friendship? What is the effect of Brockman's choice to tell the story out of sequence?

3. Brockman based Hawthorne College on her alma mater, Bates College. How does the college setting act as a pressure cooker?

4. Can we excuse the terrible actions of someone who was "ruined" by his or her upbringing, as Malin says John was? Or are some people, like Levi, simply born bad?

5. "I hated how Ruby kept things from me, how she alluded to things and then pulled back, as if she was teasing me, casting a line and then taunting me with her truths. Pulling me close and then keeping me at a distance. Her own special method of control." Discuss the various ways in which the characters exert power over one another. What do you think it says about them?

6. What do you make of Max's friendship with Malin? Do you feel that she loves him in her own way? Or does she use his love for her as a tool to manipulate him?

7. "By the time I am forty, I will have killed five people." Did this confession shock you? Or did you expect this ending for Malin? Why?

8. List some of the signs that foreshadow the dark turn of events. Would you have seen all the signs that the group misses about Malin?

9. Think about the novel's chilling final line, "Nobody knows who I am, except me." How well do you think we can ever *truly* know someone? Will there always be limits to our understanding of others?

10. Netflix has acquired film rights to *Tell Me Everything*. Who would play the main characters if you were to cast it?

CAMBRIA BROCKMAN grew up in Houston, London, and Scotland and attended Holderness School in New Hampshire. She graduated from Bates College in Lewiston, Maine, with a degree in English literature. She owns an award-winning wedding and portrait photography company, Cambria Grace, along with its popular Instagram account. Brockman lives in Boston with her husband, son, and dog. *Tell Me Everything* is her first novel.

Twitter: @cambriabrockman
Instagram: @cambria_grace